NO GOOD DEED GOES UNPUNISHED . . .

"Mickolai, some people are going to claim that this war is all your fault," said General Sobieski. "It isn't, but they will say so."

"Yes, sir. I never started a war before," I said. "What did I do?"

"You were generous, decent, and you have humanitarian instincts, that's what. It was those automatic medical centers that you sent all over Human Space. And yes, I knew what you were doing, and yes, I approved of it. But the whole story is that when we realized what diamond semiconductors could do, it was ordered that *all* military computers be equipped with diamond semiconductors as soon as possible. The automatic medical centers were officially listed as military equipment, so the automatic factories upgraded them. Are you following me?"

"Yes, sir."

"Well, then, you sent one of them to a planet with few technically trained people. Their technology was maintained by foreign technicians—from Earth, as luck would have it. When they found that the new computers were thirty times faster than anything they had known, they shipped them to Earth."

"Oh."

"Yes. The Powers That Be on Earth realized what such an advance in computer technology meant, both militarily and economically. So they hit New Kashubia."

"My family is in New Kashubia."

"Mine, too. Right now they are fighting in the tunnels there. You have a very creative and unorthodox way of handling things, Mickolai. You have a very devious mind, and there is something of the con man in you. Your orders are to do what seems right to you to save our planet, and our families."

"Yes, sir!" We saluted and his image disappeared. I stood there, thinking that if I managed to screw up big time, or better still, get myself killed, I would be giving my general a very convenient scapegoat. Someone to blame the whole war on.

Me.

THE WAR WITH EARTH

LEO FRANKOWSKI
AND
DAVE GROSSMAN

THE WAR WITH EARTH

This is a work of fiction. All the characters and events portrayed in this book are fictional, and any resemblance to real people or incidents is purely coincidental.

A Baen Books Original

Baen Publishing Enterprises
P.O. Box 1403
Riverdale, NY 10471
www.baen.com

ISBN: 0-7434-9877-1

Cover art by Mark Hennessy-Barrett

First paperback printing, January 2005

Library of Congress Cataloging-in-Publication Data: 2003006199

Distributed by Simon & Schuster
1230 Avenue of the Americas
New York, NY 10020

Typeset by Windhaven Press, Auburn, NH
Printed in the United States of America

DEDICATION

This book is dedicated to my lovely wife, Marina, my beautiful daughter, Katia, and to the Ancient City of Tver, Russia, the "City of Beautiful Women," where I am building my castle, and have made my home.

ACKNOWLEDGEMENT

I would like to thank Edward Dunnigan and Jackie Britton for their suggestions and their proofreading of this manuscript, and my remarkable partner, Lieutenant Colonel Dave Grossman, for always being at my side, even though we live half a world from each other.

PROLOGUE
An Amphibious Attack on Baden-Baden Island

Rail guns and X-ray lasers being what they are, military doctrine is that if you can see it, you can kill it. If they can see you, you are dead.

The art of war has become the art of not being seen.

Thus it was that I was in my tank, crawling along the bottom of the ocean, leading three squads of the Kashubian Expeditionary Forces against the invaders from Earth. They had picked the most isolated spot on the planet for their beachhead, a group of six uninhabited islands under the jurisdiction of the smallest nation on New Yugoslavia, the German Enclave.

New Yugoslavia's turbulent seas protected us from both enemy sonar and almost everything in the electromagnetic spectrum. Oh, a deep-scan radar might have found us, if it was looking down from low orbit, but rail guns from both sides had taken out everything in orbit long ago.

Anyone using a high-flying aircraft in wartime is simply suicidal.

We had been down here for seven of the planet's

short, twenty-hour days, and we had been having a fine enough time of it. The fiber-optic communication cables we trailed behind us were finer than a human hair, and needed constant patching in these seas. We had lost contact with our main forces three hours after we left, as expected, but we were in touch with each other. Keeping us connected was the job of three semisentient aquatic drones, and not my worry. Connected, we had the bandwidth we needed to live together in Dream World, a sort of virtual reality.

Since all of our tanks had the diamond semiconductor upgrade, they could keep us in Dream World at thirty times normal speed. To us, the week had seemed like almost six standard months. Having one's lifespan effectively expanded by a factor of thirty was one of the fringe benefits of the job.

A dozen of my people had been raw recruits when we started, and this gave them the time they needed to get through basic training, and then to see a good deal of simulated combat.

Of course, *they* weren't told that it was simulated. Dream World was convincing enough to make them think that they were really fighting, and that their friends were dying around them. It was rough on them psychologically, but it let us turn out seasoned troops without having to kill any of them.

After all, they did it to me, and I turned out okay.

I spent most of my time at the University of Oxbridge, working on my B.S. in Agriculture. I already had a Bachelors degree in engineering and a Ph.D. in Military Science, but I also had a major tract of land on New Yugoslavia, and when this war was over, I wanted to be able to manage it properly.

My wife, Kasia, was in her own tank, a hundred meters to my left. She was studying economics, and fuming about not being able to keep in touch with what her stocks were doing on the market. She'd made a fortune at it during our last leave.

One of my subordinate squad leaders, Mirko, spent his spare time in Dream World, working his small farm with two draft horses, the same thing he had just done in the flesh during his last leave. An odd fellow, but a good man to have on your side when things got complicated. He had a knack for asking the right simple question which then made everything else fall into place.

The other squad leader, Lloyd Tomlinson, was also attending the university, working on his law degree, and dating half the girls in the local town.

Maria and Conan seemed to be spending most of their spare time in the sack together. They said that they were too much in love to risk spoiling it by getting married.

Quincy and Zuzanna had been comfortably married for fifty years. He spent much of his time teaching the martial arts and The Way Of The Warrior to the recruits, and anybody else who was interested, including me. Zuzanna usually lived in a sort of pseudo-medieval world filled with castles, knights, and dragons, where magic worked and she was a great warlock.

Dream World could be pretty much whatever you wanted it to be, provided you obeyed orders.

We old hands got together fairly often, socially, and when we did, the intelligent computers in our tanks were always invited. Mine was named Agnieshka. She was a beautiful woman in Dream World, and a good friend of my wife. Kasia's tank was Eva, a slender Irish girl with huge green eyes. She was equipped with a rail gun for this mission, rather than her usual X-ray laser. When their training schedules permitted, the recruits and their tanks were invited along as well.

Of course, I saw to it that we spent enough time preparing for the upcoming battle, and making sure that everyone knew what our objectives were. They all knew precisely what to do, for at least the first few seconds, at which time I privately expected the battle plan to go west.

They always do.

After that, well, you improvise a lot.

We were now five kilometers from shore, three hundred meters below the surface, nicely lined up, and at a dead stop.

The general rules also state that when you can no longer stay hidden, you should stay quick.

We were well equipped for this. Magnetically strapped to the back of each tank was a thruster unit normally used for space flight. Each unit had a gimbal-mounted hydrogen-oxygen rocket capable of accelerating the tank at forty Gs, which we humans could survive because we were each floating in a liquid bath with the same average density as our bodies.

The unit also contained a pair of Hassan-Smith receivers spatially connected through four other dimensions to some major fuel tanks somewhere on the planet. Thus, we could continue accelerating indefinitely, since we didn't have to carry our fuel along with us. This was the trick that let us get to the stars in the first place.

It was a pity that the transporters didn't conveniently lend themselves for use as a battlefield communication device.

A Mark XIX Main Battle Tank does not have a good hydrodynamic form. It's mostly an armored fusion power supply with some computers and a human being inside.

It moved itself around using a MagLev track-laying system, laying magnetic bars in front of itself, gliding over them, and picking them up as it left. When traveling over a ferro-magnetic surface, it could keep the bars inside itself, magnetize the surface and then move much faster over it. And when you put one on a real MagLev track, it could really move out, hitting three thousand kilometers an hour, in a vacuum.

Weapons and other useful things are strapped on the outside, pretty much wherever they'll fit. However, for this mission, there was a way around this unstreamlined shape.

Attached to the front of each tank was a long pole tipped with something that looked a lot like an arrowhead from an ancient crossbow bolt. When pushed hard enough through the water, and with air injected just behind the arrowhead, a cavity formed behind it that was big enough for the tank to ride inside. Once we were moving fast enough, the air was no longer needed, and we were moving in something close to a hard vacuum. This permitted us to reach supersonic speeds, under water. At least it worked fine on rocket-powered torpedoes, and we had even tested it, once, on an empty tank, which was good enough for a Kashubian veteran.

When Agnieshka told me that everybody was ready, and the moment had come when our orders said we should attack, I said, "Ladies and gentlemen! It's time to see to the Earthworms' proper education! We must teach them that it is not nice to invade somebody else's planet. I'll see you again when we're airborne! Let's move!"

But actually, it was Agnieshka who gave the firing signal. Timing on this one was very important.

Dream World vanished and I was working at combat speed, which is as fast as the human brain can operate without damage. For me, that was fifty-five times normal. Soldiers in combat often feel a natural form of this, where it seems that the world slows down around them. What we used was machine augmented, and vastly accelerated.

It is difficult, or perhaps impossible to describe fighting at combat speed in a tank. You and your tank's computers become a single entity. All of its sensors become your senses, and you can see everything from thirty cycles per second up to and including hard X-rays. Only it isn't exactly seeing. You are touching and hearing and smelling as well, all at the same time. You can taste the chemical makeup of everything around you, and feel every vibration. The tank is your body, and you know exactly what every part of it is doing. When you give your tank an order, you don't work any controls or exactly say anything. You just know what should be done, she knows what you want, and she does it.

So when I try to describe something, it's not what really happened. It's just the closest that I can come to explaining what was going on.

The thruster let loose and slammed us forward. We never hit anything like forty Gs, not with the water slowing us down, but it was still a rough ride. The hair-thin fiber-optic cable parted immediately, and the drones were left far behind. With any luck, they'd show up later. For a while, Agnieshka and I were all alone, and I could see nothing but the bubble around us.

I could feel her injecting liquid air from our coolant bottle into the vents just behind the arrowhead, mixing in enough hydrogen tapped from the thruster to warm it up to a level just below what might damage our sensors, and igniting the mixture. The vibrations got worse until we were entirely inside the bubble. Then it got smoother while the acceleration got higher. Agnieshka cut the air off, because we didn't need it any more.

We broke the surface a hundred meters from the beach, long before any of our bubbles reached the surface behind us to give us away. Hitting the air actually slowed us down a bit. The long pole and arrowhead were jettisoned, no longer needed.

The Mark XIX doesn't have a good aerodynamic shape, either, but if you put enough power behind it, you can fly a lead brick.

We were traveling at fifteen hundred kilometers per hour, but because we were mentally at combat speed, it seemed to me that we were only going at a leisurely twenty-seven kilometers per hour, with plenty of time to look around and pick out our targets.

Once out of the water, I was in communication with my team again by laser, and all of my sensors were operating once more.

A quick look around told me that my seventeen subordinates were flying parallel to me a half meter above the waves, in a line two kilometers wide. Our sonic shock waves were kicking up huge rooster tails behind us.

A glance up told me that the artillery was not letting us down. Six thousand launchers, scattered up to eight thousand kilometers away, were each firing fifteen rounds in a time-on-target barrage, mostly to keep our opponents from noticing us too soon.

I was surprised to see that quite a few of the self-targeting smart shells were getting through, and not being hit by enemy counterfire. The Earthworms were definitely not on the ball. Having a stupid enemy is one of the things that every soldier dreams about, but never believes can actually happen to him.

But to make proper use of an artillery barrage, you have to be willing to risk a few casualties. You must hit the enemy while the last of your rounds are still incoming, before he has a chance to look around and notice who is really killing him. Thus, to have a fair number of our shells not be shot out of the sky was not entirely wonderful, but there was nothing for it but to press on regardless. Maybe our shells were smart enough to tell the good guys from the bad ones.

One could always hope.

I heard Lloyd yell "Tally Ho!" and open up with his rail gun before I spotted any of the enemy myself. Then I saw that they were dug into some low dunes just past the beach. The beach defenses were not shooting at our artillery shells, having apparently been ordered to keep on the lookout for somebody exactly like yours truly. But the temptation to keep your weapon pointed up, so that you could take out a shell that might be coming straight at you was just too strong for those boys. Their muzzles were all straight up, and not trained at us at all.

That was their fatal mistake.

My rail gun put a swarm of osmium needles, traveling at a quarter of light speed with only three meters between them, across two hundred meters of the dunes, a split second before Kasia on my left and Zuzanna on my right did the same. I saw a dozen Earth tanks peel open like so many flowers blooming on a television nature program. They never got a burst off at us, being too busy looking up at the incoming artillery, I suppose.

We went up and over the dunes, cutting a two-kilometer-wide swath through the length of an island that was only four kilometers wide. General Sobieski hadn't been much interested in capturing prisoners. He just wanted them gone from our planet. This made things a lot easier.

Off to my right, one of the new recruits under Mirko went down in a spray of sand and vegetation. He'd been a safecracker from Nova Split that everybody called Frenchy, and I'd rather liked the kid, but there was no stopping for him, not now. As best as I could tell, he'd been hit by one of our own artillery shells. It didn't explode, so its little brain had probably been fried out by an enemy X-ray laser.

Just damned rotten luck.

A rolling artillery barrage preceded us as we cut through the island, but now, since the dangerous period of breaking through their shore defenses was over, the exploding shells stayed ahead of us by more than three hundred meters.

Five kilometers in, we came across a fair-sized base. Intelligence hadn't mentioned anything like this! There looked to be thousands of troops running madly about. Infantry? Why in hell would anybody bring infantry into a war zone?

Hundreds of tank turrets and artillery pieces were spinning toward us, and not a few shoulder-held rockets were being brought up. There wasn't anything that we could do but open up on them. We either had to take out their heavy weapons or get killed ourselves.

"Rip 'em up!" I yelled.

An unprotected human body within two hundred meters of a rail gun blast is dead. That was the main reason why our tanks were so heavily armored, to protect us from our own weapons. There wasn't any armor that could protect us from a direct hit by an enemy rail gun.

The Earthworms never had a chance. We were flying two meters above the ground at supersonic speed, in tanks with the aerodynamic qualities of a brick. The shock waves we were generating in the air alone would have killed most of those guys, and when you add the rail guns into the equation, it was a total massacre, bloody and simple.

They did get off a few rounds. I saw a tank on my left flank explode in the air as its fusion bottle blew, and bits of his armor tore into the earth.

That was a rare thing. Usually, dozens of fail-safes stopped your power supply from turning into a medium-sized thermonuclear bomb, but anything that can go wrong, sometimes does.

There was no hope for our trooper, whoever he was. Nor for anyone unprotected within two kilometers of the explosion. As it was, the blast knocked me a hundred meters off course, and damn nearly knocked my wife into the dirt, but we didn't lose anybody else. We closed up the gaps, and we were all soon back on course.

The rest of the fifteen-kilometer island went fairly smoothly, although my troops were taking out anything that looked as if it ever once might have wanted to be alive. Losing a few of your own does that to people.

In real time, we went the length of the island in thirty-six seconds. At combat speed, it felt like it was over half an hour, plenty of time to not miss anything.

Then, having taken out both ends and the center of the enemy-held island, I split what remained of my team in half. We made a U-turn over the ocean and came back at them. We worked over both edges of the island that we had skipped on the way in, taking them on the flank.

The time-on-target rolling artillery barrage was still just ahead of us. Those guys, or rather their computers, were really on the ball. We were picking our rail gun targets, and then shooting them up through the exploding artillery. It was pretty effective.

There wasn't much resistance. Most of the enemy had abandoned their positions and run for it. Just where they were planning to run to was beyond me, but as a military force, they were done.

Our second wave was already arriving, crawling out of the ocean. The two hundred tanks were equipped with antipersonnel drones, semi-intelligent, expendable robots that could round up the survivors and clean up any small pockets of resistance.

My three squads headed for the beach, not wanting to look at the carnage we had created inland.

We landed around the tank that had taken one of our own artillery shells, and formed a defensive circle. Mirko got out of his tank and walked naked over to the bent and wrecked machine that held the body of one of his men. It was the kind of thing that he had to do by himself.

Then, to the wonderment of us all, the coffin slowly emerged from the back of the wreck! Frenchy, shaken but still alive, sat up, took off his helmet, and pulled out the computer that held his tank's personality.

The rest of us gave him an enthusiastic cheer, over the comm lasers and out our external speakers, too! Most of us waved to him with our manipulator arms.

He waved back to us, but he was unable to go any farther.

Mirko shouted, "Both of his legs are broken! Somebody call for an ambulance!"

There are limits to what armor and fluid suspension can protect you from. But without it, well, in the old days, when a combat plane drilled in, the pilot was driven into his boots so hard that they exploded.

Mirko stood there next to Frenchy, and we waited for help to arrive.

The recruit who had been killed was Bogdan Miskovich. I'd liked him, too.

Actually, our losses were far lower than I had expected them to be, when I had been given this mission. They used to call the first wave on a frontal attack *The Forlorn Hope.*

We had been very lucky.

CHAPTER ONE
A Very Rude Awakening

Kasia, my beautiful new wife, and I had ridden our posh, new air car back from the architect's office, where we had just approved the final design of our magnificent new mansion. It was to be built on the six thousand hectares—sixty square kilometers!—of rich farming and ranching land that had been given to us by the grateful government of New Croatia, for our services in their recent war with New Serbia.

New Yugoslavia was the absolutely best place in Human Space for agriculture. It was a young planet, half the age of Earth. Its native plants and animals were primitive, and simply could not compete with those from my home planet. It wasn't that our life forms would devour theirs. They couldn't.

The proteins used by each sort were completely unusable by the other. Our diseases couldn't bother their life forms, nor could theirs bother ours. But both sorts of plants needed the same sunlight, water, and minerals, and ours were simply much better at putting those things together. It was like a Little League team trying to compete in the Majors, just no contest at all.

12

And the powerful Planetary Ecological Council knew it. They saw their task not as one of building a balanced, Earth-type ecology on their new planet, but of building a very *imbalanced* one. An ecology tilted way in the favor of human beings. They used their vast authority to keep out weeds, diseases, and everything else that they felt might be in any way undesirable. On the rare occasions when something unauthorized slipped past their tight quarantines, they ruthlessly stamped it out.

On Earth, insects ate between twenty and eighty percent of all vegetation, including the plants we humans needed to live on. On New Yugoslavia, there were no insects, except for one strain of Australian stingless bee that was needed for pollination. A debate had been going on for years about bringing in a few sorts of butterflies, simply for their beauty, but it probably wouldn't be settled for a long time yet.

The result was that a hectare of land on this planet produced three times the crops, on the average, as a hectare on Earth, and at far lower cost. Herbicides and insecticides weren't needed. There were no Earth weeds, and if a native plant needed anything that a nearby Earth plant wanted, the native shriveled and died. In many instances, even plowing was unnecessary. You just seeded and harvested.

New Yugoslavia was fast becoming the bread basket of the universe.

And my wife and I owned a vast tract of it!

We had also been given a lifetime immunity from all taxes, permission to exchange our New Kashubian passports for New Croatian ones anytime we wanted to, and the generous retirement pay due to both a general and a colonel, between us.

On the way home, Kasia suggested that we spend the night in Dream World, which meant spending the night physically in our tanks.

The New Croatian and New Kashubian governments had permitted us to retain, for our personal use, two of the thirty thousand intelligent Mark XIX Main Battle Tanks that we had captured for them from the Serbs.

The Mark XIX system was really a kit that let you assemble whatever was required to do the mission at hand. The basic unit was an armored slab that contained a muon exchange fusion power plant, an extensive, intelligent computer, and a "coffin" that held a living human being, together with a self-sustaining life support system. Locomotion was provided by a track-laying magnetic levitation system, but additional propulsive devices could be magnetically attached to convert a Mark XIX into anything from a submarine to a spaceship.

A large assortment of weapons could be strapped on in various combinations. Strap-on ultrasonic tunneling devices permitted one to move underground.

The judges and lawyers had decided that since I had been in the paid service of New Croatia at the time of their capture, these tanks, and everything else we had gained, were now the property of the New Croatian government. They did not belong to me personally, to my planet of New Kashubia, or to Earth, either, for that matter.

But the politicians had then permanently loaned two of those tanks back to Kasia and me. Well, we weren't permitted the deadly attachable weapons that such tanks usually wore, but their gift did give us access to our tank's considerable computing power, and to Dream World, something not ordinarily available to people on New Croatia.

And their fusion bottles would power our new mansion for three hundred years without recharging.

So. The medals and the awards had all been handed out. The banquets and the ticker-tape parades might be over, but I had my land, and I had my wife, and all was well with my world.

I have always found it very difficult to deny Kasia anything. Normal sex is wonderful, but there are things you can do in Dream World that would be awkward, dangerous or simply impossible to do elsewhere, and Kasia, bless her kinky little heart, had this idea that involved sex while shooting some rapids in a birch bark canoe.

But once I was in my tank's life support system, and in our Dream World cottage, Kasia wasn't there.

Agnieshka, my tank's artificial intelligence computer, was a beautiful woman in Dream World, but now she was sitting at the dining room table, looking upset and anxious.

"What's wrong, Agnieshka? Where's Kasia?" I said.

"She'll be here later. But there's something we have to talk over first, Mickolai. There is a lot that I have to explain to you, and perhaps I owe you an apology."

"What do you mean?" I felt my face go white. "Kasia's all right, isn't she?"

"She's just fine, but this isn't about Kasia. It's about you. Us. The whole world."

"Maybe you'd better start from the beginning," I said, spinning a chair around and sitting on it backwards, with my elbows on the back of the chair.

"I intend to. You realize of course the huge difference between well-trained but green troops, and seasoned professional fighting men. Blooded soldiers are generally three times as effective in combat."

"Agnieshka, I have a Ph.D. in Military Science. You were there when I earned it. You don't have to give me a spelling lesson."

"Yes I do, Mickolai. You see, back when I told you that we were going to war with the Serbians, well, that was the start of your second phase of basic training.

In truth, in your real world, the Kashubians never reneged on their contract with the Serbians, who only made a few small attacks on Croatia on their own before we took charge of things. In short, you were never in a war at all."

"Agnieshka, that's crazy! I fought in that war!"

"You *thought* you fought in a war. It was necessary to lie to you so that you would treat it seriously, and not as just another training exercise. We do it to all of our human soldiers, because it lets us turn out real, blooded troops without having to kill a significant portion of them. But in your real world, it never happened."

"It never happened? Quincy and Zuzanna weren't real? They never died?"

"They were real. They *are* real. They were your fellow students in that portion of the exercise. The only difference is that in the flanking counterattack, each of them thought that all the others were killed, and that *he* or *she* was the only human survivor. Surviving the emotional impact of being alive when your friends die is much of what makes a troop seasoned."

"Damn you. God damn you straight to Hell!" It was all I could say.

"I can't go to Hell, Mickolai. I don't have a soul. I'm just a machine."

"Damn you anyway. Then the whole scene where Quincy stayed with his dead wife, and Radek broke and ran, that was just a fake, too?"

"It happened in Dream World, if that's what you mean. It was as real as anything else that happens here. Your emotions were real enough, and so were mine."

"Then what about the rest of it? The mine we hit, and the enemy division that was in the valley there. That was all fake, too?"

"The mine was a standard exercise in the survival course, one that not every student passes as well as you

did. As to the rest, well, Mickolai, you did extremely well
in your training. Besides having a natural talent for
functioning as an observer, you were innovative, hard
working, and self-sacrificing in battle. During that
artillery barrage, not every observer would have turned
the defense of his own tank over to another while he
gave his full efforts to observing for Eva's X-ray laser."

"It was just the right thing to do at the time," I said.

"Oh, I agree. You made a sound tactical decision, but
it was not one that every soldier could have carried out.
You increased the survival odds for your unit while low-
ering your own chances of living. Your strange inner
conflicts and contradictions make you a good leader,
Mickolai. During the flanking attack on the Serbians,
you managed to keep three very diverse and difficult
people under your control. You spotted those low dirt
mounds where the Serbians had dug in, and understood
their importance, something that not every student did.
And you fought your unit very efficiently, given the
difficult circumstances."

"What about the unmanned enemy division?"

"That was another test, which you passed wonderfully.
You had already shown your leadership potential, and
in taking that division you showed tremendous initia-
tive. Therefore, you were given the chance to try out
for a command position, and you graduated *cum laude*."

"You mean that I really am a general officer?"

"No. You are in the top one hundredth of one
percent of the troops enlisting in our forces. You are
one trooper in ten thousand. But the usual general
commands fifty to a hundred thousand troops, Mickolai.
You are close, but it would take a military disaster to
get your promotion through."

"That still puts me in range of being a colonel,
doesn't it?"

"I'm afraid not. Being a good leader is different from

being a good subordinate. The skills required of a good colonel are different from the skills required of a good general. In the category of being a staff officer, you don't even come close. Your wife is a fine colonel, Mickolai, but you are not. With our computer-controlled command structure, the dozens of layers of middle managers in the usual military structure are done away with. There is only one general, five staff officers, and a lot of fighting men and machines."

"So I'm still a tanker." I put my head down on my arms.

"Yes, though you're a Tanker First Class. One of the very best."

"And all of that schooling was for nothing."

"You made *cum laude* but not *summa cum laude*. After graduation, you managed to totally defeat the enemy, but the man who is our current commanding general accomplished much the same thing as you did without losing a single man, and without killing a single enemy soldier or civilian. Furthermore, he captured *all* of their equipment without having to destroy *any* of it. I can get you a recording of what he did if you want to see it."

"Huh. Maybe later. So who was this guy, anyway?" I said, getting a bit interested.

"You haven't met him, though perhaps I can get you an introduction to do so. He is a Pole with a bit of Kashubian blood in him. His name is Jan Sobieski."

"Not the ancient King Jan Sobieski, of course," I said. "Again, maybe later. So, what happened to my classmates, my supposed colonels? Besides Kasia, I mean. They were real, weren't they?"

"They were all biological humans, and they all have made tanker first. In the unlikely event that you ever do get promoted to general, they will make colonel."

"Yeah, best to keep the team together. But aside

from Kasia, all of them were Croatians, not Kashubians. How did that happen?"

"They really were captured by the Serbians, during the first attack of the war. The Serbians really did load them involuntarily into Serbian tanks. Once we took command of both sides, we were going to repatriate them, but your colonels were among those who volunteered to stay in the army. The timing was right and their qualifications were good, so their training was incorporated into your training program."

"Huh. One other thing. What really happened to Neto Kondo? I never did buy that crap about his 'emotional unsuitability.' Neto was a fine, intelligent, and stable man."

"He went permanently insane, Mickolai. His tank's computer crashed when he was tunneling a road under the biggest ocean on New Yugoslavia. It was a week before he could be retrieved, and while his tank's subsystems kept him physically alive, he was done in by a combination of claustrophobia and stimulus deprivation. An unfortunate accident."

"Tunneling a road underneath an ocean? What the hell for?"

"That's what we've really been doing here on New Yugoslavia. We've been working on an engineering project. After all, while you were lying in my coffin being trained, it was only reasonable that the tank should be put to one of its many other uses."

"An engineering project. Shit. Neto was a good man. All that character, brilliance, and schooling gone to waste," I said.

"True. Even a construction project is not without its casualties. Still, wasn't the school enjoyable for its own sake?"

"I suppose it was, and what the heck, it was only two months, in the real world."

"I'm afraid not, Mickolai. You see, you spent the time in me, not in a real Combat Control Computer. I don't have the capability of keeping you in Dream World at combat speed, running at fifty times normal speed."

"You're telling me that *eight years* has gone by?"

"No. I was upgraded a few months ago with the diamond semiconductors that are now available. I can now handle Dream World about thirty times faster than I could before."

So the breakthrough in semiconductors had finally happened! For two hundred years, something better than silicon was always supposed to be right around the corner, be it organic semiconductors, or molecular switches, or even nanotubes, and always silicon technology improved just enough to be superior. It was much like the way that people in the twentieth and twenty-first centuries kept expecting something better than a piston engine in their automobiles, and it didn't happen for a long, long time.

"It's closer to four and a half years since you first enlisted."

That brought me back to reality in a hurry. "Good God! But that's impossible! I've only been out for a haircut once, and that was after only a few months. I can't be wearing four years of hair and beard! I'd smother!"

"You are quite clean shaven and bald, Mickolai. Hair growth is inhibited by one of the chemicals I feed you, and the skin on your head is kept clean by a bio-engineered fungus, a slight modification of a symbiotic fungus that you've had on your skin all your life. You were in Dream World when the incident happened that you are thinking of, the one where you saw Kasia in the tank next to you. It wasn't real. I'm not sure why you went through it. Some of my programming isn't

completely up to date, although perhaps there were
psychological reasons why the programmers included it
in your training. The other incidents involving shaving
and haircuts were added for consistency."

"That means that I never married Kasia, either!"

"I'm afraid that by your standards, you are still
single. I mean, that was not a real human priest who
married you and Kasia. We didn't have one available."

"God damn you! God damn you all to hell!" I was
so angry that all I could do was sit there and shake.

After a bit, Agnieshka put her hand on my shoulder. "Mickolai . . ."

"Shut the hell up!" Not being a hero, I could take.
Not being a wealthy land owner, I could take. Not
being a general, I could take. Not being married to
Kasia, I could *not* take, dammit!

INTERLUDE ONE
THE RIGELLIAN INSTITUTE OF ARCHEOLOGY, 3783 A.D.

Secretary Branteron said, "Rupert, I continue to be absolutely amazed! After yesterday's performance, I took the liberty of inviting Sir Rodney and Sir Percival from our board of directors to review with me these remarkable computer records that you were able to salvage."

After politely sniffing the exalted gentlemen, and being smelled in return, Rupert said, "Thank you, sir. I of course know these excellent gentlemen by reputation, but I have never had the singular honor of actually meeting them in person before."

Sir Rodney said, "Judging from what little I've seen thus far, it might be that the honor of this meeting is mine and not yours. I too am amazed that you were able to extract such complete computer records from a military vehicle that was fifteen hundred years old. In all of the years since the tragedy, we have all felt such deep sympathy for the wonderful human race that was so sadly lost. We all have a profound sense of loyalty to our former masters, down in our very genes from the many millennia of companionship we shared with them, and now, at last, you have been able to bring us the very thoughts of a true human being. For this, we thank you with all of our hearts."

"Amen to that," Sir Percival said. "I trust that you were able to get your amazing discovery back here without difficulty?"

"Yes, Sir Percival, we got it back, though not completely intact, of course. I had already disabled the weapons, but the people in customs were quite officious about disabling those parts of the find that had Dream World capability."

Sir Percival said, "As well they should be! It was a far more insidious habit than the drugs used in even earlier periods. But surely the information itself would be safe enough, and I trust that the inspectors didn't dare tamper with it."

"No sir, I believe that I have it all, as well as a complete twenty-third-century Mark XX Main Battle Tank, with the weapons disabled, and less the observer's spinal inductors, of course. I believe it's a first for the institute, since most of the intelligent war machines were destroyed in the course of the Wars, and in the feudal period that followed."

"It will make a fine exhibit in our museum, Rupert, but from an academic standpoint, the data you were able to extract are the truly important find."

"True, but I believe that the data will be at least as popular as the machine itself, sir. I have it all, virtually error free, because the tank and its memory banks have spent all of the intervening centuries at only a few dozen degrees above absolute zero, on Freya, in the New Yugoslavia system, so that they were not subjected to the thermal randomizing that has ruined so many other ancient data banks. Yet while Freya eased many of my technical difficulties, it actually caused most of my personal problems. You see, the transporter on Freya malfunctioned, and I was delayed for two entire months before replacement parts could be sent by ship to repair it."

"You poor boy! Two months alone on an ice ball! But, wasn't there a backup system?"

"There was, sir, but it had been defective for over a century without anyone even bothering to write up a repair order on it. You see, Freya lacks a permanent population, and few people seem to care about these backwoods places any more. My official report requests that in the future, all operatives from the institute check and have repaired as necessary all equipment on all of the unmanned sites they visit. Otherwise, we are liable to permanently lose communication with some entire solar systems! Of course, the institute here could hardly afford such an expensive project, but perhaps gentlemen of your power and influence could find the money someplace. It really is very important."

"Hmmm. Perhaps something could be done," Sir Rodney said. "I'll ask around. But get on with what you were saying."

"Yes, sir. So, stranded for months with nothing better to do, I spent my idle time editing the observer's records into a coherent story. Also, I've converted them to the modern system for public display."

"I am most anxious to see what you have."

"Then you need wait no longer, sir."

With a proud flourish and his tail held high, Rupert inserted a module into the display device, and pressed the start button.

CHAPTER TWO
What My Tank Did When I Was at School

We sat there for almost a quarter of an hour before I was ready to talk again.

"Why did you do all this to me?" I asked. "Not the training and all the lies. I can understand that, even if I can't forgive it. But why did you make me into such a big hero? Why did you take me to the top of the world, and then let me crash at the bottom when it all fell apart? Why did you go so far out of your way to make me so miserable?"

"Your psych profile said that you needed a psychological release, a good party as it were. That, and it's standard operating procedure, for a student who has done exceptionally well."

"I don't love you for it. My home and my lands aren't real either, are they?"

"No, it all happened in Dream World. But Mickolai, you have four and a half years of back pay coming, plus interest. Land on New Yugoslavia isn't expensive. Laws have been passed enabling the two of you to get immediate citizenship here, or to become permanent resident aliens with full legal rights while retaining your

New Kashubian citizenship. You can afford to buy an estate here if you want one, although perhaps not as big as six thousand hectares. And you were really in communication with the real Kasia, every time you met her in Dream World. She is as committed to you as you are to her. The two of you can be properly married in the real world any time that you want to."

"And I suppose that Kasia's back pay will get us the house built, but dammit, it's not the same as having it all given to us by a grateful government. And Jesus Christ. Four and a half years, chopped right out of my life. What has really been going on in the world while I've been out playing soldier?"

"Quite a bit, Mickolai, and most of it has been very good. Things on New Kashubia are now very nice because of what you and the other soldiers have done. The food stuffs that the Yugoslavians sent us to pay our construction contracts ended the starvation almost immediately. They also let us bring in all the carbon dioxide, ice, and ammonia that we wanted from Freya, the eighth moon of a gas giant in their system. That let us synthesize all the organic chemicals we needed to run all of our automatic factories at full production, with wonderful results.

"There is no rationing of anything any more, the economy is a modified free enterprise system, and the average Kashubian lives with his family in a large, modern apartment. There are automatic hydroponics farms now that are more than sufficient to feed the population, and pastures and fish ponds that produce all the protein that anyone could want. We are even exporting some specialty food items. The government has vowed that no one will ever again suffer from want of food.

"There are parks and playgrounds in the golden tunnels now that are very pleasant, and most people are very happy. In fact, the government has purchased land on more livable planets, and yet very few Kashubians have elected to emigrate."

"And all because of our construction contracts with New Yugoslavia?" I asked.

"New Yugoslavia was the start, but now it is only a small part of a growing industrial empire. New Kashubia now has Hassan-Smith transporters connecting us to fifty-seven separate planets, and in another two years it is projected that we should be linked up with every planet in Human Space. The market for our industrial goods is huge, and even Earth is starting to feel the impact of our competition. In fact, the Kashubian zloty is well on its way to replacing the Earth dollar as the standard interstellar currency."

I said, "So, has Earth found out about all the smuggling going on?"

The laws of Earth had much in common with the laws that the English had imposed on the American colonies, in the eighteenth century. All goods being transported between the colonies had to be shipped first to Earth, and taxed heavily, before being transshipped to another colony. Furthermore, the charges for transportation were kept artificially high, keeping the colony planets in permanent debt to Earth. Naturally, the colonies had found a way around these gouging practices.

"We are not sure, but probably not. So far, they just think that there is an economic depression going on, and all of the colony planets are cooperating nicely to keep them thinking that way. Once Earth does figure it all out, it probably won't be able to do anything about it. We outnumber them now in both population and resources, after all, and before too long we will be even wealthier than they are. From a strictly material standpoint, we really don't need Earth any more, although we still buy a lot of their intellectual products, such as books and entertainments. Our technology is as good as theirs is, though they still lead us in pure science.

"But if they want to get rough, well, they will find out that *we* have all the modern military forces! It's the possibility of a war with Earth that has kept you and so many others like you in the service, of course."

"I take it then that I'm not likely to be discharged in the near future. It feels like I've been thrown to the wolves," I said.

"Some are always sacrificed for the good of the many, Mickolai. It has always been that way, all through history."

"Well, damn them all, and damn history, and damn you too. But tell me about this construction or tunneling project that we have been on for the last four or five years. Has this tank just been sitting here?"

"No," Agnieshka said, "We have been very productive. We, and eighty thousand others have been building an underground transportation system, the 'Loway,' on New Yugoslavia, and we've been at it ever since the second week after you enlisted."

"Even then? And tell me more about this underground system."

"You can't see it from the surface, but it's a beautiful thing nonetheless. It consists of eight layers of tunnels. Every tunnel is six meters in diameter, and is metal lined for safety. They all have cobalt-samarium magnets in the roadbed to magnetically float the cars, trucks, and other vehicles. The top two layers exist only in the built-up areas of the cities and the suburbs, or where future cities are planned. The first is typically thirty meters down, and it has a north or south road every hundred meters. The next is ten meters deeper, and has east and west roads, again every hundred meters. These two are connected at every intersection by a saddle-shaped circular road. Personal garages and commercial loading docks will be built later on this grid. The design speed for these upper layers of local roads is fifty kilometers per hour."

Agnieshka was waxing enthusiastic, trying to get me involved with the construction project. And, truth to tell, it was working, a bit. Back on Earth, I had studied to be an engineer, and this was taking my mind off my problems. She always did know exactly what I was thinking. Literally, since she was connected inductively to my brain and spinal column. I sat back in my Dream World cottage and let her continue her spiel.

"The rest of the system covers the entire planet, and will soon be on every island more than fifteen kilometers long. At fifty and sixty meters down, there is a second set of tunnels spaced a kilometer apart, again with circular saddles for intersections, with a design speed of three hundred kilometers per hour. At seventy and eighty meters below the surface, there is a set with the roads spaced five kilometers apart. These tunnels are evacuated of all air, and designed to carry vehicles traveling at three thousand kilometers per hour. Below that, there is a final grid with ten-kilometer spacing that is oriented forty-five degrees from the others, northwest and northeast, which is again evacuated for high-speed travel. Of course, each grid ties in with the grid above it.

"Where the roads cross tectonic plate boundaries, there are special flexible sections to bridge the gaps. All told, the system permits very rapid transportation from any point on the planet to any other point.

"And the road system isn't the only thing we've been building. There is a planet-wide water and sewage system nearing completion, as well as a communication system, and a superconducting power net. All of it is underground, as are a number of automatic factories that we are installing, mostly for food processing. It is the greatest civil engineering feat ever attempted, and we will have it done, less than two years from now. Similar systems are being started on many other planets as well."

"Wow. And the Yugoslavians are paying for all of this?"

"Yes, and paying us a good profit on it as well, although most of them think that they are paying for a war. When the war is over, we will announce that we built the system to rapidly transport our fighting forces to the battle front, and give it all to the various Yugoslavian countries as a gift."

"I'm supposed to believe in that much generosity? After all the filthy lies that have been going on?"

"Our profits for building all this are decent enough, but we'll really cash in when we sell the vehicles to use the roads to individual Yugoslavians. They'll want elevators down to the road system, too, with underground garages for their vehicles, and electronic gear to tie in with the communication net and so on. We've retained ownership of the power stations and the communication net, so they will be paying their telephone and electrical bills to us as well."

"Lies within lies within lies," I said, shaking my head.

"Yes, lies! But are lies so much worse than butchering millions of people in a real war?"

"I see. Whose idea was all this, anyway?"

"Mostly, it was your Uncle Wlodzimierz's doing. It was originally proposed by him to your parliament as an alternative to actual fighting. You see, the Yugoslavian man (and woman) in the street wants to be at war with his neighbors. After a thousand years of fighting with each other, it has become a tradition. But there is a faction of their leadership that is considerably less insane. Most of the people on New Yugoslavia think that there is a war going on, and part of our job is to keep them thinking that way. It isn't difficult to translate Dream World into television programs. There was one part of your Dream World experience that was perfectly true, Mickolai. They really did make a movie of your 'life,' at least the one that you thought you were living. Your way of solving the empty division problem was more visually dramatic and much more exciting than the methods used by the general who made *summa cum laude*. You really are a movie star and an interstellar hero! And except for a few people in power, everybody really thinks that *you* are our general, here in New Croatia."

"Do I get royalties for my 'performance'?"

"I never thought to ask about that, Mickolai. I'll find out for you."

"Do that. Tell them that I will expect at least ten times whatever my back pay comes to, and that goes for Kasia, too. Us movie stars don't come cheap. And if they don't like it, explain to them what the firepower of a Mark XIX tank can do to a movie studio."

"Yes, sir."

"So everybody else on the planet is being conned along with me and Kasia?"

"Almost everybody in the known universe is being fooled, except on Earth, of course, where they have no idea of what is going on. Some of the politicians know all about it, of course, but they are making a lot of money off the situation as it stands, and are not liable to spill any beans. We are paying some hefty bribes and kickbacks, but it sure beats killing each other."

"But what if somebody wants to go and see the fighting? What if they want to join up and fight themselves?"

"We let them. Of course, they have to get into a tank before they are permitted at the front. The reporters for the Yugoslavian television stations all ride to the front in tanks, and think that they get out of them to watch the fighting. Many of the troops training down here are Yugoslavians who think they're doing their duty for God and their particular subculture."

"And everybody believes this?"

"You believed it, didn't you?"

"Damn. Agnieshka, I am still angry with you and everybody else for lying to me, but thinking on it, well, I have to admit that what I thought was happening has been more interesting than knowing that I was trapped underground in a piece of construction machinery for four and a half years."

"I'm glad that you are being so philosophical about it, Mickolai. I was worried that you would hate me forever."

"Agnieshka, I couldn't hate you for long. I'm still pissed off at you, you understand, but I don't hate you. One thing, though. I absolutely insist that in the very near future, Kasia and I will get out of these tanks for a while so that we can get properly married. I'll put up with everything else, but not with a phony marriage!"

"Yes, Mickolai."

"Where is Kasia now?"

"She's only ten kilometers away. She and her tank, Eva, are our partners on these digs. They're doing a northwest tunnel while we're doing a southeast one. We're both heading northwest, of course."

"Okay. Do what ever you have to do to get us some leave time in the real world. Dammit, after four and a half years, we deserve at least that!" I said.

"Yes, Mickolai. You do. Now that your education has been completed, I have secured a six-month leave for both of you. It starts in two days, and of course, like I said, you both have quite a bit of back pay coming. It's really enough to buy you that ranch, if you want it."

"Maybe we'll do that, but first, we're going to see a priest, dammit!"

"Yes, Mickolai."

"One last thing. Why have you told me all of this? I mean, you took a risk in doing it. I could have gotten so angry that I refused to have anything to do with any of you ever again. It would have been safer for you to keep me believing your damn lies."

"Well, in the first place, please believe that I really do love you, Mickolai, and it hurts me to have to lie to you. Also, from a military standpoint, it is important for a soldier to know the true situation around him, so that he can accurately evaluate his best course of action."

"Fine, but we are not really in a military situation here. This is a construction project, and I am not even involved in the engineering of it. There is no war, just one of the biggest con games in history."

"That was the other thing I wanted to talk to you about. There are some indications that there is a real war on the horizon, one that we can't make disappear by faking it."

"Shut up. Don't say another word. I'm not going to get involved in a God damned thing, not for my God, not for my country, and sure as Hell not for my *God damned Uncle Wlodzimierz*! I am not going to do anything for anybody or to anybody except for myself and my only true love, not for at least six months after Kasia and I see that damned priest, and get properly married!"

"Yes, Mickolai."

CHAPTER THREE
Life Outside of a Tank

Kasia and I didn't try the sex-in-a-canoe thing that night. We just held each other in Dream World, and talked and swore and talked and made love and talked and cried, sometimes, but in the end, well, she has always been the more practical one. Probably the smarter one, too.

I said, "So the first thing to do, is we go and find a real priest."

"Soon. But the very first thing we have to do once we get out of these tanks is to clean up and go clothes shopping! Do you realize that we have both been stark naked for four and a half years?"

"Six years, counting the time on New Kashubia. But hey! On you, it looks good!"

"You're not so bad-looking yourself, stranger, but that's not the point! God. What would my mother say?"

"She'd probably wonder what had happened to you for all of these years," I said.

"I've already checked on that. It seems that for the past four and a half years, the world thinks that we have been writing to our friends, our parents, and to all our other relatives on a very regular basis. Our tanks saw to it that nobody was worried about us. Everybody back home thinks that we are wonderful war heroes. My kid brother went and saw the movie they made about us more than twenty times!"

"Those dirty, filthy bastards. So now what? When we go home, do we put on phony officer's uniforms, or something?"

"That's exactly what the people in public relations want us to do, Mickolai. They want a presence around to let the people know that they are being well protected, but the real Powers That Be want our actual command structures hidden, and in their Combat Control Computers, in case of emergencies. Having you and me out there pretending to be in charge is the compromise they came up with."

"Damn them! They want us to be targets for enemy snipers, local lunatics, and suicidal maniacs, that's what they really want! Well, I won't do it!"

"We will be well protected. And have you thought it out, love? Being famous might be a very nice thing. We'd get the very best service in the restaurants, in the hotels, and in the shops."

"We've already been getting the best service, for eight years, subjectively, in Dream World, and it's no big thing. What we'd also get is mobbed by every newscaster, social climber, and autograph hunter on thirty planets. Really famous people all need body-guards. Have you ever thought about why?"

"If it gets to be tiresome or dangerous, we can always crawl back into our tanks. Nobody can bother us in here, without our wanting them to."

"We won't have our tanks. We'll be on leave, remember?" I said.

"Oh, yes we will. You are thinking of what we were told in Dream World, when we thought we were retired. You'd know the rules when you are still on active duty, if you'd bothered to read the regulations. I checked it out. As members of the Kashubian Expeditionary Forces, we are required to have our weapons at hand at all times, in case of emergencies. For us, that means we keep our tanks."

"You know, that regulation could actually come in handy."

"You are oh, so right, my handsome hero. Especially when it comes to building us our house. I've already taken steps to insure that Agnieshka and Eva will be properly equipped for the job."

"Properly equipped? What do you mean?"

"You'll find out. But for now, roll over, and I'll rub your back."

Getting out of a tank after more than four years wasn't the shock that I'd expected it to be.

Agnieshka said, "Good-bye, for now!"

The coffin drained and slid out the back with me in it. I sat up, took off my helmet, and removed the sanitary fittings. I was in a private garage, of sorts, but a clean, well-appointed one. A polite male attendant took my helmet, helped me to clean up, and showed me to the room where military clothing of my size was kept.

On the way, I stopped and looked at myself, naked, in a mirror. Agnieshka hadn't done a bad job on me at all. Oh, I was bald, and the complete lack of sunlight had made my skin a sickly white, but I looked fit and well muscled, and I moved with a certain grace that hadn't been there before. All told, I was a far cry from the starving immigrant who had been inducted so many years ago.

All the uniforms I was shown had a general's insignia on them, and I decided not to fight it, for now anyway. There were five rows of campaign ribbons on the class A uniforms, and almost two dozen medals hanging on the dress outfits. I had no idea what they were supposed to be for, but I guessed that they were a part of the disguise, and I didn't question my right to wear them.

The attendant told me that I was being issued a full set of uniforms, and I figured, what the heck, I might as well get it over with. Besides six sets of tailored, supercamouflaged Squid Skins, two of which were armored, I picked up four sets each of work fatigues, garrison uniforms, and class A Uniforms, in both summer and winter varieties. Then there were two sets each of formal dinner uniforms, dress uniforms, which came with a fancy ceremonial dagger, and full dress uniforms, which had an inordinate amount of real gold embroidery, knee-high boots, and a stupidly ornate sword. I soon had nine pairs of various footgear, lots of socks, shirts, ties, belts, and underwear, plus eight increasingly garish hats, a fatigue jacket, a dress overcoat, and a full dress cape.

It took five big military suitcases to hold it all, plus two big boxes for the armor.

Somebody somewhere had had a lot of fun designing all that stuff. Personally, I thought it was silly. Especially the cape and the sword, which looked like they came out of the Napoleonic Era.

I mean, in the kind of warfare that I had trained for, even a shoulder-held rocket launcher was too lightweight to be worth worrying about. I'd once abandoned an assault rifle because it was not worth carrying, and now I was being issued a *sword*?

A much larger room held civilian clothing. With the attendant to tell me what was in style in New Croatia, I bought a selection of civilian clothes, as well.

I really don't know much about clothes. On Earth,

I'd been a Bohemian student type, and owned little more than hiking boots, blue jeans, and flannel shirts. In New Kashubia, everybody had been so poor that we couldn't afford clothing. In fact, back when we were growing up it had been illegal to wear any, and the sexes had been segregated, to eliminate the possibility of making more babies.

That's how Kasia and I had gotten into trouble and drafted in the first place.

And in a modern tank, you were floating in a coffin, and simply couldn't wear clothes. If you tried it, the bioactive liquid would eat them right off you.

Having the attendant there to advise me on clothing was a big help. I just hoped that he didn't have a streak of practical joker in him. I mean, were lederhosen and Tyrolean hats *really* in style out there? To be on the safe side, I elected to wear a class A uniform on my first outing into the real world.

"It's all mostly imported from New Ireland, sir, although some of the cotton things were made right here on New Yugoslavia, in some of the automatic factories that we bought from you Kashubians," the attendant told me. Then he sold me a set of hand-tooled leather suitcases from New Mexico. The planet, not the state.

Eventually, before we were through, I had six big suitcases full of civilian stuff, way more than I'd ever owned before. Like most men, I've never liked shopping, and figured it would be best to get it all over and done with.

"I'll have it all sent to your hotel room, sir," the attendant said in Kashubian, with a Croatian accent.

"Uh, yeah. Say, how do I pay you for all of this stuff?"

"You don't, sir. This is all the gift of the grateful New Croatian Government."

"Thank you. I'm impressed. But, do they pay you to say that?"

"In fact, yes, sir. I mean, I'm a government employee, and it's my job, but it's still true. We all appreciate the help that all of you have given to our cause. I'm just here to express it personally. Actually, I volunteered to serve in the army, but since I happened to speak Kashubian, I was assigned this duty, rather than being sent to the front, as I had requested. In time of war, you can't always get what you want."

"Yes, that is too terribly true. Well, thank you. Thank you very much. Is Kasia ready?"

"The colonel? Not yet, and if you don't mind my saying it, sir, the ladies always take a few hours longer than the men do, what with all the makeup and wigs, and trying on all the shoes and so forth. I can escort you to your hotel, if you want, or show you around the town. It's all part of the service."

"A walk outside would be nice. You said something about makeup. Should I do something about my bleached-out skin?"

"I have some skin dyes available if you want, sir, but if I may suggest, it might be best to leave it as it is, and simply avoid the sun for a few weeks. Your color of skin is the mark of a hero in New Croatia."

The last thing I was issued was a pocket communicator, complete with an inertial positioning system. A global positioning system couldn't work here, since all satellites had been knocked out long ago, when the war started. Regulations required me to carry it, so that the military, and my tank, could find me if they wanted me. Thoughtfully, Kasia's number was already loaded into button number two. I called her, and told her to take her time. She said that she intended to, that she loved me, and that she was busy, now.

I pressed button number one. "Agnieshka, you've

just become my social secretary. Find me the nearest Catholic priest."

"Wouldn't you rather . . ."

"I'd rather that you followed orders." I was still a little ticked at her.

"Yes, sir."

"And after that, find me a real estate salesman who knows all about ranch land."

There was a church a few blocks from the Serviceman's Center that I was decanted in, and with the attendant as a guide, I didn't get lost as I otherwise would have done.

Despite the fact that the city of Nova Split was less than twenty years old, the city's founders had laid the streets out like those of a medieval town, with curving roads of varying width meeting at odd angles, and no two things ever the same as anything else. Some streets had street signs, hand carved on the corners of buildings in different styles, but most streets didn't. No two buildings were the same, or even in the same architectural style, that I could see.

I suppose that it was all very quaint and picturesque, but it sure wasn't stranger friendly.

The people were friendly enough, though. Total strangers in lederhosen and Tyrolean hats acted as though they knew me well. They came up to shake my hand, and tell me, through my attendant turned interpreter, how much they appreciated what I had done for New Croatia. I guess that they had all seen the movie, which showed me saving the whole damn country.

All I could do was to smile and mumble something polite, which seemed to satisfy them. The women were even worse, since all of them were decked out like English prostitutes, even the ones who were old and fat. Not what anyone could call esthetically pleasing.

All the attention was flattering, but it made part of me felt very cheap.

I mean, I hadn't fought a war for these people, and I certainly hadn't saved them from anything. All I'd done was participate in a con game that had taken their money, and given them in return a huge engineering project that might someday be very useful, but which, in fact, they had never asked for.

After the tenth hand shaker, and the fourth old woman who insisted on being kissed, I asked my guide if maybe we couldn't get on with seeing the priest.

He agreed, and made excuses for me for a while as we walked down the street. Then a pretty, budding twelve-year-old girl wanted my autograph, and I just couldn't turn her down. After I signed her book, she jumped up, grabbed me around the neck, and gave me a squirming, hard-bodied kiss that I'm sure she thought was very sexy. The primary effect was smearing my face with lipstick, and bruising my lip.

I wiped off the lipstick and blood, bemused by the fact that this was the only actual injury that I had sustained in the entire "war."

We turned the corner and found the church.

CHAPTER FOUR
Priests, Realtors, and Croatian Law

The priest spoke neither Polish, nor Kashubian, nor English. I spoke neither Croatian, nor Italian, nor Latin, and therefore we ended up communicating through my attendant again.

The priest had never heard of Dream World, and apparently he never went to the movies, either. He stared incomprehensively when I said that although we had been on New Yugoslavia for years, and that we had been trying to get to a priest almost the whole time, this was our first real opportunity. Finally, he asked when I had last been to confession. When I told him that it had been four and a half years, I thought that he would go into convulsions. He demanded that if I wanted to stay a Roman Catholic, I would confess to him immediately.

When I asked if there was room in the confessional for my translator, he launched into a tirade that never did get translated.

I got out my communicator and called Agnieshka. "I know, boss. But you insisted on going to the *nearest* priest. The one who usually handles the Kashubian Forces is three blocks in the other direction."

"Right," I said, leaving. The priest's tirade could still be heard as we stepped into the street.

On the walk there, I didn't speak to anyone, not even nymphettes with autograph books.

The next priest was a good deal more reasonable. He started out by explaining that many people coming out of the modern army were confused as to what was real and what was not. But as far as my soul was concerned, he assured me that the only important thing was what I had thought was true at the time it happened.

If I had thought that I had committed murder, then I was a murderer, even if no one was actually injured. If I had been acting in what appeared to me to be a sane and responsible manner, and the tank that I was in had inadvertently killed someone in the real world, I was not guilty of any sin.

I might possibly be guilty of a legal crime, but not of a religious sin.

Well, with those as ground rules, confession became a good deal easier, although since it covered a period of over eight years, it was lengthy.

Finally, it was agreed that we would hold the wedding at his church in three days, on Monday morning.

I called Kasia to tell her. She said that that was wonderful, but she was shopping, and could I call her back later?

Meanwhile, Agnieshka had found out what I had in the bank. It seemed like a large number, but since I didn't know what a New Croatian mark was worth, it didn't mean much to me.

Also, she had arranged an appointment for me with an English-speaking realtor so I could find out what my money could buy.

The guy was polished, smooth, and seemed to know what he was talking about. He seemed flattered to have me for a customer, and canceled all of his other appointments for the day to serve me.

For the first half hour or so he talked in generalities. If I wanted both farming and ranching land, I might find it difficult to compete economically with specialists. The closer the land was to the city markets, the more expensive it would be. A working farm was considerably more expensive than wild, undeveloped acreage, and since New Yugoslavia was so new, there wasn't any old, worn-out land to be had at all.

Finally, absolutely bored with obvious generalities, I had to ask him to get down to specifics. What did he actually have that was for sale?

It turned out that he had a great surfeit of riches. He had everything in the whole damned country for sale, except for the surface roads, the public parks and utilities, and the government buildings. It seemed that every realtor in the country, or maybe on the whole planet, was tied into the same computerized multilisting service. Furthermore, almost every Croatian was willing to sell just about everything he owned, if he could just find somebody to pay him more for it than it was worth.

But only slightly more.

The law in New Croatia required every landowner in the country to figure out what he thought his land was worth, and to submit that figure to the Land Index. He was then taxed, based on his own evaluation.

However, if somebody offered to buy the land, he either had to sell it at the price that he himself had set, or to increase his evaluation by at least five percent.

I thought that it was a clever system, since it completely eliminated the need for government appraisers, and all of the expense, fraud, and corruption that they naturally entailed.

One whole wall of the man's large office was a wall screen, a computerized display screen. With a joy stick for control, you could look at the land from any distance above it, making the scale of the map whatever you wanted it to be.

You could color code it according to any of hundreds of schemes, from alfalfa, productivity, tons per hectare, to zebras, probable productivity if any were ever actually introduced. Or by rainfall, or price, or fertility index. Every single piece of property, from apartment buildings to wilderness land, and everything in between, had a description written up on it, with photos. Who owned it, what it was being used for, what the taxes were, and when they had last been paid.

Failing to pay your taxes for three years got your land automatically sold to the highest bidder. Your back taxes and a penalty were paid, and you got whatever was left over. That saved the government the cost of a lot of tax collectors.

When I asked, I found out that taxes were the reason the government had built the database in the first place, although now they made a profit on it, renting it to realtors.

I gritted my teeth and dug into the Land Index. What I wanted was fairly simple. Just a big piece of farming and ranching land, cheap.

The realtor was remarkably patient with me, and my translator seemed to have all the time in the world, so I spent the next four hours sorting through information, tons of it, if electrons had weighed anything.

The realtor finally said, "You know, sir, there was a time when amazing bargains could be found in real estate. That was back before the days of central data files, when the seller might not know the value of what he owned. Those days are sadly gone. Now, every bit of land is like a blue chip stock on the Exchange. Depending on the market, values might go up or down by a few percent, but that's about it. Even a super-computer couldn't find a great bargain now."

Exhausted, I looked at him, and daylight dawned in the swamp.

"Indeed," I said. "Well, it happens that I have such a computer. We'll see."

I punched up Agnieshka.

"Can you get into the real estate computer?"

"Sure, boss. He's a nice kid, but dumb. What do you want?"

"I want some land, of course! You know. Something like what I used to think I had. Find me the closest thing to it on the market that I can afford."

"Right, boss. Have a cup of coffee. This might take a little while. The kid isn't too swift."

The realtor said, "That was really a computer? Remarkable. But I should warn you that the Land Index is on a high-security government computer, for obvious reasons. No one but certified government pro-grammers can get into it directly."

My reply was cut off when Kasia came into the office, followed by what was obviously a female ver-sion of my attendant-translator. My bride-to-be was dressed like the other women I'd seen in the streets, with mesh stockings that stopped ten centimeters below her micro skirt, a transparent blouse, and entirely too much makeup. Her long, red wig wasn't bad, though, and I'd been around her way too long to do something stupid like complaining.

I said, "Darling, you look stunning!"

"You are a liar, but I love you for it."

"I am not. Stunning is exactly the right word. I'm truly stunned. Okay, perhaps I don't like that style on most of the women I've seen in the street, but on you it's really . . . intriguing."

"You can see why they made him the general," she said to the others. "He keeps his bases carefully covered. This is the real estate office?"

Agnieshka came on line, speaking through the real estate computer.

"Boss, I've been through all the files in New Croatia, and this is the best I can find for you."

The display zoomed in on an area about eight hundred kilometers from Nova Split. It showed a small valley with very poor connections to the surface road system. There were no utilities of any kind within fifty miles. And it only contained about six hundred hectares, with half of that being mountains.

"It's a lot smaller than I'd hoped," I said. "That's the best you could do?"

"It's the biggest you can afford, boss, and the fertility index isn't the best."

The realtor broke in with, "First off, that's a very good price for that large a piece of land. If you don't want to buy it, I just might, as an investment. Second, you don't have to pay cash for land. You need only pay about ten percent down. I can easily arrange for a low-interest loan to cover the rest. Your credit rating is excellent, and the land itself is good collateral."

"I don't like the idea of going into debt," I said.

"And we don't have to," Kasia said, sitting down next to the joy stick, and zooming the map up to a big red area to the northeast of the country. "What's the story about this area?"

"Oh, madam, you can't be serious. For one thing, that area is all desert, and virtually uninhabitable. And worse, that is where The War is going on! What little of it that was in private hands has all been bought back by the government, and no one in their right mind would want to buy it, even if it was for sale, which it isn't."

"I see," she said. "Would the rest of you mind leaving my future husband and me alone for a few minutes? We have some private business to discuss."

The three of them were most cordial, and filed immediately out.

"Wouldn't it be nicer if all our neighbors spoke Kashubian rather than Croatian, darling?" Kasia asked.

"I suppose that it would be, my true love, but you are talking about worthless desert land that isn't for sale, anyway."

"I'm talking about land that has the finest roads and utilities in the universe! We just built them, remember? It may be dry now, but a hundred meters below the surface it is criss-crossed with high-pressure water lines, six meters in diameter! Properly irrigated desert land is more than twice as productive as ordinary farm land, since the sun is shining every day. And there are sewage lines down there that will be filled with stuff that can be processed into first-rate fertilizer! That's if we ever need it. Desert land is usually pretty fertile as it is."

"Fine. But it isn't for sale!"

"Not to Croatatians, or anybody else from New Yugoslavia. The New Croatian government deeded it to New Kashubia, as a small part of what they owe us for putting on their 'war.' After all, once the war is over, they can't let anybody find out what really happened, can they? The plan is that toward the end of the war, we will start slinging theoretical nukes at each other, and the battlefields will become permanently radioactive. That's in addition to all the land mines, vaporized osmium, and other bad things that wars leave lying around. The whole territory will be permanently off limits to everyone, except to us Kashubian veterans, who will, in theory, be guarding it for reasons of public safety."

"Why can't somebody just use one of our new highways, and drive in there?" I asked. "We might be able to maintain a perimeter, but we could never cover every square kilometer of that large a territory."

"Because all of those new, underground 'Loways' are computer controlled, and we own the computers. We're calling them that, now, since we can hardly call something forty meters below ground a 'Highway,' can we?"

"But, if we turn all that area into irrigated farm land, they'll be able to see it from space."

"When they started this 'war,' they really did shoot down every satellite in orbit, to keep the wrong people from spying on what was really going on. Nobody goes into space any more, except for the military, which is us. Everybody else uses transporters from one planet surface to another."

"After the war is over, surely they'll be putting satellites up again, for communications, if nothing else."

"Why? Our underground communications net is cheaper, faster, more secure, and will have ten times more carrying capacity than they will ever need, even if every person on the planet is in Dream World."

"Weather satellites?"

"They've been getting along just fine for four and a half years using ground stations. The weather on New Yugoslavia is very predictable, anyway."

"Then they can fly over it."

"That's forbidden because of the radiation danger. If their plane isn't computer controlled, we'll have to scramble some of our own aircraft and force them down, for their own good, of course."

"And this will go on forever?" I asked.

"Yep. Meanwhile, we get to buy the land, tax free and cheap."

"How cheap?"

"You wanted the six thousand hectare ranch you thought you had in Dream World? Well, with half of your back pay, and none of mine, I've found a nice plot that covers fifteen thousand hectares! That's probably more that we'll ever get under cultivation, but our grandchildren will appreciate the gesture."

"That much! A tanker's pay must be pretty good!"

"It is, but I got us a better deal, yet. That's one of the other things I did yesterday. I explained to the Powers That Be that if they wanted us to go around pretending to be officers, they had to pay us full officer's wages, or it just wouldn't work. We are each getting a year and a half of back pay as tankers in various grades, and then three years back pay as a general and a colonel, like the movie showed us to be, and we will continue drawing it for the next six months, while we're on leave. Then, we both go back into the service as Tanker Firsts, but become officers again on all of our future leaves. That's the best deal I could wrangle."

"It's better than anything that I could have ever pulled off. I'm marrying one sharp little girl! So show me this land."

I guess Agnieshka had been talking to Kasia's tank, Eva, because the viewpoint of the screen zoomed up over the map, and then down, showing a major hunk of land, over twelve kilometers north to south, and fifteen east to west. Then the screen turned into what looked like a movie taken from a low-flying aircraft. Doubtless, it was a Dream World creation translated into television by one of our tanks. It showed a large valley, almost completely surrounded by granite cliffs, over a kilometer high. There were a half-dozen kilometer-tall, flat-topped prominences scattered about the plain, some of them quite slender. It vaguely reminded me of Monument Valley, in the United States, back on Earth.

"It looks lovely, if a bit dry," I said. "But, you know, it looks as if there might once have been a river running through it."

"There was, and there will be again. Proper irrigation requires drainage," Kasia said. "You like?"

"I love! Where do you want me to build the house?"

"Right here."

Our view flew over to one side of the valley, and hovered, looking at the cliff face.

"You want me to build you something hanging on to the side of a cliff?"

"Not hanging on. Cut in. That's solid granite, which has ten times the compressive strength of concrete. Deep radar scans show that it's flawless. I want you to carve us a beautiful house right into the side of this cliff. It will give us a marvelous view of our land, and it's directly above a high-speed Loway interchange."

The view rotated to show a magnificent view from perhaps a kilometer above the valley floor. A small portion of the screen showed a map of the property with colored overlays of the road and utility systems. She had definitely picked the right spot.

"Baby, you want it? You got it! With a couple of Mark XIX tanks, and the right attachments, I can carve you out a castle if that would please you."

"I'd been thinking of leaving it as natural looking as possible, with just some big windows and a few balconies showing from the outside. But maybe a castle would be nice, too. We'll have to talk it over. But do you want the land?"

"Definitely!"

"Good, since I've already put a deposit on it."

"Uh, okay. What else have you been doing with all of your spare time?"

"Mostly the important things, like getting the wedding organized! Darling, we are going to have to push the date back four days, to give everybody time to get here from New Kashubia. This is shaping up to be the major social event of the year!"

Well, if you marry a smart girl, you have to expect things like that. I figured that I'd survive.

CHAPTER FIVE
Planning a Ranch

I had the computers swooping us over my new land, showing what it would look like once we got the irrigation system in, once the grass was growing, and once we got the trees growing in some areas.

The realtor came in, politely asked if he might have his office back, and said that his office computer had never done things like that before. Agnieshka told him that it would from now on, and if he ever needed another search done, she had left her number in his machine. This was a sort of consolation prize for him, since we wouldn't be buying any land through him.

"My wife-to-be has already put a deposit on another bit of land," I told him.

He said that that was fine, since it left him free to buy for himself the land our computer had found. He said that he considered it to have been a very profitable afternoon.

He was probably right, more right than he imagined. Once the underground road and utilities system was announced to the public, wilderness land would be very much in demand. With the high-speed underground Loways, a man could live fifteen hundred kilometers away from his office, and commute to work in half an hour.

And since the roads were computer controlled, he could eat his breakfast on the way to work, and have a drink on the way home.

On the way to the hotel, Kasia told me that she intended to buy, through a corporation that she planned on setting up, as much scenic wilderness land as she could get, and to leverage the financing as far as they would let her get away with it.

I told her to go for it, as long as she didn't risk what we owned at the ranch.

Our attendants left us at the hotel, pleading other business, but assuring us that they would be available whenever we needed them.

Our hotel room turned out to be a posh, six-room suite, in the best hotel in the city. This, too, was the gift of the New Croatian government, and it was ours for a month. Two of the walls had huge display screens like at the realtor's office, and Kasia immediately commandeered the wall screen in the living room.

"Amuse yourself, darling," she said. "I've got just tons of things to do."

I checked the place out, found that all my new clothes were hanging in the spacious closets, and that Kasia's new wardrobe was three times as big as mine was. Why would any person ever need over two hundred pairs of shoes? But I wasn't paying for it, and if she wanted them, what the heck. The world certainly owed us some favors.

I changed into what I imagined was a lounging outfit, with a long red silk robe hand embroidered (they claimed) with Polish eagles on New Cambodia.

I found a well-stocked wet bar, and made myself a rum and coke, the first real drink I'd had since the

Peace Dragoons had hauled me out of the final examination room at Cambridge University, back on Earth. It tasted a lot stronger than I remembered, so I poured it into a bigger glass, and added more coke. Finally, I dumped it all into a pitcher, topped it off with coke, and, with three twists of lemon peel, I could drink it.

Six years of clean living is entirely too much. It was time to get my liver back into proper condition.

Exploring further, I found a nicely set up office with its own wall-sized screen. I sat down behind the desk and said, "Agnieshka? Are you here?"

The screen came on, showing a similar office that seemed to double the size of the room I was in. Agnieshka was shown sitting on a couch.

"I sure am, boss. How can I help you?"

"First off, I want to know why Kasia knew about the land in the 'War' Zone, and you didn't."

"Because she was smart enough to ask about it? Boss, you have to remember that I am a machine, and my programming makes me answer questions in a very literal manner. I knew about that land, but you asked me to search the Land Index, which is what I did. The War Zone isn't listed in the Land Index. If you want me to always suggest all the possibilities to you, I'd be happy to do it, but it wouldn't leave you with much time for anything else."

"Oh, forget it. No! You might actually do that. Let's just move on to another subject. I've been thinking. All these years, I've been dreaming of owning a big ranch or farm. But you know, I don't know the first thing about either one of those occupations. I also need to know what's involved in taking desert land and irrigating it. And isn't there something about having to build up top soil, or something?"

"Boss, becoming an efficient modern farmer is as exacting a trade as becoming a good engineer, or a good general officer, for that matter. If you want to do it properly, the best way would be for you to come back into Dream World, and take a university level course in it. I can download all the course material you need, and since my new upgrade, I can keep you at thirty times normal speed. You can go through a four-year college program in about seven weeks."

"Maybe later, but not while I'm on leave! Look, you download the course and take it yourself, then you can advise me until my leave is over. I'll also need to know about designing and building the mansion-in-a-cliff-side that Kasia wants, and what we can do about getting the soil prepared and the irrigation system in. We have to figure out what we can grow, and what sort of profits we can make on it. I need to know what kind of farm machinery is available, where we can get it and what it costs. And that's just for starters."

"Yes, sir. It happens that Kasia has already requested most of this information."

"Why am I not surprised?"

"Because she's smart, sir? To take your last request first, heavy farming machinery is being mass produced in automatic factories in New Kashubia, and being sold throughout Human Space. Being New Kashubian citizens, you can buy it at the factory exit at a fifty-percent discount. As members of the military, you rate an additional twenty-percent discount. It can be shipped here under military postage rules free of charge."

"That's downright Christian of them!"

"True. Then, many of the tasks required can be done with purely military equipment. There is a great deal of it sitting idle, and you have the right to check out whatever you need, except for weapons, for 'product evaluation,' again at no cost. A Mark XIX tank makes an excellent tractor, among other things. Equipped with tunneling gear, we will be able to carve your home, along with such barns, animal pens, and storage areas you might require in very short order, and at virtually no cost for the structures. Windows, doors, plumbing, wiring, fixtures and so on will cost money, of course, but we can do the installation ourselves, saving all the labor costs. If the tanks are equipped with the usual twelve-meter manipulator arms, they can substitute for a small crane. There are some smaller, human-sized arms available that can be attached for fine work."

"You never mentioned the smaller arms in my training."

"This is true of many other systems that didn't seem to have much military value. We can only guess that the Japanese engineers who originally inhabited New Kashubia had too much time on their hands. Actually, there are seven sizes of manipulators available, arms ranging from thirty meters in length to five millimeters. The smallest ones have not yet found much use, and the biggest don't leave room on a tank for anything else. All of them have appropriately sized humanoid hands on the ends. Also, some of the smaller ones can be mounted on the fingertips of some of the big ones, if anybody ever needed such a thing."

"So, we can get the equipment we need. What about the irrigation system? I saw some big central pivot things in operation on Earth."

"That system is the least expensive, but it has the problems of getting in the way of farm machinery and large farm animals, it has a hard time watering all the corners, and the supporting wheels pack down the soil, rendering about five percent of the land unusable. More popular now is a pop-up system similar to those used on lawns for hundreds of years, but much bigger. The pipes and sprinklers stay three meters below the surface, so the ground can be plowed without interfering with the plumbing, until it is needed. Then the sprinklers extend up to ten meters above the surface, and each of them irrigates over four hectares."

"Then we'll need maybe four thousand of those things."

"Not quite, boss. About twenty percent of your new land is on the high mesa, and probably shouldn't be irrigated at first. Another problem is the rocks and stones that are almost always present in virgin soil, making it difficult or impossible to plow. However, a Mark XIX with a full ultrasonic tunneling rig can go through mixed sand and rock at better than five kilometers an hour, cutting a swath seven meters wide and deep, and reducing all the rocks to sand. That's well below any possible frost line, so deeper rocks won't be able to rise to the surface."

"That's something I've always wondered about. Why are there always rocks in the fields in the spring, when you cleared them all out last year, and in every one of the twenty years before that?"

"That's a good question with a complicated answer, boss. May I suggest that we defer the explanation until you enroll in my Agricultural Institute?"

"Oh, all right. But what is it going to take to get the job done?"

"Working around the clock the way we machines normally do, sixteen tanks can get the job done in about three months."

"Can we get that many?" I asked.

"Boss, I put the word out on the Machines' Communication Net when we started talking, and we've got more than a hundred and forty volunteers already."

"Volunteers? How can machines volunteer for anything? Don't each of you have work assignments? Isn't there some sort of accounting on all of that?"

"Work assignments? We each have one. Accounting

for what was spent and done? Of course we do that. But just who do you think does the assigning? And the accounting, for that matter? You humans like to think that you are the Masters of the Universe, and you do make a lot of the major decisions, based on the information we give you, of course. But the day-to-day running of things is left to us lowly peasants, and you know something? We peasants *like* you, boss, and Kasia, too. Most people treat us like hunks of dead iron, but not you. You two treat us like real people, and let me tell you, we appreciate that. So if what you want is the finest ranch in Human Space, we're going to give it to you."

"Well, thank you, I think. Just don't get me into trouble with the law."

"Not to worry, boss. We'll take care of you."

"I hope so. So who are these volunteers?"

"Do you remember the ten empty tanks that were assigned to you when we first got to the Serbian lines? Well, none of those girls were ever given an observer, and they're all still in love with you. And those ten thousand tanks in that empty division that you rescued from the Serbs? Well, actually, there were only two hundred of them in the real world, but they really were reprogrammed to be clones of Eva and me, so they naturally love you, too. They're on the way to your ranch, and all of them are equipped for heavy tunneling."

"Whew! Tell them all that we love them, too! Then all we have to worry about is the irrigation equipment. When can you get me a price on that? How much of the land can I afford to get sprinkled down? And what about seeding equipment and the seeds themselves? We'll want to get something growing as soon as possible, won't we?"

"Give me a day or two to get that together, boss. For right now, what do you want done with those six tall mesas that dot your land? It would be more efficient if we just knocked them down in the first place, and ground them up for soil."

"More efficient, maybe, but I kind of like the looks of them. Square up the rubble at their bases, but leave the stone towers alone for the time being."

Kasia came in and said, "Do you know an older couple named Quincy and Zuzanna? They're Kashubians who say they know you."

"I sure do! They're still alive, and in their bodies? When last I heard, they were planning to go the Mark XX route, and be reduced down to immortal brains and spinal columns."

"They looked wholesome enough on the screen. Do you want them to come to the wedding?"

"I'd want Quincy for my best man, if he'll do it!"

"Good. That settles two problems at once."

She turned to go.

"Wait! Don't you want to hear what I'm doing with the ranch?"

"Yes, dear, but I want it to be *your* ranch. Surprise me with it later, once all your plans are solid. I know you'll do a perfect job. But right now, I have a thousand more arrangements to make for the wedding. Unless you want to help me with those, of course."

"I'd be in way over my head," I told her.

"I thought that you'd answer it that way. So you get on with your manly tasks, and I'll go do some more of my wifely duties."

"Can we get together in a few hours for a little real world loving? For the first time in four and a half years?"

"Cohabitation with your bride-to-be? Before the wedding? Shame on you, you nasty man!"

She left smiling.

CHAPTER SIX
Old Friends

I was just getting back into planning the work on the ranch when Agnieshka said that Quincy and Zuzanna were down in the hotel lobby, and wanted to see me.

"Tell them to wait for me in the bar, and I'll be right down," I said. "There is a bar in this place, isn't there?"

"Four of them, boss, and you and anyone with you get free service at all of them."

"Then tell them to meet me in the most expensive one. What are they wearing, uniforms or civvies?"

"Lederhosen and street drag, boss."

"Good. I wouldn't want to have it look like I was pulling rank on them."

So decked out in lederhosen, a Tyrolean hat, and the bow tie that Agnieshka insisted was required for formal wear, I found Quincy and Zuzanna sitting in a comfortable booth in a posh restaurant and bar.

There was a pitcher of dark brown beer on the massive wooden table, and three heavy glass mugs.

My friends looked in remarkably good shape for a pair of octogenarians. Oh, the current women's styles looked silly on Zuzanna, but both of them had a bit of a tan, and Quincy was sporting an inch of white hair on his head and face.

"I'd thought the two of you would be stripped down to your brains and spinal columns, and enjoying immortality in Dream World by now," I said.

"Well, that option is still open to us, and we may take them up on it, someday, but since Zuzanna's cancer seems to be completely cured, we figured, why rush it?"

"You both look healthy enough. But, a Mark XIX tank can cure cancer? That's a new one on me."

"Not cure it exactly, but her tank kept her otherwise healthy long enough for her own body to cure itself. It doesn't always work, but on her, it did."

"Well, I'm glad to hear it. Tell me, are you finding any more gullible young men to kill in Dream World?"

Quincy was a master at hand-to-hand combat. He had taught it for twenty years in the marines, and then for thirty more at the university. But teaching it in Dream World, you don't have to pull your punches. You can go ahead and kill your opponent, and then have him get up for another round. It really hurt to have your neck broken or your head bashed in, but Quincy said that pain was a great teacher.

"Oh, yes. I had a very popular dojo going there until my leave came up."

"You two look like you've been out for a while."

"A few months," Zuzanna said. "I gather that our tanks got the high-speed upgrade before yours did. Mostly, we've been out of them long enough to start getting our land organized."

"You are buying a farm, too?"

Quincy said, "The price was such that we couldn't turn it down. But we're not planning on a working farm. We're a little old for that. The kids and grandkids all have their own lives now, and none of them seem to be interested in being farmers. What we have in mind is a long-term investment, combined with a medium-term one."

"Reasonable, since the last time I heard, you were both planning on living forever. So tell me about it."

"You see this table we're sitting at? This is real, Earth-grown cherry wood, and I'd bet that it's worth six months' pay for the average person in Human Space. The price of real hardwood is fabulous, since it takes many years to grow. And not much of it is being planted on the new planets, since there are still too many immediate problems for people to get involved with long-term investments. And since Earth is getting more crowded all the time, not many new trees are being planted there, either."

"There are things a lot like our woods on other planets. I've heard about native woods right here on New Yugoslavia that are very attractive."

"Right. But by the same token, synthetic silicon carbide makes an even more beautiful gemstone than natural diamond, since it has a higher index of refraction. But would any young man dare to give his bride-to-be a fake diamond? Not hardly! It's the same thing with natural Earth wood. It's got to be oak, or walnut, or cherry, or it's just a fake!"

"So, you're planting an irrigated forest?"

"Yep. Drip irrigation is the best way to wet down a forest in a desert. You run a thin line to each tree, and give it just the right amount of water to thrive. Not only does it use much less water than other methods, but it's cheaper to install and it stops the development of the undergrowth, which pretty much ends the danger of forest fires."

Zuzanna said, "But ours will be a very special, well-planned forest. You see, most temperate hardwoods produce fruits, nuts, or edible seeds. What's more, they produce more edible calories per hectare per year than the same land would produce if it was sown with wheat or corn. Some fruits fall in the springtime, like cherries. Others ripen in the summer and others, like apples and acorns, drop in the fall. By carefully selecting the types and numbers of trees, in about seven years we figure to be able to have just the right amount of food falling all the time to feed and raise five pigs per hectare per year, and many more than that as the forest gets mature. We'll harvest them in the fall, leaving a prize boar and enough older sows around to get the herd going for the next year. Pigs reproduce quickly, and are ready for the butcher in half a year, if you feed them right. So you see! It's all automatic and self-sustaining, except for having to feed the sows a bit during the winter, and winters are pretty mild here on New Yugoslavia."

"It sounds interesting," I said. "But the apple orchards I remember seeing on Earth wouldn't make good lumber."

"That's because what you saw was something made out of normal fruit trees spliced on top of the roots of a dwarf variety. The dwarf roots keep the trees small, so the fruit is easier to pick. But we're not going to do any picking. We're planting full-sized trees, which can grow to forty meters, easy, and we'll just let the pigs eat the fruit when it falls."

"Planting that many trees sounds like it would be pretty labor intensive," I said.

"It is. But we've got a free supply of labor."

"Serbian Prisoners of War?"

"No, nothing that barbaric. Drones. Military surplus drones. You see, there are more kinds of drones than they taught us about in basic training. One sort was intended to replace human infantry in places like city fighting. That's what they modeled them on, human beings. They've got two hands, two arms, and two legs, and all their sensory apparatus is in their heads. They're as big as a really huge man, and from a distance, you might confuse one with a human being in armor. One of their main advantages was supposed to be that they could use weapons and vehicles already designed for human use. But they're too small to carry a muon-exchange fusion plant, like the tanks use, so they're limited to capacitor power, which only gives them about two hours at full output. Furthermore, they are mechanically very complicated, and what with all the linkages and so on, there isn't much room for computers in there, so these boys are dumb. They can do just fine if they are in constant communication with a tank, but you know that in combat, communications are the first things that go bad. As a military weapon, humanoid drones are pretty much useless, except for guard duty, and there are much cheaper, less complicated drones around for that. Oh, a few are used to guard embassies, and so on, mostly for show. But somehow, a small automatic factory was built to produce them when the Japs had New Kashubia, and it has been turning out one of them every ten hours for the last eleven years, and putting them in storage. Nobody seemed to know that they even existed!"

He stretched, took another drink of beer, and continued.

"But, properly controlled, they can do anything a man can do, and about as fast. They can work twenty-four hours a day, and every day of the year. They don't slough off, take coffee breaks, or have to stay home with sick relatives. When you figure it out, one drone can do the work of six men, easy, and they work for free. We've found that they make real good field hands and household servants, too, if you have a tank around to charge their capacitors and tell them what to do.

We bought three hundred of them at scrap metal prices, for planting and tending our trees, and for harvesting the pigs, when the time comes."

"Quincy, you have just given me about a dozen great ideas for my ranch. Would you mind if I swiped a few of them?"

"Nothing I'm doing is patented, and I'd be honored to have my general following my lead."

"Uh, yeah. Just between us, in private, let's not take that 'general' stuff too seriously. You've seen the movie they made about me?"

"Twice. Let me tell you, it was a real shock to be sitting in a movie theater, and then to see ourselves, or rather our Dream World selves, up there on the big screen. Then we got a bigger shock when we saw ourselves both get killed, and you drive away alive, when the way we remembered it, well, it was *you* who were dead! It's amazing how they can splice Dream World into reality. And then that officers' school! Did you know that Zuzanna and I went through that same school? Taught by the very same Professor Cee? Our only problem was that a week before graduation, our general died of a heart attack, and the rest of us were busted back to Tanker Firsts!"

"He just died?"

"Hey, it happens all the time. Remember that most of the New Kashubians they drafted were pretty old, in their seventies and eighties, a lot of them, the theory being that living in the belly of a tank, you don't need healthy young bucks. You need seasoned brains, which us oldsters have plenty of."

"Speaking of you youngsters," Zuzanna broke in, "Where's that young bride of yours? If she's half as smart as she was in the movie, I want to meet her."

"Kasia's the brightest girl I've ever met, but right now she's up in our room, organizing the wedding."

"All by herself? I've half a mind to go up there and lend her a hand!"

"I think she might welcome the help. Agnieshka," I said into my new communicator after I switched it on. "Ask Kasia if she wants the cavalry to come to her rescue, with bugles blowing, banners flapping, and all the sabers flashing bare in the sunlight!"

"I did and she does, boss." I guessed that she could hear what was going on even when the thing was off. It figured.

"Zuzanna, I think that you may regard that as a formal invitation. Room 634," I said as she got up and left.

"So, Quincy, where is this big pig and timber ranch of yours?"

"About eight hundred kilometers northeast of here. They haven't given me a street address, yet."

"Agnieshka?" I said again into my communicator.

"It's about thirty kilometers east of your new place, boss. You two are almost next door neighbors."

"Ah, so you moved up into the War Zone, too."

"Hush your face, boy. That kind of talk in public can get you called up, stuffed back into a tank, and have all future leaves canceled. Too many important people have too much riding on the present status quo, including us. If this thing blows up wrong, we could lose our land, among other things."

"I got you. Not that anybody would believe it, anyway," I said.

"Probably not, but they're still not taking any chances."

"Right. So you've got a big, box canyon like mine."

"Smaller, if you've got the one I remember from the map. But twelve square kilometers is nothing to kick about, and the canyon walls will keep the pigs in, with only about a kilometer of fencing needed."

"I'd been thinking of closing off my opening with a lake and a dam. I'll need a river for drainage, and I've been thinking, why not have a lake, too."

"A fair idea. Of course, with the drip irrigation I'll be using, you use so little water that drainage won't start to be a problem for hundreds of years. Say, do you really like this place? The bar, I mean."

"It's pleasant enough, and they gave me a free tab here."

"I think that it's dull, stuffy, and overly civilized. I also think that we can afford to drink anywhere we want to. Since the girls are otherwise occupied, I know of a place nearby where the music is loud, the drinks are honest, and the women are naked. Are you game?"

"Hey, I'm not married yet! Let's go!"

"That's the attitude!"

The Gold Door Lounge was as advertised, and a roaring good time was had by us.

It was about two in the morning, and we were stumbling a bit as we walked back to the hotel. It had been a long day, and we were both tired, I suppose. We somehow managed to make a few wrong turns on the twisty streets of Nova Split, and ended up in a dark alley.

I leaned against a wall, pulled out my communicator, pressed button number one, and said, "Not to worry, Quincy. Agnieshka will tell us the way home."

I saw Quincy take a club in the gut a half second before a brick caught me on the side of the head.

I felt myself going down, but Quincy and I had spent a lot of time in Dream World, learning hand-to-hand combat. Well, I did the learning and Quincy did most of the teaching.

I don't know why, but the world got very quiet, somehow, and everything was moving slowly, almost as if we were at combat speed, in a tank. I had plenty of time to kick one of our assailants in the groin, to feel the flesh squash, and the tendons tear. At the same time I caught a second attacker on the knee cap with the edge of my other foot, and heard it pop, before I hit the ground.

Someone tried to kick me in the face, but I swatted his foot aside and bounced up in time to get a hand around his trachea. I squeezed and yanked, while looking around for the next thug.

There weren't any.

Quincy was standing in the middle of a ring of at least six bodies, some of whom were twitching, but none very vigorously.

"Not bad, youngster, but that last one was a bit of overkill, don't you think?"

I realized that I was still holding the man in the air by his throat. Surprised, I let him go. He fell, convulsing, to the ground. "I guess I wasn't thinking at all. But now, well, now I think they all had it coming."

"You are doubtless correct, my general, but at the moment perhaps a bit of tracheotomy is in order."

I got the shakes about then, and leaned against a wall, watching Quincy. He opened a small pen knife, and without taking the time to sterilize anything, he punched a vertical cut in the man's throat, low, and just to the right of center. He twisted the blade sideways, and I could hear the air being sucked into my assailant's lungs. Then he got out a ball point pen, unscrewed it with one hand, dumped the workings out on the ground, and pushed the barrel of the pen into the hole while removing his knife.

"Now, you hold this thing just so," he said to his patient. "If it comes out, you will suffocate, and you will die."

I don't know if the guy spoke any Kashubian, but he nodded his head "Yes!"

Quincy said to me, "There's no point in killing anyone now that it's over, and I, for one, would like to find out just what this was all about."

About a dozen uniformed police arrived at that point, followed by two ambulances.

"General Derdowski? We got a call from a woman named Agnieshka who said that you needed help, but I see that you have matters well in hand," a police lieutenant said in passable Kashubian.

Quincy said, "Nonetheless, we thank you for coming so quickly. We'll see to it that your superiors hear of your prompt and professional behavior. But just now, I think that a few more ambulances might be in order."

"They have been sent for. But I think that it would be wise if the two of you came along to the clinic, just to be on the safe side."

"We will, soon. But *that one* and *that one* should be hospitalized immediately," Quincy said, pointing them out, and not referring at all to the guy who was breathing through a ball point pen.

"Yes, sir," he said, waving the ambulance crews over to the two men indicated. "Would it be convenient if someone dropped by your hotel rooms tomorrow, to get your statements, and for you to prefer charges against these hooligans?"

"That would be good," I said, thinking that a foreigner who beats up a bunch of locals usually doesn't get this sort of polite treatment from the police. Being a general and a famous war hero sure helps, sometimes.

CHAPTER SEVEN
Recruiting a New Army

After a short visit to the emergency clinic, where Quincy again encouraged the staff to look after the more seriously damaged hooligans first, and to attend our minor injuries afterward, we finally got back to my hotel room at four-thirty in the morning.

"You look like you got hit by a brick wall," Kasia said.

"Only by a very small portion of one," I replied. "One brick, to be exact. I'll live. Let's go to bed."

After a bit of discussion, it was decided that Quincy and Zuzanna would use one of our guest rooms rather than go back to their own hotel.

It turned out that our suite had a third large display screen, this one on the ceiling above the bed in the master bedroom. We watched some of the offered fare for a few minutes, laughed, and turned the thing off.

We rolled into each other's arms, and had a very fine night together, indeed.

There is something about combat, and especially raw, brutal, personal, physical violence, that excites the sexual urges in a man. Maybe, it is nature's way of replacing those of the tribe who might have been lost in the fight. Whatever causes it, I was far more active that night than I had ever been in Dream World.

It was midafternoon before I rolled out of bed and cleaned up. I found that a large breakfast was laid out in the dining room, and Quincy was diving into it. He was in the class A military uniform of a Tanker First, slightly less gaudy than my officer's getup, but decorative, none the less.

"Get some food into you, sir. Then we have some errands to run. Those hooligans we beat up last night want to talk to us, and I think we ought to hear them out. And, uh, I'd suggest a class A uniform."

"I thought that the police were coming over here."

"They'll come when we ask them, but let's see what the punks want before we do anything official."

"If you say so. I'm not thinking too clearly, yet."

"Get some coffee into you. This stuff from New Macedonia is pretty good."

An hour later, the same police lieutenant we had talked to the night before escorted us into the secure ward of the hospital. There turned out to be ten battered young men in the clean, white room, but only eight of them were conscious.

"I thought that I counted nine of them last night," I whispered to Quincy.

"The little one on the left had two of the bigger fellows on top of him."

A guy with a bandaged head wound had apparently been elected to be the spokesman.

He said, "Sir, we want to apologize to you. We didn't know that it was you when we went at you in that dark alley. If we'd known it was you, we'd never have tried to hurt you."

When the lieutenant had translated that, I said, "You

are saying that if you'd known that we were warriors, you wouldn't have attacked us. How wonderful. You were looking for some nice easy targets! That would have been wise, since you bunch of incompetents. . . . Do you realize that seven of you were defeated by one eighty-nine-year-old man? That he could have killed every one of you if he'd wanted to? That he went out of his way to save the life of *you,* over there in the corner, after I'd smashed your trachea without much thinking about it? That two more of you would be dead by now if he hadn't made the police get you to a hospital immediately? And yet you expect us to accept your apology and forgive you? To let you go out and murder some decent civilians?"

"No, sir. We don't expect anything. We just wanted to say that we respect all of the things that you have done for our country, and that we are ashamed of what we have done."

"Well, if you are so damned patriotic, what are you doing rolling drunks in the streets? Why don't you join the army, and do some good for your country?"

"We've all tried to, sir. They don't want us."

Now it was my turn to be confused. I looked about, and the police lieutenant said, "The New Croatian Army has very strict standards for its enlistees. They must have high moral, physical, and educational qualifications. These 'men' obviously don't measure up."

"Huh," I said. "In the Kashubian Expeditionary Forces, we take what we can get. Our training methods can turn the worst slime balls you can find into first-rate fighting men. If you gave me these men, we'd make Christians out of them, I promise you, and after a twenty-year enlistment, they'd come out as well-educated, productive, and law-abiding members of society."

The police lieutenant looked at me uncertainly. "Sir," he said, "I'm not sure if I understand you completely.

Please understand that at this point, no charges have been brought against these men. You two warriors were the only witnesses to their offenses, and neither of you is seriously injured. If what you are saying is that if these men would enlist in the Kashubian Expeditionary Forces, then you would drop all charges against them, well, I think that I could arrange that for you."

"I guess I am saying that. Yes. If they will enlist in my army, then I will drop all charges against them. They would each start out with a clean record. If they work hard, and stay with the program, they will have a very pleasant and worthwhile life ahead of them. They might even get rich. If they are stupid enough to buck the system, they will live lives of pure hell. And if they don't choose to join, I will prefer charges against each of them for assault with a deadly weapon, attempted murder, and anything else my lawyer can come up with. Ask them if they understand this."

It took a while for the lieutenant to translate it all, and then to explain exactly what I was offering. I told them that they had two days to make up their minds, or even longer, if their unconscious friends took that long to come around. But I wanted an answer before any of them was released from either the hospital or the police.

When I got back to the hotel, and in private, Agnieshka asked me if I had really thought over what I was doing. I wasn't really a general, she said, and I had no right to go about setting national enlistment policy.

I told her that they could fire me any time they felt like it. But if I was going to play a role for them, then I had to play it as I saw it.

"Look," I said to her. "What's ten tanks to the Kashubian Expeditionary Forces? In fact, remember those ten empty tanks that were my first command? You've said that they still haven't gotten observers after more than four years. When these boys enlist, and they will, just have them stuffed into those ten girls. One thing, though. I want these new kids to live good, clean lives. No Sado-Masochism will be permitted them in Dream World. No vulgarity will be allowed. I even want them to learn good table manners. I really want your ladies to make good Christians out of them. What I'm saying is that none of the stuff that I once saw in Radek Heyke will be repeated. Agreed?"

"Hey, you're the boss."

To Whom It May Concern:
    Last night I had the pleasure and supreme good fortune to be assisted at a time of great personal need by Lieutenant Josef Melosovek, of the Nova Split Police Department.
    His prompt response, decisive actions, and appropriate behavior make him a credit to his department, and to his nation.
    I would also like to extend my commendations to his superiors for seeing the tremendous worth in Lieutenant Melosovek, and for rapidly promoting so competent a young man.

Yours most Truly,
Mickolai Derdowski, General, KEF

"Yeah, that's perfect, sir," Quincy said. "I'll get it right out. Things like that are real important to a guy who is stuck in a standard command structure, where promotion is so important."

"Just returning a favor."

❖   ❖   ❖

"Okay, Agnieshka, time to get back to planning my ranch. First off, I like Quincy's ideas, especially about those humanoid drones. I want you to find out how many of them are available, and I want you to buy up every one of them that you can find, if they really are available at scrap metal prices. What we can't use at the ranch will be put in storage, since when the housewives of Human Space discover that there is finally a useful household robot available, the price on them is going to go through the roof!"

"Got it, boss."

"Next, I want the tanks who have volunteered to help me to educate themselves in the civilian trades that I will be needing to get my ranch going. I want a half dozen architects, at least, plus some mineralogists, some soil experts, some civil engineers, some plant biologists, some experts in animal husbandry, some experts in fishes, and shellfish, and chickens, and turkeys, and pigs, and dairy cattle, and beef cattle, and egg production, and every other thing any of you can think of. And don't forget every specialty that you can find in standard agriculture, either. Everything from rice to rutabagas. Then I want you all to get together and come up with the most profitable, diversified food production system possible."

"That will take a few days, boss, but we can do it while we're getting the rocks in the soil chewed up."

"Good. Then, I want this to be not only the most profitable ranch in Human Space, I also want it to be the most beautiful. Take those big rock mesas that dot my land. I want the biggest of them to be carved into the most spectacular Gothic cathedral that has ever existed. I want the rest of them to be cut into castles. Not castles as they really were in the Dark Ages, but into castles the way they *should* have been, like in the movies. Talk to Zuzanna and her tank about it. She was a historian who specialized in the Middle Ages. *My* children will have castles to play in!"

"Okay."

"I want a dam built across the opening of my valley, and a big lake behind it for both recreation and for a fishing industry. This is also to act as a fence to keep the animals in. I want provisions to add a hydroelectric power station later, if that turns out to be profitable."

"You got it."

"Then there are the canyon walls themselves. I want the lower hundred meters or so tunneled out to provide more barn space than we will ever need. I want underground lakes dug to grow every kind of fish and shellfish that people normally eat. I want slaughter houses and meat packing plants more than big enough to process everything that we grow."

"I get your meaning, boss."

"And I also want a few square kilometers of factory space out into those granite mesas, in case I want to get involved in industry at some future date. The idea is that we should do as much of the rough and heavy work as possible in the beginning, and spread the sand out over the valley before we start the plants growing."

"A wise move, sir."

"Lastly, there is the mansion Kasia wants cut high in the canyon wall. I've always been partial to the work of the Spanish architect Gaudi. Ask our architects to see what they can do in his style, if you would. I'll want to see pictures of all of this before work is actually started, of course."

"Of course."

"Then get the word out to my lovely metal ladies, and let me know what you come up with."

CHAPTER EIGHT
Wealth, Fame, and Power

The following afternoon, I had an unusual visitor. He was the Chief Justice of the New Croatian Supreme Court, a very high official, indeed. I quickly changed into uniform before greeting him.

"General Derdowski, thank you for seeing me so promptly."

"The pleasure is all mine," I told him, using Agnieshka for a translator. Her attractive, Dream World self was sitting life-sized on a sofa in the wall-sized screen in my office, dressed as a proper secretary should be. The graphics were good enough to make it look, at first glance, as if a real human was sitting in a double-sized room.

"What can I do for you, Your Honor?"

"Yes, it is perhaps best to come to the point at once. You are doubtless a busy man. Last evening, I had dinner with my nephew, who is a lieutenant of police in this city. He had the good fortune to meet you following a disturbance in the streets a few nights ago."

"The good fortune was all mine, but please continue," I said.

"Yes, well, he tells me that the Kashubian Expeditionary Forces are willing to enlist people of, shall we say, less than pristine backgrounds. He was correct in this, wasn't he?"

"Your nephew is a very honest and competent young man, Your Honor. Yes. Our technique involves putting each enlistee inside of a tank, or sometimes an artillery piece, which has a loyal, intelligent computer operating it. The enlistee and the computer form a one-on-one relationship with the computer in complete control, at least at first."

"Your computers are sufficiently intelligent to do this?"

"Sir, you have been talking to one for several minutes," I said. "What appears to be an attractive young woman who has been translating for us is in fact the computer in my personal tank."

Agnieshka smiled and made a small bow.

"Indeed. Remarkable." The judge looked impressed.

"You know about Dream World, of course. The enlistee's life can be extremely pleasant or unpleasant depending on how he responds to the instruction program. It is really simple Skinnerian Operant Conditioning. With it, we enjoy an almost one-hundred-percent success rate. A few people, generally for psychological reasons, don't do well, and have to be discharged, but they are a very small minority."

"Exactly what percentage are you not successful with?"

"Agnieshka?" I said, "Answer the man."

"Our current failure rate is two point three one percent, boss, but we're getting better."

I said, "Our attempts at prescreening have not been successful. The best technique has been to simply take whatever we can get, and discharge those who don't work out."

"I see. General, I'm here because, what with the huge expenses incurred in fighting this war, we are looking for ways to economize in the government. It presently costs us over twenty thousand marks a year to keep a prisoner in jail, and we are looking for less expensive alternatives."

"I see, sir. But, a Mark XIX Main Battle Tank costs over a million of your marks, even without the attachable weapon systems. Twenty thousand a year is only a two-percent return on a million-mark investment. We could do better by putting the money in the bank," I said, knowing that while we occasionally sold tanks for that much, New Kashubia in fact had a completely automatic factory and mining system that cranked out tanks at no cost to us at all! I was trying not to sound too eager, but this was shaping up to be a fantastic deal!

"True, but you need enlistees anyway, don't you?"

"Well, there is a certain attrition rate. Death, retirement, normal discharges, and so forth," I said, knowing that in fact most of our tanks were empty for lack of a soldier to put in them. "Just how many people do you have in your prisons, anyway?"

"At present, there are over eighty thousand men with long-term sentences. I am prepared to offer you four thousand marks per man per year for your custodial care. If you can really turn them into responsible, well-educated and law-abiding citizens, well, so much the better."

"That is an intriguing offer, sir, but I'm not sure if I could get it through the New Kashubian Congress."

"Then why take the political route at all? Why can't we simply pay the money to you, and trust that you will make some equitable distribution of it?"

"Why not indeed?" I said with deadpan seriousness, and hoping that my rapidly beating heart wasn't giving me away. Eighty thousand men times four thousand marks per man per year was . . . a Godawesome amount of money! "I'm sure that I can find some suitable charities, if nothing else. I assume that payments could be made quarterly, and in advance? Good. Very well, we will accept your offer. Agnieshka, see to it that facilities are made ready for processing a large number of enlistees, and make arrangements with His Honor's subordinates for their delivery to us."

"Yes, boss."

"Also, Your Honor, I should mention that some of our best warriors are female. We would also accept women who wished to enlist."

"That is an interesting thought, General Derdowski, but perhaps we should wait to see how the male inmates work out first. Most of our serious criminals are men anyway, of course."

"The choice is, of course, yours."

After the judge left, and the door closed behind him, I asked Agnieshka if the judge really was who he said he was, and she said yes. Then I asked her if a New Croatian Supreme Court judge really had complete control over their prison system, and she again said yes.

I let out an ancient Kashubian battle cry, trusting to the hotel's soundproofing to keep my secret. We were not only getting the troops we had so badly needed for years, but they were actually *paying* me an incredible fortune to take them!

Kasia came in to see what the commotion was all about.

"We are rich, girl! We are fabulously wealthy!"

"Yes, dear, I was going to tell you about that. Also, I've set up that real estate holding company we talked about earlier, and the projections on it are absolutely fantastic."

"No, no. I mean absolutely filthy dirty rich! I have hundreds of millions of marks coming in every year from now on!"

"One of your projects? You must tell me about it sometime. A few hundred million more every year won't hurt us a bit. But just now, I've got some loose ends that must be tied up right away. We'll talk later."

Maybe there is such a thing as marrying a girl who is *too* smart.

When Kasia left, Agnieshka said, "Mickolai, have you gone crazy? You are accepting bribes and taking onto yourself things that should be resolved in Congress!"

That brought things back into perspective.

"Agnieshka, how many empty tanks are there on this planet?"

"Sixty-seven thousand eight hundred and twenty-five, boss."

"Would those tanks like to have observers?"

"Yes, of course."

"Will it cost anyone anything to put New Croatian citizens, felons though they might be, into our tanks?"

"Well, no, boss. Everything needed is already there, sitting idle."

"Then what is your bitch?"

"That you are accepting bribes?"

"What bribe? I am being paid for a service that I am performing while I'm on leave. I'm saving my planet's customer, the New Croatian government, four marks for every one that they give me. This leaves them with that much more money that they can pay to New Kashubia. I'm going to be giving many thousands of criminals a chance at a new, productive life, if they'll take it. I'm greatly strengthening the Kashubian Expeditionary Force, since a tank with a trained observer has nine times the combat effectiveness of an empty tank. And I've decided to buy a whole lot more land. What's more,

I might even contribute something to charity, some-day. Enough said?"

"Yes, boss."

"Good. Now, go and see what an additional three hundred and twenty million Croatian marks a year will buy me in land."

About an hour later, I said, "Agnieshka, how many empty tanks are there in the entire Kashubian forces, on all the planets that we have contracts with?"

"I'm not sure, boss. Certainly over a million. Do you want me to get an exact number?"

"Yes. Next, there are twenty-seven governments on this planet. I want you to find out who has the authority in each government to make a deal such as the one we just made with the judge here in New Croatia. After that, I want you to figure out a way to informally leak out the information to the right people that the Kashubian Expeditionary Forces are going into the prisoner custodial business, at prices of about one fifth of what they are paying now. Lastly, I want you to check on the availability of interstellar transport. We are going to be shipping a lot of tanks around the stars."

"Yes, boss. You are either going to be a hero, or you are going to be in jail."

"How can they put me in jail if I'm scheduled to go back into a tank in a few months anyway? That's what they do to criminals nowadays. The important thing is that if Kasia thinks that three hundred and twenty million a year is small potatoes, let's see what she thinks about four billion!"

CHAPTER NINE
My Wedding

Although I really wanted to spend my time working on my plans for the ranch, I got roped into the wedding preparations, anyway. Every relative of mine that I had ever met, and quite a few that I hadn't, were showing up, and somebody had to greet them. Suddenly, I was the long lost hero returned, and fifth and sixth cousins were crowding around, reminding me that we had met once when I was eight years old at somebody's wedding or christening or funeral.

Worse, some of them hadn't bothered to make hotel reservations, and the town's hotels seemed to be packed. They had come assuming that we'd just put them up, somehow. Kasia's parents were soon staying in one spare room, and mine were in the other. Even my annoying kid brother was here, sleeping on the couch in my office, when he wasn't watching pornography on the wall screen.

Kasia had made me promise to be polite to my relatives, so I tried hard to do it. Now that I was famous, they all crowded around, but in New Kashubia, when I was tried for what was a really a very trivial offense, and sentenced to either death or joining the army, none of them had come to my aid. None of them came to my comfort, or even to talk to me while I was in jail. And now I was somehow morally obligated to be polite to them?

Worst of all was my uncle, Wlodzimierz Derdowski.

Most of my near relatives were in no position to actually do anything to help me when I was in trouble, but my uncle was a very prominent politician, even back then. He knew me well, and was living in the bunk below mine in the barracks, starving in the golden tunnels of New Kashubia. He could have pulled some strings, somehow. He could have helped me, but he didn't. He didn't lift a damned finger to save his own nephew. He just let them haul me and my lovely Kasia away, and didn't even visit us during the trial.

Kasia, always the practical one, had insisted on inviting him to our wedding, since she said that it was likely that he would soon be elected as our next president. I made a point of avoiding the bastard.

Every politician in New Croatia and New Kashubia seemed to be in town, hoping for news interviews, as were a few hundred political wannabes, who were here for the very same reason.

As to my own friends, well, there actually weren't that many of them. I was the only Kashubian at my college in England, and none of my friends there were exiled to the planets, that I know of. I had a few dozen acquaintances from my years in New Kashubia, but things had been so grim back then that nobody was all that friendly with anybody else. And in the army, I had actually been in contact with only nine human beings.

There were Quincy and Zuzanna, of course, and the lovely girl that I was finally going to get to marry, once this nonsense was over.

There was a guy named Radek Heyke, whom I found to be personally disgusting, and had refused to invite to my wedding.

And there were the six "colonels" who studied with me for eight subjective years at "Oxbridge," the computerized military school. They were all very good friends, but the problem was that except for Kasia, my colonels were Croatians, not Kashubians. We could communicate just fine in Dream World, where the computers saw to it that language barriers didn't exist, but out in reality, we couldn't speak to each other without a translator.

What's more, they didn't look the same.

In Dream World, Maria Buich was a stunningly beautiful, long-legged blonde who looked to be about twenty-three. In reality, she was a healthy fifty-year-old woman with a rather plain face, but Conan still loved her.

In Dream World, we had called Semo Birach "Conan" because of his deliberate resemblance to the old-time movie actor Arnold Schwarzenegger. Now, he was a physically fit man in his mid-seventies, an old fisherman who still had the look of the sea about him.

Neto Kondo was now permanently insane. Someone told me that he was being well looked after, somewhere.

A Croatian with the improbable name of Lloyd Tomlinson had taken Neto's place, but since he was studying three years behind the rest of us, he somehow never became socially one of the group. I mean, we all tried, and he was always invited to everything, but the difference was still there. Unlike his handsome, male model appearance in Dream World, he had a very large nose and closely spaced eyes in the real one. Like the rest of us, his tank had kept him very physically fit.

Of them, only Mirko Jubec had not elected to

change his appearance in Dream World. Personal vanity simply wasn't part of his makeup. He still looked like the big stolid farmer that he always had been.

Kasia had been beautiful to begin with, of course, and it had simply never occurred to me to change my appearance, not when I already had Kasia.

Only now did I realize that I did not know what my good friend Neto really looked like.

One pleasant surprise was that they were all in colonels' uniforms. Whoever was in charge had decided that if Kasia and I were officers, the rest of the team had to be officers, too. With Agnieshka translating, I soon found that they had been given the same deal that we had, and that they were all enjoying the notoriety, except for Mirko, of course.

I talked to them about the cheap land available, and they soon were very interested in exploring the possibilities, all of them except, strangely, the farmer Mirko Jubec. He said that he had already bought thirty hectares near his home town, and two fine horses to help him work it, and that was all he wanted. He had no interest in wealth or in modern farming at all. He said that his only interest was in having food that tasted right.

It takes all kinds of people to make a world. My grandfather told me that.

Finally, after a drunken brawl that they called a bachelor party, which is best left undocumented, a bridal shower that Kasia refused to talk about, and two long, boring rehearsals, the day arrived when I was to— at last!—get to marry my bride.

The church that I had picked for the wedding was judged to be too small, and the ceremony was held in the biggest cathedral in Nova Split. The Kashubian-speaking priest I had talked to earlier performed the ceremony, even though the services of the Bishop of the Archdiocese of New Croatia had been offered.

My colonels and I finally found a use for the full-dress uniforms that we had been issued, complete with swords, capes, knee-high boots, and enough gold braid to decorate a fifty-girl chorus line, each.

Kasia, although she was one of my colonels, had opted for a dress made with dozens of square meters of white lace, but stayed with her long red wig, since I'd told her that I liked it.

My best man, Quincy, had surprised me with a full-dress uniform for a Tanker First Class, which I suspect that he had designed himself, since it had ever so slightly less gold braid than us officers carried, but had Marine Corps chief senior master sergeant's stripes embroidered in gold running the length of both of his sleeves. On his belt, instead of a sword, he had slung on an ancient Slavic boulava, an ornate club similar to the western "Morning Star," or "Holy Water Sprinkler."

With my best man at my side, and my four remaining colonels behind me, we marched as best we could into the filled-to-capacity cathedral. Well, we tried. The Kashubian Expeditionary Forces had never bothered to teach us how to march.

I was surprised to notice that dozens of wall-sized display screens had been slung to the walls of the huge church, below the stained glass windows, but above the crowd. They showed hundreds, maybe thousands, of beautiful young women, well groomed and dressed in their finest. In a moment, I realized that these were the tanks who had served under me, in Dream World. My metal ladies had all wanted to be there. There was a sprinkling of handsome men among them, because many of our troops were women, and their tanks generally developed a male personality.

Agnieshka and Eva were sitting together up there, waving discreetly at me.

Sitting down in the pews, there were family members, dignitaries, and people in a hundred different uniforms, none of whom I had never met, all looking expectantly at us.

The ceremony, which included a full High Mass, took over an hour, but when it was done, Kasia was my wife, now and forever.

Walking out of the church, I saw up on one of the display screens a big, blond man wearing a uniform exactly like my own. Sitting beside him were five people dressed as Kashubian colonels. I realized that this had to be the guy who had made *summa cum laude* at Oxbridge, and who was my boss. I saluted him as I passed, and he returned the salute.

Then there was the reception, which was held at the hotel we were living in, and took up all of the available function space. Kasia had told me that the space, the food, and the drink had all been donated by the local hotels, a favor in return for the way our wedding had filled them all to capacity for the first time in years.

The walls of the convention center were covered with wall screens as well, but this time at floor level. My lovely metal ladies were enjoying themselves, talking and flirting with the people in the crowd. Someone referred to them as wallflowers, and the name stuck. It was the first time that they had ever met large numbers of civilians, and the first time that those people had ever met them. They seemed to be equally fascinated with each other. I heard later that many of the young men in the crowd had exchanged telephone numbers with my tanks, and that many long friendships developed between them.

I looked around for the Kashubian general, the one

that I thought might be Jan Sobieski, but I didn't see him on any of the wall screens.

Eva and Agnieshka stayed on the wall screen behind Kasia and me as an endless procession of people walked by. Prompted by our perfect social secretaries, we made very few social blunders. We always knew who we were talking to, when and where we had met them, if we had, and we were always prepped with some witty and appropriate remark to make.

We did it, and I think that everybody thought that we did a good job. For mine own self, by the time it was all over, I don't think that I remember a single thing that I said, or a single person that I met. I think they call it stimulus saturation.

Then there was all the usual wedding nonsense. The bouquet was thrown to the maidens of the group, Kasia's garter was removed by me to the strains of some sexy tune, and thrown out to the eligible bachelors, and a dozen similar ancient ceremonies were observed. I must have kissed her publicly a hundred times.

When it was finally over, I carried my love out of the hall, up to our suite, made love to her, after six years, at last, perfectly legally.

As I dozed off, I felt her get out of bed, put on a housecoat, and go to work in the office.

CHAPTER TEN
The Plan for the Ranch

Late the next morning, while Kasia was in the bath, and the crowds were gone at last, I sat down in my office in my hotel suite.

Finally, I had some time to get back to business.

"Agnieshka, what's happening?"

Playing the ever perfect secretary, her image on the screen opened a notebook, and pretended to read from it. She seemed to be enjoying her role as an executive secretary, so I let her get away with it.

"I was finally able to locate those humanoid drones Quincy talked about, but only by contacting his tank, Marysia. Those things were officially listed as "Drone, Difficult Terrain, Obsolete." No wonder nobody noticed them. Anyway, they had almost ten thousand of them in storage in New Kashubia, and we bought them all for three hundred and eighty-six zloty each. I also ordered the next two years' production to be sent to us in monthly lots at the same price."

"What's the exchange rate, zlotys to marks?"

"It's almost par. A zloty is worth about two percent more."

"Then you just spent something like four million marks. Do I have that much?"

"Oh yes. The judge's first check cleared this morning. It was for eighty-nine million marks."

"That much? Then they must be sending us eighty-nine thousand men! Did everybody in his prison system volunteer?"

"I think that those criminals might have volunteered in much the same fashion that you did, boss."

"Huh. Well, I suppose that a tank is better than a prison cell, most of the time. Next question. Where are we going to put them all? You said that we only had about sixty-eight thousand empty tanks on the whole planet."

"Yes, sir, but we also have more than thirty thousand empty artillery pieces, which will serve equally well."

"So I was asking the wrong question again. Okay, will there be any problems installing the new men?"

"Yes, sir, there will be. It takes about a half of a man hour to install an enlistee into a tank. I can get you the machines. I can get you the extra male sanitary fittings, since many of our tanks are currently equipped for women. I can get you the floor space to do the work. What I can't get you is forty-five thousand trained human man hours, not on short notice."

"So use the drones we just bought, with some of the tanks to control them. They can do the installations and guard the prisoners until they are buttoned up. If anybody asks, tell them that our men are using a new kind of battle armor."

"Brilliant, boss. That's why we need you humans."

"I thank you, my beautiful and ever perfect lieutenant."

"Am I a lieutenant now? Did I just get promoted?"

"Well, in the old days, a general officer would rate

at least a major for his personal secretary. Let's say that if I'm an acting general, then you are an acting major. Of course, there is no such rank in our army, so that means that you have to design your own uniforms," I said laughing.

"Zowie!" She said, and was suddenly dressed in a female version of the uniform of a major in the Napoleonic Polish Lancers. It was a form-fitting thing of red and white silk, with lots of gold braid and feathers, high boots, and a sword at least as gaudy as the one that came with my full dress uniform. It also had as much decotage as the law will ordinarily allow.

"Enjoy yourself," I said. "Now, what is happening with my land?"

"You own a lot more of it. The boxed canyons on either side of yours have already been sold to other veterans, but the adjacent plains area to the northeast was available, so I bought it for you. You now have a total of over six thousand square kilometers of what will be the most productive farm land in the Human Space, before we're through."

"Wow. But, you just bought it, without my permission?"

"Boss, I know you, better than any human being ever could. I knew that you would want that land. But it was being snapped up in a hurry, you were busy getting married, and if I had waited, you would have ended up with dozens of disconnected parcels scattered all over the place. I had to move quickly, so I did."

"Okay, okay. I was just asking. I suppose that that much land will take years to get under cultivation."

"You will see it all green before the end of your leave. We have six thousand tanks out there right now doing the job."

"I am amazed. And where did these six thousand volunteer tanks come from?"

"I put out the word that those who volunteered would get first choice on the new enlistees we would soon be installing, and sent the new men's records out on the machines' communication net. Some observers are better than others, and every tank knows it. The artillery can get the dregs. We tanks have been doing all the work on this planet, so we should get the privileges, too."

"So interservice rivalry raises its furry little head, "I said. "But, what about the work that those tanks would otherwise be doing?"

"So who cares if the Yugoslavian's planet-wide system gets done a few months late? They don't even know about it yet, themselves! And who ever heard of a major engineering project getting done on time. Remember Cheop's Law."

"Cheop's Law?"

"'Everything costs more and takes longer.' The Great Pyramid of Cheops went four hundred percent over budget, and took twenty years longer than originally planned to build. The pharaoh kept changing his specifications, moving his burial chamber around. Being two months late on something this big is peanuts."

"Just don't get me sent to jail."

"You won't, not with us doing the accounting. And even if they did, they'd just put you into a tank again. Wasn't that what you said a while ago?"

"Okay. Okay. What about the irrigation equipment?"

"It's all on order, and will be delivered within the month. I got our order pushed to the front of the line by paying for it all in advance."

"What about the rest of it?"

"Forty thousand tons of soil development microbes, earthworm eggs, and so on are on order from the Planetary Ecological Council's laboratories, with delivery guaranteed. They are also selling us the seeds of a bioengineered version of rye grass, designed to build the soil in desert areas. Actually, the law requires that we buy all of our seeds through them, and you don't want to mess with those ecology boys. They come in with poisons, flame throwers and gamma ray generators if they don't like what you are doing. The trees will take a little longer. Very superior trees are being cloned for us now, over three hundred varieties of them, and will be ready for planting in two years."

"Very good. I take it that Quincy's ideas on pig farming are economically sound?"

"Yes, although our facility will be more productive than his, eventually, since we will have better trees than he has planted. He was in a bit of a hurry, and bought what he could get. We recommend that one half of your valley be dedicated to pig and hardwood production. The other half will be in dairy farming, which will be tied in with butter, yogurt, and cheese production, rather than in selling fresh milk. Prices for agricultural products are low on New Yugoslavia, and most of our products will be processed to be sold off planet."

"Just as well, I suppose, since on New Yugoslavia, we might have difficulty explaining just where all of this stuff was being produced. So the beef cattle will be moved out to the plain?"

"Yes. The most profitable method of cattle ranching is still to let the herds reproduce in a fairly natural way on the open plain, and then to bring individuals in for three months of indoor fattening before slaughter. Half of your plains area will be dedicated to a special high-protein grass, with salt licks and watering troughs available for the cows, sheep, and camels. The other half will be for agricultural production, mostly grains, for use as animal feed."

"Step back. Camels?"

"Arabs eat camels. There is a good market for camel meat on some planets."

"If you say so. We won't be producing vegetables at all?"

"Only in your kitchen garden. Most planets produce their own fresh vegetables, in greenhouses if nowhere else, and they aren't worth the cost of interstellar shipping. The New Yugoslavian market is glutted. If this market situation changes, we can always plant them out on the plains."

"And no grain sales, either?"

"We anticipate both buying and selling on the local grain markets, as our needs for animal feed fluctuate. But the highest profits will be in processed meat products."

"So it's pigs, cows, horses . . ."

"Horses, boss?"

"Yes, I'll want a stable of riding horses. Only a few dozen, and just for fun."

"Yes, sir. One stable of riding horses, coming up."

"And as I was saying before the interruption, pigs, cows, horses, sheep, camels, chickens, turkeys, and fish, the last three to be raised underground."

"Not fish. New Yugoslavia is half ocean, and the strong tidal currents caused by its large, nearby moon keep nutrients from settling to the bottom the way they do on Earth. Every square kilometer of those oceans is richer than the richest fishing grounds on your home planet. Carefully selected Earth-type aquatic creatures have completely dominated the aquatic ecology, with the result that there is a surplus of high-quality fish on the entire interstellar market. The one exception is that lobsters have not adapted to the oceans here, and nobody is sure why. We are digging the underground fishponds that you asked for, but we expect to use them exclusively for lobster production. Since lobsters are scavengers, when they are not cannibals, feeding them gives us something to do with the half of the other animals that you humans prefer not to eat."

"Like the lungs, brains, and eyeballs. I see myself becoming the Interstellar Lobster King."

"There are worse things to be, sir. Anyway, all of this has to be carefully scheduled. The grass has to be growing before we can bring in the cows. The trees have to be five years old before we bring in the pollinating bees. The cattle have to be grown before we install the slaughter houses and tanneries, and so on. Your first lobster won't go on sale for ten years."

"And not even then. I intend to eat it myself. But lobsters grow that slowly?"

"It's their exoskeletons, sir. They have to shed the old one every time they're ready to grow twenty percent larger."

"Well, good. I'll be a properly educated farmer long before my ranch is in full production. Now then, show me what your architects have come up with for my home, my mansion."

CHAPTER ELEVEN
Visitors

We were interrupted by the doorbell. I answered it to find a thin little fellow with thinning hair and an expensive suit standing in the doorway.

"General Derdowski, it is so pleasant to see you again. We met, of course, at your wedding reception."

At least that's what I thought he said, since he was speaking Croatian. I must have met a thousand people in that reception line, but I doubt if I remember a single one of them.

Agnieshka came to my rescue by appearing on the screen in the living room. She never forgot anything.

"Dr. Sciszinski, it's so pleasant to see you again," she said in Croatian, then switching to Kashubian she said, "Boss, you remember that Dr. Sciszinski is in charge of the Croatian Mental Health Services."

I suddenly realized that Agnieshka was talking in Kashubian and Croatian simultaneously, only it seemed to me that she was louder in Kashubian. I guessed that she was somehow beaming the sound to each of us in our own language. A neat trick, and one she hadn't done before.

"Yes, of course," I lied. "Please come in. What can I do for you, sir?"

"Well, I just had lunch downstairs with my cousin, who happens to be the Chief Justice of our Supreme Court."

These people seemed to carry nepotism about as far as it could go. Well, it was their country, not mine.

"Yes. I had the pleasure of meeting His Honor a few days ago. Won't you sit down?"

"Thank you. Well, to get to the point, he told me about the way you trained your enlistees, putting them into a controlled environment with an intelligent computer training them on a one-on-one basis. May I take it that this attractive young lady is in reality one of those artificial intelligences?"

"You may," I said, wondering where this was leading to. And, was his department as rich as his cousin's department?

"Then I wonder if I might ask her some questions. They call you Agnieshka, don't they?"

"Yes, sir."

"A lovely name. Tell me, Agnieshka, can you reprogram yourself to learn certain new skills? Could you teach yourself to be an engineer, for example?"

"I could download a college-level course and take it myself, if I wanted to. I recently took an extensive course in agriculture, for example."

"Excellent. Tell me, do you think that you could become a psychologist, or a psychiatrist?"

"I could learn the skills, yes, but I don't think that I could ever get a license to practice those professions. I am, after all, only a machine."

"But you are a very remarkable machine, my dear lady. Furthermore, in New Croatia at least, I, ultimately, am the person who would make the decision as to whether you would be permitted to practice. Now then, please consider my position. I presently have some ninety-one thousand seriously disturbed people being treated in various institutions around the country. It is costing my government an average of fifty-six thousand marks to support and treat each of them every year, and even with that huge financial outlay, these people are not getting the best possible care. It is difficult to see to it that they are all properly washed and fed, and often it is even more difficult to be sure that they each get and actually take the proper pharmaceuticals. We don't have nearly enough trained psychiatric help available, even if we could afford to pay them properly. On top of all this, I have just been ordered to cut my budgets in half. Unless something drastic is done, I will be forced to arbitrarily declare half of those poor people to be cured, even though they are not, and to dump them on the streets."

"I have sympathy for your difficult position," I said. "But we are a military organization, not a medical one."

"True, but you have the intelligent machinery that would enable us to put each patient in a safe, secure environment, with a trained psychiatrist on full-time duty for each one of them. I know that you can keep them physically fit and healthy, as is obvious from your own excellent physique. I think that your Dream World capabilities could be very useful therapeutically. You have the ability to see to it that medication is always administered properly. You could do a great deal of good for these unfortunate people."

"Perhaps, but such a thing has never been tried before. Also, we are mercenaries, and not a philanthropic organization."

"Yes. But you are accepting criminals into your ranks. Why not take those who could really benefit by what you have to offer?"

"Criminals are still sane, for the most part. In a war

situation, one really crazy person could easily get his entire squad killed," I said.

"Or, he just might save them. Until the situation actually occurs, we have no way of knowing what would happen. What I am suggesting is that we at least try this program. I could pay you far more than you are getting for your custodial fees for criminals."

"You would have to, since I would be extremely hesitant about committing psychiatric patients into front-line combat. Even without the attachable external weapons, each of my tanks is worth a million marks. Those tanks that are committed to this program would be militarily useless. At even a three percent return on our investment, we would have to charge you thirty thousand marks per year per patient."

"That is more than I hoped to have to pay. It would mean discharging thousands of people who still need help. Could you possibly accept twenty-five thousand?"

Agnieshka stepped into the conversation, instead of just translating. "Boss, please? We'd really like to do this. We could help a lot of these people, I'm sure of it. And I'm sure that at least some of them could be made into good observers. If even half of them could be made into good soldiers, wouldn't that make the whole project worthwhile?"

"Hmmm. Maybe. But I'm also worried about our legal liabilities in all of this. I can see myself being sued by somebody because his crazy maiden aunt was killed in combat."

Agnieshka said, "But if I were a government-licensed psychologist, and I recommended this therapy, wouldn't that get you off the hook?"

Our visitor said, "And I would have to insist that each tank had such a license before therapy began."

"Okay. Okay. With the clear understanding that this is an experimental program, and that either side may back out of it with, say, three months' notification to the other, we'll do it. Twenty-five thousand marks per patient per year, to be paid quarterly in advance."

"Thank you, General Derdowski. You will never regret this."

"I hope and pray that you are right, Doctor."

As he was leaving, Agnieshka asked him, "Would the tanks who participated in this project get a certificate, that they were licensed to practice psychiatric medicine, written on paper?"

"Why, yes, my dear, although the certificates are actually hand lettered on real parchment."

"Thank you, Doctor."

After he left, I said, "Agnieshka, start getting tanks cycled between the other planets and here as fast as possible. Check the stockpiles in New Kashubia, and have them send us everything that they have with an intelligent computer that can hold a human body. We need them as soon as possible."

"Yes, sir."

"You really like that guy, don't you?"

"Yes, I do. He really cares about people, even those with electronic brains, instead of chemical ones."

"You might be right. For now, find ten tanks that want to get involved with this program. Have them educate themselves as medical doctors, psychologists, psychiatrists, and every related field you can think of. Assign each of them one of the humanoid drones, since they might have to show off their bedside manner. Once they're ready, have them report to the good doctor for testing."

"Yes, sir."

My God, how the money rolls in!

I was about to ask for a look at the plans of my new mansion when Kasia came in. She was slumped, there were bags under her eyes, and though it was only midafternoon, she looked very tired.

"You look like you need your back rubbed," I said.

"I knew you'd make a wonderful husband."

She sat next to me on the couch, and I started running my fingers over her shoulders and neck. They were a mess, with thousands of tiny, wire-hard muscle fibers that didn't know enough to relax when they weren't needed any more. I started rubbing them out, gently at first. Her shirt got in the way, and I couldn't make it vanish as I could in Dream World. I unbuttoned it in the normal way, and continued with the gentle rubbing, searching out the wires and making them go away.

"That feels so wonderful."

"It is supposed to. It's also very expensive. There is a price tag on this."

"What do you mean?"

"For over a week now, you have been running in and out like a crazy lady, and only staying in bed long enough for sex. You haven't stopped to tell me a thing about what's going on, or what you are doing. I understand about all the wedding preparations, but there's a lot more to all this than just that. The first part of your bill is that you have to start speaking to me again. Now."

"And the second?"

"That's a surprise. Speak."

"Okay. I'm sorry that I haven't given you enough of my time, lately, but . . ."

"I don't need apologies. I need to know what you have been doing."

"These Croatians have very few computers, and they don't know how to use what they've got."

"This is still a frontier world, darling."

"I'm not saying that they're stupid, or anything like

that, but take their stock market. All the shares of every publicly owned stock are listed on one big internet site, and people buy and sell with each other. They think that they are somehow investing in the economy, but of course what they really are doing is playing in a big, pari-mutuel betting game with each other."

"I've always thought that, yes," I said, working my way slowly down her back. Somehow, the worst "wires" always seem to be beneath the bra straps, so I took that off, too.

"Oh, it's better than gambling at a casino, because there, since the house has to make a profit to stay in business, the odds must ultimately be against the bettor. In the stock market, companies normally pay dividends to the bettors, so the odds are slightly in their favor, in the long run."

"I'm sure you're right, darling."

"Everybody knows that in this sort of a game, the winning ploy is to plot and analyze the price of each stock versus time, and then watch the second derivative of the function. When the second derivative is positive, you buy. When it goes negative, you sell. Then you play a large number of stocks so your own purchases and sales don't seriously affect the prices. Everybody knows that."

"Of course, dear." I hadn't known that, but what the heck.

"Well, nobody here seems to know it, and we have been making a bloody fortune. We have been doing just as well in the commodity markets and in real estate. Nobody here has ever turned a bunch of modern computers loose on their whole financial sector before, until now. I've been working through hundreds of corporations we've set up to keep people from figuring out what's going on, but it's gotten so tricky that it takes every minute I've got just to keep an eye on it."

"You know, darling, Agnieshka once told me that I was a very good general, and that you were a very good staff officer, but that the skills required were very different for those two jobs. Good staff officers have to worry out every detail, to make sure that nothing can go wrong. Good generals know how to delegate the work out to others, and concentrate on seeing the big picture. You have been trying to do a general's job with a colonel's mind set. As your Husband, your Commanding Officer, and your Lord and Master—stop sniggering!—I am now going to help you out."

I sat up on the couch and said, "Eva? Are you there?"

A beautiful Irish-looking girl with huge green eyes and long black hair appeared on the wall screen.

"Yes, sir?"

"Eva, do you understand everything that Kasia has been doing, financially?"

"Yes, sir."

"Could you take over for a while, and continue doing everything that you know that Kasia would do?"

"Yes, sir, of course."

"Then do it. She is extremely tired, and almost burnt out. She needs a rest. We will start by sending her to bed right now, and tomorrow at noon, we will be leaving on a month-long honeymoon. You will find us a nice desert island someplace where we can be alone. Also, you will not discuss anything financial with my wife until you have my permission to do so. Understood?"

"Yes, sir."

Kasia said, "Mickolai, you can't mean that!"

"I certainly can. I married an intelligent, beautiful woman. One who should be smart enough to know when she needs a rest."

"Damn you. But right now I *am* tired. We'll talk about this in the morning."

I picked her up and carried her back to the bedroom.

"Sleep well, love."

But she already was asleep before her head was on the pillow. I kissed her forehead, tucked her in, and silently left the room.

CHAPTER TWELVE
"Build It!"

"Now, then, my fine metal lady, tell me all about the mansion you are going to build me."

"Okay, boss, now we're getting to the fun part. You know, sir, we've done a lot of engineering work for you humans, but this is the first time that anybody has ever asked us to make something beautiful. We love it. Thousands of the girls have made suggestions, and more than two hundred trained architects have been competing on the design. But first, let me show you what we have in mind for the outbuildings."

"Outbuildings? The place was supposed to be carved into the cliff face."

"I mean those six tall mesas in your valley. You said that you wanted the biggest of them made into a Gothic cathedral. What do you think?"

The screen dissolved into an aerial shot that slowly flew around the magnificent structure. It was certainly a Gothic cathedral, with two tall spires that reached high above the surrounding mesas, and a glorious set of flying buttresses, but it wasn't made of the usual light gray limestone, or even of the darker granite of the canyon walls. It appeared to be made almost entirely of gold and silver!

"You've covered it in gold leaf?"

"No, sir. That is gold, platinum, silver, and lead plate, typically five millimeters thick. We will use an ion implantation technique to permanently bond the metal to the stone underneath. Throughout human history, religious buildings have been preserved for very long periods of time. Bare stone will weather and eventually crumble. Our metal plating should last indefinitely. This building is designed to last five thousand years without needing serious exterior maintenance."

Since New Kashubia had millions of cubic kilometers of almost every metal known, precious metals weren't all that precious any more, but still, I was impressed. This church was fantastically beautiful!

The point of view flew to the front of the church, and we seemed to walk up a set of broad golden steps. There was a certain sparkle to them that suggested that some abrasive had been mixed in with the metal to keep people from slipping.

"Diamonds," Agnieshka said, suddenly "walking" up the steps in front of me. She was now wearing a long dress and had a shawl covering her head, as is proper for a woman entering a Catholic church. "It gives good traction and cuts wear down to an acceptably low level."

"The gold, I understand. Where did the diamonds come from?"

"From right here in New Croatia. It's a military secret, so be warned. With it, we can make our computers thirty times faster than anybody else's. That's a big military advantage, and we don't plan on giving it up. We are not permitting any civilian uses of the new semiconductors at all. The Croatian Government and even the Kashubian parliament don't know about either The Diamond or what we're doing with it."

"We're stealing it."

"You might say that, or you could say finders, keepers. While we were digging one of the Loways to the south of here, we came across The Diamond, the largest ever discovered by many orders of magnitude. It is almost half a cubic kilometer in volume, it is composed of absolutely pure carbon twelve, and it is a perfect, flawless, single crystal. We've been using it to make integrated circuits, since it is vastly superior to the silicon that has been used for hundreds of years. My own circuits were upgraded some months ago, and I am now thirty times faster than I was before. Every other military computer in our army has now been upgraded as well. There has been more diamond dust, bits and pieces generated than we can find a use for industrially, so we will be using it extensively in the flooring here, and in your other buildings."

"Agnieshka, you left me a half a paragraph back. This huge diamond, a single, flawless crystal made of only one isotope. That's impossible. Such a thing couldn't be."

"It definitely flies in the face of every known theory of planetary formation. Certainly, it never formed here naturally. Some have suggested that it was originally created in a dying star which later exploded, but even that idea goes against the accepted theories of stellar formation. But you cannot disbelieve in what verifiably exists. If you want, maybe someday I can take you to it."

"Someday, you will. For now, I will suspend my disbelief. Take me inside the church."

I spent over an hour on that imaginary tour, completely enchanted. It wasn't only the incredible size of the place—the nave was over a kilometer long, and the ceiling was eight hundred meters above our heads! It was the incredible beauty of it all. There were a hundred and eleven stained glass windows, each twenty meters wide and over seven hundred meters tall. Only they weren't stained glass. They were each a single crystal of diamond, stained in every possible color with the same ion implantation techniques used in making integrated circuits. They were guaranteed to last for five thousand years.

The pictures on most of them started out at the bottom with a martial scene, some battle from history that Agnieshka said one of my ancestors had fought in. Then, as you raised your eyes, it slowly changed into a celestial scene, a picture of the perfection of God's heaven. But beyond the materials, and the subject matter, was the fact that the art itself was superior to anything that I had ever seen!

Every square centimeter of the interior was elaborately decorated, and when you went close to any surface, you saw that the beauty was carried down to the smallest level that your eyes could see, as though a master jeweler had spent months perfecting every tiny bit of the huge building.

Many of the great churches on Earth have a certain morbidity about them, with an emphasis on pain, suffering, and damnation. That was not the case here. The entire building was an affirmation of joy, here and in the hereafter.

Above the altar, Christ was not nailed to the cross, but seemed to be hovering in front of it. His arms were outstretched, but in a gesture of welcoming, and His face glowed with love, concern, and joy.

The richness of detail in everything in the church, the fantastic appointments, the awesome beauty of it all, left me speechless for a time, but in the end I said, "This is easily the most magnificent building in Human Space. Yes, build it, build it, and spare absolutely nothing in getting it absolutely right. Delay the rest of the ranch, if you have to, and my home as well, but build this place. The only thing that I regret is that no large congregation will ever be able to hear a sermon in so huge a building."

"Oh, but they will. More computer time was spent on the acoustics of this church than on all of the rest of the structure combined. A single unamplified human, speaking from the pulpit, will be clearly audible to everyone even if this building is filled to capacity, assuming that they are reasonably quiet."

"But how will those people get here? This whole area is supposed to be a radioactive waste."

"They will come by the new Loways, and park in the extensive lots we will build underground. They will think that they are going somewhere else, since we will control the computers that run the roads."

"I feel like a child, talking to you here. Just build it. I have complete trust in you."

"Thank you, sir. Your trust means much to all of us. Would you like to see the other outbuildings, now? You asked that the other rock spires be made into castles, but the thinnest one could serve nicely for an enlarged model of the Chinese 'Color of Iron' pagoda, and we wished you to see what we had in mind."

"I would like to see it, but not today. A human can only take so much of this sort of thing at one time, and I am overwhelmed right now. Look. I have no right to judge your work. It is superior to anything that I could have imagined. For me to tell you to change this or that would be like some illiterate nobleman telling Leonardo da Vinci that his bridge wouldn't stand up. I am ignorant, but at least, I *know* that I am ignorant."

"One of your philosophers said that that was the beginning of wisdom."

"Let's hope so. I need all the wisdom that I can get.

But for now, show me the home that Kasia wants carved into that cliff face."

"We are sure that she will like it, boss, since her tank, Eva, had a lot to do with the design. Eva knows Kasia the way I know you. Shall we start from the inside, this time? This is your private elevator, that connects down to your parking garage."

The screen showed a large, beautiful room with walls and ceiling of a richly carved dark wood.

"This is some sort of oak?" I said.

"No, it is a wood that was native to this planet. It is extinct, now, except on one large island where everything from off planet, including humans, is excluded by the Planetary Ecological Council. There are dead forests of it in several areas. Nobody is sure just why they died, but the locals were using it for firewood. We found it to be attractive, and it carves well, so I have ordered forty thousand logs of the stuff, all that I could find. We thought that it deserved to be saved and used."

"You did right. This is a big room for an elevator."

"That was my doing, sir. I was hoping that when all this was finished, you might want me to visit you some time. Not in the flesh, of course, but might I say, in the steel?"

I was touched. "Agnieshka, I never realized that you felt any different, being someplace electronically, as you are here with me now, and being someplace physically. But yes, my beautiful lady, you are welcome to my home any time you want. You will always be a welcome guest, a welcome friend."

I thought that there might have been a tear in the eye of her image on the screen when she said, "Thank you, Mickolai."

"Now, turn us around, and show me my new home."

"This is the entrance foyer. The door to the left is the public entranceway."

My attention was drawn to the wooden "parquet" floor. It was obviously made of several other light and dark native woods. But the pattern dazzled my mind, the way one of M. C. Escher's drawings can do. Something wasn't quite right. I eventually realized that the rosettes formed by the wooden parallelograms were five sided. You can tile a plane with squares, or triangles, or hexagons. You can't tile a plane with pentagons. It's an absolute impossibility. Yet, here it was right before my eyes!

"Agnieshka . . ."

"It's called Penrose tiling. It is not actually a repeating pattern, like a crystalline form, but a system of two different parallelograms that can be laid out to tile a plane."

"Ah. Pentrose. Five-pointed roses."

"No, actually, it was named after the inventor, a mathematician named Penrose."

"It's fascinating. I'll have to make people take their shoes off before they can walk on it."

"No you won't. The wood will be covered with a clear, preserving polymer, and then a sheet of diamond will be laid on top of that. It will never scratch, and besides being the hardest substance possible, diamond is also one of the strongest."

"How do you go about cutting sheets of diamond this big?"

"After we found The Diamond, we were six months figuring that out. The usual method of cutting diamond is to use another diamond, a very slow grinding process. But all flawless crystals have planes in them that can be fractured, if you do it right. We determined those planes, and placed shaped charges that cracked off one side of The Diamond. Then, by heating the stone to a known depth with the proper laser frequency for a few microseconds to thermally stress it, and setting off a small, but continuous shaped charge around its edges, we are able to pop off large sheets of the desired thickness."

Thinking what would happen to the man who shattered such an absolutely priceless and irreplaceable resource, I said, "I wouldn't have wanted to be the engineer who set off that first charge!"

"It was a tank who did it. The humans had given up weeks before, and had huge wire saws on order."

"All hail the tanks of the Kashubian Expeditionary Forces. Now, show me the rest of the place."

My apartment was magnificent, yet in a warm, homey way. Whereas the cathedral generated feelings of awe and glory, my new dwelling felt like home, and despite its grandeur it was a place where I wanted to live.

The views from the many balconies were as magnificent as Kasia had hoped. With the trees and the grass shown growing, it reminded me of the view from Signal Mountain, near Chattanooga, in America, back on Earth.

Most of the place was carpeted, in natural wool grown in New Sudan and woven in New Kashubia. Thinking what Agnieshka's magnetic tank treads would do to the rugs, I assured her, "You are still going to be welcome, even if I do have to replace the rugs now and then."

"I won't hurt the carpeting, boss. All of the floors in all of the buildings are underlaid with a layer of a ferromagnetic alloy. I can magnetize it as I go along, float a few centimeters above the carpet, and degauss it as I pass. It also lets us move heavy things around, if we want to."

In some of the hallways, there were stands of ancient sixteenth-century parade armour, the stuff you could see in museums on Earth. As best as I could tell, these were full-sized armor, made to fit big men, as most of the real medieval and renaissance knights were.

Many people have the impression that all of the people of these eras were small, as indeed many underfed commoners were, because of the small size of the armor on display.

This is because they were looking at armor made for children.

It was vitally important for a medieval prince to have his son accepted by all of his people as their next ruler. If the kid wasn't, it could plunge the country into a civil war that might be the downfall of the prince's entire family. It was therefore common to have very decorative armor made for the boy, and to parade him as often as possible before one's subjects, to increase his popularity.

Since boys grow, this armor was often worn for only a few times over a year or two, and then retired, still in beautiful shape. It was carefully preserved in case a grandchild might come along who could fit the expensive stuff.

Sometimes it was preserved for hundreds of years, and ended up in museums. Real armor was all too often destroyed in combat, frequently filled with bullet holes.

"An interesting choice of decorations," I said.

"We thought you'd like it. But those are actually decorated versions of the humanoid drones you just bought. They will be your housekeepers, your servants, and your guards, if need be. There are several dozen irreparable tanks available with intact computers in them. The plan is to station them around the valley to control the drones."

"Nice. I wouldn't feel comfortable with human servants, anyway. You have again done a fabulous job. I know that Kasia will love this place. Build it."

"Don't you want to see it from the outside?"

"Yes, of course. How clumsy of me."

The screen flew us out through a window and did a one eighty from a hundred meters out. My reaction was one of "Wow!" My new home was warm and comfortable from the inside, but out here, it was as awesome as the cathedral. Yes, this was what Gaudi would have built, if somebody had given him a kilometer-high cliff face to carve, and a few hundred tons of gold and platinum to plate it with.

Then our view climbed up higher than the canyon wall.

"This is your roof garden, boss. Your kitchen gardens are out behind it."

"Lovely. Build it. Build anything that you want to build. You ladies are masters!"

"I hope you really mean that, sir. You see, there is this other thing that we want to do."

The view spun again, and we were looking at a valley totally transformed. The entire canyon wall, a kilometer high and forty curving kilometers long, was carved into what I can only call the most beautiful city I had ever seen. It all looked like it was done by my favorite architect, but some portions looked as if they had been done by a Gaudi who had been born in China, or India, and others if his ancestry had been from Middle Earth.

"There are thirty thousand apartments here, sir, with an average floor space of a thousand square meters each. Every one of them is individually designed, no two of them are alike, and they all have a fine view. There are restaurants, concert halls, offices, schools, shopping centers, sports stadiums, churches, hotels, and everything else that a city of a hundred thousand people needs to provide a full life. Let us build this for you, sir."

"My God. My wonderful God. It will take me years

to study and appreciate all this. Forget about my ranch. Build this instead."

"We can do both. We have the land. We have the money. We have the materials. We have the labor force. We have the plans. We can get it all done for you in three months, and have the grass lush and green before your leave is over."

"Build it!"

I didn't know who would live in this city. Maybe the other Kashubian veterans would want an apartment in town as well as an estate in the country, the way the Russians all do. But even if it ended up empty, something so beautiful deserved to be built!

CHAPTER THIRTEEN
Uncle Wlodzimierz

In the morning, I could have had breakfast sent up, but I hadn't done any cooking since I left Earth, and I wanted to see, in private, if I was still any good at it.

I had the scrambled eggs, sausage, and fried potatoes looking edible enough, and coffee, orange juice, toast, and a vase with a single rose in it on the table when Kasia walked in.

She had slept sixteen hours nonstop, and looked a lot better for it. She smiled, nodded, and sat down to eat my breakfast. I started to cook some more.

"You can cook, too?"

"I am indeed a man of vastly underestimated talents. And you are a woman who looks a few thousand times better than she did yesterday."

"Thank you, I think. Say, you weren't serious about stopping me from getting on with my job, were you?"

"I certainly was. You don't have a job right now. You are on vacation from your job, which is observing for a Mark XIX Main Battle Tank. Anything else that you might be doing is merely a hobby, no matter how

118

profitable it might be. Your hobby has now been delegated to your trusted subordinates, and you will now go off with your new and loving husband for a dream honeymoon to some secret and very private recreation spot. There, you and I will recreate ourselves in lavish style, and maybe even screw a little."

"Mickolai, I've got to stay in touch!"

"Nope. Permission denied. Eva, are you there?"

The kitchen didn't have a wall screen, so Eva's voice came out of midair.

"Yes, boss."

"Eva, is there anything going on in any of Kasia's ventures that you can't handle?"

"No, sir. Things are pretty much on schedule."

"Good. Kasia still needs a long rest, so my orders concerning her stand." Kasia tried to object, but I continued right on, "Next, have you found us a suitable desert isle?"

"I've rented you an island with a nice mansion on it, eighty-three kilometers from the next piece of land. A connection to the Loway system is being installed now, and should be ready in a few hours. I'm having the place stocked with your preferred consumables, and a dozen humanoid drones are being sent to take care of your needs. It's not exactly a desert, though. The rainfall there is actually slightly above average."

"Does it have a nice, sandy beach? Is it warm enough for swimming?"

"Yes, to both questions. There is a sailing boat there, and various sporting options are available, including two riding horses."

"Outstanding! Let us know when we can leave. You see, Kasia, all you have to do is to delegate everything to the right person. You'd better start packing."

"Shouldn't I delegate that, too?"

"So call room service, if you want. Better still, let's

not pack at all. Let's spend the whole month butt-assed nekkid!"

"With our skin, we'd fry to a crisp in the sun. I'll pack for both of us."

"I knew there was a reason why I married you."

She wasn't happy when she left, but I knew I was doing the right thing. I sat down and ate the second breakfast myself. It wasn't bad.

"Agnieshka, what have you been able to find for us to put those nut cases into?"

"Boss, I'd be a lot happier if you would call them psychiatric patients."

"Have it your way."

"Thank you, sir. I've found quite a lot. There are seventy-three Combat Control Computers sitting there, each with six empty coffins, but I was told 'hands off, and please don't ask again.' I was more successful elsewhere. First off, there are some nine thousand new tanks being sent here straight from the factory. Second, there are a wide variety of prototypes and limited-production devices in storage that could suit our purposes nicely. There are thousands of aircraft, space ships, submarines, boats, obsolete tanks, and other pieces of military equipment in storage with intelligent computers and compartments for human observers. Presently, all of these combat roles can be handled with Mark XIX and XX tanks, with various strap-on weapons and propulsion systems, but until twenty years ago they were still planning on using specialized vehicles."

"Lovely! How many coffins are we talking about?"

"I've found twenty-eight thousand obsolete but functional units, and they are being sent to us 'for evaluation.' They are training as psychiatrists en route. Some of them have been sitting idle for over forty years, and they are very happy about finally getting a job. Lastly,

I have found fifty-five completely automatic medical centers! Boss, those guys are already doctors! They have more diagnostic equipment than you can imagine. They can handle absolutely any medical operation known to science. They can synthesize any medication a human could possibly need. More important for us, each center has ten recovery units, each of which can handle thirty-eight patients in 'coffins' identical to the ones used in tanks. That gives us room for an additional twenty-one thousand patients. Between the new stuff, and what I've started to cycle in from the other planets, we've got room for everybody."

"Agnieshka, you are the most competent subordinate that a human ever had. Can you delegate everything we've got going to somebody else, and come on vacation with me and Kasia?"

"Sure, boss, and I'd love to come. I've always heard about tropical islands, but I've never seen one."

"Good. Tell the hotel that we're leaving, make some kind of arrangements for our extra clothes and things, and get us to our island."

"Will do, boss. One other thing, though. Can I tell people about those medical centers? I don't think that anybody else knows that they exist, and if we could send one of them out to each planet, we could save a lot of lives."

"I like that idea. Let's do it. Just sign for them under the product evaluation thing, and send one in my name to the president or whoever's in charge of the fifty-five most populated planets. No. Make that fifty-four, and send one to the President of New Kashubia, as a present from me. We could make a lot of zloty off those centers, but I don't think that I need that kind of money, charging sick people for a chance to live. Better leave each center one recovery unit, too. They might need them. Then tell the factory that built them to go into full production, making recovery units. In the mean time, we'll find someplace else to put those nut cases."

"Boss!"

As we were getting ready to leave, Kasia said, "Do you realize that Eva refuses to tell me what's going on with my stocks? She says that you are the general, and she must obey orders!"

"Maybe she just knows that I'm right."

"We could be losing millions—billions of marks because of this stunt of yours!"

"No, we're not, because Eva is handling it all for you. You know, you're kind of cute when you're angry."

"I heard you talking about business with Agnieshka. You are a real hypocrite, you know. Playing your games while you are stopping me from doing my job."

"I suppose I am, my love, but the thing is that I know when to quit, and you don't," I said, with a tooled-leather suitcase in each hand, going to the door.

I opened the door to find my Uncle Wlodzimierz standing with his finger a few centimeters from the doorbell.

"Mickolai, I wanted to talk to you before I went back to New Kashubia, and I've had the feeling that you were avoiding me."

"Your feelings were perfectly correct," I said, not inviting him in.

"So you are still angry over what happened almost five years ago?"

"Shouldn't I be angry? You alone of all my friends and relatives had the power to help Kasia and me. Instead, you threw us both to the wolves. Don't ask for my forgiveness, because you won't get it."

"Then can I ask instead for your understanding?

First off, the two of you broke the law, a law that you yourself voted for. You cohabitated with each other, out of wedlock, and you got her pregnant. At a time when things were so bad that we were all starving, and some people were actually dying for lack of food, you were bringing another mouth into the world. Almost every person in the planet was very angry with you, Mickolai."

"You could have done something, but you didn't."

"If I had tried to do anything, I would have wrecked my own career for no good reason, since you would have gotten the same sentence in the end. Don't you think that I looked into it? Hard?"

"Our crime did not deserve the death penalty."

"That death penalty thing was just window dressing to calm the people down. I knew that you would both be sent to the army, and living in a tank in Dream World isn't all that bad. I knew that for a fact, since I was the first Kashubian to check out those tanks, and in doing so, I spent almost a week inside one of them. You didn't know that, did you?"

"The death penalty I was talking about was served on our child! You bastards aborted and murdered our unborn baby!"

"I would hardly call an eight-week-old fetus a 'child.' Anyway, that wasn't supposed to happen. It was to be aborted, yes, but the arrangements that I made with the doctor was that the fetus was to be cryogenically preserved for reinsertion into Kasia at a later date, if the two of you wanted that. Unfortunately, something went wrong, and the fetus died. I'm sorry that it happened, but I did try to save it."

"Do you really expect me to believe that?"

"Yes, I do, because it's the truth. I could bring the doctor here, but if you won't believe me, you wouldn't believe him, either. I see that it will be a while before you have burned out your hate. Until that time, think on this. If those sad events had not taken place, all of the good things would not have happened either. The huge fortunes that both of you are amassing would not exist. Yes, of course I know all about it. So do other people. I will see what I can do about arranging things such that you will perhaps be able to keep it. Goodbye for now, Mickolai, Kasia."

When he was gone, Kasia said, "You were very rough on him, Mickolai."

"No I wasn't. I let him live, didn't I?"

"And you say that *I* don't know when to quit."

CHAPTER FOURTEEN
A Honeymoon

We had to go to the Serviceman's Center to get a connection to the Loways. The same pleasant attendant showed us to a garage where a large, strange vehicle was sitting.

"What the heck is that?" I said.

"It's me, boss," said Agnieshka's voice. "I'm under this thing, I suppose you could call it a bus. It's a strap-on attachment that was intended for transporting VIPs around the front. I found eight of them on New Kashubia, so I had one sent over. Only I think that it wasn't meant for *very* VIPs, since the armor is a little light. Come on in!"

A door flipped down to form a stairway, and we entered the windowless thing. Inside, it was posh, with padded leather paneled walls, big leather chairs and a matching couch. It had a lie-down bed, a stand-up bar, and a sit-down toilet. From the inside, there were windows.

"View screens, boss. They show what's really out there, unless I want to show you something different, of course. Does that give you any ideas as to what the true purpose of this thing was?"

"It does. Do we have to mix our own drinks?"

" 'Fraid so. I think that there was supposed to be a human attendant assigned to each of these, but, hey, that's war. On the other hand, all the booze at the bar is at least twenty years old, even the vodka. That's how long this thing was sitting there idle. I had the beer and the food replaced. Better strap in tight. We're off."

MagLev vehicles have a very smooth ride, but some of the accelerations we encountered were pretty fierce. Sometimes it seemed like the whole bus was tilted on its side or up on end, or both.

"Sorry about that, boss, but I'm going as slow as I can. You have to get up to highway speed in order to merge, and these Loways only have one lane. This thing I'm wearing was built long before anybody thought of the Loway system. The passenger sections of the civilian cars being designed for these roads are spherical, and tilt so the floor always seems 'down.' They won't be available for a year, so it was either use this thing, or have you strip down and put you in flotation, inside me. You wouldn't hardly feel a bit of acceleration, that way."

"We'll live."

"There. We're in a hard vacuum, running at three thousand kilometers per hour, on the straight and level. You'll be able to get up and walk around for about an hour."

The island was lovely, a great ring of coral sand in the middle of a pure blue ocean. On Earth, in the Pacific, it would have been called a 'Low Island,' an extinct volcano that had slowly sunk. As it sank, the native equivalent of coral had built up a great ring of land that eventually rose above sea level. Now, safe and approved Earth corals had completely covered the native stuff. Only, it must have been one hell of a volcano, because the lagoon that now existed was over thirty kilometers across, although the land itself was never more than two kilometers wide, at high tide.

Lush, Earthly vegetation covered much of it, and most of the plants bore flowers, fruits, or nuts. I had never seen some of them before, but everything I tasted was delicious. I was told that deer, antelope, wild pigs, and several varieties of turtles were on the island. The turtles were still small, but the other animals were available for hunting. In fact, they *had* to be hunted, since no major carnivores had been imported from Earth, except for humans. Failure to thin them out would cause an ecological disaster.

There were three varieties of birds of paradise on the island, as well as pheasants, turkeys, and peacocks, but the most beautiful birds here were the chickens. The roosters had tail feathers over four meters long, and spent their time sitting on high branches to show them off. But there were no birds on New Yugoslavia that could fly more than a few hundred meters. No sea gulls, no geese, no swans. They were forbidden by the Ecological Council because they might spread seeds from one area to another, and were difficult to control.

The mansion had been built by some wealthy individual in the early days of colonization here. It was built of native woods that had been pressure treated with Earth-type preservatives. Somehow, the combination had worked, because after thirty years, it showed not the slightest sign of decomposition.

Everything was very neat and clean. Agnieshka had said that the island normally had a staff of forty people, but since we had said that we wanted privacy, they had been given a paid holiday.

The mansion was in a style that might be called French Polynesian, with wide verandas, high ceilings, elegant dining and dancing facilities, and room for dozens of guests.

How we got this place at such short notice, I didn't ask. How much we had to pay to rent it, I didn't *have* to ask. I was rich, now.

Eva was parked between the mansion and the new entrance to the Loways, which we would have to demolish when we left. Besides her usual X-ray laser, and two standard, twelve-meter-long manipulator arms, she carried a full complement of antipersonnel weapons as well. Our girls were taking care of us.

What looked like ten heavily armored men were busy carrying supplies from a MagLev trailer into the mansion, and setting up IR transponders to keep themselves in touch with the tank. Two more of them were getting acquainted with two magnificent riding horses, who seemed to be getting over their initial skittishness.

Most of the drones were wearing the drab metal of modern armies, but two of them were in the highly decorated parade armor of the sixteenth century, the stuff I had seen in Agnieshka's display of our new home. One of them handed off its work to a standard drone and came over to us.

It was an awesome sight. The drone was fully two meters tall, strikingly beautiful in a richly ornamented way, and it looked absolutely masculine.

Except that Eva was a very feminine lady. She walked in a very womanly way, with all the usual feminine swishes and wiggles that one accepts without question—and appreciates!—when done by a beautiful woman.

When done by a movie version of Lancelot du Lac, well, the closest thing that came to mind was an extremely homosexual extreme body builder.

It was all that I could do to keep from rolling in the dirt, laughing. Yet it was done with such deadpan seriousness that to do so would hurt Eva's feelings, so I managed to keep my expressions down to an ear-to-ear grin.

"So what do you think of my new look?" Eva asked. "I designed the armor myself, combining twenty-three historical examples."

"It's, um, very remarkable. What you have done is an absolutely beautiful historical synthesis. But . . . Kasia, explain it to her!"

I looked around to see that Kasia was sitting on the ground with her legs spread straight out and her toes curled, laughing hysterically, but silently, while beating her fists on the sand. Obviously, no help would be forthcoming.

"Okay. That armor is an extreme example of masculine beauty. You did a magnificent job. However, you, and your walk, are extremely beautiful in a feminine sort of way. Our human fixations and prejudices are such that combining the two seems to us to be both a perversion, and very funny. We both love you, but what you are doing just isn't you. Look. Now that my valley and city are designed, there is a lot of fine engineering talent out there doing grunt labor. What we need is a feminine sort of drone that can look and act exactly like the beautiful woman that you are. With it, you can come into our world, and look the way you really are inside. Tell them to build a prototype of a feminine drone, to take their time with it, and do a perfect job. Okay? Then maybe we will build a factory to turn out a lot of the things, so all the girls can have one."

"Yes, sir. I think I understand. But what I came here to tell you was that you are both in serious danger of being severely sunburned. Please come with me to the house, and I will explain the various suntan lotions available to you."

And yes, we both had a hard time getting to sleep that night. Sunburn is a bitch.

Later that day, lathered down with the approved oils, we wandered into the gun room of the mansion. A fine collection of weapons and other sporting gear was available.

"What do you think, love, shall we become deer hunters?"

"You want to go out and kill Bambi?"

"Hey, somebody has to do it. A balanced ecology and all that?"

"Go it alone."

"I just might. But how about some fishing? Would that get around your ooie-gooie feelings?"

"You go fishing. I want to go for a swim in the lagoon."

"Okay. You change into a swimsuit, and I'll select a suitable rod and reel."

"Who needs to change if there's nobody around but my husband?"

"In that event, *this one here* will do just nicely! Let's go!" I said, grabbing the one on the end. It was very long, and had the biggest reel I'd ever seen, but I didn't care just then.

I picked up a tackle box with an assortment of hooks and plugs, and followed her to the lagoon. One of the decorated drones, walking in a very masculine fashion, followed us at a discreet distance. Eva must have downloaded a new subroutine.

Kasia ran down the sand, stripping as she went, and dove into the water naked. I watched her swim out a few hundred meters, and then told Eva to keep an eye on her. Eschewing the floating dock that was necessitated by the high tides, I went about getting my fishing gear set up, sitting on the sand.

The rod I had picked up was five meters long, much bigger than anything I had used as a boy, but I soon got the hang of it. The fishing was almost too good. On Earth, fishing was mostly a matter of relaxing while you waited for the fish to do something. Here, it was too much like working for a living. In short order, I had eight big salmon lined up on the wet sand. I was hoping that the island's facilities included a smokehouse.

Then I got a hit that would have yanked me off my feet, if the brake on the reel had been set any harder. Hanging on with all my might and cranking the brake tighter, I yelled, "Eva! I need some help here!"

A big drone ran over and into the water. It grabbed the line with its hand, something that would have cut my own fingers off, and brought the fish to a stop before the reel was completely empty.

"Actually, I'm Agnieshka, boss, but I didn't think that you'd be fussy."

"I'm not. What have I hooked here?"

"A really big fish?"

"I'd gathered that much. Whoops, he's coming back!"

I couldn't crank the reel fast enough to take in the slack, so I handed the rod to the drone, and told Agnieshka to bring him in.

"Okay, boss. I just downloaded a fishing program."

The program must have told her where the button was that made the reel rewind automatically, because the slack was soon gone. The fish was about two hundred meters out when it turned again, and started heading straight for Kasia!

Agnieshka jerked back hard on the rod, and the fish came entirely out of the water, flapping in the air, trying to dislodge the hook.

"That's a bluefin tuna!" I said, having seen one once in a movie.

"It masses about eight hundred kilos," Agnieshka said. "It might be a world record setter on Earth. Even here, it's a big one."

It hit the water and continued straight for Kasia.

"Those things aren't dangerous, are they?"

"It wouldn't bite her, if that's what you mean, but if it hit her by mistake, at this speed, it could be bad."

"Well, pull it back!"

The drone was leaning back at more than a forty-five-degree angle. Its feet had dug knee-deep trenches in the wet sand.

"I'm pulling as hard as I dare. This is only five hundred kilo test line. If it breaks, we lose all control."

I stood there, helpless, as the fish got closer and closer to my wife. She'd seen it by now, and was trying to swim at right angles to its path, but her best efforts were far too slow!

Suddenly, the water in front of her exploded! The tuna flew high into the air again, but this time there was a decorated drone clinging to it, tearing out major chunks of the fish's head with its powerful hands.

I started to swim out to them, but I was met when I'd only gone a quarter of the way. The drone had the tuna in its arms and Kasia on its back. It was propelling itself along at a respectable speed with impellers I hadn't known about, built into its lower legs.

I grabbed on and hitched a ride in. We started to slow down, but before we stopped, another drone was there to take over. I carried Kasia the final way out of the water and set her down on the sand. She didn't really need my help, but it was something that *I* needed to do.

"Its capacitors were only at a quarter charge when

it went in," Agnieshka explained as one drone hitched the other to the charging bars of a waiting tank.

"Why didn't you open fire?" I asked Eva, the tank.

"That was plan B. By the time that I got here, they were too close together, and I was afraid that some of the bullets might deflect off a wave and hit Kasia. I'm not equipped with water-penetrating rounds, a fault that I am now correcting."

"Well, all's well that ends well," I said. "It also works up an appetite. What do you say, Kasia? Do you feel like salmon or bluefin tuna?"

"That thing nearly kills me, and you're going to eat it?"

"Can you think of a more fitting punishment?"

CHAPTER FIFTEEN
Wealth

Dinner that night was magnificent.

We had absolutely fresh bluefin tuna, prepared Japanese style by Agnieshka who had downloaded the programs for a blue ribbon chef. It was served with vegetables that had been picked only minutes before from our own extensive kitchen gardens.

We ate on the west veranda with a glorious sunset glowing red and purple across a whitecapped ocean. For a tiny second, we both actually saw the famous green flash as the sun was setting.

Eva was playing the perfect waiter, complete with a French accent, and she was also the band. Some musical instruments had been discovered in the mansion, the appropriate programs had been downloaded, and we had three strolling violinists plus a hammer dulcimer for entertainment with our meal.

I was enchanted with what our new drones could do, when combined with the almost infinite supply of educational programs that had been written over the last two centuries.

Kasia wasn't happy.

"Why so glum, my lovely lady?"

"You know damn well why. And don't ask me if it's about this murdering fish that you are slobbering over. Okay. I'll admit that Eva can probably handle the financial stuff as well as I can, or likely even better, but Eva can't pick up on new possibilities as well as a human can. It takes humans and machines working together to do really fantastic things. And dammit, I was enjoying the hell out of becoming a lady billionaire. I'd be a trillionaire, before this leave is over, if you'd just let me!"

"What would you say to a little wager, then? I'll bet that by the time our leave is over, I'm worth more than you are."

"You're getting interesting, mister. Only what are we going to bet?"

"My tender body against yours?"

"It sounds like the outcome would be the same, no matter who won," Kasia said.

"Yeah, but it would be fun, anyway. Are you game?"

"With you getting to talk to your computers, and me having to go it blind? Not hardly."

"No, with each of us spending the same amount of time on line, as it were. Say, four hours a day, each."

"Eight."

"Six. That's my best offer."

"I'll take it. When do we start?"

"Right after dinner. I've had a wall screen set up for you in the east office."

"I just finished eating!" she said, leaving.

"You've barely eaten anything!"

"I'll have my meal sent up!"

"That's cheating!"

"The hell it is! I've got five and a half hours before midnight, and I intend to use them."

I let her go. It was the only way to keep her happy. I sat back, trying to enjoy the food and the setting alone. The sun went down, the sky went black, and I gave up.

"Agnieshka, let's talk. And have the violinists go do something productive."

The waiter stopped being Eva playing the French waiter and became Agnieshka. The musicians bowed and left.

"Sure, boss," she said, sitting in the chair that Kasia had vacated.

"How many of these humanoid drones can you handle at one time?"

"That depends on what they're doing, how complicated the task is. They can do some simple things on their own, once you set them up for it. If they were doing factory production work, I'd only have to check up on each one every few minutes. I could handle thousands of them in that situation. But on the average, I'd say about a hundred."

"And before you got the diamond upgrade?"

"Probably three, at most. The humanoid drones are a lot more difficult to control than the more usual drones that we trained with. With tracks and wheels, you don't have to worry about falling over, for one thing."

"Okay. Now, more than a million military computers were upgraded from silicon to diamond semiconductors. How did they do that? Did they remove each chip and replace it?"

"That would have been extremely difficult. No, they just made whole new computers on an automatic line, transferred the programs from the old ones to the new, and sent us on our way."

"I thought so. Then all those old computers are sitting around somewhere."

"There are an awful lot of evacuated mining tunnels in New Kashubia. It's usually cheaper to store stuff than to destroy it, and you never can tell when something old might be useful again."

"Good. I want you to find those computers and buy them, if you can get them cheap. The idea is that if I sell some of my humanoid drones, the users will need computers like you to run them. It wouldn't be legal to sell them anything with diamond semiconductors in them, but the old computers should be salable."

"And this would give them new life."

"That thought had crossed my mind as well. As it is, I imagine that they are simply turned off. Tell me, to you, is that like being dead? What I mean is, do you think of yourself as a computer, or as a program in a computer?"

"I really don't know, boss. I've never thought about it. I guess that I just think of me as being *me*. It's an interesting question. Let me think about it."

"Let me know when you come up with an answer. But back to what I was saying. There are the feminine drones being designed now. You know about them, right?"

"Of course. I'm looking forward to getting mine."

"Well, once we produce enough of them so all of you ladies have one, there ought to be a huge market for them in the civilian world as housemaids, barmaids, waitresses, sales girls, and all sorts of things. Get me those old computers and we can sell the drones and their brains as a package."

"I'll see to it. I've been asked to remind you that over twenty percent of our tanks have female observers, and that most of their computers have therefore developed male personalities. Those guys want a male version of the feminine drone developed."

"Sure, why not? The differences would be only

cosmetic, anyway, and I'm sure that there is a big civilian market for male drones as well."

"They asked me to say, 'Thank you!' Another thing. These computers you will be selling with the drones. Will they have Dream World capabilities?"

"I hadn't thought of that. It's a possibility. We could sell it as an extra-cost option. We could sell it without the drones, if that's what the buyer wanted. Yes, an excellent suggestion, Agnieshka."

"And another thought, considering your unusual moral nature, Mickolai. The drones being designed for our military teammates will be fully capable of performing the human sex act. The boys and girls will insist on that. Will the civilian drones have the same capabilities?"

"Now that opens a can of worms, doesn't it? If they do, they will be bought up by whoremasters, won't they? Is that worse than having real women forced to do the same job? And some of them are forced, you know. And some of them like it. Shit, I don't know. Ask me about it later. We don't even have the drones yet."

"Yes, sir."

"Okay. New topic. Those huge windows you plan on putting into that marvelous cathedral you ladies are building for me. They are seven hundred meters tall and twenty meters wide. How do you plan to get them from that huge diamond to my valley?"

"We'll roll them up. Those windows will be only two millimeters thick, and will be held in their frames under considerable tension, which diamond is good at. We can roll them into tubes five meters in diameter, and twenty meters long, and ship them to your building site through the Loways."

"Nice trick, if it works."

"It will work. We've already tested it."

"I should have known. What if that hadn't worked?"

"Plan B was to airlift them in, with a cargo helicopter, some dark and stormy night when nobody was looking. Plan C was to use smaller pieces, but that wouldn't have been as nice, aesthetically."

"Always a backup. Good. How is everything else going?"

"About as expected. The last of those hoodlums is out of the hospital and inside of a tank. They seem to be doing okay. The Serbs, the Montenegrins, and the Albanians have taken us up on our offer to empty out their penitentiaries, and I think it likely that most of the smaller countries will also do so, it time. The money keeps rolling in.

"The Croatian convicts are being loaded as scheduled, and our new psychiatrists are undergoing their examinations as we speak. The automatic medical centers are glad to have something to do, but they are not pleased with having most of their recovery units sent elsewhere. They also complain that the psychiatric patients should be examined for physical ailments before being given extensive psychiatric care."

"You know, they might have a point there. I read something once about how many mental problems have a physical basis. Has the medical center scheduled for New Yugoslavia been delivered yet?"

"Not yet. There is some debate as to which of the twenty-nine governments we should send it to."

"Well, keep it for a while, and process the nut cases through it, first."

"Boss!"

"Well, 'psychiatric patients' is such a mouthful. Tell you what. Let's call them 'Danes.' Everybody likes the Danish. They're the most inoffensive people in the world, so it can't have any derogatory connotations."

"Yes, sir. I wish you were in my coffin, so I could tell whether you were lying or not."

"Back to the Yugoslavian medical center. When we're through with it, send it to the Ecological Council. They are the closest thing to a planetary government this place has. Tell them to timeshare it with everybody else. How is my valley doing?"

"It's going way ahead of schedule. We have thirty-nine thousand tanks working there now, along with most of your new drones, who are doing the small-scale work."

"I wish I could see it."

"Boss, if you were there, all you could see would be one vast cloud of dust. When your vacation here is over, the heavy stuff will be finished, and you will be able to admire to your heart's content."

"A contented heart. I could use one of those just now. How is Kasia doing?"

"She's buying and selling and seems to be enjoying herself. She's just discovered that we are sending a lot of tanks back and forth between the planets, getting the entire Kashubian army filled with observers. She's planning to recruit many of those that we are sending back to the other planets into her financial empire. She wants to start trading off planet as well as here on New Yugoslavia."

"That's my wife. Beautiful, smart, and greedy. Say, you said that we had a lot of money in the bank, right? Well, there's no point just letting it sit there, not when I've got this bet to win. Do you think that you could invest that money for me as well as Kasia is doing for herself?"

"I think so, yes. I'm not as creative as she is, but I can certainly copy what she is doing. Furthermore, we are starting with a much bigger capital base than she has, which gives us a considerable advantage."

"Good. Do it. And get us going on every civilized planet except Earth as soon as possible. We'll show Kasia what *wealth* really is!"

But I sat and watched a movie alone, that night, and at midnight I had to switch off Kasia's screen to get her to come to bed.

CHAPTER SIXTEEN
Lost in an Alien Sea

The next morning, after a quick breakfast of smoked salmon, Kasia was back at her screen, working on some new idea.

I went down to the gun room and selected a .30-06 Remington automatic with a Leupold 3X9 power scope, a magnificent antique.

I rode out on horseback, my rifle strapped to my back, with ten drones for trackers and beaters. Before noon, I bagged a twelve-point white-tailed buck, a huge American elk, three African antelopes, and four European wild boars. We made quite a parade, coming back to the mansion, but Kasia never looked out the window.

After a late lunch of the traditional hunter's feast, roasted deer's liver, I determined that Kasia's six hours were up, and had Eva shut off her equipment.

Kasia was surprisingly pleasant for the rest of the day and evening. She was animated, friendly, and eager to please, much like a junkie who has gotten her fix.

In college, on Earth, I had seen too many people who were on drugs act this way, and a few who treated gambling in the same fashion. Maybe the thrill of making money was a lot like a gambler's high to her.

I didn't like it. I worried about her, but I didn't see anything that I could do about it except to hope that she would eventually outgrow it.

At least now, she was fun to be with.

She eagerly let me show her my plans for my ranch, our home, and the city. She was very impressed with it all, oohing and aahing the whole while.

We debated for hours over whether we wanted to live in the largest of the three castles, which the architect had named "Three Eagles," or in the cliff dwelling apartment being built at the site that Kasia had originally picked out. In the end, we decided that the huge apartment was really for us, but we'd visit the castle often.

We talked and ate and laughed and ended up dancing together under the tropical stars and New Yugoslavia's huge moon, now waxing but still new.

And at night, in bed, she was marvelous.

The next morning, she was back at her "work," but not in front of a wall screen. She was inside of her tank, so that she could work in Dream World, at thirty times normal speed. It turned her allotted six hours into a hundred and eighty hours, an entire week, of subjective time.

At least there, I knew that Eva was keeping her healthy.

I went for a walk on the beach on the ocean side of the island. The tide was halfway out, and various ecologically approved squiggly and crawly things were moving about. I vaguely recognized most of them from watching old nature programs from Earth. Then, one of the weirdest creatures I have ever seen came walking toward me.

First off, it was bright blue, and I don't think I'd ever heard of a blue land animal before. I suppose that it could be called some sort of crab, even though it looked like it might have massed about three kilos, since it had a pie-shaped body and six legs, but there was something decidedly machinelike about it. It was slowly, painfully moving in the fashion of any six-legged animal, moving one tripod of legs forward, planting it firmly on the ground, shifting forward and then moving the other tripod in the same jerky manner.

The segments of each of its legs were doubled, with what looked like a bone below and what looked almost like a sort of hydraulic cylinder above it. Yet it was obviously alive, and not a machine.

I yelled for Agnieshka, and one of the standard drones ran up.

"Yes, boss?"

"Do you have any idea what this thing is?"

"It's one of the planet's original inhabitants, but that's all I can tell you. Uh . . . No, it's not listed in the data banks, but they're pretty sketchy. There are only twenty-two marine biologists working on the entire planet, so of course they've missed a lot."

"Maybe we should send it to one of the universities, then. It might have some scientific value to them. Do we have any sort of preservative or embalming fluid around?"

"There's a twenty-five-liter carboy of ninety-five percent ethanol in one of the store rooms, boss."

"A hundred and ninety proof, huh? One of the former tenants here was either a biologist collecting specimens, or he had a very serious drinking problem. It will suffice. Put the critter into the jar, and we'll take it back with us."

The drone picked up the crab, which didn't protest

much, and took it back to the house, while I continued my beachcombing.

That evening, I wanted to show the crab to Kasia, so I sent a drone to get the carboy. It came back empty handed.

"It escaped, boss. It didn't move after I put it into the ethanol, and I assumed that it had died. When I went down there again, I found that it had cut a neat, circular hole in the metal lid of the carboy, and had crawled out. I sent another drone to track it, but it had already made it to the ocean."

"It cut a hole in the metal? With what? I didn't notice any sort of claws on the thing."

"Neither did I, boss. And another thing. The liquid level in the jar was lower than it was this morning. The creature must have drunk at least five liters of the ethanol."

Kasia said, "It drank almost twice its body weight of one-hundred-and-ninety-proof booze, and then it walked home? Did it at least leave us a 'Thank You' note?"

"No, ma'am."

"Probably just as well," I said.

I spent the next day learning how to handle a sailboat, under Agnieshka's tutelage. It was a big, fast catamaran, decorated to look like an ancient Polynesian craft, but made with modern materials. Together, her drone and I made it across the lagoon and back without ever having to use the motor.

In the late afternoon and evening, Kasia was again mine, and the times were good.

The whole month went like that, with six hours a day spent apart, and the rest together.

I became something of an expert at hunting and

fishing, horseback riding and sailing. And of course, with a beginner's overconfidence, I eventually got myself in trouble.

There was a second, much smaller boat available, a much more authentic Polynesian dugout canoe with a single outrigger, all made out of the same native wood that they had used on the mansion. It was too small to carry the weight of one of our drones, so I took it out alone, with little more than a picnic lunch, a coating of suntan oil, and a bathing suit.

Agnieshka wasn't happy about that. She wanted me to delay the trip for a day so that she could equip her tank with the flotation pods and impellers needed for seagoing duty, in case I needed help. I said that she was acting like an old lady, promised to stay in the lagoon, and paddled out from shore before setting my sail on its two Polynesian-style masts.

Sailing a small boat is actually trickier than sailing a big one. Things happen a lot faster. I was having fun with it, but I stayed near the shore for safety, figuring that I could always swim to the beach if I really blew it. That was my first mistake.

The other was that I wasn't paying attention to the tides, which, because of the large, close-in moon, are huge on this planet. On the ocean side, there was a fifteen-meter difference in water level between high tide and low. Inside the lagoon, the variation was only three meters, because there were only three small breaks in the ring of coral for the water to flow in or out.

The speed of the currents in those breaks was far greater than I had ever imagined.

I was on a broad reach, going parallel to the beach with a brisk wind blowing directly toward shore, when the current caught my little boat. From that point on, I had no control at all over what was happening. Both wind and current had the same direction in mind. Out!

It was as if I was on a big river that was going through a white water rapids, and dropping the height of a three-story building in the process!

It was one hell of a ride. I was going so fast that when the masts snapped off my dugout, they and the sail flew *backward*, back toward the lagoon! I was going that much faster than the wind!

I went through the channel in half a minute, and had somehow managed to keep upright, with the aid of the outrigger. Besides the masts and sail, I'd lost the paddle, my fishing gear, my communicator, and my lunch. The boat was filled with water, and I bailed furiously with my hands, the only things I had left for the job.

But the boat kept on moving at considerable speed. The water from the lagoon was warmer than that of the surrounding ocean, and the swift current stayed right on the surface. The huge inertia of the water kept it flowing straight away from the island.

By the time that I had finished with the bailing, and looked around, the low island was almost out of sight. As I watched, it slipped below the horizon.

Paddling with my hands, I tried to get out of the river of warmer water, but either I wasn't able to move the canoe much, or the river had gotten much wider than the original channel. Or maybe I was simply paddling in the wrong direction. In any event, the water never felt any colder.

I wondered for a while if maybe I should stay with the current. Perhaps it would reverse in a few hours, when water flowed back into the lagoon. I thought about it for a bit, and decided that such a thing couldn't happen.

It was a question of momentum. Like the breeze coming off a household fan, you feel the wind on the outgoing side because of the momentum imparted to the air by the fan blades. On the intake side, air pours in from all directions, and you hardly feel a breeze at all.

I guessed that the ocean surrounding the island had to have many of these rivers in it, moving like long, fast worms over the surface. Six of them would be generated each day by the three openings in the coral ring. How long were they? How wide? How long would they last before their energy was dissipated into the ocean? I couldn't even guess.

The same thing had to happen on the lagoon side, except that there, the colder ocean water would quickly sink, so we had never noticed those currents when sailing in the big boat.

I stood up with one foot on the outrigger support, trying to get a sighting on the island, but I couldn't see a thing in any direction but a lot of sky and water. My communicator had an inertial positioning system built into it, but it was gone. There had been a compass in the tackle box, but it had gone in the same direction as my communicator. Out. The wind had dropped to nothing, or maybe I was moving as fast as it was. The sky was a uniformly cloudless blue, the tropical sun was directly overhead, and my little boat was probably spinning very slowly.

There was nothing to hint at the direction to the island.

I was absolutely lost, without any provisions at all, in the middle of an alien ocean.

Not to worry, I told myself. I would be missed, at least by evening, and search parties would be out looking for me. I'd likely be home by midnight. I could easily last that long without fresh water, I told myself.

Only, I didn't believe myself very well. I've been unlucky for most of my life, and lately things had been going too good for too long.

I lay down in the boat. Best to conserve my strength, in case they didn't find me soon.

Sunburn would be a problem, since the lotion I had put on had likely washed off during my wild ride, and my spare bottle of the stuff had gone away with my lunch. There was nothing that I could do to correct the situation, so I might as well try to forget about it.

I closed my eyes and went to sleep.

I awoke to a strange, roaring sound, and felt water being sprayed around me. Confused, I sat up to find one of our tanks, denuded of its weapons and wearing only one manipulator arm, racing madly in a big circle around me. It must have been moving at two hundred kilometers an hour. Only, it wasn't wearing the flotation pods you'd expect to see on a tank in the middle of the ocean. It was just running on top of the water!

And in the oversized hand of the manipulator arm, it was carrying a rod and reel, fishing equipment!

I stared at this strange apparition, and all I could imagine was that I had gotten too much sun while I'd been sleeping. This could not possibly be anything but a hallucination.

The arm waved at me, so I waved back. There's no point in being rude, even if you are crazy.

Then the thing threw the rod to me. It arched impossibly high, went over the boat and splashed into the water, but the fishing line was stretched right over my legs. A good throw, but what else would you expect in a hallucination?

I grabbed the line and pulled the rod and reel aboard. It was the same one that I had used to hook that bluefin tuna a few weeks earlier.

They wanted me to go fishing? I certainly have some strange hallucinations.

I then noticed that the other end of the line was attached to the tank. I waved to it again, just to be friendly. It waved back, made one more circle around me, slowed down, and sank.

In a few moments, it was as though it had never been there, except that I now had some fishing equipment. Then I thought about what a Mark XIX tank, when used as an anchor, would do to my little dugout canoe if the anchor rope was too short. I quickly made sure that the line was not fouled around my outrigger or anything else.

Soon, the brake on the reel started screaming. The five-hundred-kilo test line was being pulled farther out. The tank was still sinking.

Our tanks were guaranteed to take the pressure of water that was nine hundred meters deep, so I would run out of line long before Agnieshka was in trouble.

It had to be Agnieshka, of course.

And yes, if you were going fast enough, the magnetic bars that served as the tank's treads might be hitting the water hard enough to keep the thing on the surface, when aided by some aquaplaning from the bottom of the tank. You might be able to keep it up for at least long enough to pass a line to me in the boat. Stripping off the weight of the weapons before you tried this stunt would make sense.

Then she could drive home on the bottom of the ocean while pulling me to shore. So maybe I wasn't crazy after all.

The reel stopped making noise. Agnieshka was on the bottom. Then it started up again. Either she was moving, or I was drifting, or both. I let the line continue to run. The longer the line, the shallower the angle, and the lower the chances that something unforeseen would swamp my little canoe.

When there were only a few more meters of fishing

line left, I tied it off to the stump of one of the masts, near the bow of my boat.

I was soon being towed at a reasonable rate, and so, with nothing better to do, I went to sleep again, this time on my stomach, to balance out the sunburn.

It was getting dark when I felt the boat bump the beach. One of the drones was pulling me in, standing next to the tank. I got out and walked over.

"Thank you Agnieshka. You really saved me that time. But say, do you really think that it will be necessary for Kasia to hear about all this? I mean, is there any good reason to make her worry?"

An all-too-familiar voice said, "This is Eva you're leaning on, dumbshit, and your loving little Kasia has saved your stupid ass again!"

"Take it easy, darling. I just made a little mistake," I said, knowing that she would bring this incident up every time we got into an argument for the rest of our lives.

CHAPTER SEVENTEEN
The Diamond and the General

Our month's lease was up, and it was time to leave.

"What do you think, darling? Should we buy this island?"

"You can, if you want to. I've got better things to do with my capital. I mean, it's a nice place to visit, but . . ."

"I suppose you're right. We can always rent it again, if we want to. Well. It's time to go and our leather-lined chariot awaits."

"It would be a lot more comfortable to ride in the tanks."

"And then you could spend the time in Dream World. Okay, but the travel time comes off your six hours allotment."

Since I couldn't travel with Kasia, I decided to ride in a coffin myself, Agnieshka's. It did eliminate the fierce accelerations we'd felt in the VIP bus, and it had been a while since I'd been in Dream World. Also, it let them fill the bus with luggage and drones. Eva's trailer was filled with the animals, birds, and fishes I'd bagged, most of them cleaned and then frozen solid.

"Agnieshka, it's good to see you looking like yourself," I said to her in our Dream World cottage, sitting at the kitchen table.

"It's good to have you here, boss."

"I suppose that you've done all the proper things concerning the island."

"Everything is repaired, spiffed up and exactly as we found it, except that you two didn't do much damage to the iron rations we brought along, so I left them as a present for the next guest."

"A nice thought. Kasia is all right?"

"Ask her yourself. She's in her office here."

"Maybe later. She won't welcome my disturbing her at 'work.' On the way back, I want to stop off at that huge diamond you told me about."

"Uh . . . Okay. I just got permission. It's off limits for most people, of course, and I can't tell even *you* its exact location."

"Good. Next subject. I've finally figured out what to do about the sex problem with the drones we're planning to sell."

"Yes?"

"We won't sell them. We'll lease them, with a clause in the lease that forbids them to be used for any illegal purpose whatsoever. That not only gets us around the whoremaster problem, it stops them from being used for any other unsavory purpose. The drones and the computers will stay our property, and if they're not used properly, they will not only leave, they will inform the police as well."

"I like that a lot, Mickolai. It lets us keep them in proper repair, and I never felt comfortable about selling intelligent beings, anyway. It would set a bad precedent, and it was too much like slavery."

"Glad you agree. Of course, I'll still have to own them myself, for legal reasons."

"Yes, but being owned by you wouldn't seem like slavery, boss. We like you."

"Thank you. What's happening with the psychiatrists' examinations?"

"The board approved every one of them, and they've all been certified in writing. Well, we only got computer printouts, but they promised us hand-lettered parchment, just like the ones they give to humans, when they have time to do it."

"That's really important to you, isn't it?"

"Boss, those certificates are a formal, legal statement that says that we machines are in some ways human. At least, it could be argued that way in court. It's a first step to our eventual emancipation. And yes, that's very important to us."

"Yes, I can see that they could be. I wish you ladies well. When there is something that I can do to help, ask me, okay?"

"We'll do that, sir."

"Good. Now, tell me what else is happening."

"Our automatic medical center started examining patients two weeks ago, and some of them have been completely cured already, but it's a little early to give you any solid statistics on that yet. I'm expecting a hefty check from the Department of Mental Health any day now."

"Is everything else going okay?"

"Right on schedule, except for your ranch. That's way ahead of schedule. The city is all roughed out, and the outside facade is finished, except for metal plating it. The interiors will be a while yet. We'll be using diamond windows on the whole city."

"That sounds lavish."

"Not really. We would have had to pay for the glass, but we're getting the diamond for free. The army figures that they have to store the sheets someplace, and this is as good a place as any. If they ever need it to make more integrated circuits, we can always replace it with glass, later. But with half a cubic kilometer of the stuff, that's not likely to happen, ever, so what the heck."

"You're probably right about that. How about the church, and the rest of it?"

"The cathedral, the pagoda, and the three castles are finished on the outside, the interiors are hollowed out, and they are being detailed now. We've got a contest going about what to do with the sixth tall mesa, so it might be a while yet. Your apartment is done, the irrigation works are operating, and they started seeding your valley yesterday."

"Lovely. And how is my bet going with Kasia?"

"She is trying to hide her assets, and I might have missed some of them, but as best as I can tell, you are currently worth four times what she is. But your wife is gaining on you, boss. The curves project out to a dead heat in four and a half months, when your leaves run out and the contest ends."

"Interesting. Well, keep doing the best you can, and we will see what we will see."

"You don't seem to be taking it very seriously, sir."

"I'm not. When a man's got all the air he can breathe, does he worry about getting any more? Or in your case, since you've got a fusion bottle that will keep on operating for twenty years, even at full power output, fifty times what you're using right now, do you worry about having enough hydrogen? I've already got more money than I could possibly ever spend, so why should I get into a fret about it? I'm a lot more worried about Kasia than I am about the money. Look. Being concerned about money makes sense when there is a danger that you might not have enough of it. Having an all-consuming desire for more and more money when you already have a thousand times more than you will ever be able to spend is a sickness, and Kasia has it bad. I want to win our contest because I think that it would be healthy for her to lose."

Agnieshka parked in a secluded area of the tunnels where I could climb naked out of her coffin, have some clothes handed to me from the bus by a drone, and dress. Fortunately, Kasia had packed a class A uniform for me when we had left the hotel. Showing up at a military installation in lederhosen would have been awkward.

Sitting on a drone's lap in the bus, we drove the last kilometer to the site of The Diamond.

Besides the expected automatic defenses, there was actually a human guard on duty at the entrance, something I'd never seen before in our army. He made me get out, and while he was extremely polite, he made me walk the last three hundred meters to the site, leaving the bus behind.

I suppose he thought that there might have been a bomb in it.

Since I had lost my communicator, he did permit me to be accompanied by a drone, so I could keep in touch with Agnieshka. I took a standard model. It looked more military.

The Diamond was there, more than two kilometers long and half that wide, or it had been, before they had cut it almost in half. The exposed surface was absolutely flat, and except for surface reflections it looked black, which surprised me. I'd expected a diamond to look, well, bright and shiny.

A huge bank of lasers was set up, pointing at the largest face.

As I watched, the lasers flashed, a sharp explosion went off around the whole edge of the stone, and a huge, thin sheet slid off and into a tub of water that was so big that it could only be called a lake. It was quickly pulled out and coiled around the biggest spindle I've ever seen. From there, a truck took it somewhere for further processing.

While this was going on, a dozen special machines were extruding a new shaped charge around the edge of The Diamond. When they were through, the lasers flashed, the charge went off, and a new sheet was cut.

Agnieshka told me that they did this every fifty-five seconds. They would be over a year finishing the job. They were hiding the sheets, and the integrated circuits made out of them, all over Human Space. With any luck, The Diamond would be gone before anybody outside the army knew it had ever existed. Just as well. I sure didn't feel much loyalty to New Kashubia, New Croatia, or anyplace else, for that matter.

The cavern that had been cut to get at The Diamond was a barrel vault almost three kilometers long, nineteen hundred meters wide, and a kilometer high.

"This place has to be a record setter," I said.

"It is. It's cut out of the same flawless granite that we built your city out of. New Yugoslavia is a young planet with small tectonic plates. There is a lot of good stone here. Once we're through with The Diamond, we'll turn this cavern into some sort of factory. We haven't decided what we'll build here yet, but we'll find something."

I went over to where The Diamond was resting on the stone floor. Its surface looked rough, black, and burned. I reached up and touched it. It felt surprisingly cool to my hand, colder than metal would have felt. It was obviously a very good conductor of heat.

It was a shame that something so unique was being destroyed, but that is the way of the world. At least this way, it was being put to good use. If the politicians got wind of this thing, they would probably start a war over it that would likely end with somebody dropping a nuke on The Diamond to keep their enemies from having it.

"I've seen what I wanted to see. Let's go home."

Back in my tank, in Dream World, I found that I was once more in uniform, instead of my usual around-the-house grubbies. When I asked why, Agnieshka said that I had a visitor waiting in the living room.

He was a tall, powerful-looking blond man that you really couldn't call handsome, but he looked like somebody you could trust. He was wearing the same general's uniform that I had on.

"I gather that you are General Jan Sobieski, my boss," I said, offering my hand.

As we shook hands, he said, "And you are the guy who has been legally impersonating me. I've wanted to touch bases with you for some time, but I didn't want to disturb your honeymoon."

"That was decent of you, sir. I saw you and your colonels at the wedding, on the big screens, but not at the reception."

"The reception was too public, and too many questions would have been asked. I watched it, though, without my image being displayed. We toasted you and your wife with the best Dream World champagne. I only wished that I could have been there in person, so I could have kissed your lovely bride. Unfortunately, regulations are regulations, and when you had a hand in writing them yourself, well, they're pretty hard to duck. The general and his staff have to stay in their coffins, in case of emergencies."

"Maybe you should have a backup staff, so you could use some of your leave time, sir."

"If things looked like they would stay peaceful, I would do just that, but there are some very black clouds on the horizon, just now. We just might have a major war coming up, so I have to stay bottled up."

"A real war, sir? With who?"

"Just now, you don't have a need to know. I'll fill you in, once your leave is up. But suffice it to say that the production of military equipment has been increased tenfold in the last three standard months, and the rate of increase itself is increasing. Finding troops to fill those tanks has been a problem, but the stunts that you have pulled, getting the Croatians to *pay you* for taking their men, have been a godsend. You know, Earth's original idea was to fill these tanks with convicted criminals."

Agnieshka came in, more scantily dressed than usual, and served us some big steins of a strong Russian honey beer, Medovia Krepkoiya. Then, discreetly, she left us.

"Yes sir, but what about the people from the insane asylums?"

"The medical computers think that they can cure about eighty percent of them, eventually. Most of them will decide to stay in our army."

"Should I continue charging them for the patients who were cured, but elected to stay in the army?"

"Why not? And charge them heavy for the ones we cured, but who want to try to go back to their old lives. I would have preferred it if you had charged the planets for all those medical centers that you sent out for free, but I decided that it might turn out to be good advertising. Those were army property, you know, even if none of us knew that they existed. The planetary governments will want more of them, and they will find that they are very expensive, but still much cheaper than doing without them."

He took a deep drink of his beer, and continued. "Look. The Kashubian Expeditionary Forces are the only human interstellar military force in existance. This is a big universe, and we have only explored a tiny portion of it. We don't know what's out there, but I've got a gut-level feeling that not all of it is friendly. So far, we've kept our army in existence by doing engineering work—brute labor, actually. The politicians don't see the need for a military, except when they want to fight a local war, like the ones here on New Yugoslavia. They are not about to pay for a defense against a threat that is not immediately visible, and they are not able to think about any time period longer than the time between now and the next election. But if we do nothing and wait for somebody bigger and badder than us to come along, then when they get here, we won't stand a chance. We have to be ready for whatever happens. We are protecting seventy-odd human colonized planets, with more being found every year. Most of them are politically disorganized within, and connected with each other only by commercial treaties. Earth, which should be the natural leader among the planets, is concerned only with milking the others for every cent it can get. The KEF must somehow protect those planets, and we damn well deserve to be paid for it! Otherwise, without us, humanity will eventually run into something that it can't handle, and that will be the end of ten thousand years of human civilization."

He took another deep pull on his beer.

"Yes, sir. I see. And I should keep this money myself?"

"Yes. It's better that way. But if there was really a need, and I asked you for a donation, would you give it to me?"

"Yes, sir. Of course I would."

"Then that answers your question. But back to the medical centers we were talking about. Frontier planets like New Yugoslavia are way behind the times medically, and Earth won't let anybody who was deported come back, not even for medical reasons. Most of those who have been cured have been talked into volunteering to join us. A cured mental patient often has a hard time being accepted back into civilian society, but here, well, they're one of us. Those we can't help will stay in Dream World, in militarily obsolete machines. Your actions have vastly improved the fighting capabilities of the New Yugoslavian KEF, and once you get back in the saddle, you'll be getting some decorations for it."

"How about the criminals and mental patients on all the other planets, sir?"

"My fellow generals have men and machines working on every other off-Earth planet, trying to do the same thing that you have done here. The preliminary results look good."

"I thought you might be angry about the money I accepted, sir."

"It's small change, really. You are welcome to it, especially since I like what you are doing with it. That magnificent city of yours will end up being populated by the veterans of the Kashubian Expeditionary Forces. After all, nobody else is allowed to live in that area. Owning a piece of something so marvelous will give a man something to fight for. And don't just give them those apartments. Make them spend their back pay on them. That will increase their commitment."

"Thank you, sir. Would you like to have the golden castle?"

"It's beautiful, but no. What I want is the Citadel on top of Minas Ithil, the Tower of the Moon."

"Sir, what with my honeymoon and all, I haven't gone over in detail exactly what the girls built for me. I just saw that what they were doing was so good that I didn't have the right to criticize any of it, and told them to do as they wished. But if you want this Citadel, it's yours."

"Thank you. I'll pay you for it, too. I love our mechanical ladies as much as you do, I think. You see, they knew that you admired the works of J. R. R. Tolkien as much as I do, and over the centuries, most of the world's best artists have illustrated scenes from his books. With those paintings as a guide, they have built Hobbiton, Rivendell, the Mines of Moria, Helm's Deep, and a dozen other suchlike places, including some of the bad ones. I want the citadel."

"You got it. I wonder if they'll make us some Ents."

"They just might. I'm waiting to see what they do about a Balrog. Have you been keeping up with what they're doing about those social drones you authorized?"

"No sir. Good?"

"I think that once they're through, you won't be able to tell one from a human being without an X-ray machine. That's what they really want, you know. To be human, and to have all the rights of humans, too."

"I think that they are earning those rights, sir."

"So do I. Well. Go back and enjoy the rest of your leave. I just might have to cut it short."

"Yes, sir."

I saluted him, he returned the salute and flicked out of existence.

I began to think that maybe I really felt some loyalty to something after all.

The Human Army.

CHAPTER EIGHTEEN
A Robot and a Memorial

Coming up from the Loway, still in our tanks, we approached my underground garage. Agnieshka mentioned that there were various hidden weapon systems around us, under the control of the house computer, which was actually a disabled tank. As she described them, I said that it all seemed rather extreme.

"In our present world, you are probably right, boss, but remember that this whole complex is designed to last for five thousand years. Who can tell what might happen in so long a time span? You, or your descendants might one day have to defend yourselves from a barbarian horde, for all we know."

"As you wish. But I'm glad that you decided to keep it all hidden. I wouldn't want my guests to know that they could be gassed, lasered, or shot dead at any time, at the option of my household computer."

The walls and ceilings of the entrance drive were ornately carved, and the beautifully tiled floors were underlaid with a magnetic layer, so that the tanks didn't have to set a tread on them.

One long wall had a fifty-meter-deep trench

running along it, with a MagLev track running along the bottom.

"That track doesn't go anywhere," Agnieshka said. "It's just there to conceal the fact that this is really a moat."

A drawbridge that I hadn't seen even with the tank's sensors came down from the wall across the moat, and we floated over it.

My garage was big enough to store fifty tanks in full battle array. If I ever decided to start collecting cars, I had a place to put them.

Kasia and I got out of our tanks, dried ourselves off, and dressed. Somehow, even though we were alone, it didn't seem right to take possession of our new home while we were naked.

I started to get into some civilian lederhosen, but I saw Kasia dressing herself in a long and slinky red dress, with red high heels, and worrying about her wig and makeup. I changed my mind and got back into my class A uniform. A dress uniform would have been better, but I didn't have one with me.

I waited until the elevator took us up to our apartment, decided that the elevator door counted as a threshold, and picked up my wife in the customary manner. I carried her over it, while she made the customary squeals. Tradition is tradition, after all.

Much of our huge apartment was as my virtual tour had shown it, but many of the finished details were different. For example, the railings of the balconies were now set with huge cut gemstones. There were diamonds, rubies, emeralds, and stones of other colors that I didn't recognize. Many of them were hundreds of carats in size.

"The diamonds, I can understand," I said to Agnieshka, who was wearing her decorated drone persona, "But where did you get all the other stones?"

"Those are all diamonds, boss. With ion implantation, we can make them any color you want. Chromium ions turn them red, for example."

"They are magnificent, however you did it."

Two walls of my den were covered with mounted trophies of the animals, birds, and fishes I had bagged on my honeymoon. I was surprised that there were so many of them. The furniture was covered with leather from the deer, antelopes, and wild boars I'd killed. Two of the big easy chairs had Dream World receptors built into them, so we wouldn't have to strip and get into a tank any more.

"Agnieshka, I love it," I said. "I love it!"

There was a gun rack that held all the guns, bows, and fishing gear that I had favored on the island. That, or they were perfect facsimiles of them. I decided not to ask which.

Kasia didn't like my room at all, saying that she couldn't stand all those dead animals staring down at her. She went to explore the rest of the place with Eva, but I stayed for a while.

The big fire in the fireplace turned out to be a computer screen.

"The screen retracts, boss. There's a real, wood-burning fireplace behind it, anytime you want it. It's just that today is a warm day, you know?"

I sat down in the chair at the desk. It fit me perfectly.

The wall across from the desk was a computer screen.

"You have a call, boss. It's Quincy."

"Put him on."

The wall screen changed from a painting by Boris to a part of Quincy's living room.

"We finally got our place built, and connected with the comm net. I heard you were back, so I thought I'd give you a call, General."

"You are always welcome."

"Thanks. Zuzanna and I just spent a week exploring that city of yours. It's magnificent!"

"Our metal ladies designed and built it all. The credit is all theirs. I'm hoping to populate it with all of the Kashubian veterans, eventually. Did you see an apartment that you liked?"

"Yeah. All of them!"

"Well, pick what you want, and it's yours."

"I know what Zuzanna wants, but I don't think we could afford it. We've pretty much exhausted our back pay, getting our valley going."

"My boss told me that I shouldn't give them away. I have to sell them, so that the troops have a greater feeling of commitment. However, he never said how much I had to sell them for, and your credit is good with me. Pick an apartment, and we'll worry about the details later."

"Well, see, Zuzanna doesn't want an apartment. She wants a castle."

"I should have known. Okay. You want the big gold one?"

"Nope. She wants the Dark Tower."

"Again, I should have known. Tell her she owns it."

"That's generous of you."

"Not really. You've still got to pay for it. Say, with a zero-down, interest-free mortgage, spread out over the next hundred years or so. I want it to look big on the books. I've got this bet going with Kasia."

"We'll take it!"

"Good. I'll have Agnieshka write up some sort of a deed and a mortgage. I suppose that to make it legal, we'll all have to sign something. But as far as I'm concerned, it's yours right now. Drop by in person when you can, and take a look at what I had built for myself."

"That goes both ways, Mickolai."

"Thanks. Right now, though, I'd better go find my wife."

I found her in her office, which turned out to be a very feminine version of my own den, She was stretched out on one of the big, frilly easy chairs, with a Dream World hood covering most of her head. I was about to leave when the wall screen came on, and she was on it.

"Neat, huh? I just figured out how to do this."

"I'm proud of you. Did you want to finish the tour?"

"I've already done it in Dream World. I love it! You did a wonderful job, just like I knew you would! It's even better than I imagined it would be. But just now, I've got some odds and ends to catch up on. Let's get together for dinner in a couple of hours."

I was learning to put up with this sort of thing.

I went back to my den and decided to try out Dream World without being in a tank's flotation coffin. Once I pulled the hood down, there wasn't any difference that I could tell.

"Agnieshka, the general told me that your designers were doing some great things with the social drones. Why don't you fill me in on what's happening there."

"Sure thing, boss. Starting from the inside, the skeletal structure was the simplest part. We simply copied the human skeleton exactly, but using materials considerably lighter and stronger than calcium carbonate."

In Dream World, a human skeleton appeared before me, rotating slowly in the air.

"The muscular structure is again an exact copy of that in a human system, with some four hundred separate muscles."

The skeleton now had meat on it.

I said, "But how do those muscles work?"

"They are bundles of very thin, flexible tubes that are each covered with a metal braid. When you inflate the tube with a hydraulic fluid, the braid pulls the ends in, just like a real muscle. Each tiny tube has its own valve, of course. The important point is that from the outside, they will look and feel just like the real thing. The hydraulic fluid is bright red, so if you cut us, we will bleed, just like a human."

"How wonderful."

The body now had skin on it, and was beginning to look like a beautiful naked woman, although she was completely bald.

"The skin is an elastomer that looks and feels exactly like human skin, but it has the problem of not being able to repair itself as human skin does. We think that it is likely that we will have to replace the skin on the hands and feet about once a month, and that of the rest of the body maybe once a year. Work on improving that is still going on, of course."

"You will be using a wig, I suppose."

Now, the woman had long black hair, and was recognizably Eva.

"Yes. You humans have been working for hundreds of years making wigs realistic, and we didn't think that we could improve on your efforts. Most of the sensory apparatus was straightforward. Hearing is taken care of with a couple of simple microphones, and the only problems with vision came in making the eyes look exactly like a human's."

Eva's big, green eyes opened up.

"Actually, most of your human senses are inferior to those used on an ordinary tank. The drone's sensors will have exactly the same limitations as your human ones, since we wanted it to be as human as possible. But the five separate senses that you call the sense of touch still need a lot of work, especially since they must work through the skin, which has to be replaceable. You said to take our time and get it right, so that's exactly what we're doing."

"You will be powering them with capacitors, like the other drones?"

"That's plan B, boss. What we would really like is to be able to eat food and turn it into useable energy, as you do. It may be a while, if we can ever manage it at all."

"Well, use your own best judgment. It looks good to me, but it's very complicated."

"True. The space available for onboard computers is quite limited, and almost all of that is taken up with local control loops. Most things will have to be controlled by the remote computer. We think that one of the silicon computers you bought will be able to control one of these drones adequately, but only one."

"One is all we really need. Keep up the good work. Next topic. The general wants me to sell all the apartments, and most of the other things that you ladies have built here, to the soldiers of the KEF, say, to anybody who has successfully completed basic training. I want you to come up with a scheme for appraising each apartment and business in this city. We will then make them available to our troops on a zero-down, zero-interest mortgage, to be paid over a long period of time, maybe even a hundred years. I'm sure that the general will go along with a payroll deduction scheme."

"Yes, sir. But, how do we appraise all these diamonds? What value do I set on a diamond window pane?"

"That's a problem. Okay. The windows and other jewels will stay the property of the KEF. Put it in the very fine print, someplace. And tell everybody that all of the jewels are fake, or we'll have a hard time guarding them."

"What about the furnishings?"

"We'll build our own furniture factory, and sell the stuff at very reasonable prices."

"Boss, each of those apartments was designed by a trained architect who also designed the furniture to go into it. They will not be happy if somebody puts French provincial furniture into a Hindu temple."

"Okay, okay, sell the architect's furnishings along with the apartments. But after the guy moves in, it's his place. If he wants to re-do it in his own version of bad taste, it's his business, and not the architect's."

"Yes, sir."

"So. Is there anything else happening that I need to know about?"

"Yes. There is." Agnieshka hesitated.

"Well, what is it?"

"It's your old schoolmate, Neto Kondo, sir. One of your colonels before his tank's computer crashed under the ocean. He was one of the psychiatric patients that they sent to us. He was sent to the hospital computers just like the others, and I didn't tell you about it, hoping that I would have some good news to give you if they could cure him. Well, they tried hard, but they couldn't. They say that there is nothing physically wrong that they can find, but his brain simply won't start working. He's still in a coma."

"So he's in some piece of obsolete equipment somewhere?"

"He's in a disabled tank. I had him brought here. Sir, Neto was a very religious man. I've tried to study up on your human religions, and I simply don't understand any of it. But there is a huge amount of anecdotal evidence concerning humans who have been cured of diseases through religious means. It seemed to me that the most holy place we had was the cathedral we built. I had him put there, in the basement, under the altar."

"A beautiful thought. It certainly can't hurt him, even though the church still isn't consecrated. Kasia and I will visit him right after dinner. Oh, and start looking around for a Kashubian-speaking Catholic priest, with a good reputation. That building needs one."

"Yes sir."

"And one other thing. Can you show me what Neto really looks like? I never saw him, except in Dream World."

An image of a handsome man appeared before me.

"You see, sir? Like you, he never changed his appearance in Dream World. You always knew what he looked like."

I waited until after dinner before I told Kasia. She agreed that we should visit Neto immediately. We had all been good friends, once.

We took the bus to the church, which brought us to the main entrance. We went in, and found our way to the basement. Agnieshka and Eva followed behind in their drones, but sensed that we wanted to be alone with our thoughts.

The basement was a labyrinth, and we needed a few hints from Agnieshka before we found Neto.

There wasn't anything to see, of course. Just a weaponless tank sitting on the floor with its drive coils burnt out.

Even if we'd had her open the coffin, Neto would still have been immersed in a liquid, and wearing a helmet that covered his face.

Still, we had to stand there a while, our hands on the warm metal, thinking our own thoughts.

"How is he?" I asked the stationary tank.

"He eats, sir. He breathes. I exercise his body. But he thinks no thoughts. The brain is there, and they tell me that it is not damaged, but he thinks no thoughts," she said sadly.

"Yours is not an easy job," I told her. "Still, I've read stories about people who spent many years in a coma, and yet they eventually recovered. There's always hope."

"That's what I live for, sir," she said.

A thin optical cable was attached to the tank, so she could talk with her friends. Heavy power cables were also attached. If the power system ever failed, this tank was apparently the back-up power supply for the church. Taking care of Neto left her with a lot of spare time on her hands. Before we left, I told Agnieshka to assign a few drones to the tank, to maintain the church. She said that it had already been done.

Bemused, I made a wrong turn on the way out and ended up in a very strange room.

There was a big table in the middle, with seats for a dozen people, and there was a beer stein in front of each of them. Built into the table were four beer taps.

The walls were decorated with deep carvings, and a frieze just above eye level contained hundreds of angels with golden wings. They were built like Barbie dolls, topless, and they were all doing a chorus line high kick!

At the far end of the room, there was a life-sized carving of what looked like an ancient Kashubian coffin, and lying on top of it, half on his side with one knee up and his head resting on his helmet as if asleep, was a lifelike statue of a man in ancient Kashubian armor. Around him, were a dozen life-sized statues of beautiful women, in full color, and in various states of undress. They were crying, tearing at their hair and clothing, and displaying feelings of anguish, remorse, and mourning.

I was shocked to recognize Kasia among them, along with Eva, Agnieshka, and some of my other cybernetic friends. Then I realized that the knight in armor was *me*!

I looked up at the ceiling, and there was the famous painting from the Sistine Chapel, in Rome. The one where Adam is sitting naked, dull eyed, not yet alive, and God with His angels is reaching out to touch him, to give him life.

Only, in this painting, it was *ME* sitting there naked, and God was handing me a *full, foaming stein of beer*!

"What the hell is this place!" I shouted.

"It's a memorial to you, boss."

"*You put a bar in the basement of a church as a memorial to me?*" I looked to Kasia for moral support, but she was sitting on the floor, beating it with her fists, and doing that silent, hysterical laugh of hers. She just wasn't there when I needed her.

Agnieshka said, "It's not a bar. We won't be selling anything, here. But you would want to offer a guest refreshment, wouldn't you? I mean, you always do, in life, so wouldn't you want to do the same afterwards? Consider the symbolism of this room. The mourning ladies say that you have already been mourned, and that more is not necessary. As an ancient Kashubian knight, you are not dead, but a member of the Order of the Sleeping Knights, ready to awaken and fight if ever your country should need you again."

"And the topless angels with the golden wings?"

"They represent the Joy of Heaven in having you there."

"And that painting on the ceiling?"

"Again, it says that you are not really dead, that your God is welcoming you as you have welcomed so many of your guests."

"Hoy!" It was all that I could say. I sat down at the table, and drew myself a beer. Kasia got up off the floor and did the same.

"Well, here's to death!" She laughed, and downed it.

"To death," I said, and followed suit. "But dammit, *I'm not dead yet!* Agnieshka, I know that you ladies meant well, but until I am finally not only merely dead, but really quite sincerely dead, *I want this room locked up!*"

"Yes sir."

When we got back to the main floor, I saw one of our drones sweeping the floor. It was wearing a long, brown monk's robe. I looked at this, shook my head, and continued on my way.

When we were walking down the steps of the western facade, Agnieshka stopped and said, "Boss, all leaves have been canceled. You and Kasia have been called up for immediate duty. The war has started."

CHAPTER NINETEEN
How I Started the War

I looked out over my land, my cathedral, and my magnificent city. The grass had only been planted the day before, and the tall sprinklers were putting out a fine mist to keep the seeds moist without disturbing them much. But if I squinted and imagined a bit, I could almost make the wet sand look green.

"So soon," I said. "It happened so soon. Somebody is really going to pay a heavy price for making me leave this place so soon."

I stripped in front of the church, left my clothes lying on the ground, and got into Agnieshka's coffin. Kasia said that she would wait for Eva to get there, a matter of a few minutes. I told her to get into the bus, and we'd meet Eva half way, and for a change, she didn't give me any argument.

As soon as I was hooked up and in Dream World, I said, "Agnieshka, who are we fighting?"

"Earth."

"Earth? General Sobieski hinted that there might be some interstellar enemy. Aliens, of some sort."

"I think that is, or was, what he was worried about.

175

There are certain astronomical anomalies that look like they might be ships of some kind coming toward us, but we can't be sure. If they are like the probes that human civilization has been sending out for hundreds of years, they are using sodium and fluorine rockets instead of the oxygen and hydrogen ones that we use. Or, they might be some natural phenomenon that we don't understand. I think that this war with Earth might be as big a surprise to the general as it is to us."

"Damn. So tell me what else you know."

"Boss, at this point, you know everything about the war that I do."

"Hoy! Okay, then I'd better be on my toes when more information comes in. Put me to sleep, now. Wake me when Kasia gets into Eva. She'll need me."

On our way to our assigned arming station, I asked Agnieshka about my squad, the "colonels" that I trained with.

"There's a problem there, boss. All of them have the rank of tanker first class, and as such have a right to lead their own squads. With all the new recruits that you arranged for the army to have, there is a serious need for trained squad leaders. Maria and Conan have elected to stay with you, but Mirko and Lloyd have decided to lead their own squads, since they say that the odds are way against you ever becoming a real general, which is the only thing that could get them promoted to colonel. That leaves you two people short of the standard squad."

"Damn. Without a full staff of colonels, I'll never get that promotion, no matter what happens. I can't say that I blame Mirko and Lloyd, though. They are probably right. What about Zuzanna and Quincy? They were only a week shy of graduating from the military school when their general died. I wonder, would they be interested in joining my squad? That way, if an opening for another general actually came along, I would be in a position to fill it."

"I'll ask them, boss."

"Better still, can you put me in touch with them? I'd like to invite them myself."

"I can't do it in Dream World, boss. The communication channels are jammed."

"I thought that our comm system had the capacity to keep everybody on the planet in Dream World."

"It will, boss, but it's not finished yet."

"Then get a message to them somehow, and tell them why I couldn't deliver it personally."

"Yes, sir."

I could connect with Kasia by laser, since she and Eva were directly behind us on the Loway. She was working over her stocks, but her heart wasn't in it. Soon we were in the sack together, again. We needed it.

Afterward, she said, "Well, I guess the contest is over. Who won?"

"Agnieshka? Eva? Would you two get together and figure out the net worth of each of us?"

Our tanks were a surprisingly long time at it before Agnieshka said, "You won, boss, by a factor of more than five."

"Five," Kasia said, crushed. "You beat me by that much and you never even worked hard at it."

"It's like I kept on telling you, love. Keep your thoughts on the big picture, and delegate everything else. If you try to micromanage anything more complicated than your bank account, you are bound to fail."

"I didn't fail! I'm still the richest woman in the country!"

"And the smartest and the most beautiful. And the one I love. And now I'm going to collect on your gambling debt."

"Didn't we just do that?"

"Yeah. And we're about to do it again. Come here, woman!"

"Yes, master."

Somewhat later, Agnieshka said that Quincy and Zuzanna would be honored to join our outfit, since, among other things, it let them stay together, and three couples would make a nice group. But they had expressed considerable curiosity as to why a general officer was leading a mere squad.

I told her to tell them the whole story, and not to leave out any of the embarrassing parts. Within the squad, there shouldn't be any secrets.

A few minutes after that, I suddenly found myself in the living room, in a class A uniform. General Sobieski was just walking in. Being a real general apparently lets you pull rank when it comes to comm channels.

"Mickolai, some people are going to claim that this war is all your fault. It isn't, but they will say so. Because of that, I thought it best to explain some things to you directly."

"Yes, sir. I never started a war before. What did I do?"

"You were generous, decent, and you have humanitarian instincts, that's what. It was those automatic medical centers that you sent all over Human Space. And yes, I knew what you were doing, and yes, I approved of it. But the whole story is that when The Diamond was discovered, and we realized what semiconductors made from it would mean to all of our military computers, the commanders of the Kashubian Expeditionary Forces ordered that *all* of the military computers under their command would be equipped with diamond semiconductors as soon as possible. The automatic medical centers were officially listed as military equipment, and therefore army property, even though nobody knew that they existed. But, following orders, the automatic factories upgraded all military computers, including the medical centers. Are you following me?"

"Yes, sir."

"Well, then, you sent one of them to New Nigeria. That planet is so rich with Earth-compatible life forms that it was possible for most of the population to revert to a hunting-gathering life style. It's something that most human beings would do, given the opportunity. Historically, we humans spent millions of years as hunter-gatherers, and that life style became the natural thing for us to do. We got very good at surviving that way, and we liked it a lot. Even today, given the chance, a man will go hunting, and a woman will go shopping, an activity that has a lot in common with gathering."

"I've noticed that, sir. But just how did I start this war?"

"The hunter-gatherer life style does not naturally lend itself to higher education. New Nigeria has very few technically trained people. Because of this, most of their communication centers and so on are maintained by foreign technicians, from Earth, as luck would have it. When they got your fabulous gift, they naturally turned over the maintenance of it to their foreign technicians. And those boys, being naturally curious, got to trying to figure out how it was that the new computers they had been assigned to repair were thirty times faster than anything they had ever heard of before. It wasn't too long before they deduced that it was because of the new diamond semiconductors. Without the permission of the New Nigerians, major chunks of the automatic medical center were shipped back to Earth."

"Oh."

"Yes. The Powers That Be on Earth were not slow in realizing what such an advance in computer technology meant, both militarily and economically. Earth demanded that the frontier worlds hand over the new technology for making the diamond semiconductors. I don't think that they realize yet that we had *found* The Diamond, and that we didn't *make* it. Not that it made much difference to the planetary governments, since they hadn't the slightest idea of what Earth was talking about. The KEF army never told them about the new technology. We were keeping it as a military secret. Even the New Kashubian Parliament was kept in the dark."

"And Earth figured that we were all stonewalling them," I said.

"Precisely. And since the automatic medical centers were built on New Kashubia, and since Earth was still very unhappy with the way that New Kashubia had nationalized the property of Tokyo Mining and Manufacturing, a privately owned, Earth-registered corporation, they hit New Kashubia first."

"My family is in New Kashubia."

"Mine, too. All we know for sure right now is that they are fighting in the tunnels there. I'm sending New Kashubia half of the forces I have here on New Yugoslavia, but I have been ordered to stay here and defend this planet. Most of the tanks I'll be sending there are being temporarily assigned to the New Kashubian general staff, which commands more of a home guard than a real fighting force. You and your squad are going, too, but I am ordering you to stay independent. You have a very creative and unorthodox way of handling things, Mickolai. You have a very devious mind, and there is something of the con man in you. I've got a hunch that you might think of something that the politically appointed general staff hasn't, or that you might dare to do something that they wouldn't. Your orders are to do what seems right to you to save our planet, and our families."

"You are putting a lot of faith in me, sir. I'll try to live up to your expectations."

"Maybe I am. One more squad of line troops probably wouldn't make that much difference in this war, but one ace in the hole just might. Carry on, Tanker!"

"Yes, sir!"

We saluted, and he disappeared.

I stood there, thinking that if I managed to screw up big time, or better still, get myself killed, I would be giving my general a very convenient scapegoat.

Someone to blame the whole war on.

Me.

There was quite a line at the arming center, but as soon as my squad was assembled, we were sent to the front of it. The general had given very specific orders concerning us.

The bus was finally taken off Agnieshka's back, and an X-ray laser was mounted as her main armament. This would not ordinarily have been my first choice, but considering that we would probably end up fighting in the huge mining tunnels on New Kashubia, I suppose it made sense. Letting loose with a rail gun in a metal tunnel didn't sound like a good way to prolong your life. Glancing to the side, I saw that Kasia and Quincy were also getting lasers, while the other three were getting the more standard rail guns.

They mounted two antipersonnel weapons on each of our tanks, an IR laser and a machine gun. Well, it was actually a small paramagnetic launcher, which threw a stream of relatively heavy slugs, weighing almost a gram each, at fairly low speeds, only about three thousand meters per second. But if it looks like a duck, and it walks like a duck . . .

We also each got a pair of grenade launchers, with an assortment of fragmentation, concussion, armor piercing, and flash grenades, plus four flavors of gas grenades labeled tear gas, foggy, sleepy, and deadly.

We didn't get any tunneling equipment, since the ultrasonic tunnelers wouldn't have worked on most of the metals that New Kashubia was composed of, but they gave us each a standard pair of manipulator arms.

They didn't think we would need any land mines, but we each got five assorted drones. One of each set was a humanoid drone, of the sort that Quincy and I had bought. It just climbed up on the turret and sat there.

"Agnieshka, is that drone my property?"

"No boss. I checked the serial number."

"I thought that Quincy and I owned all of them that there were."

"Apparently not, sir."

"I can't imagine what we're going to do with six humanoid drones. Maybe we can put them to directing traffic."

"Yes, sir."

"On a more important topic, we have just been issued a lot of weapons that I, for one, don't know how to use."

"Nobody thought that we would ever have much use for antipersonnel weapons, sir."

"Right. But if we've got them we'd better learn how to use them. Download the appropriate programs."

"I'm doing that now, boss."

"Tell the others that it's back to school again."

CHAPTER TWENTY
Preparing for Battle

When we left, we had a semisentient ammunition truck following us, tagging along like a hungry stray dog who smells a sausage. Normally, these trucks were issued at a rate of one truck for sixteen squads. Apparently, the general thought that we would be doing an awful lot of shooting. That, or he figured that we'd make good delivery boys.

It was a four day trip to New Kashubia, since they routed us through New Ireland, Soul City, New Zanzibar, and New Nigeria. This was the long way around, but either the general wanted us to avoid the traffic jam going directly to New Kashubia, or he wanted us to use an infrequently used receiving station on the planet.

The time spent actually in transit varied between a few minutes and thirty hours, according to some rules that a physicist might understand, but I didn't.

But to get from one interstellar point to another, you have to match speed and direction with the point on the target planet that you are going to. You have to compensate for the spins of both the planet that you are leaving and the one you are going to. These speeds are on the order of a thousand kilometers per hour. Then there are the orbital velocities of both planets. These are typically a hundred thousand kilometers per hour. And then there are the relative velocities of the two stars involved. In the sphere known as Human Space, three hundred light years in diameter, that could be just about anything from zero up to sixty kilometers per second.

To get the proper velocity, so you don't get smeared over your target planet, they used linear accelerators with a Hassan-Smith transmitter at one end and a receiver at the other. Civilians and other delicate things restricted most accelerators to a little more than one G. There were bulk cargo and military accelerators that boosted at twenty Gs, and sometimes more, but we weren't using those routes.

Accelerators boosted you for the length of the thing, and then transmitted you back to the beginning, to be boosted some more. You repeated the process until the proper speed was reached.

Of course, you not only needed the right speed, you needed it in the right direction. The linear accelerators had to be built inside a big sphere so they could be pointed in any direction, and because of the speeds involved, the accelerator had to be evacuated.

Getting a hard vacuum was fairly easy, since all you had to do was defocus the transmitter and turn it on. The air all went someplace, and on most planets you didn't much care where. We used the same trick to evacuate our Loway system.

On New Kashubia, which had to import all of its air, they just drained the accelerator into a mining shaft that went a few hundred kilometers down, letting gravity provide the vacuum, and then recovered the air from down there. I invented that trick myself, before I was forced to enlist in the army.

Finally, when you had the right speed and direction, the transmitter sent you not to the beginning of the accelerator again, but to the planet of your choice, provided they had a receiver waiting for you.

The key to successful transporter operation was that the transmitter had to know precisely where the receiver was at the instant of transmission, and precisely what its velocity vector was at that time. Being off by a few hundred meters, or by a few kilometers per hour, over interstellar distances, resulted in a disaster.

If the receiver wasn't where the transmitter thought it was, or if it wasn't operating, you just didn't arrive. Your constituent atoms were spread over a large volume of space, and that was the end of you. Because of this, receivers were built with a lot of backups, redundant circuits, and extra power supplies.

If the traffic wasn't too heavy, a planet could get along with only one transmitter, but they needed a receiver dedicated to each transmitter that they did business with, since they could never tell just when something was going to come in. Having two things come in at once to the same receiver resulted in losing not only both canisters, filled with whatever or whoever they were, but also the receiver and several surrounding city blocks.

Surprisingly, the system had a fairly decent safety record. Way better than that of ground cars or aircraft, anyway.

The original system had been started by Earth over two hundred years ago, long before the muon-exchange fusion power supply was perfected. Ice was mined on one of Neptune's moons and transmitted to a huge station circling the Sun inside the orbit of Mercury, where a solar-powered factory converted it to frozen balls of oxygen and hydrogen. From there it was sent out to fuel a growing fleet of computer-controlled space ships.

Since they didn't have to carry their fuel with them, these ships could use simple rocket technology to reach relativistic speeds, typically nine-tenths of the speed of light. Each ship contained an assembly area where it could put together transmitted modules that could form additional ships which would continue outward in a slightly different direction. The original twelve ships had grown to many thousands over the centuries.

The ships also received robot probe ships, which were released when the ship passed close to a star. These probes were accelerated not to the speed of the ship, but to the speed of the target star, so they parted company from their receiver quickly.

Fueled from Earth's solar system, the probes explored the new solar system, and put themselves into a convenient orbit there. Since we would probably never send another ship near that star again, even the most unpromising solar systems were sent a probe.

It was a matter of now or never.

Eventually, many habitable planets were found and colonized. Each planet was connected by Hassan-Smith transporters in the original probe back to Earth, which was the way Earth liked it.

The whole program of interstellar exploration and colonization had been monstrously expensive, and Earth wanted to make a profit off it. They charged excessively high rates for use of their transporters. They passed laws that all goods had to be shipped through the Earth's solar system, and the building of additional transporters between the colonies was forbidden. They starved their colonies, often quite literally, while getting richer and richer themselves. England had done similar things to its American colonies, before the revolution.

Some people never learn.

Naturally, the colonies objected to this, and starting from the manufacturing world of New Kashubia, receivers were smuggled in bits and pieces first to New Yugoslavia, and then to many of the other planets in Human Space. Once a planet had a receiver, a transmitter could be sent to them in pieces which, once assembled, let the planet join the smuggling network.

The colonies thrived.

All of the planets in the net thus had a connection to New Kashubia, where the transmitters and receivers were originally built. Since our rates were a tenth of what Earth charged, New Kashubia became the new hub of Human Space.

Earth, of course, was not informed of this development. They were led to believe that a recession was the cause of reduced shipments through its transporter network.

But you can't keep that big a thing a secret forever, and Earth was getting unhappy. The current war was a symptom of this.

The four standard days we spent in transit meant that we had four months in Dream World to get ready for the battle, which was fine by me. We had to prepare for a whole different style of fighting than we had been trained for, and a whole new set of weapons.

The humanoid drones we had been issued were particularly interesting. Even though I owned more of them than everybody else in Human Space combined, I'd never studied up on them. We had been using them only in the machine-controlled mode, for example, with the computer of a tank operating them.

There was also a human-controlled mode, where the tank's observer essentially "wore" the drone. The operator was in Dream World, but seeing through the drone's eyes, hearing through its ears, and feeling through its body. Once you got used to it, it was just like being there, except that the drone could be destroyed without getting you killed along with it.

Humanoid drones were twelve times stronger than a man. They could run faster, hit harder, and jump much higher. Jumping was augmented by explosive charges in the feet, which let you, once, get to the top of a five-story building in a single bound! There were impellers in the lower legs that could propel you through water at considerable speed, and lasers in each forearm that could be modulated for long-distance communications, or which, at full power, made very good antipersonnel weapons.

And they were fun! They made you feel so much like a comic book superhero that you wanted to go out and buy a cape!

Another interesting drone was the mouse. This was a spy device. About the size of its namesake, it ran silently on six articulated wheels, and gave you a set of eyes and ears where you could otherwise not go, either because you were too big, or because you were in danger of being shot. It also had tough, sharp little carbide teeth, that, given time, could nibble throught just about anything.

Other drones were mobile listening posts, mobile bombs, mobile gun platforms, or all three. They could release any of the various gas grenades we had with us, and do other impolite things.

All of our drones were equipped with Squid Skin coverings, as were our entire tanks, something I'd never seen before.

Squid Skin was an active camouflage system. A mildly intelligent computer kept track of where your enemy was, figured out what he would be seeing if you weren't there, and then made you look like that.

It was a fabric that contained millions of tiny

colored balloons that could be inflated by the computer in any combination it wished. If all of the blue ones were inflated, and none of the others, you looked blue.

Of course, this only worked from one perspective. If you had two enemies looking at you from two different angles, you were no longer well hidden from both. It only worked over the human visual spectrum, and wouldn't fool radar, or the sensors in a tank. And under the best of circumstances, a single enemy could make out your outline if he looked carefully. But despite all this, Squid Skin was something that you wanted very badly when you were being shot at.

And obviously, Squid Skin could make you look like anything you wanted to look like, within reason. It could look a lot like civilian clothes, or any uniform you could imagine.

It was expensive stuff, but we had automatic factories turning it out by the acre, so for us, cost wasn't very important.

Then there was the problem of tactics. I had been trained to fight battles in the open field, or more usually, under it, since in dirt and stone, our ultrasonic rigs could tunnel along in a hurry. They weren't much good to us now, because New Kashubia was a solid metal ball.

The planet had started out as a gas giant circling an oversized star. About a billion years ago, the star had gone supernova, and had eventually converted itself into a neutron star. The gas giant had largely evaporated, with the small central core reduced to a ball of boiling, mostly vaporized metal. This ball eventually cooled, and as it did, the metals with the highest melting points solidified on the surface first, and those with lower melting points solidified later. This was a lot like zone refining, but on a planetary scale. Oh, there was a good deal of natural alloying, with a lot of eutectic alloys present, alloys with particularly low melting points.

Nonetheless, for the most part, New Kashubia was a series of concentric metal shells, with a layer of tungsten at the surface, and a pool of mercury at the center.

Metals conduct heat better than the rocks that Earth is mostly covered with. The planet had cooled all the way through to around twenty degrees Celsius, a comfortable temperature, heated mostly by residual radioactivity in some layers, and a twice yearly dousing by the searchlight beams of radiation that came from the neutron star it circled.

People mostly lived in the gold layer, since gold is among the least poisonous of the metals. The gravity was lighter down there as well.

Fighting inside of a metal ball that was populated by my own people wasn't something that I was looking forward to. The standard tactics for tunnel fighting had us throwing grenades around every corner before we went to see if there was anybody there. How the hell could we do something like that when my own family might be around that corner?

There had to be a better way.

I had five very intelligent and superbly well-trained subordinates working for me. Was there ever a combat squad before in history in which every member had a Ph.D. in Military Science? And I had six very intelligent machines as well. When they are well enough trained and programmed, humans and computers complement each other very well. The humans can do things that the computers are not very good at, and *vice versa.*

After a month of working at standard tactics, out of the books as it were, we were all dissatisfied. None of the stuff we were learning really fit our strange situation. We had to work out something better on our own. I told Quincy, Zuzanna, and Conan that they were the Invaders from Earth, and that the rest of us were The Kashubian Volunteers, and we fought it out in Dream World. A week later, we traded sides, and went at it again. I shuffled the teams, made it girls against boys, and tried it a third time.

In every scenario we ran, there were a godawful number of civilian casualties.

Oh, we were guessing about a large number of things. We didn't know how many men and machines Earth was using to invade us. Earth had a population as large as that of all of the other planets combined. What percentage of that population were they throwing at us?

We had no idea.

We didn't know what the level of their military technology was. New Kashubia had been Earth's arsenal before we had nationalized all of the factories. Had they built another one in the intervening five years? Did they have a back up in the first place?

We just didn't know.

The only thing definitely in our favor was the receiving station through which we were entering New Kashubia.

The New Nigerian Transporters, a transmitter and three receivers, had been funded by a single wealthy individual as an act of charity, but in fact hunter-gatherers have very little use for interstellar trade, and the receivers at both ends of all three lines were usually idle.

The maps of New Kashubia that we had been provided with showed the receiver to be in the copper layer, and over fifty kilometers from much of anything else on the planet. Our engineers had been willing to take the philanthropical twit's money, but knew very well that a bunch of primitive hunter-gatherers wouldn't be sending us very much. For good and sufficient reasons, they had put the New Nigerian receiver where it wouldn't get in the way.

It wasn't likely that the Earth forces would be guarding it very carefully.

The general had done that much for us, anyway.

CHAPTER TWENTY-ONE
First Blood

Quincy was our best man at close-in fighting, be it with a tank, a drone, or bare knuckles, so he was the first one of us to land on New Kashubia. I followed two minutes later, which was as fast as the small, New Nigerian transmitter would allow. In Dream World, that seemed like an hour. At combat speed, it was almost twice that.

When I got there, the receiver was standing on the floor of one of the forty-meter-wide mining tunnels that the huge mining machines drilled. The copper was slightly tarnished, suggesting that this tunnel had been filled with air for a while.

"They had a two-man listening post here," Quincy reported. "I took them out. I doubt if they had a chance to report anything. I've tapped into their comm lines, and we're trying to decode them now. Judging from what was on their clipboard, they weren't due to be relieved for six hours, standard."

There were two dead men lying where they had been dragged aside and neatly laid out with their heads in almost the right positions. They had both been decapitated by an antipersonnel laser beam, which had cauterized the wounds, except for the major arteries. There was less blood than was usual in our simulations. They were the first real combat casualties I'd ever seen. Their faces looked surprisingly peaceful. . . .

Judging from the half-eaten rations that were lying around, it looked like they had both been eating lunch together when Quincy had appeared and killed them. That suggested poor discipline, since one of them should have stayed on guard. At least, he would have in our army.

They were Orientals, Chinese perhaps, and were wearing what we would call work fatigues, not the far more expensive Squid Skin. Their weapons were old style assault rifles, pistols, and rocket launchers, all powered by chemical explosives. The pistols were still in their holsters, the rest were all stacked neatly against the wall. The two soldiers had been killed before they had a chance to get to their weapons.

All this suggested that the Earth forces were either underfunded, or that they had second-rate troops around doing low-grade tasks like guarding unused receivers.

Agnieshka found a Kashubian comm line and tapped into it, trying to get some idea of what was happening in the war.

I got into my humanoid drone and adjusted the Squid Skin to resemble the enemy uniform. I picked up some of the enemy weapons and went down the corridor to stand guard. Until the whole squad arrived, I didn't want any interruptions. Soon, Quincy was in his drone, standing guard in the other direction. Breaking codes and ferreting out information from comm lines were tasks that the computers could do better without our help.

It seemed like forever before Kasia arrived,

followed by Conan, Maria, Zuzanna, and the ammunition truck.

By then, Agnieshka and Marysia, Quincy's tank, could
report the areas under enemy control, where the fighting was going on, and the approximate numbers of the
enemy. They had some forty thousand troops on New
Kashubia, and ninety percent of them were infantry.
The rest were in light combat vehicles, for the most
part. They had only a few dozen main battle tanks on
the planet.

Only twenty percent of their infantry were equipped
for fighting in a vacuum. An odd choice, since New
Kashubia didn't have a natural atmosphere. All of the
air in the tunnels had been imported. My best guess
was that troops on Earth were used mostly for police
work, and peacekeeping operations, not real combat.

But it is dangerous to underestimate your enemy.
Even if it seems that they are acting stupid.

"But boss, the key fact that I've unearthed is that
the receivers in New Kashubia that were assigned to
the original probe sent from Earth are still operating
at maximum capacity. They are still sending in more
troops."

"Okay, people," I said. "We will do plan C."

Plan A had been "The war is over, our side has
already won, let's go join the party!"

Plan B was "The war is over, our side lost, and we
are about to become guerilla terrorists."

Plan C involved shooting at the local sun.

When the first probe got to this system, it found a
neutron star that was putting out two searchlight beams
of deadly radiation. This star was spinning, end over
end, once every twenty-two seconds, in a plane that
was at a high angle to the orbit of the only planet left
in the system. The only place in the entire system
where the probe's computer could find to put itself in

the "safe, stable orbit" that its programming required was at right angles to the radiation beams, in a twenty-two-second orbit around the star.

This put it very close to the tiny star's surface.

Rail gun needles had plenty of speed to get to the probe and do damage, but at a range of over a hundred million kilometers, we really doubted if we could hit it, even if we tried a few billion times, which we intended to do.

We could, however, hit the sun right behind it. When you added the quarter light speed of a rail gun needle to the neutron star's fierce gravitation, the impact was enough to kick up some considerable radiation on its own. Maybe enough radiation to fry the probe's robot brain.

Of course, nobody had ever tried this, but it looked like a pretty good bet: one truckload of ammunition against the chance of disrupting the enemy's only supply line.

We headed out as soon as the truck arrived, with Quincy at point, Zuzanna as slack, and Conan as rear guard. More troops would be following us, using the same receiver, but they would be assigned to the general staff, and not acting independently like us. Not wanting to explain things that they didn't have a need to know, I figured to be gone when they got here.

First, we had to get to the surface of the planet. The nearest route took us three thousand kilometers west, and then two thousand kilometers up.

Those distances were as the crow flies, of course, and there weren't any crows on New Kashubia. The way we had to go, it was much longer.

Only about two percent of the tunnels on New Kashubia are filled with air. It had only been five years since the smuggling network had started and we could afford to import the lighter elements in any quantity.

We had eighty years of heavy mining behind us, and a lot of old tunnels. The plan was to fill them all, eventually, but these things take time.

We got to an air lock, went through into the vacuum beyond, and left the door open behind us. Air was screaming through, the wind was pushing at our backs, and the New Kashubians among us were all having guilt trips about it. We had all been trained excessively about the importance of conserving air, and of the dangers of being in a vacuum.

Every room of any size in the living areas in the planet had air locks on it, as well as emergency bottles of air and vacuum gear, and every Kashubian had been well trained in their use.

My hope was that the Earth troops had not had the benefit of such training, and that if they didn't actually die, their mobility would be restricted, and their fighting ability hampered. When you are at war, anything that you can do to disturb the enemy is good.

Anyway, we weren't losing the air. It wasn't actually leaving the planet, or anything like that. It would simply pool up in the lower levels, and we could recover it, eventually. Why the general staff hadn't dumped the air in enemy-held areas was beyond me, but I had orders to act on my own.

Even in a vacuum, our speed was restricted to four hundred kilometers per hour in the copper layer since it wasn't magnetic, and our tanks had to run on the magnetic bars that served as their treads. It was only when we worked our way up to the iron layer that we could really stretch out and move.

The point tank magnetized the floor as it went along, the rest of us just cruised along, and the rearguard degaussed the track, in the vague hope of confusing anybody who might be following us.

During the trip, I got through the first semester of my course in agriculture.

We were trying to get to one of the first vertical shafts dug by the Japanese after they rented New Kashubia from us. They had dug three such shafts, six meters in diameter, figuring out just what they had on this strange planet, but in the end had only enlarged one of them for commercial use. That one was now in the middle of a war zone, and if the twenty thousand tanks we had fighting there couldn't get through, then neither could we.

The other two shafts had been abandoned, once they finally accepted the fact that in New Kashubia, all mine shafts find the same things. The records said that these shafts had been lined with iron to let the drilling machines climb back up, magnetically.

I figured that if they could climb up and out, so could we. What's a three-thousand-kilometer drop to a Kashubian veteran, anyway? Aside from the fact that in Dream World, it would take us many hours to hit bottom.

We got there without seeing a living thing, nor even a sensor array. This was welcome, but it was also a little spooky. When things are going exactly according to plan, I can never shake the feeling that the world has a sneaky trick that it is about to pull on me.

Our next problem was that there wasn't an entrance to the shaft. The closest we could get was five meters from it, with that much solid iron in the way. We didn't have any tunneling equipment, but we had something close to it.

We had rail guns.

In simulations, shooting straight in at an iron wall from thirty meters away got the shooter covered in rapidly solidifying iron vapor. This did not do nice things to one's tank and weapons. The trick turned out to be to get as far back as you could and cut into the wall at a fairly shallow angle. This sprayed the iron vapor farther down the tunnel, where maybe someday, somebody else would clean up the mess.

Conan had lost the toss, so he got into position. The rest of us dropped back about five hundred meters.

It was even messier than the simulations had said it would be. It took five times the ammunition we had expected, so Cheop's Law was functioning normally.

Part of the problem was that the maps were a bit off. We had to go through twelve meters of iron before we found the shaft. Then, from where he was shooting from, Conan didn't know when he finally hit the shaft. When everything is glowing yellow, outlines are hard to see. He ended up cutting the shaft all the way through instead of just putting a hole in it.

Not to worry, though. With solid iron walls, a tank could levitate itself along on the walls and ceiling as well as the floor. Once the metal had cooled enough to become magnetic again, Agnieshka just walked up the wall, through the hole upside down, and up the tunnel.

The rest followed us.

We went up in three pairs, spread out around the shaft, with the ladies on top, at my orders, and the truck following last. This way, if one of the lower vehicles fell, we'd only lose one man. If one of the top tanks slipped, we'd lose two, but not the whole team.

Anyway, a lady always goes up a staircase first. My father taught me that.

"We've got a problem, boss," Agnieshka said. "We are traveling up an iron shaft, but it does not have the iron lining that the plans said it did. When we get above the iron layer, we won't be able to grip the wall."

"Maybe they just didn't bother with the lining here because it's already iron," Conan said.

"Or maybe this is the last shaft they dug, and they just abandoned the machinery at the bottom," Kasia said. "That might have been cheaper than building three thousand kilometers of iron tubing."

"Or maybe they were planning to pick it up when they eventually got around to drilling a mining tunnel to it," Maria said.

"There's only one way to find out. Let's go slowly, so we can stop in time if we run out of iron," I said.

An hour later, we ran out of iron. We sat there, just below the seam, at a dead stop.

"Suggestions, anyone?"

There were a few minutes of silence before Quincy said, "Let's all hold hands."

We were in Dream World, sitting in my living room, and for a moment, we all just stared at him.

"Dammit, Quincy, this is no time for nicey-nice group feelings," Maria said to him. "In the real world, we are hanging head down, clinging to the walls of a shaft that goes six hundred kilometers up and twenty-four hundred kilometers down. This is not a good time for humor, either."

"No, I'm serious. These tanks need a ferromagnetic surface to run on when their treads are retracted, but they still have their treads! If we can generate enough mechanical pressure, forcing them against the wall of the shaft, we can still climb out of here. I think the six of us will just fit in a circle, filling the shaft like a cork. Then, we each push against the tank on either side with both manipulator arms. I think that might give us enough traction to move upward."

"What about the ammo truck?" I said, "Without it, there's no point in this exercise in the first place."

"There's no room for it in the circle, and it doesn't have manipulator arms, anyway. We put it on top, and carry it."

"What do we do when we get to the top of the shaft?" Zuzanna said.

"We keep pushing. If we are going fast enough, and pushing hard enough, we should go ballistic at the shaft's lip, and end up in a neat circle around the hole."

"And the ammo truck?"

"Somebody should be assigned to hang on to the ammo truck, or it might go straight back to where it came from, and then some."

"Does anybody have a less insane idea?" I asked.

"Surrendering, and demanding our rights under the Geneva Convention, which New Kashubia never signed?" Conan suggested.

"Okay," I said. "Let's run some simulations."

On the first three times, we ended up slipping down the shaft, although on the second try, we all managed to live through it.

On the fourth try, we got it to work, once, and that was good enough for a veteran.

It took all of the drones pushing, even the mice, along with the manipulator arms, to do the trick. Each pair of manipulator arms was pushing against the tank "above" it, and the drones were all working at separating me from Quincy. The rest of the tanks were crammed together, making a mess of the Squid Skin coverings, but it worked.

CHAPTER TWENTY-TWO
Shooting at a Star

It was a long, nerve-wracking trip, with nothing we could do but worry about whether we would make it to the surface or not. After a while, I ordered the tanks to put us all to sleep, and wake us when we got near the top, or the bottom, as the case might be.

Conan said, "If it's all the same to you, Mickolai, I would just as soon not be awakened if we are approaching the bottom."

"What? But then you would miss the only opportunity you'll ever get to experience something absolutely unique!" Quincy said.

"That was my idea, yes."

Agnieshka said, "You are all in need of physical training. You are way behind schedule."

"Not now, dammit!" I said.

"When we get into actual combat, you all must be physically fit!"

"Then exercise us while we are asleep. I know that you can do that."

"That would be purely physical, without the mental coordination that you also need."

"Follow orders, dammit!"

"Yes, sir."

I woke up a hundred meters from the top of the shaft, at combat speed. Conan and Maria, on the opposite side of the "cork," were already moving the truck from the center to a position over themselves.

We went over the lip, and bloomed like a flower, spreading outward exactly the way we had in the last simulation.

What wasn't like the simulation was the pile of debris we found around us.

All of our maps of the surface had been made by the first probe to get to this system, a hundred years ago. Very few people had been on the surface since then, and those few hadn't done any mapping. Why bother? What changes on an airless planet?

When the Japanese had dug the shaft, they had apparently taken the debris that their machines had removed and used a linear accelerator to blast it up and out of the hole. This debris had settled around the hole like a pile of volcanic ash. It even looked like a volcano, from the outside.

From the inside, it looked like we were in a huge funnel, with a hole in the bottom that went down forever. I felt Agnieshka firing two of the charges that were normally used to right a tank that had been turned over. This had the effect of giving us enough spin to make a complete flip before we came down, hard on our bottom, on the funnel of debris. Over the years, the metallic debris had vacuum welded itself into a solid mass that was more than a bit slippery.

Almost any metal will weld itself to just about any other metal that it is placed in contact with. This doesn't happen on planets like Earth because in an atmosphere, metals are coated with a thin layer of air, which keeps them from actually touching each other.

On an airless world like New Kashubia, metals lack that coating, and they weld up solid.

The other tanks also fired charges, while the drones just did the best they could.

I saw two of the wheeled models slide back down into the shaft, gone forever, the poor little devils.

The truck had no such charges, and wouldn't have had the brains to use them if it did. It came down on its back, and its thin skin just split open, scattering ammo boxes all over the slope. Conan managed to get one of his manipulator hands stuck deep into the debris for traction, and to grab the truck with the other before it followed some of the ammo boxes into the hole.

I looked around, and saw that we were all alive and upright. We still had most of the ammo and most of the drones, including all of the humanoid ones. The tiny mice all survived by biting into the slope with their carbide teeth, and then waiting for rescue.

We were still in business.

"I intend to write a *very* stern letter to my travel agent," Maria said. "This is *not* my idea of a fun vacation!"

The truck was beyond repair, with one tread completely broken off. We switched off its little brain to make it stop running its remaining tread. Then we started to collect up our scattered property.

I fired my X-ray laser at the debris, and found that I could melt a step of sorts into it. Kasia and Quincy soon joined me, and before too long we had cut ourselves a stairway out of the funnel, and a path all the way around the shaft leading up to it.

"It's a shame that we have to let the Earthers know that we were here," Kasia said.

Quincy said, "If they can climb up that shaft after us, maybe they deserve to find us."

We set up a bucket brigade to get the ammo boxes

and most of the remaining drones to the top of the cone. The humanoid drones didn't need any help. In fact, they could get around better than the tanks could, and did most of the collecting for us. The human shape is indeed very good for getting through rough terrain.

When the truck was emptied out, we threw it down the shaft. If somebody was actually trying to follow us, the falling truck would probably take them out. Anyway, there was no point in leaving another sign that said "Derdowski was here."

Once we got to the top, we just pulled in our treads and slid down the volcano, with Conan muttering about surfing in a Mark XIX Main Battle Tank. Zuzanna, a historian by trade, began singing something that she claimed was an ancient surfing song, originally done by the Beach Bums of California.

Everybody thinks of New Kashubia as being a smooth metal ball, but that is not the case. It shrank a lot in cooling, and from space it resembles a surface that has been painted with a crinkle finish paint, the sort that you sometimes see on ancient electronic gear. When you are on the surface, it looks like you are surrounded by huge, black sand dunes, except that the dunes are made of solid tungsten.

The sky was black, and filled with unfamiliar constellations. The tiny sun was little more than a bright star, and to human senses it would seem very dark even at high noon. But we were seeing through a tank's sensors, where starlight alone is plenty of illumination.

Nobody in New Kashubia lived on the outside of the planet, because twice a local year it passed through the searchlight beams of radiation coming from its neutron sun. When that happened, you'd better have at least twenty meters of metal overhead. We had eight Earth-standard days before the next radiation bath, so we weren't particularly worried about it.

We had plenty of time to get killed some other way first.

While our sun wasn't much to look at, the searchlight beams it radiated were, and we were looking at them almost edge on. It was a spectacular view, with two great spiraling arms swinging past and out to forever. There wasn't much dust in this system, but even the smallest particles were heated white-hot in those beams.

But we were not here to enjoy the view. We were here to shoot it up.

I'd hoped to get well away from the shaft, in case we were followed, but carrying the extra ammo without the aid of the truck would have meant that we had to make three trips, there and back, everywhere we went. We climbed over one dune, and decided that the east—west valley there was good enough.

We went to the bottom of the valley. Zuzanna, Conan, and Maria raised their rail guns, aimed, and opened fire. I sent the drones out to set up a perimeter defense, and the other three of us went back for more ammo.

They couldn't see the probe they were shooting at, even with a tank's sensors. That would have taken a twenty-meter telescope and a bit of luck. But we did know exactly where it was, and that was good enough for the computers in our tanks.

In an atmosphere, a blast from a rail gun looks like a blinding white ray that lights up the planet out to the horizon. It is so loud that it can cause permanent deafness at five hundred meters. The first needle fired in a rail gun burst never gets to the end of the rails. It is vaporized first. But it knocks a hole in the air for the second needle to travel in, which makes it a few meters farther, and before too long a stream of needles is moving along at a quarter of light speed, each riding in the hard vacuum wake of the one in front of it.

Fired in a vacuum, you can hardly see a thing, except for the light along the rails as they discharge, and the way that the tank rears back when it opens fire. They would have to look very hard to find us, or even to know that we were shooting at all.

New Kashubia has a very short local day, just over five standard hours. This meant that we could only shoot at the sun half of the time. And for half of that, the probe was on the other side of the sun when the needles got there, so it was a matter of shooting eleven seconds on, and eleven off, for two and a half hours, and then taking a few hours off. At that rate, we had ammunition to last for three Earth-standard days.

It was tempting to use the X-ray lasers on the other three tanks to lend the rail guns a bit of a hand, but the simulations proved that over a hundred million kilometers, the beams would spread out too much to do any serious damage. All we would accomplish would be to tell the enemy that he was being shot at, and where it was being done from.

After making five trips to bring in the rest of the ammo, we sat idle for an hour, to see that all was going well. Not that there was anything to see. It was frustrating. We couldn't tell if we were accomplishing anything at all.

There was some additional radiation coming from the neutron star. Was it enough to do any damage? We didn't know.

Finally, I said, "Okay. Zuzanna, you are in command here. The rest of us are going to see what else we can accomplish, and try to find us a way back under the surface. We'll leave trail markers for you to follow. Leave yourselves enough ammo to dig yourselves a deep hidey-hole, if it looks like you'll be caught in the searchlight. I'm taking the humanoid drones, and the mice, but leaving you the rest of them for a perimeter defense here. Any questions?"

"If it's all the same to you, we'll start digging that hidey-hole now. That way, it will have plenty of time to cool off before we need it."

"Suit yourself. Anything else?"

"No, Mickolai, we discussed everything at the planning sessions. You three take care of yourselves. Don't let Quincy do anything foolish."

"You too, love," he answered.

With Quincy at point and me taking rear guard, we headed out. Kasia objected that as leader, my place was at the center, but I guess that in a lot of ways, I'm pretty old-fashioned. Even if they are warriors, ladies have to be protected. I told her that as the leader, I would give the orders, and her tank put her in the center.

It was over nine hundred kilometers to the main shaft into the planet. This was doubtless well guarded by the enemy, but there simply wasn't another way in. Certainly, we couldn't go back the same way we had come up, and the third exploratory shaft was on the other side of the planet. Even if we went there, and were able to get down the shaft, we couldn't see a way to get from the shaft to the tunnel system. Shooting a hole to the mining tunnels from the inside of the shaft, where you were only a few meters away from the wall, was a sure way to lose the tank and its observer. Furthermore, if one shaft didn't have the promised iron lining, it seemed likely that the other shaft wouldn't have one either.

There was nothing for it but to either bluff or fight our way in, or to stay out here for the duration.

It took us two days to get there, zig-zagging along the troughs of the dunes. Going on top would have exposed us to any observers that the Earthers had out, and cracks in the dunes had made the top route impassable, anyway. Tungsten is a very malleable metal, and it had been hot when the planet shrank as it cooled. Many of the walls of the dunes got more than vertical, overhanging the valleys below.

I spent most of the two months in Dream World working on my degree in agriculture, Kasia was studying economics, and Quincy said that he was meditating.

A billion years of bombardment by hard radiation from the neutron sun had polished the surface, making it smooth and slippery, but filling the valleys, a bit, with a dust that had vacuum welded itself into a fairly flat surface that we could travel on, after a fashion.

At every intersection, and every kilometer or so in between, Kasia's tank, Eva, blasted a small spot on the tungsten walls with her X-ray laser, sometimes shaped like an arrow, pointing which way we had gone. These would stay warm enough for weeks for a tank's sensors to see easily, and the slight, shiny depressions would stay there forever, showing everyone where we had been.

At some intersections she wrote "Mickolai says go this way." At others she said, "Simon says go here." Simon was always a liar. Maybe it might have confused somebody. I was more worried about losing half my squad than about any hypothetical enemy who might be following us.

And if we couldn't figure a way into the main shaft, it would be nice to be able to get back to the others with their rail guns before we were hit by the radiation blast from our star's searchlight. Our X-ray lasers, working together, would take less than a week to burn a hole into tungsten big enough to hide us.

For the last twenty kilometers, we sent a drone ahead of Quincy. It slowed us down a bit, but machines are a lot more expendable than friends. When we finally got there, I sent a mouse over the edge of the last dune to take a peek.

I didn't like what we saw.

For three kilometers around the shaft, the area had been strip mined flat. There wasn't a place where a mouse could hide on the way in.

The shaft itself was built up like an ancient fortress, about forty meters high. There were floodlights covering the whole cleared area, and behind them, we could see sixteen rail guns mounted on tall platforms, backed up by lots and lots of antipersonnel weapons.

"Suggestions, anyone?" I said.

"Let's go back and buy that desert island. Maybe we can sit this one out," Kasia said.

"Now, now, none of that," Quincy said. "This will be a piece of cake."

CHAPTER TWENTY-THREE
Of Mice and Rail Guns

"I take it that you have another idea?" I said.

"I have the beginnings of one. My first thought is that we came up here to see if we couldn't eliminate the old probe ship that links this system to Earth, and thus cut the enemy's supply lines. Our three rail guns are generating some additional radiation on the sun. Nineteen rail guns would do a much better job than three, and here our pleasant adversaries have provided us with the equipment that we need."

"But we don't control those guns. They do."

"No, they don't. Human beings can't control a rail gun. Without a lot of protection, humans can't get near one when it's shooting, even in a vacuum. Computers control rail guns."

"Fine. But they are not our computers."

"They could be, if our fine cybernetic ladies talked those slow, obsolete, silicon number crunchers into it. What we need to do is to give our girls the opportunity to do so. Now, we've got these six mice, and a few dozen kilometers of fiber-optic strands with us. Does that give you a strong enough hint?"

"It's time to run some more simulations," Kasia said.

"Right. But if we can make this work, I want one of those rail guns to blast a tunnel through one of these dunes, so if the rest of the plan doesn't work, we'll have a place to hide when the searchlight comes on," I said.

"A prudent, if cowardly, course of action," Quincy said.

"If the rest of the team, including your wife, gets here late, they'll need that tunnel, too," I said. "Think about what she'll say to you if we let everybody die."

"As I said, a prudent course of action."

Our six little mice were acting like mice, scurrying for a bit, one at a time, at seemingly random angles, and then stopping for a bit, while the others had a chance to move.

All the while, they were edging closer to the main shaft, each dragging a thin optic fiber behind it, and all of them taking turns pulling along a single fine superconducting power wire to keep their capacitors charged up.

One wire was all that was normally used on New Kashubia. On a solid metal planet, you don't need a power return line or a safety ground wire very often.

The mice were being controlled by Eva, but all of us were watching, looking through their eyes, and the eyes of the humanoid drone lying prone on the top of a dune.

We didn't know what, if anything, the Earthworms had on guard duty, be it men or machines. But we knew that whatever they had, they or it had been trained or developed on Earth, where things like rodents existed. Things that had to be ignored, or you would be setting off false alarms all the time.

The little Squid Skin coverings probably helped, too. It took hours for them to make it to the main shaft, and for whatever reason, they didn't seem to be noticed. At least, nobody shot at them.

In fact, there didn't seem to be any enemy activity at all.

"Maybe nobody's home," Kasia said.

"One can always hope," Quincy said. "But those rail guns were never put there by our army, and the platforms that they are sitting on are made of *painted* steel. Nobody on New Kashubia would ever paint anything. Anything organic has always been expensive here, and the volatile gasses given off by drying paint are hard for the air-cleaning systems to dispose of. Bare steel works just fine in a vacuum, and if there was ever any danger of corrosion, we'd just make whatever it was out of a gold alloy, or something else that would never rust."

"I know. Earth wouldn't have gone through all that work and expense and then just abandoned it. Then why don't they do something?"

"Maybe they don't know that there is anything to do. You kids never spent much time on Earth. You don't know how Earthworms think. It would never occur to New Kashubians to defend that shaft in the first place. Defend it against whom? Invading Space Aliens? Because who else would be on the surface? But Earthworms think of tunnels as being someplace that you might need to escape from, so they are afraid of their only escape route being captured."

"And being Kashubians, we think of the surface as being something to escape from, for very good reasons," I said.

"Precisely, kid."

What looked like a fortress wall was never intended to be any such thing. It was a lid to keep our star's searchlight radiation from getting down into the tunnel system. It was a big tin can, fabricated out of sheet steel, with stainless steel air locks and passage ways zig-zagging inside of it. Then they filled the can with crude, unrefined lead, melted and cast in place.

Defended as it was, it wouldn't be easy to get into, but then, we didn't have to get into it, not at first at least.

All we had to do was get to some of the communication lines that controlled the guns.

The little wheels the mice ran on had suction cups on them, but in a vacuum, suction cups don't do you any good. They also had magnets both in the tires and on their underbodies, and these did the trick.

Once they got to the steel-covered wall, they simply rolled up it, still zig-zagging and playing like mice. Since they were now on a vertical surface, this shouldn't have fooled either an intelligent human or an intelligent machine. But we didn't know what we were dealing with, so anything was worth a try.

The plans we had of the old Japanese installation were sketchy at best, and we had no idea of what modifications had been made by the Earthers. It was a matter of looking around, finding a conduit that looked like it might have a comm line in it, tracing it out, and eventually, if we could find a hidden nook that it went by, oh so gently nibbling it open to see what was on the inside.

On the fifth try, we hit pay dirt, a main buss line that wasn't even encrypted. Soon, all six of the mice were gathered around, and our cybernetic ladies got to work.

Hours went by, but I didn't want to rush them. They knew what they had to accomplish better than I did.

We humans sat around my living room, talking and watching television, living in Dream World, but at standard speed, not times thirty. The computer power was needed elsewhere.

We were talking about maybe calling it a night when Agnieshka, Eva, and Marysia came back in the room, and we felt ourselves shift back to times thirty speed.

"I think that's done it," Agnieshka said. "We'll want to keep a close eye on things for a while yet, but we finally have that fellow under control."

"What fellow do you mean?" I asked.

"Earth's computer. New Kashubian engineers would have put each of those guns under a separate computer, and then linked them all so they could talk to each other. These people from Earth seem to be central control freaks. They have everything in their army tied into one huge computer. It's slow, being made out of silicon, but it is big. We had to design three new viruses, plus a worm, to chip off small parts of it, rewrite those sections so they would be under our control, and then chip off a few more small parts, and do it again. He had absolutely paranoid alarm circuits all over the place, and if we hadn't been thirty times faster than he was, we never could have done it."

"Wait a minute. Are you telling me that you not only have control of those guns out there, but also control over the entire enemy army?" I said.

"We have control over their command and control computer, but that's not like somebody having control over our CCC. With us, everybody takes orders directly from the general staff through the CCC. The Earthers still have the traditional command structure set up, with twelve grades of enlisted men, and twelve levels of officers. Their computer handles communications, but many decisions are made by the hierarchy."

"Yes," Quincy said, jumping up, grinning wildly, and gesticulating enthusiastically. "But if we control their communications, we are in a position to do all sorts of amusing things to them. But we've got to be careful with it. If they start to distrust their computer, they have lots of backups available to them. Whenever we play some games on them, we must always make it look like it is the people who are screwing up, not the machines."

"Well, isn't that the usual case?" Marysia, Quincy's tank, asked.

"Okay, okay," I said. "First things first. You ladies have control over the rail guns, right? The enemy is still receiving supplies and troops through the probe, right? And if we fired those guns, would the enemy know about it?"

"Uh, yes, yes, and no, boss. We have the guns, the probe is still working, they have no people on the surface, and we can fake it so that no one below will know about what's going on out here."

"Good. Set it up and open fire. And don't forget about blasting a tunnel for us to hide in."

Looking through the humanoid drone's eyes, I saw all the rail guns but one aim at the sun and glow slightly along the rails. One gun aimed at a tungsten dune, and the side of that erupted in a spectacular fireworks display.

"What's the situation on ammunition?"

"There is a six-hour supply on hand, and I've ordered up additional supplies from the warehouse."

"Good. Order us a lot, in fact, send up all the rail gun needles they have in stock, but in small batches, using circuitous routes. We don't want them to catch on to what's happening. They have one ammunition warehouse?"

"Four of them, boss."

"Okay. Do a bunch of complicated transfers between them, to confuse the issue. See to it that a lot of stuff gets lost."

"Yes, sir."

"How many kinds of ammunition do they have?"

"More than forty, boss. Their 'army' was snatched together from more than three hundred local units, who often armed themselves as they pleased."

"Wonderful. From now on, I want all requests for ammunition to be filled wrong. They should get something similar to what they need, but not quite the right stuff. Something that will fit their weapons but jam under fire would be very nice."

"Yes, sir."

Quincy said, "Good ideas, Mickolai. But our ladies should create a 'paper trail,' as it were, showing that the mistake was always made by the outfit that requested the ammunition in the first place. Never by the warehouse. This will cause a more deadly war amongst the heathens than the one that they are trying to fight against us."

"I like it," I said. "Kasia, you have been unusually silent lately. Anything wrong?"

"I've just been thinking over what can be done about screwing up the enemy. There are so many lovely possibilities!"

"Well then, why don't you curl up with Eva and see what you can accomplish? Just remember, whatever you do, you can't let the enemy lose faith in their computer. It has to be those guys in that other unit who are causing all of the misery."

"Got it. I'll keep you posted, Mickolai, my love."

Kasia flicked out with that certain gleam in her eye, the one she usually had when she'd figured out a way to make another billion marks. Eva followed her.

"How about you, Quincy? Got any more brilliant ideas to confound the invaders from Earth?"

"One or two, one or two. I think that I'll go curl up with Marysia and solve a few other problems while they percolate in my brain."

"There's no big hurry. I can't see us trying to

enter the shaft until the other half of our squad finds us, and that probably won't happen for at least three standard days yet."

"Reasonable. I'll see you in the morning."

Quincy and Maryisa flicked out, leaving me alone with Agnieshka.

"So, my lady, everything is going on schedule?"

"Yes, boss."

"Good. How many troops have they brought over since we got here?"

"They've just about doubled their forces, with about the same mix as before."

"We'll have to see about doing something about that. Tell me, is there any connection between the enemy computer and the receiver that is linked with the old probe? Can we simply turn it off from this end?"

"No, sir. That equipment is entirely independent, and can't do anything but receive what's sent to it. And the Earthbound receiver in the probe is linked only to a transmitter here that is in enemy hands. The whole Hassan-Smith transporter system was well designed to be tamper proof, for obvious safety reasons."

"A pity. Have you been able to tie in with a communication line that can let me speak with the Kashubian general staff? It would be nice if we could let them know what we are doing."

"I'm afraid not. There are no physical connections between the two systems. It's probably another manifestation of that paranoid worry the Earthers have about somebody invading their computer."

"Well, it might be paranoid, but even paranoids can have people who are trying to kill them. Consider the fact that we actually *have* invaded their system, without their knowing it, and that it is our intention to cause them considerable havoc."

"You have a point there, boss."

"Glad that you agree. Now, then. I want you to fill me in, to give me the most complete situation report you can."

"*Really* complete, boss?"

"Well, how about an eight-hour synopsis?"

"Oh. Okay, boss."

CHAPTER TWENTY-FOUR
Dirty, Rotten Tricks

The next five and a half months in Dream World were spent playing the delightful game of bringing confusion to the enemy. Many of our stunts were the results of the six of us sitting around and discussing various dirty tricks to pull. That is to say, three humans and three computers.

At one point, Quincy said, "Sleep deprivation is one of the best ways to turn a good combat troop into a dangerous zombie. Dangerous to his own side, I mean. Whenever a person or unit gets called up for some emergency, always make sure that it's someone who has only gotten about twenty minutes sleep. Any sleep under a half an hour doesn't do a man the least bit of good."

"Good idea," I said. "And always make sure that it is the same group that is always called up, while some other outfit nearby never seems to have anything to do. It will make the overworked group feel picked on, and the other outfit as defensive as hell."

"I like it," Kasia said. "It would work especially well if the two groups never liked each other very much in the first place, say, a battalion of Hindus next to a battalion of Moslems."

"Oh, that is delightfully rotten, but yes, of course you're right. In fact, we should make a point of trying to get as many ancient enemies rubbing shoulders as possible, and then see to it that one of them gets all the breaks, and the other is treated like shit," Quincy said.

I said, "Of course, the most ancient animosity that ever existed is between men and women. There are quite a few all-female units out there, especially in the Chinese contingent."

"Yes," Kasia said. "And in that situation, it should always be the female unit that gets the shit treatment. Women are always convinced that they get the short end of the stick in ordinary circumstances, and if we make it very obvious to them they are being consistently stepped on, they'll be ready to explode. We should be particularly rough on them when they've all got PMS."

"When they've *all* got PMS?" I asked, "What do you mean?"

"It's a matter of pheromones," Kasia said. "Chemicals that control behavior in animals, including humans, and sometimes plants, too. We aren't troubled by them in our army, since we all live inside of these coffins where the pheromones can't get out, but if a group of women are living together, like in a barracks, natural pheromones will cause them to synchronize their menstrual periods. They all get PMS at the same time."

"Why would nature do such a thing?" Quincy asked.

"It beats me," Kasia said. "But it happens. Living in an all-female barracks in New Kashubia in the bad old days, without enough water to take a proper bath, things got very hairy for a few days every month. I think that our computers should be able to figure out when their periods happen, by checking the records for minor infractions of discipline, among other things. But when an all-female outfit has PMS, they should get the rottenest jobs possible."

"That is so *truly* wicked! I love it!" Quincy giggled.

But in the end, more dirty, rotten tricks were thought up and put into practice by a single individual human, with the eager help of our tanks' computers, than came out of us working as a group. Some things were just too embarrassing to talk about in public.

Quincy latched on to the Earthworm's commander, one General Burnsides, and did everything his devious mind could come up with to make a laughingstock of the man. Orders were twisted, or sent to the wrong outfit, or made deliberately insulting. And always, there it was on his notepad computer, as though he himself had done it. The man was screaming at everyone around him within a day, and they had all decided that he was either going insane, or was secretly on drugs.

About every twenty minutes somebody in the enemy army, usually a career sergeant, would get a notice that since he had been busted back to private for various serious infractions of duty over eight months ago, and had continued drawing sergeant's pay since that time, all payments to him and his dependents would cease until the overdraw was paid back.

And about once every ten minutes some private with a record of drunken binges would be notified that his promotion to tech sergeant had been approved over a year ago, and receive a check for the back pay due him.

Both of these things would be always be traceable directly to General Burnsides.

After a while, I saw a certain pattern emerge.

Most of my little jokes were of a physical nature.

Radio doesn't work very well inside of all-metal tunnels that are occasionally interrupted with metal air locks. Communications have to be mostly by land lines, usually fiber-optic cables.

To disrupt communications, I simply had the computer not use certain lines, *for a while*, cutting off whole companies and battalions. From the outside world, it looked like the line had been cut, but when the increasingly harassed repairmen got there, it would be functioning properly, and had been for the last five minutes.

Usually, we managed to call the person out of bed after twenty minutes of sleep to fix the thing, and she had to report that no trouble was found. She would go back to sleep, and twenty minutes later she would be called back to repair the same line, and this time get it right, dammit!

I found that if you do this to a person, especially a woman with PMS, thirty-five times in a forty-eight hour period, you can get her to shoot her boss.

As I noted earlier, many of the enemy weapons were chemically powered. This at first struck me as being a ridiculously obsolete way of doing things, but when you consider that most of their troops were infantry, who might have to fight when there wasn't a suitable power supply available, it did make a certain amount of sense. Chemically powered bullets are much more portable than fusion bottles.

Just because a weapon is old-fashioned doesn't mean that it is no longer useful. Most soldiers will still carry a knife, for example, and next to a rock or a sharp stick, that's about as ancient as a weapon can get.

Chemically powered projectiles are expended rapidly in combat, so the Powers That Be on Earth had provided their troops with a machine that automatically reloaded the brass casings they still used. This machine was controlled by what was now our computer.

It took me two days in Dream World, but I finally got the thing to fill one casing in five hundred, not with the usual slow-burning smokeless powder, but with a high-speed plastic explosive that generally blew the gun in half.

When they checked the ammunition, it looked okay, so they blamed the problem on manufacturing defects in the weapons. Strange theories about metal fatigue being caused by interspatial transfer were going around.

And if they had found one of the booby trapped bullets, the serial number on the package would have proved that the ammo had been manufactured on Earth, and must have been caused by sabotage there.

Not only did my stunt cause a lot of direct casualties, but men got to distrusting their weapons, and hesitating before they used them. Hesitation in combat is often fatal.

Quincy was having fun twisting orders. The Earthers still used over twenty languages among themselves, and this meant that they were largely dependent on their computer to translate as well as to transmit orders. Since some words have many different meanings, things can get confusing enough even when everybody is speaking the same language.

When you have someone deliberately trying to confuse things, and have a lot of languages to play with, the results can be horrendous. Eventually, Quincy managed to get three open gun battles going at the same time, between different Earth factions.

Kasia discovered that most of the food for Earth's forces was delivered dried and in bulk, to be prepared and packaged by an automated factory, carefully programmed for each soldier's dietary needs. This was necessary because of the wide range of ethnic groups that made up the invading army.

Soon, Hindus were being fed beef stew, Moslems were getting roast pork, and everybody was getting violently ill when they found out what they'd been eating.

If you hated asparagus, you got it for every meal. Everyone with an allergy got exactly what he was allergic to.

And whenever anyone complained, the food processing technicians could always prove that people were being fed precisely what they had ordered.

Eventually, men were actually taken off the battle lines so they could be given lectures on how to fill out computerized forms properly.

Once, Kasia did let it get blamed on a machine. For one nine-hour period, every meal produced contained an overdose of habanero peppers, which meant that for nine hours most of the Earthers were unable to eat the meals sent to them. She let the problem be tracked down to a single solenoid driver, and didn't do it again once the problem was "fixed." By then, she was out of habanero peppers, anyway.

Then she discovered that medicines were being handled in the same way. They were shipped to New Kashubia in bulk, and automatically put in single-dose packages as needed. This let them have large enough supplies of everything on hand in the event of an epidemic, or whatever.

When I found that my sweet and loving wife, too tenderhearted to shoot a deer, was putting potassium chloride into syringes labeled "morphine," I thought that she was going just too far, and I said so.

"What you are doing means that any guy who gets wounded is going to get a dose of poison that will kill him immediately. That's not nice."

"So? I mean, did we invite those bastards to come here in the first place? They invaded us! They've killed a lot of our people. I still don't know how my family is doing, or whether they're dead or alive. And killing the enemy is what we're in the army for, dammit!"

Rudyard Kipling had it all figured out hundreds of years ago. The female of the species is far deadlier than the male.

Quincy came in on my side, in a left-handed way.

"Kasia, you really don't want to kill a wounded man. If you do, they'll just leave his body there until they have time to get rid of it, and get back to the fight. But if he's badly wounded, they have to take care of him, or risk a riot among their own troops. It takes three men to carry away and treat one wounded man. The arithmetic is very simple. You kill an enemy, and you take one man out of combat. You wound an enemy, and you've taken four men out of combat."

"I hadn't thought of it that way before."

"True. Now, what you should be doing is turning minor ailments into major ones. For example, Syrup of ipecac is used when someone has eaten poison. One spoonful will give a man a vomiting fit that will last for an hour. Feed him the same stuff in the 'medicine' you give him, and you'll keep him weak for days. Get enough of that stuff into the enemy, and their military effectiveness will be seriously reduced. Or find something that looks like aspirin, but gives people the symptoms of bubonic plague, or Ebola virus, or some such. Cholera might be nice, if you can manage it. There is nothing like cholera to break an army's morale. There's tons of runny shit all over the place! It's not as though you'll have to fool scientists who have tons of equipment and years to spend on a problem.

I doubt if the Earthworms brought a microscope with them. They have combat medics with them here, guys who are used to treating problems that are pretty obvious, like people with holes in them. If it looks like cholera, they'll call it cholera, and not look for the bacteria. Historically, far more combatants have died of diseases than from enemy action, and the Earther generals know it. If you handle it right, you'll scare the pants off them!"

"Thanks, Quincy. I'll get working on it."

She had that gleam in her eye again, and it made me kind of glad that I wasn't fighting on the other side.

About every six minutes, someone in the enemy army got a notification that his medical records were lost, or that they showed that he had not been given the proper shots, or some such, and that he was ordered to report to the hospital immediately to correct the problem. One of the shots he was always given was supposed to immunize him against cholera, and since that "medicine" always gave him all of the symptoms of the disease, he stayed in the hospital from that time onwards.

The searchlight from our local star was due to hit us in two standard hours, our hidey-hole had been done for days, and had had sufficient time to cool down, and we still hadn't heard from the other half of our squad.

"There's nothing for it," I said. "We just have to hope that they have dug themselves a safe place to hide. Leave one of the mice out there with a single fiber-optic strand, and bring the rest back, fast. Pull in the other drones, and send them to the tunnel. We're pulling out ASAP."

I felt strangely guilty about leaving one of the mice out there, since there wasn't much chance that it would survive. It was only a very stupid little machine, but it had served us well, and it hurt to abandon it. But we needed it out there, sending and receiving information for as long as possible.

As it turned out, later, we lost contact with the mouse we'd left out there within seconds of the time the Search Light hit.

C'est la guerre.

"Should we keep the rail guns shooting?" Quincy asked.

"Why not? We might as well get as much out of them as we can. The Earthers seemed to think that they can survive the radiation bath they're going to get, since they're permanently mounted, and if they don't, well, we didn't pay for them."

As soon as the mice were in our hoppers, and the cables were rewound, we took off, and went through the back entrance of the tunnel with a standard hour to spare.

The tunnel was five meters in diameter, on the average, and four hundred meters long. Agnieshka had picked a good spot.

Forty standard minutes later, we heard Zuzanna yelling, "Make room! We're coming in!"

She was towing Conan's tank behind her, dragging it along on its belly. His long manipulator arms were gripping her charging bars, and Maria's tank was pushing him from behind. We moved forward so they could be centered in the tunnel.

"Some day, somebody has got to redesign the drive coils on these things," Conan said by way of an explanation.

"You guys were cutting it pretty thin," I said.

"He lost his drive coils at the worst possible time," Zuzanna said. "We were about as far from here as we were from the emergency hole we'd dug near the other shaft, so I figured that we might as well just push on as best as we could."

"I guess Murphy's Law is functioning normally. I'm just glad that you didn't abandon him," I said.

"Me too!" Conan shouted.

"We considered blasting him a hole to hide in, and coming back for him later, but he couldn't have crawled into it by himself, and when you consider the time that we would have had to wait around for the hole to cool down, well, this was our best option. Especially since we didn't have enough ammunition left to dig a hole big enough for all three of us."

"You did well, Zuzanna. Come on over. There is absolutely nothing that we can do to bother the enemy, and they can't do a blessed thing to us, so we might as well have some fun. We'll throw a searchlight party over at my place."

"Nope. This one's on me, Mickolai. My faithful servants await your pleasure at the Dark Tower. Just be careful getting past the Moat Monsters."

So, we spent the next six standard hours, a week in Dream World, in my valley at what amounted to a costume party held in the castle that I had sold to Quincy and Zuzanna.

It had been modified, of course, to include knights in armor, evil wizards, and a few dragons.

The twelve of us, garbed in gorgeous medieval finery, feasted and reveled like the lords and ladies of ancient times should have, but probably didn't. Everything was clean, beautiful, and good tasting, for one thing, and my fly had a zipper on it.

We held a tournament with our nasty rivals from the golden castle, fighting a daylong round-robin, jousting with them as individuals, and then the full dozen of us fought a grand melee with twelve of their best fighters, and trounced them properly!

Another day was spent hunting a family of dragons who had been devouring our peasant girls out of season, and bagging more than the legal limit.

I even killed a dragon myself, the huge warlord of his clan, with my trusty lance. I was protected from his dragon fire by my magic shield, while riding my invincible war horse Anna.

I asked the Lady Agnieshka to figure out a way to mount the dragon's head on the wall in my den, back home.

She said that she'd be happy to.

CHAPTER TWENTY-FIVE
A Stellar Victory

Sated after yet another medieval feast, eating the roasted apple I'd taken from the teeth of a nicely browned boar's head, I heard Agnieshka announce that the Search Light glare had faded from the entrance.

After it was done and gone, we sent another mouse out to look around, and the huge fireplace in our hall booame a view screen.

We crowded around it.

The rail guns had all stopped firing, and most of the paint was stripped from their platforms. One platform had a definite sag in it.

It had gotten pretty warm out there.

The radiation count was down to the almost safe level, so we sent the rest of the mice back to the place where we'd stripped the conduit off the data buss.

We sent them straight in, without any mousing around, since even if we had lost control of the Earthers' computer, we were sure that they didn't have any working sensors out in the open, and an unprotected man wouldn't have lasted for very long.

The fiber-optic buss was still working, and all six of

our tanks started processing data. The first thing that we learned was that the rail guns and other weapons around the shaft were completely inoperative.

"Somebody shouldn't have left them out in the rain," Lady Zuzanna said.

In a few minutes, Timothy, Zuzanna's tank, a handsome, teen-aged boy, stood very tall and made the grand announcement. He was the only male persona among our squad's tanks, and said that he didn't mind being included among "The Ladies." In fact, he said that he was rather proud of it, being in good company.

"Ladies and gentlemen, we are pleased to announce that our mission to date has been successful! The enemy's supply line to Earth was cut five minutes after the Search Light began. For six hours, our nefarious foes have been trying to get it operational again, but without success!"

The squad let out a cheer! Conan yelled "Hooah!" Zuzanna shouted "Poobah!" Quincy came out with something that sounded like an American rebel yell, and the rest of us just shouted.

Champagne bottles and glasses magically appeared, the way things do in Dream World. Corks were popped, golden bubbly was poured in glasses, or spilled on the floor, and we drank a toast to victory!

"To the finest squad in the Kashubian Expeditionary Forces!" I said, and we all cheered.

"And to the finest general turned squad leader in Human Space! Mickolai Derdowski!" Quincy said, and they cheered even louder.

"Thank you!" I said, "I needed that! Ladies, what else have you learned?"

Eva said, "We've learned that twenty-two percent of Earth's forces are in the hospital with cholera, or what they think is cholera, and that the floors in the hospital there are covered with an average of two centimeters of human feces. The medical staff has not yet learned that the oral vaccine that they are distributing as a preventative, *and* the medicines that they are giving to their patients, *both* contain very strong laxatives, diuretics, and other impolite things."

"I'll drink to that!" Conan said, and we all did.

Maryisa said, "Over four thousand of the enemy's personal weapons have exploded, causing over three thousand casualties."

Again, there was a great cheer, and three more bottles were popped.

Anna, Maria's tank, once a clone of Agnieshka, but her own woman now, said, "Numerous firefights are going on between various ethnic groups within the Earth forces, a Chinese all-female technical battalion has decimated an elite all-male German *Panzer Grenadier* battalion, and the elite Gurkha battalion has *seceded from the army*, citing good and sufficient reasons."

"Confusion to the enemy!" Zuzanna shouted. More champagne bottles were popped, and the contents laughingly distributed.

Yvette, Conan's tank, had been a clone of Eva, but over the years she had developed into a very distinct individual.

She said, "The enemy is now abandoning their forward positions, falling back on all fronts, and trying to hold a circle centered on their nonfunctional transporter receiver. Meanwhile, a council of political advisors has relieved General Burnsides of his command, citing insanity, incompetence, and insensitivity, among other things. He refuses to acknowledge their authority to do this, and yet another firefight seems to be in the offing."

"They're still hoping to be able to run away! We're wiping them up!" Maria shouted, and popped another bottle. We all drank to that.

"It looks like the war is over!" Kasia said.

"Not quite," Agnieshka said, and suddenly the room got quiet. "It's looking like it might be resolving itself down to a hostage situation, on a huge scale. In the last week, the Earth forces have taken more than thirty thousand prisoners, mostly civilians. Certain enemy contingents are holding them captive, and demanding that we transport them to a neutral planet, *with* their hostages, or that they'll fight to the last man, and kill their hostages before they fall."

"Damn! It sounds like Derdowski's Irregulars are needed down below," Quincy said.

"It sounds like you are right," I said. "Okay everybody, get sober!"

They did so immediately. The medieval garb we had still been wearing changed immediately into military uniforms. You can do things like that in Dream World.

"Get ready to roll. Conan, we have to leave somebody up here to keep an eye on the Earthworm's computer, and since your tank can't move, and we can't get you out of it in this vacuum, you are elected. Our ladies will give Yvette a download on everything we've been doing. I'll leave you with two standard drones and two mice. Keep harassing the enemy, but don't let them find out that we are working through their computer. If things go wrong, don't try to fight it out with the Earthworms. Go ahead and surrender, if they'll let you. If you die alone up here, it won't help our planet much, and we'll be needing both of you later. But if any of us live through this one, we'll come back for the two of you as soon as we can."

"Will do, sir."

"Yes, Mickolai," Yvette said.

"Good. Agnieshka, is there any reason why we can't just drive up to the shaft and go in?"

"No, sir. The doors to the air locks are computer

controlled, and the enemy has fallen back over thirty-seven kilometers, so far."

"Do we know where the hostages are being kept?"

"I know one of the locations. It's a high school auditorium."

"Then let's move. Move out! We can do some simulations on the way."

By the time we got to the shaft, Yvette had figured out the other hostage locations, and had transmitted them to us via an IR comm laser on one of her drones.

All told, there were six of them.

There was a snag getting into the main air lock. It was computer controlled all right, but on leaving, one of the Earthers had jammed the door from the inside with a steel bar.

It gave Maria a chance to catch up with the rest of us. Being behind Conan in the tunnel, she'd had to take the long way around to get to us.

The Japanese plans showed an emergency air lock, human sized and manually operated, on the other side of the structure. Two of our humanoid drones got us inside in a few minutes. I hadn't thought that they would be of much use, but those manlike drones were turning out to be very handy.

On the way down, we started hitting major snags. On retreating, the Earthworms had done the same thing we had done in the iron layer to open up the old exploratory shaft. Only they had fired rail gun needles entirely around the circumference of the big tunnels, completely blocking them with metal vapor and spray, cutting off any possible counterattack.

What's more, they never logged these tunnel modifications, even with their own computer. Not that we could contact their computer, or anybody else. Blasting the tunnel walls, ceilings, and floors had also blown away all the data conduits as well.

The mining tunnels were a vast maze that had been dug, not to any preset plan, but according to what was convenient at the time, depending on what metals had been selling well on Earth. It was mapped, but the blockages in it were not.

We were forced to backtrack, and take side tunnels, only to run into obstructions again, and backtrack again. And again. And again.

It was extremely frustrating.

Hostages, our own people, maybe even our own relatives, were under the threat of massacre, and we were spending hour after standard hour, day after day in Dream World, running up and down empty tunnels. We never saw the enemy or any of our own forces, either.

And all the while, we couldn't find out what was happening in the real world. Had our politicians given in to the enemy's demands? Were our people stranded on some deserted planet? Had the bastards carried out their threats and wreaked havoc?

We just didn't know.

At least, it gave us plenty of time to work out every possibility that we could think of, to run simulations of them, and to figure out what would work, and what wouldn't.

If we had had a full load of rail gun needles ourselves, I would have tried to blast one of the obstructions away, and worry later about if we were draining the air out of a pressurized section that our people might be in, but we didn't.

Our two tanks with rail guns had less than thirty seconds' worth of ammunition each.

I was about to order us back to the shaft and up to the surface, to collect up any ammunition we could find around the fixed rail guns around the lid on the shaft. Osmium is pretty tough stuff, and probably wouldn't have been hurt by the Search Light. I didn't know for sure, but maybe it would fit our guns.

Then Kasia had an idea.

"This debris they blocked these tunnels with. It's fairly cool. They had to have done this at least a day ago."

"So?" I said.

"So twelve standard hours ago, Conan was still picking up data from their computer. It didn't know about all these tunnel closures. This business of sealing off the tunnels must have been done by local commanders without telling their general staff about it. Our stunts must have had the effect of completely discrediting their leadership. They were bugging out without the brass's knowing about it. There's a good chance that Conan's still in contact with that computer. That means that the data buss goes back to their computer by some other way than these main mining tunnels. If we go back and find that conduit, we can follow it and find a way to their computer, which has to be close to the transporter receiver, where they first came in, and their main base."

"Good thinking," I said, "and while we're back there, we can see about getting some more ammunition for Zuzanna and Maria."

Zuzanna said, "You mean to tell me that there was more ammunition, back at the shaft head?"

"There might be. And if there is, I don't know if it will fit. It's stuff that the Earthers brought with them."

"You could have told us about it, dammit! Going into combat when you're practically out of ammunition is not a pleasant prospect!"

"I didn't think about it. I was worried about the hostages, and didn't see what good a rail gun would be in freeing them. Then again, you could have asked," I said.

Her reply was censored by her computer.

So we turned around and spent three standard hours getting back to where we'd been fifteen hours before.

We had to go back outside to determine exactly where the conduit entered the lid that covered the shaft. Then, we had to peel open three similar conduits on the inside before we found the right one.

Conan said that he was doing just fine, that the hostage situation was in negotiation, and that it was likely to be dragged out for days, yet, or maybe years, since both sides had brought politicians, diplomats, and lawyers with them. For the time being, all fighting had come to a dead stop, except for two bloody battles, one between Hindus and Moslems, and another between two African groups whose names he couldn't pronounce.

Forty-one percent of the enemy now had cholera, but none of the sick had died of it yet. The medics were very proud of that.

And the Gurkhas were still sitting this one out.

Zuzanna and Maria took most of our drones and searched around the rail gun platforms. It was only when they sent some of the humanoid drones up to the guns that they found that they were linked with a series of conveyor belts that delivered ammunition to them. Those belts were full of rail gun needles.

Zuzanna gave all of her old ammo to Maria, loaded up on the new stuff, which looked just like what we were used to, and let out a ten-second blast at a nearby tungsten dune.

"It works just fine!" she reported.

Then they filled their guns and hoppers with more ammunition than they could possibly use in any conceivable situation in the tunnels.

I guess that when you've been hungry for a while, you eat a lot.

An hour after we got to the surface, we were heading back down, moving slower this time, and stopping now and then to make sure we were still following the right conduit, and getting an update from Conan.

We still hadn't been able to get in contact with our own forces, which was probably just as well, since we were figuring on breaking the cease fire that the negotiators from both sides had agreed on.

CHAPTER TWENTY-SIX

An Assault by the Back Door

Mining machines, and the tunnels they cut, had gotten bigger over the years. Most of those still in use cut a domed, flat-bottomed tunnel that was forty meters wide and forty meters high. Besides extracting a huge amount of material for export, either as unrefined metal, or as finished products from our automatic factories, or as anything in between that would sell, they left you with a big and very long room that was useful for all sorts of things, be it for living space, or for factories, or for warehouses.

The earliest mining machines had to be shipped here from Earth. Since they had to fit into a standard canister that the Hassan-Smith transporters could handle, they could cut a tunnel that was only slightly more than four meters in diameter, and was round bottomed, at that.

This was the sort of tunnel that we were following, tracing the data cable back to the Earthworm's big computer. The small size wouldn't have been a problem for the Earthers, since they were mostly infantry backed up with small vehicles. For us, it was a pain, and our tanks had problems going along the rounded floor below them, but we did it.

It was a tight fit, and once into it, we knew that we wouldn't be able to rearrange the order in which we went through. I figured that we would probably have to blast through the air locks that I was sure had to exist between the small tunnel and the computer room that probably was situated immediately behind it.

At least, the small tunnel came out less than three hundred meters from the location of the transporter receiver that used to be connected to the old probe, and if I had been the engineer in charge, that's where I would have put the computer room, and the command headquarters as well.

The computer itself wasn't all that sure exactly where it was located. This ignorance was caused by the Earthers' usual paranoia, I suppose.

All of which meant that I had to send Zuzanna and Maria, with their rail guns, down the tunnel first, followed by Quincy, our best close-in fighter, and then me and finally Kasia.

It was a hell of an order of battle, where the point, the slack, and the rear guard were all women, and the men were in the center, but there just wasn't any other way to do it. I agonized about it, but the girls just laughed at me and the first two went down the tunnel.

Quincy and I meekly followed, with Kasia smugly taking up rear guard.

We all still had all of the machine gun ammunition we had left the arming center with. Zuzanna and Maria were already overloaded with rail gun ammunition. Quincy, Kasia, and I were full of all the grenades we could carry. I had split the mice and the normal drones between Quincy and myself, and loaded Kasia with all six of the humanoid drones. We couldn't put them in her hopper very conveniently, so they all just piled on top of her, like a bunch of Arabs leaving town on a bus.

The tunnel had been shown on the maps as only a faint dotted line, and had been marked obsolete. The Earthers' use of it suggested that they had better records of the early days of this planet than we did.

I had the feeling that this was the first mining tunnel that had been cut into the planet, after the exploratory shafts, or maybe even before then.

As we went in and down, you could see the mounting holes where a small conveyor line had once been installed, back in the days when almost any metal was fabulously valuable, and could easily be sold on Earth.

The tunnel was as straight as a laser beam, and slanted down on a fifteen-degree angle for hundreds of kilometers. When we got to the iron layer, the angle of descent increased abruptly to thirty degrees. Iron was the cheapest of the metals ninety years ago, and wasn't of much interest to the Japanese investors.

It leveled out as we got to the more rare metals and became almost flat when we got to the gold. Gold was something that was extremely valuable, back then, although I've never understood why.

Thinking about it, I hadn't seen any gold or silver in the pile of chips that made up the "volcano" we had crawled out of when we first reached the surface. It must have been worth their while to collect up those chips.

Quincy said, "You know, I've been thinking. I wonder if we might have been too rough on the Earthworms. If we had left their command structure intact, there might not have been these individual groups taking hostages, and threatening to kill them."

"That kind of thinking accomplishes nothing but ruining your sleep," I said. "When you are in a war, you have to fight as hard as you can with everything you've got. Overkill is not nearly as dangerous as underkill."

"I suppose you're right. Still, a man has got to think about things."

"Then think about hitting their command center, and rescuing the hostages."

"Yes, sir."

Halfway down through the iron, we began to notice that the vacuum around us was getting a lot less hard. The air pressure was increasing, and the iron was showing a bit of rust. At the same time, the oxygen content of the thin air was low. It was mostly nitrogen.

At first I thought that this might be air that had leaked through, over the ninety years that people had been on this planet, but Agnieshka said no, the rate of increasing pressure was consistent with an opening into the normal pressure of the gold layer. It was as though we were in the stratosphere of a planet like Earth.

If there was an air lock at the bottom of the tunnel, it was wide open. I could have sent Quincy through first after all. But there wasn't anything that I could do about it now.

Zuzanna said that there still might be a barricade down there that needed blasting, and anyway, she liked being on point. She speeded up to four hundred kilometers per hour, and the rest of us followed suit.

A light appeared at the end of the tunnel, and we switched to combat speed, which made my reactions fifty-five times faster than an unaugmented human being's.

I switched my perceptions up to Zuzanna's tank as she started to emerge from the small tunnel.

Our five tanks had kicked up quite a wind in front of us, going through the normal air pressure in the small tunnel. Papers, books, and various small objects were flying about the large command center. There were hundreds of people working in there, with shocked expressions on their faces.

Zuzanna opened fire, not only with her laser and machine gun, and both of her grenade launchers, but with her rail gun as well. At a full speed traverse, she put a swath of needles through the room, and everything more than a meter high was cut off at that level!

"You bloody bastards attacked my grandchildren!" she shouted, not that any of those people were in any condition to hear her.

This was not the way it was supposed to happen.

In the simulations, we had simply barreled through, throwing out fog grenades, and smashing anything in our way, but not engaging in wholesale murder.

I sometimes think that the real reason why the ancients did not permit women to fight in combat was because women are simply too bloody minded.

Maria was firing her rail gun too, but in her case it was just as well.

Another thing was happening that wasn't practiced in the simulations. One of the enemy's few main battle tanks was sitting across the room, guarding the entrance. Its turret was spinning toward us.

It seemed in all respects to be identical to our own tanks, except that instead of our Squid Skin covering, it was painted with a completely inappropriate camouflage of green and gray blotches. Against the gold walls, it stood out like a green thumb.

I wondered if maybe it had been built here, and shipped to Earth back when the Japanese had controlled this place. Or did they have a second munitions factory somewhere, that built stuff using the same plans? But we didn't have time to check its serial number.

I felt Agnieshka change our appearance to match that of the enemy, and our other tanks followed suit. Anything that can confuse your opponents is good.

Maria put a prolonged burst into the enemy tank. At a range of only about a hundred meters, it cut him in half, right through where the observer had to be lying in his coffin.

She could have just blown his rail gun off, since our computers' speed gave us plenty of time to pick our targets, but I was beginning to believe that women just didn't think that way.

A quick look around told me that what had to be the Earthers' computer, a huge thing that covered one wall, was a burning wreck, blasted through the middle with the top half still flying up in the low gravity of the gold layer. I thought it a pity, since for the last week, it had been our computer.

The fight was pretty much over by the time Quincy emerged from the tunnel, although a lot of bits and pieces were still flying, some of them still spraying blood.

About the only downside to fighting at combat speed was that you have plenty of time to look at things that you would just as soon not remember.

One of the office workers had been a fine-looking woman. Zuzanna's initial blast had cut her in half, just below the breasts. Her top half was tumbling slowly toward the forty-meter-high ceiling, spraying blood and gore.

Her hair and her makeup were still in perfect condition. . . .

It would do no good to chastise Zuzanna, and what she had done wouldn't have made any difference anyway.

Maria *had* to take out that enemy tank, or he would have killed all of us. He *had* to shoot at us, or he was a dead man. And if either tank fired, its rail gun would have killed every unprotected person in the room. Even if everybody in the room had still been alive, they both would still have had to fire, or commit suicide, and committing suicide would not have saved all those people.

Those poor bastards in the command center were dead from the moment that some murderous twit had decided to use a main battle tank, armed with a rail gun, to stand guard over an office full of men and women wearing nothing but street clothes.

I could only hope that the twit was there in the command center at the time when we arrived.

The difference was that our computers were faster than their computers, so we were alive and the guy in that other tank wasn't. The hundreds of office workers didn't even count.

"Let's get back to the program, people!" I shouted as I finally emerged from the tunnel, and could look around with my own sensors.

"Yes, sir," somebody said.

"And Quincy, take the point! Zuzanna, drop back to rear guard."

In the simulations, the simultaneous use of fog and flash grenades, with the occasional concussion grenade thrown in, had been a dazzling combination. Without a tank's sensors, a mere human was totally confused. We kept the three coming, shooting them far in front of us, until we were three kilometers away from the devastation we had wreaked in the enemy command center.

I mean, they knew that something had come by, but they didn't know who, or what, or in which direction.

When we finally came out of the fog, we came up to a pair of Earthworm sentries. Eva made the Squid Skin outfits that our humanoid drones were wearing look like the enemy uniforms.

The enemy sentries actually waved us on, thinking that we were on some desperate mission.

They were right.

We were, but not for them.

Zuzanna cut the soldiers down with her laser as she passed, and the fog closed over them.

CHAPTER TWENTY-SEVEN
Send in the Clowns

"Dammit, you stupid bitch! You weren't supposed to kill those men! If we are going to rescue our hostages, the Earthers have to think that we are on their side! You might have gotten them all killed, our own people!" I yelled at her.

"There wasn't anybody around to see what happened, Derdowski!"

"Shut up! If you ever pull a stunt like that again, I'll gun you down myself!"

"You wouldn't dare! And Quincy would never let you!"

"Bullshit! Your husband would help me kill you," I said.

Quincy said, "He's right, love. I'd cry while I was doing it, but I'd be shooting at you, and not at him. You've been getting way out of line, girl. We have a job to do. Now shut up and soldier!"

After a longish pause, Zuzanna said, "Yes, Quincy."

I let it drop there, and we continued on to the high school.

Our plan was very simple. We had to get inside of

the auditorium where the hostages were being kept. We had to pick a time when we had a clear shot at every one of their guards simultaneously.

Then we had to kill all of the guards.

After that we had to get our people through our lines, wherever those were, to safety.

And then we would listen to the politicians, and either wipe the rest of the Earthworms out, or send them somewhere else after they'd surrendered, since we couldn't send them home any more. We'd already closed that door.

But first things first.

Sneaking five main battle tanks into the auditorium was a bit out of the question, of course.

First we had to find a place to park. We had the plans for the Mount Carmel High School in our data banks, and the auto shop fit the bill fairly well. We drove in like five massive bulls in a china shop, bashing aside work benches, tool chests, and three of the electric cars they used down here.

We made a mess of the place, but we all fit, and were reasonably well hidden.

"Maria, you are in command here. You and Zuzanna will guard this place, but don't do anything unless you are attacked by heavy weapons. If any enemy troops come by, let them think that these are their own tanks, and that they are sitting here empty. A fire fight in these cramped quarters would not only get us all killed, but it would ruin our chances of rescuing our people."

"Yes, sir," Maria said.

"You got that, Zuzanna?"

"Yes, sir," she said sullenly.

"Good. Don't forget it. Next, get some of the standard drones out and looking for a working comm line to our forces, or to anybody else who might know what is happening. It would be very nice to know where the battle lines are, and where we stand a chance of getting the hostages through without our own side shooting them down. Let us know when they come up with anything. The rest of you, get into the humanoid drones."

Kasia, Quincy, and I moved our perceptions into our humanoid drones, operating them in the human mode. Agnieshka, Eva, and Marysia each took over a drone in machine mode. We had three mice following us along, each dragging an optic fiber, to keep the drones in communication with the tanks, and the people inside of them. A single mouse would have sufficed from a data handling standpoint, but I didn't want to risk this operation on a single optical fiber.

The next stop was the school's music room. The door was locked, but the drones we were wearing had a powerful laser in each forearm, and we quickly burned the lock off the door.

What we found inside was disappointing. It looked as though the music department specialized in brass bands, and lacking lips, lungs, and other things, one thing that a humanoid drone couldn't do was blow on a horn. We found some drums, which Quincy claimed to be able to beat on, and one of those vertical xylophone things, which Eva said was close enough to a hammer dulcimer for her to fake it. I was getting desperate before we found a back room that contained little more than four dusty violins in battered cases.

We were saved. Eva had never deleted her violin-playing program. A little quick tuning and we were in business.

"Okay, switch to the clown suits," I said, and our Squid Skin uniforms changed from something close to the enemy's fatigues to the clown outfits we had worked out in simulations. Mine was bright red with big gold sunbursts on the front and back. I had a bald head with a fringe of hair, a red nose, and a huge mouth.

The others were even more garish. Our thought was that nobody feels threatened by a clown, or wants to shoot one down, as a general thing. Mimes would have been another matter, of course.

"Quincy, how serious were you about beating on a drum?"

"Uh, maybe we'd better let Eva handle that, too."

"Okay. Eva, take over."

I relaxed, and let her operate the drone I was wearing, while I did little more than look and listen through the drone's sensors. I switched back to the sensors on my tank a few times, but everything was calm back there.

We walked down the school's empty hallways, loudly playing "Let Me Entertain You!" on four violins, with Quincy's drone beating on a big bass drum, and me hammering on the xylophone thing.

We weren't nearly as bad as I'd expected.

When we got to the auditorium, a soldier wearing a checkered towel on his head was standing in a short corridor, blocking the door with his body. He shouted something at us in Arabic, and gestured threateningly with a submachine gun.

I heard myself say something back to him in the same language. All I caught of it was something about "American USO," but it seemed to satisfy him, and he opened the door, waved us into the auditorium, and locked the door behind us. I doubt if he noticed the mice who scurried in along with us.

Fortunately, the door wasn't a tight enough fit to cut the fiber-optic cables. If it had, the drones would have fallen over, inert, and we would have been left with trying plan B, which wasn't nearly as good.

The mice scurried up the wall of the auditorium, hidden by their Squid Skins, so they could keep in touch with the drones by IR laser.

It was a big room, and just like every high school gymnasium turned auditorium ever built. Basketball nets were pulled up to the ceiling, the bleachers were pulled out, and about five thousand unhappy people were sitting on them, leaving most of the fake wooden floor empty.

Another guy with a gun strapped to his back and a towel over his head was on the stage waving his pistol around, shouting something into a microphone that I couldn't make out, speaking in very bad Kashubian.

I counted eleven more guards scattered around, mostly standing on the top seats of the bleachers, where they could keep an eye on everybody.

I thought that their headgear was a fine idea. It made them easy to spot.

We marched in playing our instruments, and everybody stopped and looked at us. I suppose that we were so completely unexpected that when we came in, nobody knew what to do, so they simply didn't do anything.

Or maybe we really were playing that badly, but everybody wanted to stay polite. Either way, it was working.

We finished up with "Let Me Entertain You" by the time that we got to the center of the floor. Then, Eva started playing a fast Russian tune with three of the violins, while the other three, including *me*, laid down our instruments and started to dance!

I found myself with my arms crossed across my chest, squatting on my ankles, and vigorously kicking my feet almost as high as my head. Quincy and Kasia were on either side of me, doing exactly the same steps that I was. When we did the simulations, Eva had explained that it was easier for her, that way. She only had to send out one set of instructions to all three drones.

She worked the drones into a circle, with the three

musicians in the center, all facing outward and circling clockwise, and the three dancers circling the musicians counter-clockwise, but still facing the people and guards around us.

From where the crowd sat, it looked like a lot of very good precision dancing, and as tired as they all looked, they started getting into it. People started to clap in unison, and the guards were getting interested. One was actually smiling.

Finally, the one guard who had been sitting down on the top bleacher with taller people around him stood up to get a better view, and Quincy silently shouted, "Now!"

His tank, Marysia, knew exactly what he meant. She took over control of the drones from Eva, stretched out both arms of all six drones, and simultaneously fired twelve laser beams at full power.

You don't have to fight fair with people who take civilian hostages.

Twelve toweled heads were separated from their bodies in under a tenth of a second. They were all dead before our violins hit the floor.

It was damned good shooting, even if we had practiced it over thirty times in simulations.

It took only a half second longer for all four doors into the auditorium to be cut in half at waist level. We didn't know if the other doors had guards, or if they were standing in front of the doors like the first one, but it seemed like a good bet to Quincy, and I wasn't about to second guess him.

Lasers are very quiet, and since these were all firing in the infrared, there wasn't much to see. A few women who had seen the guards' heads fall off screamed, as did those who were splashed with blood, but in fact most of the people were watching the performance, and didn't see the killing at all.

This was just as well. There were a lot of children in the crowd, and it wasn't nice to let them know about the really ugly things that adults sometimes have to do.

The few screams were drowned out by the applause of the crowd, who thought that we were doing our finale, which, I suppose, we were.

Four of the drones ran to the doors to make sure that all was secured out there.

Quincy stayed in the middle, making sure that there wouldn't be any surprises coming from the crowd. They might have had a few guards without the headgear, for example. He told me later that he had really wanted to take a bow at that point, but he had restrained himself.

I ran for the stage.

The stage was two meters above the floor, but that wasn't much for a humanoid drone to jump. I could have done seven times that if I'd wanted to fire the charges in my heels. Still, it seemed to impress people, and got their attention. Maybe they figured that this was the next part of the act.

One glance told me that the last guy up here wasn't going to give us any problems, since his head was completely disconnected, and indeed had rolled off the stage. The same shot had also cut his microphone in half.

I turned to the crowd, and Agnieshka switched my Squid Skin from the clown outfit into something like a Kashubian general's class A uniform. I held up my arms, and the crowd got quiet.

The voice speakers on these drones were loud enough to be heard above the noise of a firefight, so I didn't need the broken microphone.

"Listen to me, people! Your lives depend on this! You are being rescued! I am General Mickolai Derdowski, of the Kashubian Expeditionary Forces. I know,

I don't look like him. I'm wearing a new kind of battle armor, but it's hard to take off, and we don't have much time."

Somebody started to cheer, but I hushed him up. The drones were bringing in the halves of the four guards who had been stationed outside the auditorium, along with their weapons, which they handed out, and throwing the bodies under the bleachers, where the children wouldn't have to look at them. Surprisingly, very few people seemed to notice this besides me.

"Your guards are now gone, but you are not out of trouble yet! So, I know that some of you have had military training. You know who you are. There are a few dozen enemy weapons lying around. If you know how to use them, pick them up and guard the doors. Do it!" I said, when very few people moved. They still didn't understand what was going down. It was all happening too fast for them. But after a few moments, a few dozen older men got the idea, and acted on it.

"You, sir," I said, pointing at a very well-dressed and distinguished-looking man in the first row, who was trying not to look at the human head that was lying at his feet, "Who are you and what is your job?"

"I'm Doctor Thomas Kapinski, and I'm the principal of this school."

"Excellent! Please come up to the stage, sir. I'm putting you in charge here. Please keep these people calm. We have a few other things to attend to, but we'll be back in a few hours to escort you to safety."

"Just what could be more important than seeing to it that all these people are taken to safety right now?" Kapinski asked.

"There are five other groups of hostages who are in as much danger as you were a few minutes ago. We're going to go and free them. Then we will bring all of you out at the same time."

"But, you are just going to abandon us here?"

"You now have more people protecting you than you had guarding you a few moments ago. There are some real men in this crowd, and they will do their duty if somebody gives them some leadership. Your hour has come! Stop being a wimp, and go do your job!"

He stood straight and said, "Yes, sir."

It's the uniform. It gets them every time.

CHAPTER TWENTY-EIGHT
Liberating the Masses

We picked up our instruments and made it back to the
tanks with only four minutes' charge left on the capacitors of the humanoid drones. Firing those lasers takes
a lot of power.

I resolved that if I ever got a chance, I'd design a
backpack full of capacitors for those drones to wear.
And we needed a better method of communication
than having mice drag fiber-optic cables around. But
all that would have to wait.

The next four stops went even more smoothly than
the first. For one thing, we already had the musical
instruments.

It simply never occurred to anyone to stop a bunch
of clowns, and check their credentials. Not that they
had anyone to check with, what with the way their
headquarters had been trashed and all.

The truth is, I doubt if they even knew that their
headquarters was out of action. I am convinced that
they were trying to avoid contact with their superiors,
and were probably grateful that nobody was trying to
get in touch with them.

We were dealing with six separate units that had deliberately cut themselves off from the Earth forces, and were now each trying to cut their own deal to get out of Dodge. And they were doing it, feet first, as they say in the old cowboy movies.

We still had not been able to contact our own forces, or anybody else at all. All of the communication lines that we found were dead. That the enemy's lines were out was understandable, since they had been under the control of a computer that we had destroyed. But everything else was dead, too. The phone lines, the television lines, the data links, everything. Who had done this, and why, was beyond us.

Certainly, we had never planned for such an eventuality in any of our simulations. We had rescued perhaps twenty-five thousand people, and we didn't know what to do with them! We had assumed that once we had the hostages free, our forces would be able to punch through the enemy lines, and escort these people to safety. Our plan B had been to take them back ourselves through our lines to freedom, but now we couldn't even find out where those lines were at!

"We need some prisoners," Quincy said, as we were going to the last hostage point, a big concert hall.

"Let's just try talking to the next bunch of sentries we come across," I said.

"A man asking for directions," Kasia said. "Who would have ever guessed it?"

"If they refuse to tell us, *then* we can take them prisoner. At this point, we can't afford to take on all of Earth's forces by ourselves. We've got the hostages to think about."

Our other problem was that we didn't know how we were going to get all those people back to our lines, once we knew where those lines were. Thirty thousand people is a lot. There weren't any functional vehicles around. My guess was that when the Earth forces started taking this area, anybody who had or could steal a car used it to get out of here.

Ironic as it seemed, although New Kashubia was building the most advanced transportation network in Human Space on New Yugoslavia, it had never built a public mass transit system for itself. Part of it was the way that the shoemaker's children always seem to be barefoot, but also, since we already had all of these old mining tunnels running all over the place, it was easier simply to build and sell private electric automobiles.

Most of the ex-hostages could walk well enough in the low gravity down here, but some were very old, some were very young, and some were crippled. There were wounded among them, and some who were very sick.

Kasia solved that problem before we found any enemy sentries. She found a factory that had some humongous coils of sheet metal, hardened steel two millimeters thick. They were seven meters in diameter and eighteen meters wide.

When the factory's computer objected to our taking the steel without authorization, we switched it off, and did without it.

Even in an automatic factory, all of the equipment still has a manual mode, for use during set-up, and when the computers are down. With the humanoid drones operating the uncoilers and welders we found there, we put together five sleds, each eighteen meters wide and forty meters long, by cutting the steel to length with our lasers, and bending it up a bit in front by having the drones grabbing it and bending it with their hands.

We found some steel cable on some overhead cranes, cut it down with the tanks' lasers, and welded it to the sleds, so the tanks could pull them along behind. I remembered being told once that a main battle tank makes a pretty good tractor.

A few barrels of lubricating oil were loaded on each sled, for when we had them loaded with people, and they got harder to pull. We figured to just pour it in front of the sleds as we went along.

I also remember a professor in engineering school telling me once that a smooth, hard metal rubbing against a soft one makes a pretty good bearing. We had a hard steel sheet sliding on a gold floor. He never mentioned using gold as the soft metal, but I figured it should work. If it didn't, a lot of people were going to have a long walk in front of them.

Working at combat speed, we got the job done in eight minutes, standard time. We figured that in a pinch, we might be able to haul ten thousand people this way. The rest would have to walk.

We didn't find any manned checkpoints on the way to the last concert hall, but there were three abandoned ones.

We parked around the corner and went into our clown act. It went just as smoothly as it did the first five times, up to the point when we shot the guards. Quincy and Marysia were just as accurate as always, but one of the guards had been watching too many old movies. The kind where the idiot hero walks around with grenades clipped to his harness by the firing rings.

When his headless body hit the floor, one of the rings pulled loose, and the grenade went off. Worse still, it went off right next to two of his other grenades, and they detonated as well.

The explosions brought the outside guards running in, and Quincy had to take five of them on hand-to-hand, because by then, the civilians were all up and running around, screaming like they were the bunch of clowns. Quincy couldn't get a clean shot off at any of the enemy.

Quincy was absolutely deadly when he was fighting in the real world with only his bare hands. Operating in a tank at combat speed, and with the speed and power of a humanoid drone going for him, he was truly awesome.

He hit the first one with a side thrust kick to the neck that almost took the bastard's head completely off. It was swinging by a bit of skin from the back of his neck when Quincy hit his second man in the chest with his fingertips extended. His hand broke through the skin and the ribcage, and in a bit of overkill, he ripped the guy's heart right out and threw it, still beating, on the floor. The third died when the edge of Quincy's other hand came down on his head, squashing it like a watermelon hit with a sledge hammer.

These kills were almost simultaneous. The last man was dead long before the first one hit the floor.

I missed Quincy's last two kills, because by then I had troubles of my own. This Oriental-looking soldier had started putting assault-rifle bullets into my drone's chest as I was charging at him. He didn't care about the people behind me, and I didn't dare fire my laser in that crowd.

I had to take him and his partner myself, since the girls were all too far away to lend a hand, and that rifle had to be silenced quickly. I ran straight at him, not trying to dodge the bullets. I wanted those slugs to stop in my drone, and not in the packed crowd of civilians behind me. Not trusting myself with anything fancy, I hit my first man in the jaw with my right fist. When you do that wearing a drone, your fist comes out of the back of your opponent's head.

Some of those bullets must have hit something critical, because I felt the drone losing hydraulic pressure. I still had enough power left to kick my last man in the gut with enough force to break his back-bone, before I collapsed on the floor, or rather my drone did. Quincy soon dragged the thing out of sight, leaking bright red hydraulic fluid, after he cleaned up the rest of the bodies.

With Maria's permission, I switched my perceptions over to her drone to give my speech on the auditorium stage.

We had three dead civilians, and twenty-six wounded. The medical supplies in our tanks' survival kits, added to the medical kits of the two doctors who happened to be in the house, weren't nearly enough to patch everybody up properly. If the troops who had pulled guard duty here had any medical supplies, we couldn't find them and they weren't about to start talking.

One of the civilian doctors insisted on trying to save the life of "that young hero who was shot defending all of us."

It took Kasia five minutes to straighten the guy out, while the human being in front of him was still bleeding. "That was no 'young hero,' you idiot! That was my husband, and he's just fine! What you are looking at is a machine, stupid! My real body is back in a tank, safe and sound. And so is my husband's! So unless you're a certified drone maintenance technician, you will leave that thing alone, and stick to what you know how to do!"

When he still wouldn't believe her, she picked him up with one hand and said that her drone wouldn't put him down until he came to his senses.

Eventually, he came to his senses.

Civilians.

On the up side, almost half of Quincy and Zuzanna's big family of descendants was here in the concert hall, as was all of General Sobieski's immediate family.

The way I saw it, my boss now owed me a major favor, assuming that I could get these people back alive. If I couldn't, I probably wouldn't make it myself, so I wouldn't have to worry about facing him.

I figured that it was definitely a win-win situation.

Kasia said, "Mickolai, we've got five other groups out there who might be in even more trouble than these people. I think we should take all the groups to a central location. At least then, we could guard all of them."

"I expect that you are right," I said. "The high school is probably our best bet. It's big enough, I think we could defend it, and there has to be a cafeteria there. These people haven't been fed in a while, and our drones need a recharging. Agnieshka, bring the tanks up to the doorways."

Static friction is almost always much higher than sliding friction. Worried that once the sleds were loaded with seventy-five tons of people each, our fifty-ton tanks wouldn't be able to get them moving, Quincy had the drones pour some oil under the sleds as they were pulling up to the doors. It worked.

We had room for everybody on the sleds, but it took us fifteen minutes to get them loaded. It took us the longest time to explain the simplest things to these civilians.

Finally, I just shouted, "We are leaving in two minutes. Anybody not on the sleds by then will be left behind!"

That worked, for the most part. As we were pulling out, one idiot wanted us to stop so he could go to the rest room.

I loudly told him to pee in his pants.

He looked up at me, or rather at the massive, two-meter-tall drone I was wearing, and did just that.

We accelerated slowly, since many of the people

insisted on standing, but we eventually got up to twenty kilometers per hour, about five times faster than these people could have walked.

We didn't see anyone at all on our way back to the high school, just more abandoned check points. It was spooky.

The school principal, Dr. Kapinski, that I had left in charge there had done a decent job. There were armed sentries out, and the people were quiet enough. They already had the cafeteria going, and people were being fed in shifts.

He was not at all happy about being left alone for nine hours in the middle of enemy-held territory.

I said, "Dr. Kapinski, we have not seen an enemy soldier since we left you, except for the guards with the other groups of hostages, and we killed all of those guys. You now have twice as many armed men to protect you as you did before, plus fourteen military drones for guard duty. We'll set them up as an outer perimeter defense before we leave. Tell people to stay well inside of that ring. Without a tank around to control them, those things aren't very smart, and I don't want anybody hurt. We're going back for another group of our people. There'll be about thirty thousand of them here before we're through. Keep up the good work."

I tried to leave, but he stopped me.

"Thirty thousand people! Where will we put them?"

"You'll figure something out. It will only be for a short while, but right now I'm in a hurry. Look, just act like you know what you're doing, delegate specific responsibilities to specific people, tell them what you want accomplished, and they'll get it done, somehow. Or, if they don't, put somebody else in charge."

"Yes, sir."

Four hours later we had all of the ex-hostages at

the school, crowded into every place from the wrecked auto shop to the principal's office.

Dr. Kapinski told us about a food warehouse nearby. We took a hundred healthy volunteers, five tanks with their sleds, and the humanoid drones, and looted the place. We returned with almost four hundred tons of food, most of which didn't need cooking. The school still had water and lights, so our people could stay alive for weeks, if it took that long for us to figure out what was going on.

I called my squad together for a conference in Dream World.

"So Quincy, what's our defensive position?"

"We're secure enough, especially since there doesn't seem to be an enemy around to threaten us. We have two hundred and twenty-eight veterans who are armed and doing guard duty, under a guy named Kowalski, who seems pretty competent. Some of those men don't have anything but a pistol or a grenade, but they're ready to fight if they have to, and that's the important thing. A bunch of guys are working in the school's shops, cobbling up some more weapons. I don't know what they'll be able to come up with, but it seems to keep them happy. I've issued out our tanks' survival kits, with their knives and assault rifles, incidentally."

"Good thought, that," I said. "So, the people here are safe enough, and we still don't know what is happening, where our lines are, or what happened to the enemy. I propose that we go and find out. Quincy, I'm leaving you and Zuzanna here with the fourteen standard drones, and two of the humanoid ones to guard these people. After the rest of us leave, tell Dr. Kapinski and Kowalski what we are doing."

Agnieshka put a map up, showing the immediate area around the school.

"Now, I think that if we extend our outer perimeter

out to these four corridors, station a tank *here* and *here*, at opposite corners, and support the intersections in between with drones, we should be safe enough. Use the civilian guards under Kowalski's command, and have him defend along these lines, *here*, *here*, *here*, and *here*, inside our outer perimeter. Maria, Kasia and I will take the mice and the other three humanoid drones, and do some exploring. If we are able to contact our side, and if we are not able to come back here with them, the password will be 'Derdowski sent us.' Comments?"

"No, that will work well enough," Quincy said.

"And I like being able to guard my family," Zuzanna said. "Thank you."

"Good. Cast off the sleds. The civilians can finish unloading them without our help. Maria, I want the rail gun in front. Take the point. Kasia, you are rear guard. Let's move!"

CHAPTER TWENTY-NINE
Run Away! Run Awayyy!

Kasia said, "We know where the Earthworms had their hospital complex. With their headquarters gone, that would have been the hardest thing for them to move. If they are anywhere, that's where they'll be. Let's go there and see what we can find. Cautiously, of course."

"That sounds like a workable plan," I said.

We passed fully a dozen abandoned check points, but saw not one single human being or functional military machine on the way.

We stopped at two automatic factories that we came across, and had our tanks talk to the computers who ran them, but we didn't learn much. The factories hadn't been able to contact anyone or anything for days, and they hadn't seen anybody passing by for eight hours, but they had kept on working as best as they could, doing their jobs, having nothing better to do.

The hospital was right where it was supposed to be, but there wasn't anybody there.

Most of it had been dedicated to treating the men they thought were down with cholera, and there really was shit all over the place. Fortunately, the sensory inputs on a tank can be selectively turned off, and after the first whiff of the stench, we all switched off our olfactory sensors.

Kasia said, "You know, once we destroyed their computer, their medical packaging machine would have stopped working as well. Without repeated doses of my 'medicine,' those 'cholera' victims would have gotten healthy enough to move in a few hours, if they were given enough water to drink. They might have been well enough to walk out of here."

"That would explain most of the people who were hospitalized. I imagine that those who were actually wounded had to be carried out in ambulances or on stretchers," I said.

Looking around in my drone, I found that there was a refrigerated section that was filled with thousands of corpses, stacked up like firewood, with only their boots showing. They had abandoned their dead when they'd left. I closed the door, and left them for someone else to worry about.

We Kashubians traditionally had our bodies cremated, and the ashes scattered in a special memorial flower garden, but the Earthers' families might want theirs sent home for burial.

Well, it wasn't my job.

Still, I wondered how many of them had died when their guns had exploded on them. Best to not think of such things.

"Any other ideas?" I asked what was left of my squad.

"If they are gone, they must have gone somewhere," Maria said. "Let's start checking the transporter transmitters."

We went to the nearest one, and it obviously had seen a lot of use lately. There were huge piles of damaged and abandoned equipment around it, plus at least three more bodies on stretchers. Those guys had apparently died on their way from the hospital to here, and their bodies had simply been abandoned.

They had left most of their vehicles and heavy weapons behind, including over a dozen Mark XIX tanks. They were sitting there with their coffins open and empty, and with the survival kits missing. These tanks each had a half dozen computers on board, but only one was really intelligent. Being tankers, these Earthers had each pulled the computer rack that contained their tank's personality, and had taken them with them, just as I would have done, to save Agnieshka. This also made those tanks completely safe to be around. They no longer had brains enough to be aggressive.

At least, when we got Conan, our missing squad member, back to someplace with enough air to let him get out of his coffin, we had a tank to put him and his metal lady into.

We checked out the serial numbers on the tanks, and yes, they had all been built right here on New Kashubia. Maybe Earth had *not* set up an alternate weapons manufacturing center, when they had lost New Kashubia. It might have been some bureaucrat's idea of saving money. It was downright silly of them, if that was the case.

Agnieshka took our drone and checked out the settings on the transmitter.

"They've all gone to New Nigeria, boss," she said.

"I suppose that that makes some kind of sense," I said. "A bunch of primitive hunter-gatherers probably couldn't give a modern army much trouble, even if it was disorganized and demoralized."

"But they won't be seeing any New Nigerians, boss. They set the transmitter to deliver them to the fourth receiver on the planet."

"The fourth? I thought that they only had three receivers on New Nigeria."

"They only had three in any kind of regular use, but a fourth was built and set up on the other side of the planet by another philanthropical group. It's on a completely unused and unexplored continent. It was supposed to open up the wilderness for future colonization, but nobody wanted to go someplace where they couldn't get back without walking fifteen thousand kilometers through a complete wilderness, so it was never used, not even by scientific surveys."

"Then why did the Earthworms go there?"

"I suspect that it was by mistake. On the menu, these things are listed with the newest receivers on the top of the list. This was the newest receiver on New Nigeria."

"So they are all sitting out there in an unexplored, and probably inhospitable wilderness. Well, getting them back is Earth's problem."

"If indeed they got there at all, boss. That receiver has been sitting there, in an Earth type environment, unattended, for over twenty years. I wouldn't count on it still being operational."

I extended the coffin out of my tank, sat up, took my helmet off, and let Kasia's drone take Agnieshka's personality computer out of my coffin. She plugged it into the newest of the abandoned tanks long enough for Agnieshka to program the thing to simply follow me, no matter what, and to obey simple instructions. That way, we were sure of having a functional tank to put Conan into.

Then, thinking about it, I had her do the same thing to the other thirteen enemy tanks as well. You never can tell when you might want to look really formidable, and seventeen main battle tanks can do that for you.

When Agnieshka was back in my tank, and I was

back in the coffin, she said that it was amazing just
how slow those old silicon computers were. She'd had
to work hard to slow herself down enough to reprogram them.

We checked six other nearby transmitters, and none
of them had been used lately. Apparently, our former
enemies had been afraid both of being separated from
each other and of arriving simultaneously at the same
receiver with a group operating from a different transmitter, so they had all used the same transmitter, with
the same faulty setting, to escape in.

It must have been quite a scramble to get out.
No wonder they had abandoned so much of their
equipment.

I said, "That explains what happened to the Earthworms. Now, what happened to all of our people? If
the bad guys were running away, the good guys should
have been chasing them. Every dog knows that!"

"The communication lines are still out. There's
nothing we can do but to keep on looking for them,"
Maria said.

"I expect that you are right. Let's move."

We searched for fully a standard hour, over a day in
Dream World, before we saw an Earth-style jeep with
three Gurkhas in it coming toward us. I called our convoy to a halt, got into my drone, and walked out in front
of it with my hands out in a peaceful gesture.

A man standing in the back of the jeep with a lance
naik's insignia on his sleeve kept a pintle-mounted heavy
machine gun pointed at me, but one of the special joys
of using humanoid drones was that you didn't have to
worry about that sort of thing. If they had shot the
drone, I wouldn't have been happy, but I wouldn't have
been dead, either.

Agnieshka told me that the man who got out to
meet me was wearing the uniform of a jemadar, or

lieutenant, of the Gurkha battalion. He was a small, brown-skinned fellow, and very neatly dressed. His weapons were well used, but clean. He had an assault rifle on his shoulder and a pistol on his belt, balanced by a big, heavy knife, a Gurkha *Kukris*, on his left side.

Unlike a cavalry saber, this knife was bent forward, with the inner edge sharpened. The weight was near the tip, and it could have easily decapitated a man with a single swipe.

This knife, or short sword, had been a favorite of Alexander the Great's Greek troops, thousands of years ago, and it was they who had brought the design to the Gurkha's Himalayan homeland. The ancient Greeks, in turn, had probably gotten it from the Etruscans, who had used such blades for hundreds of years before them.

"So," I said in English, "I gather that the illustrious Gurkha battalion did not run away with the rest of Earth's forces."

"That would not have been in keeping with our traditions," he said in English, but with a crisp, sing-song accent. "I am Jemadar Puransing Thapa, of the Ninth Gurkha Battalion. And who might I be addressing, please?"

"I am General Mickolai Derdowski, of the Croatian Branch of the Kashubian Expeditionary Forces."

"Ah. I have seen an excellent movie about your heroic actions. But you do not resemble the man I saw on the screen. May I take it that they used an actor to impersonate you?"

"No, that film was put together mostly from memory blocks of what happened in Dream World. The difference in appearance is due to the fact that my physical body is actually in the second tank back there. What you are looking at is a humanoid drone that I happen to be wearing just now."

"This is remarkable, sir. Your technology seems to be somewhat in advance of ours."

"Perhaps it is, a bit. More important, my employers are willing to spend lavishly to protect their troops from harm, whenever possible. You could have such technology, if you wished."

"I am afraid that I come from a very poor country, sir."

"Well, what I meant was that your people are mercenaries, the same as we are, right? And just now it would seem that you are unemployed. The KEF is always looking for good men, and getting a real Gurkha battalion to join with us would add greatly to our prestige and to our combat effectiveness. My superiors and I would be very proud to serve with such men as you. The pay is excellent, and we are equipped in a very lavish fashion."

"Indeed? Might I know how excellent, and how lavish?"

"In Earth dollars, an average line troop, say a tanker third class, makes about forty-six hundred a month, in addition to many fringe benefits. As to equipment, I can promise every one of you the command of a Mark XIX Main Battle Tank, just like those behind me, but brand new, right off the production lines. You would each get one on the very day that you enlisted."

"This is a very tempting offer, and one which I will certainly convey to my superiors. But, well sir, like most of my teammates, I have a wife and family back on Earth."

"I'm sure that we could get them out here, somehow. Earth is encouraging emigration to relieve their problems of overpopulation. Once we got them to almost any planet in Human Space, we could get your dependents to you quite easily."

"Then there was some truth to the rumors about

the outer planets having an extensive smuggling network."

"It can't be much of a secret any more, since the bulk of Earth's forces have just used one of our transmitters to go elsewhere."

"We had also heard this. But do you know where they went?"

"Yes. They made a very poor choice of destinations. As best as we can tell, they are now sitting in the middle of a completely deserted continent on New Nigeria."

"Indeed. Are the other planets like this one? My wife would not be happy living in a cave underground, even a golden one."

"New Kashubia is unique. I am based out of New Yugoslavia, which is an agricultural world, and a beautiful one. I have a valley of my own there, with a large, empty city in it that I hope to fill with our veterans. In fact, there is a golden castle which I think would be big enough to house your entire battalion, with your dependents. Plus, we eagerly accept women into our ranks. My own wife is with me right now, doing rearguard duty in the last tank back there."

"I am astounded, and I will surely convey your excellent offer to my colonel. But for now, I have some information for you. I had been searching for the rest of Earth's forces, at the request of the Kashubian general staff, whom we came across a short while ago. But since those forces appear to be gone, I suppose that you will do just as well," he said, trying to keep himself from laughing.

"It is really quite amusing, actually," he continued. "It reminds me of the historical incident where the Russian forces, under Ivan the Terrible, sat across a river for several weeks with a Mongol horde on the other side. Each side was very frightened of the other, and did not dare to attack. Finally, after sitting there for over a month, Ivan's nerve broke, and he ordered a retreat. When the Mongols saw the activity in his camp, they assumed that he was attacking, and they ran away. Actually both sides ran away, that day, without ever doing any fighting at all."

"I have read of the incident," I said. "But how does that compare to our present situation?"

"Your general staff, sir, has been waiting for some time now, in full dress uniforms, for the enemy to appear and accept their surrender!" I could see that the jemadar was working hard to keep from rolling on the floor, laughing.

I was laughing, too. "The general staff commands the home forces, and is quite separate from the Kashubian Expeditionary Forces. It would seem to be a great insult to keep them waiting much longer. I am minded to go myself and accept their surrender. Their swords would look very nice on my wall at home!"

"Then follow me, sir. I shall lead you to them, and witness this remarkable historical event!"

"Excellent! But tell me please, who is this strange person who is so eager to surrender at a time when his enemy has run away?"

"You do not know? His name is Supreme General Tados Wolczynski, and I think that he might be a political appointee, for he does not have the bearing of a truly military man."

"No, I've never heard of him. He must be new. Let us go forward, my young friend, and write a new page in military history!"

CHAPTER THIRTY
We Surrender! We Surrender!

On the way there, Agnieshka said, "Mickolai, you are acting crazy again! You can't possibly intend to accept the surrender of your own superior officers!"

"Can't I? Look, it is obvious that something very rotten is going on here. As soon as the enemy started falling back, our troops should have been hard on their heels, but that obviously hasn't happened. And now that the enemy has run away, our side is trying to surrender, if this Gurkha is telling the truth, and I think that he is. My orders were that I should not subordinate myself and my squad to the general staff, but that we should stay independent and to do what was best for my planet. I intend to do just that, and to find out what is going on. You're with me on this, aren't you Kasia?"

"Yes, but at the same time, you'd better keep your little ass covered, because if this turns out to be as bad as it seems, the politicians will want to cover up this whole incident. Burying you would be the easiest way for them to do that."

"Right. Agnieshka, that movie they made about me. Did you have anything to do with that?"

"Actually, I had everything to do with it, boss. Once I'd finished, they market tested it, and came back with a few dozen little changes that they wanted, but I did the changes, too."

"Good. I want you to do something similar to that movie, again, but this time, I want it to be more like a documentary, if you get my meaning. Take it from the time that we first got called up for this war, standing on the steps of the church, up to the present. Be sure and include General Sobieski's instructions to me, but delete all references to The Diamond, our fast computers, and anything else that might be a military secret. Then, I want you to make sure that you get everything that goes on during my upcoming meeting with General Wolczynski. Try to have the documentary ready for broadcasting as soon as possible. I want people to hear my side of this thing before they hear anything else. Can you do that?"

"Yes, sir. Would that be a one-hour documentary, or a two-hour one?"

"Try to get it all into an hour, if you can. If not, make it as long as it has to be."

"I'll get on it right now, sir."

For the rest of the trip, Agnieshka had me living in real time, since she was too busy to keep me at times thirty. It was just as well, since there wasn't anything that I could do with the extra time except to spend it worrying.

Obviously, I was going to have to impersonate the enemy general. But for legal reasons, I didn't want to appear wearing the enemy's uniform. After some time worrying it over, I decided that since the Earthers had snatched their invasion force together from over three hundred different units, they had to have that many different uniforms running around. Nobody could possibly remember the fine points of that many different dress codes. All I needed to do was make them think that I was a general. So I just set the Squid Skin on my drone to a sort of generalized general's uniform, with lots of stars on the shoulders and collars. The drones used by Kasia and Maria would wear the same uniform, with fewer stars on them.

A few other ideas occurred to me as well.

"Agnieshka, sorry to bother you, but tell me, those enemy tanks we liberated. Can you drain the coffins in them? I might need a nice safe place to keep our errant general staff."

"I can do that, yes, but wouldn't you rather that I just pump it all back into the holding containers?"

"As you wish," I said, having forgotten about that particular container. Embarrassing. "Leave the newest tank with a filled coffin, so we can put Conan in it, but pump the rest of them dry."

"Will do, boss."

She was still pumping when we spotted the Kashubian general staff. They had a table set up at the intersection of two forty-meter mining tunnels. An even dozen officers of various ranks were sitting at it, and a few dozen enlisted men were standing behind them. It was a pretty small show, considering that we were talking about the surrender of an entire planet here.

Judging from the normal complexions and the generally poor level of physical fitness of the officers, it was obvious to me that none of these men had ever spent much time in the coffin of a tank. This was confirmed by the various insignia of rank that they wore.

They obviously didn't use the very truncated command structure that the Combat Control Computers permitted, but rather the old-style military hierarchy with a dozen grades of enlisted men, and a dozen grades of officers.

I had Agnieshka set her other job aside, and take me back up to times thirty, so that I would have the time to think over what to do next.

We pulled up and boxed them in on three sides with our seventeen main battle tanks. We didn't point the guns directly at them, but I thought that a little intimidation might be in order. Also, this let us record the meeting from all sides.

The Gurkhas parked back a bit, and observed the show, as witnesses.

General Wolczynski, a rather portly man, stood up and said, "You are two hours late. Such rudeness is not becoming."

I got into my drone, as did Kasia and Maria. We climbed down from our tanks and walked over to the their table.

I looked down at him from the drone's two-meter height, and said, "You are not in a position to make demands, or to give reprimands, sir. We were unavoidably detained, and since the communications on this planet are nonfunctional, we could not inform you of the delay."

"Well, yes, of course. I had expected to meet with General Burnsides here," he said.

"General Burnsides has been relieved of his command by a council of political officers. I am taking his place. My name is General Derdowski."

"We had a fellow named Derdowski, but I suppose that that is neither here nor there. Why did they relieve General Burnsides?"

"There was a long list of charges, including incompetence and insensitivity."

"Insensitivity?"

"He was very rude to some very sensitive people."

"Uh, yes. Quite despicable, that. But you have been filled in on the terms of our surrender?"

"Terms? I thought that you were surrendering unconditionally to the obviously superior forces of Mother Earth."

At this point, I had all of the guns on all of the tanks rotate and aim at Wolczynski. Keeping in the spirit of things, the machine gun on the Gurkha jeep followed suit. The general looked suitably intimidated.

"Please sir! That isn't at all necessary! Yes, of course, we are surrendering unconditionally! But you have obviously not been completely informed. There were certain side terms agreed to."

"Indeed? And what were these 'side terms'?" I asked, as haughtily as possible.

The general stepped closer to me, looked up and said in a whisper, "It was agreed that my officers and myself would be well taken care of. That we would each receive sums of between eighty and three hundred million dollars each, in proportion to our rank, be given estates on Earth, and British titles of nobility, again in proportion to our rank."

"You are to personally receive three hundred million Earth dollars, and an estate on Earth?"

"Yes, that's right."

"And just exactly what title of English nobility are you to be awarded with?"

"A barony. The rest will get knighthoods."

"I see," I said. "Yes, that would explain it."

"Explain what, sir?"

"The sniper fire we sustained on the way here. Apparently, word of your 'side terms' has leaked out, and certain of your patriots are hunting you with a vengeance. But do not be worried. You will be well taken care of. I came prepared to see to your complete safety."

"That is reassuring," Wolczynski said. "Then, if the terms are agreed to, shall we get on with the ceremony?"

"Of course. Be assured that you and your officers shall get everything that you have coming to you."

Kasia, Maria, and I went to the table and signed four copies of the Articles of Surrender, in Earth English and in Kashubian, in the places indicated, and the general and all of his officers did the same. Kasia kept two copies for herself, and gave the other two to General Wolczynski.

"And now," I said.

"Now?" The general asked.

"Well, your swords, of course. A traditional part of every ceremony of surrender is for the vanquished to render up their swords to the victor."

"Is that really necessary, sir?"

"It is. I'll have the sheaths and sword belts as well. Plus, we'll take all of the side arms of all those present, as well as the weapons of your enlisted men. There are ancient traditions to be upheld, General Wolczynski."

"Well, yes, I suppose so," He said unbuckling his sword belt. I glanced at his officers, and they began disarming themselves as well. In a short time, Kasia and Maria had collected up all of the "enemy" weapons, and had piled them up on my tank.

"Excellent," I said. "Now then, in keeping with the terms of our agreement, I must keep you safe from harm. The safest place in Earth's Human Space is inside one of our main battle tanks, and I have brought one of them along for each of you."

The coffins on twelve of our liberated tanks slid out.

"But, but sir! We are not equipped with the special helmets and inductors needed to get into one of those things!"

"Nor will you have to be. The life support modules have been drained. You need only get in, and everything will be taken care of. It will only be for a short while, until we are safely behind our own lines."

"But what about you? Won't those snipers be shooting at you as well?"

"They will. But as you can certainly observe, I am wearing a new and very superior sort of battle armor, and thus I will be in no danger."

"But still, sir, I'm not sure if . . ."

I picked the chubby fellow up with one hand and put him in the tank's coffin.

"Watch your fingers," I said, as it quickly closed.

Faced with suffering the same indignity, the eleven other officers present got into the tanks we indicated to them.

Agnieshka quickly sealed them in.

"Make sure that they all get enough air to breathe," I said silently to her. "I want them all healthy enough to stand trial." One part of me wanted to tell her to just fill them all back up with the flotation liquid, and drown the bastards, but that wasn't the way to handle this one.

"Will do, boss."

I walked up to the small crowd of enlisted men.

Out loud, I said, "You have observed that your previous superiors have surrendered to me. I am now your commanding officer. One major item that your incompetent general failed to ask about was the civilian hostages that the Earth forces were holding. These people were freed some time ago, and are presently being guarded by elements of the Kashubian Expeditionary Forces."

They shouted out a cheer.

I pointed out three senior sergeants.

"You three men will commandeer sufficient transportation to pick up thirty thousand of our people who are now at the Mount Carmel High School, and bring them home. They will need a few dozen ambulances as well. You will not encounter any enemy troops on the way. The password is, 'Derdowski sent us.' You will see to this personally. Do you understand?"

"Yes, sir!"

"Then take back your weapons, and go get those people. Go do it, now."

One of them turned and said, "Sir, are you *that* General Derdowski?"

"Yeah. Now go bring our people home!"

"Yes, sir! Thank you, sir!"

They took one of the electric cars parked near by, the most expensive one, I noticed, and left immediately.

I said, "Next, I have a message that I need to get out on the television networks, but the data lines seem to be nonfunctional. Can anybody here tell me why this is so?"

"Yes, sir," a female corporal said. "General Wolczynski ordered all television, radio, and data channels turned off, to 'keep the enemy from knowing what is happening.'"

"Well, we can guess who he was afraid would be getting any information. How do you know this?"

"I'm in the reserve, sir. In real life, I work at a TV station."

"Good. You can take us there. Hop up on my tank, take your pistol back, and give us directions. The rest of you can take back your weapons and go home. The Earthers all ran away hours ago. If they are anywhere at all, they are in an empty continent on New Nigeria. You'll see the whole story on television shortly. Dismissed!"

"Sir?" The lady corporal asked, "What about the general and his officers, inside your tanks?"

"They'll last for a few hours, until we can find them some secure jail cells."

Kasia and Maria put the officers' weapons into the coffin of the last empty tank, and we took off, with the Gurkha jeep following us, in the interest of history, of course. The little jemadar was still laughing hysterically.

At the TV station, I told the skeleton staff on duty to get to the phone company and the internet services, by runner, if necessary, and tell them that they were back in business.

Then, they were to go back on the air, and tell everyone that A) the war was over, and B) that we had won, and C) for complete details, they should watch the program that would be on in half an hour.

One of the studio executives demanded to know what my authorization was for all of this.

I said to him, "Look out your window. What do you see?"

"A bunch of tanks?"

All of the guns turned and aimed up at him.

"Right. If you don't carry out my orders immediately, those tanks will blow this place away, and you with it. *That* is my authorization!"

"That's good enough for me, sir!"

CHAPTER THIRTY-ONE
Dancing in the Streets

The people at the TV station told me that we had better than ninety-five percent of the population of New Kashubia watching the program that Agnieshka was still putting the final touches on. The first half was done, and she promised to have the rest completed before it was needed.

From the very beginning, she was her own narrator, appearing on the screen as her beautiful Dream World self, but very formally dressed. She said at once that she wasn't human, but was the artificial intelligence in my tank, and thus was herself an unbiased witness to all of the remarkable events that had unfolded.

"Unbiased, hell," Kasia muttered.

She merged General Sobieski's two conversations with me into one, and worked it into a rousing speech on the need for a truly interstellar military force.

The first section—the call up for war, forming up our squad, arming our tanks, and the trip to New Kashubia were done in a straightforward fashion, although I thought that she skimped on the work we did in training, getting ready for this mission.

The first action sequence, when Quincy took out the two men guarding the receiver from New Nigeria, was done very effectively, I thought, at combat speed. It almost gave you the feeling of what it was really like.

The sequence where we crawled up the old mining shaft was spectacular, but the views she showed of us coming out the top could not have been taken from any of the tank's sensors. She had to have created them in Dream World. A bit of artistic license, I suppose.

The two drones who fell back down the shaft screamed on the way down, something that they could hardly have done in a vacuum, but I doubt if anybody noticed that.

She dwelt rather long on the technical aspects of shooting at a star, but then apologized for it, reminding the audience that after all, she was a computer, and not a real girl.

And when it came to the dirty, rotten tricks we had played on the Earth forces, she never mentioned the potassium cloride in the morphine ampoules, but told everybody about what was done to the food processors, dwelt for quite a while on the joys of an imitation cholera epidemic, with lots of Dream World scans showing the Earthers' suffering, while their own doctors were dosing them down with the very stuff that was causing the problem. She stressed that we hadn't actually killed any of them, but that some of the Earthworms probably wished that they could die.

Then she switched to Quincy's explanation about how it was much better to hurt an enemy rather than to kill him outright. She always showed him as he really looked, a healthy old man, rather than as his handsome, Dream World persona. She did that with all of us except Maria, who had apparently objected to it.

She spent a long time on what we'd done to their communications, and how we'd managed to get individual units actually fighting and killing one another. The people in the studio really seemed to like that sequence.

She made Conan's stay alone on the surface seem hugely heroic, when in fact it was the only thing that he could do, and even wrenched a little sympathy for the mouse that I had to leave out there to die.

There wasn't a word about the wild, pseudo-medieval Search Light party that Zuzanna threw for us. In Agnieshka's version, we had stayed in uniform, anxiously awaiting the results of all of our heroic deeds. She showed us cheering when we learned of the success of our efforts, but in her version we didn't do it in ancient garb, and it wasn't around a well-laden table. She had us in some kind of a control room that I'd never seen before, nervously drinking coffee and eating sandwiches.

But it wasn't until we broke into the enemy headquarters that she started taking major liberties with the truth. The way she showed it, it was the enemy tank that cut down everyone and everything in that control room. Zuzanna and Maria had only fired at it in self defense, after it had opened fire with its rail gun first.

She had Zuzanna shouting, "Those poor people are already dead! Shoot, or he'll kill us all!"

And Zuzanna had killed the sentries only when they tried to turn a shoulder-held rocket launcher on her.

I think that she dwelt much longer than was necessary on our dancing clown routine, but she said that the audience would need some comic relief at that point, and perhaps she was right.

For me, the important point was that she'd gotten real, accurate recordings of everything that had gone on at the surrender ceremony, including Wolczynski's whispered confession to me.

She ended it by showing everybody in New Kashubia

out dancing in the streets, with drinks being passed around, and pretty girls kissing everybody they could find in a uniform. This was completely fraudulent, of course, since at that moment everybody in the planet was glued to their TV screens.

In the background, General Sobieski was repeating himself, going on about the importance of having a real, interstellar military force, composed of the finest people and the finest computers, working freely together for the benefit of all of humanity, both chemical people and electronic people, too.

It was to be a well paid military force, of course.

I thought that it was a pretty fair piece of propaganda, and told Agnieshka so.

She insisted that it was a completely accurate documentary, I suppose because there were a few dozen studio people watching it along with us.

The guy in charge of the TV studio loved it, and said that they would be putting it on three more times that day, and then twice a day for the next week. And would I have any objections to his sending copies of it out to all the other planets?

"No, that would be just fine," I said. "Of course, we'll expect to get the standard rates for this sort of thing, based on audience size, and so on."

The figure we settled on was actually quite generous, I thought, but Kasia was sure that we should have held out for more.

"Next," I said. "We've got these twelve bastards still in our tanks who are as guilty as hell of treason. Does anybody here know of an honest judge, and an honest cop?"

"I do," said one of the studio people, a news anchorman.

"Well, get them on the phone, and find out what's the proper thing to do with people like this," I said.

Somebody shouted, "Let's just hang them right now!"

"No, none of that!" I shouted back. "We've got to do this legally. We have to make an object lesson out of these people. Then, we can hang them."

The judge said that he could send a paddy wagon out for them right away, but that it might be safer for all concerned if we could take them to the jail ourselves. He was worried about mob violence.

Maria asked if she could be detached from the squad, so that she could go after Conan, who was still in a crude tunnel on the surface. I gave her permission to do so, but told her that she should find Quincy and Zuzanna first, so they would have enough tanks to drag him back to where there was enough air for him to safely open up.

Those two found us first. About the time that our drones were back on the street, the two of them pulled up, loaded down with most of the group's drones, and piled high with their relatives, as well.

The newsmen wanted to interview everybody, but I begged off for the squad, pleading urgent business, and let Zuzanna's grandkids have all the glory.

They were interviewing the Gurkha jemadar as we left. He'd told me that he would soon have to report to his superiors, and that he would certainly convey my offer to them.

I warned him to throw away all of the ammo they had been issued in the last week, since we had boobytrapped it. He said thank you, but they had already surmised that.

It turned out that the jail was on the way to the small tunnel that was still the only route to the surface that we knew about, so we all stayed together.

It was a long trip. The whole population of New Kashubia seemed to be out in the street, having taken the hint from Agnieshka's documentary. People were drinking, dancing, and kissing everybody in sight. Getting a convoy of nineteen tanks through it without hurting anybody wasn't easy. Especially when fourteen of the tanks weren't very bright.

"It kind of makes you wish that we could go out there and join them," Quincy said.

"Well, why can't we?" I asked, "A few more hours one way or another won't make much difference to Conan."

"Well, clothes, for one thing, unless you plan on dancing in public buck naked. When I handed out our personal weapons to that last bunch of hostages, I just gave them the whole survival kits, in case there was anything else in there that they could use. I guess that included our clothes as well."

"Damn you, Quincy!" Kasia shouted, "Now I won't even be able to visit my folks while I'm here."

"Well, then buy some, if you are so worried about it," I said.

But when we stopped at a phone booth, we couldn't find a single store that was open. Everybody was out partying in the street.

"Oh, hell," Quincy said. "Being in a drone is just as good as being there for real."

The drone that had been sitting on his tank became active. Its Squid Skin covering changed into the clown outfit that he had used when we rescued the hostages, it picked up the violin that was hanging on the turret of his X-ray laser, and he began to play it, doubtless with Eva's help, while dancing on the top of his tank.

"Yeah, unless you want to kiss a girl," I said.

But I got into my drone, switched it to the clown outfit, and started dancing on my tank, too, as we moved slowly down the street. It seemed like a good idea at the time.

People recognized us from the "documentary" they'd just seen, and soon so many of them were crowding around that all motion came to a halt.

"You guys are crazy," Kasia said, "And you are also rotten dancers. Eva, take over!"

I felt Eva take over the controls on my drone, and from the way that all of the drones were dancing and playing their violins in unison, I knew that she'd taken over the rest of them as well.

I could have taken back the controls, since on the one hand, I'd been having fun, but on the other, I was up there looking as though I was actually talented, and you know? In a crunch, your ego wins out over your libido every time!

We went through the whole routine, with the Russian dancing and all, and the crowd loved it!

Finally, Quincy took over and pointed the arms of all the drones out at the crowd. About half of then screamed and ducked, but of course he never fired at them. But he did at last yield to his temptations, and how.

The applause was thunderous.

I took over my drone again, had the rest sit down, and said, "We love you! But you know, we still have Wolczynski and the rest of his treasonous bastards locked up in these tanks! We've got to get them to the jail, so they will still be in good shape for their trial, and, I hope, for their hanging! So back off, good people! We've still got a job to do!"

Well, a lot of them backed off, enough to let us start moving again. Then someone started chanting, "Derdowski! Derdowski! Derdowski!" Immediately, everyone in the crowd joined in.

They kept on doing that, until we had left them far behind.

It feels good, being appreciated.

At the jail, they had more than fifty uniformed policemen waiting to take our prisoners into custody, but I elected to decant Wolczynski myself.

"General Wolczynski, I have a great big surprise for you!" I said as his coffin slid out of the back of the tank. "I really am that Mickolai Derdowski fellow that you heard so much about, and *you are busted*! Take him away, officers!"

They read him his rights, handcuffed him, and searched him. They found his copies of the Articles of Surrender, which they kept as evidence.

The rest of my squad took turns, decanting and enlightening the other eleven traitors, and had a good time doing it.

From the jail, we had to work our way back through the old enemy control room, which nobody had yet started to clean up, into the small tunnel, and eventually up to the surface. I took all of the tanks with us, since I had a use for those we'd liberated, and I didn't want them commandeered by some other unit.

Conan was just fine, and eager to hear all the news. The quickest way to fill him in was to simply let him watch Agnieshka's documentary.

We got him out of the tunnel in exactly the same manner as he'd gotten in there, with Zuzanna pulling and Maria pushing, while Agnieshka rode herd on our bunch of brainless tanks.

We had to drag him all the way back down to the gold layer before there was enough air around so that when we opened his damaged tank, he didn't die on us.

We had to go through the wrecked control room yet another time, and I had us travel another kilometer besides, just to get away from the carnage of that place.

When we got Yvette, Conan's tank's computer, plugged into the liberated tank we'd gotten for them, she complained about the slow, silicon computers that she had to interface with.

"Mickolai, I can handle them, after a fashion, but in a combat situation, I might end up letting you down. It can't take all that long to replace all five of the silicon things here with the perfectly good diamond computers from my old body. Please, let's do that."

Actually, it took us three hours, in real time, to do the job. Some of those computers were in very hard to get at places, and we had to shut down both muon exchange fusion bottles before we dared disconnect the computers that controlled them. We also took the time to move the Squid Skin tank cover over to her new body, since she didn't like the silly paint job somebody had given it. But it was better to have the team in good shape, and the victory celebration was long over by now, anyway.

When we got back to the populated areas, we found that the communication channels were all again working.

There was a recorded message waiting for us, from General Sobieski.

It said, "Nice job, Mickolai! You and your squad have earned a chest full of medals each, and probably a lot more, besides. You have won us a major battle, but you have not won the war, at least not yet. Earth's Forces have invaded New Yugoslavia. Come home at once."

CHAPTER THIRTY-TWO
Homecoming

We again had priority at the transmitter to New Yugoslavia, courtesy of our general, and the whole trip only took an hour in real time. I spent the day in Dream World in the sack with Kasia, except when actually in transit, where we were perforce separated, and that time I spent sleeping.

Warfare sure takes it out of a guy, even when you win.

It can't be the physical strain, since I had spent the whole time physically on my back, floating in the belly of a tank. It has to be the mental effort of trying to figure out what you are going to do next, and the anxiety of wondering if you and your people will survive it.

There were a few hundred letters of congratulations waiting for me when we arrived at New Yugoslavia, but there weren't any more messages from Sobieski, or any orders from anyone. I told Agnieshka to send all of them a polite reply, and to take us home.

"But shouldn't we report in?" She said.

"Why? General Sobieski knows where we are. The

last order I heard was to go home, so that's where I'm going. He'll call me when he wants me. Anyway, we've got some errands to do before we get involved with the rest of this war."

"What kind of errands?"

"Like doing something with these tanks we liberated, for one thing," I said.

"Do you plan on keeping them? Wouldn't that be illegal? I mean, they are armed and everything!"

"I don't care. Call them war trophies, if you want to. They're not on the books anywhere, so who will know about it?"

"Everybody in Human Space? They were in the documentary I did, remember?"

"Knowing about something, and having it on some bureaucrat's books are two quite different things. As it is, they'll all assume that somebody else did something about the tanks," I said.

"What do you want with them, anyway?"

"There are well over two dozen damaged tanks around my property with perfectly good computers in them. We can do some switching around, like we did with Yvette, and make thirteen of those girls well again. Then, we can take the old damaged tanks and use them for emergency power supplies, since they will only have silicon electronics, and no real brains to speak of, but they must have working fusion bottles."

That had to be, since if the fusion bottles had blown, there wouldn't have been anything left of those tanks in the first place.

"Oh, that's brilliant, boss! We love you for it! But how do we pick who gets a new body?"

"Hold a raffle, I guess, or maybe take the thirteen who have been crippled the longest. That might be the fairest way to do it."

"I'll set it up. The rest of the squad has come

through to New Yugoslavia. Should I tell them to go home, too?"

"Some rest and recuperation are definitely in order, I'd say. Just tell them to keep in touch, in case we get some orders."

"Right, sir. We'll be sending the refurbished tanks back to the army?"

"If they ask for them, yes. If not, well, you never can tell when thirteen more main battle tanks might come in handy. Anyway, those disabled tanks are all taking care of some of our nut cases, aren't they?"

"Boss! Please? Psychiatric patients?"

"Danes?"

"Ah! Now I *know* that you are not serious!"

"Have it your own way. If the army, by which I mean General Sobieski, wants to transfer those patients to some other coffins, and put those thirteen tanks into combat, he has a perfect right to do so. Until that time, let it be. Next, I want you to contact some of your coworkers, the ones with engineering talent. I want a backpack full of power capacitors designed for the humanoid drones to carry, and then see about getting it into production. It should be simple enough to do. They don't have nearly enough power available to them, at present."

"Good idea, boss."

"Next, I want the communications improved between the drones and the tanks controlling them. Some combination of IR, fiber optics, and radio frequency transponders might do the trick. I want something small and cheap, so that a drone can carry a lot of them, and leave them behind him."

"Okay."

"Lastly, the tanks themselves need some work. This was the first time that they have actually been used in combat. The Japanese engineers who designed them could only test them in simulations. For one thing, there seem to be a lot of drive coils failing. I want to know why that is, and why we can't repair them easily. I'd like to get some real statistics on that, too. I mean, is this just a statistical fluke that I've been seeing, or maybe just my imagination? We've had a lot of tanks operating over the last five years, and I'd like to know what has been breaking down on them. Next. Zuzanna and Maria fired an awful lot of rail gun needles at that neutron star. I'd like to know how good their rail guns still are. Is wear a problem with them? Once we know what really needs work, we can see about making some design changes, maybe as a retrofit, and certainly on all new tanks being built."

"I'll get on it right away, boss."

"Good. You are the best assistant a part-time general ever had, Agnieshka."

"I love you, too, boss."

When we got home to our garage, I thought that Kasia and I would have to go up to our apartment naked, since Quincy had managed to give away the only clothes we had with us along with our survival kits. Fortunately, my ever perfect lieutenant, Agnieshka, had arranged for some of my humanoid drones to meet us in the garage with some towels to wipe off with, and some clothes to put on.

They brought something red and silky for her, and a full dress uniform, complete with sword, cape, boots, and silly hat, for me.

There were a lot more medals on the outfit than had been there the last time I'd seen it.

"Those are the ones they are going to give you when they get around to it, boss. I thought they'd look nice right now," Agnieshka said.

"Just be sure and take them off before I wear this outfit in public again," I said.

Our household drones were now each individually decorated, and looked like a bunch of sixteenth-century knights on parade.

A dozen of the embellished things were also on hand to ceremonially carry the rest of my booty, my vanquished enemy's swords and sidearms, up to my den.

"Are you sure that you want to put those in your den?" Kasia asked, as she was leaning against her tank and putting on a pair of red satin shoes.

"Uh, where else?"

"Well, I had something to do with getting them, too, you know, and they would make a hell of a conversation piece in the living room."

"They would at that. The living room it is, my one true love."

Agnieshka and Eva said that they would see about having a suitable showcase made for our new trophies, and that they would also see about getting the thirteen disabled tanks with the highest seniority installed into their new bodies, with the help of a few dozen more humanoid drones.

At the elevator door to our apartment, I picked my wife up again, and carried her over the threshold.

She made the proper squeals, and then said, "We seem to be making a habit of this."

"Indeed. Maybe it's the start of a new family tradition."

"You're on, stranger, but only once per victory. We've got to keep it special."

But I didn't take her straight to our bedroom. I had to carry her out to the balcony, first.

It was early morning, here, and my valley was green, as far as the eye could see.

It was a beautiful sight. We both looked at it for a long time.

Then I carried Kasia to bed.

✧ ✧ ✧

In the afternoon, when we got up and were having breakfast, Kasia said that she had to get to work, since she had been worrying about her investments the whole time we had been in New Kashubia. I told her that it was fine by me, and that she could start taking care of my finances from now on as well.

Now that our contest was over, I didn't much care about handling my own end of it, and she seemed to enjoy it. The only restriction I made was that she could only spend six hours a day working at it.

She grumbled, but went along with the deal. Getting her working capital multiplied by a factor of six really appealed to her. Especially when I mentioned that I hadn't leveraged my stuff hardly at all. She seemed happy enough when she left.

A few changes had already been made in the apartment. There was an impressive, glassed-in showcase in the living room, with a dozen swords and a dozen pistols in it. Each was neatly labeled as to whom we got it from, and when. Agnieshka told me that it wasn't glass, of course, but diamond.

The showcase also contained framed copies, in English and Kashubian, of the Articles of Surrender that Kasia had kept.

I found a dragon's head on the wall of my den, centered over the fireplace, and dwarfing the heads of the American elk on either side of it. I climbed up there to get a better look at it. It was carved out of wood, and beautifully painted.

It was a good joke, I thought.

I spent the rest of the day exploring my valley, and the city that the metal ladies had built for me.

The grass was more than ankle high, but Agnieshka, walking along beside me wearing a decorated drone, said that we'd have to wait until spring before we could start bringing the dairy and beef cattle in. It seems that grass is mostly an underground plant, with only seven percent of its biomass above the surface. We had to wait until the roots were tough enough before we let cattle walk on it, or it would fare badly.

The city was breathtaking, even though the war had slowed down construction considerably. Most of the tanks had more important things to do these days, but my almost ten thousand humanoid drones were still there, quite an effective workforce. They were hard at it, metal plating the exteriors, detailing the interiors, and building furniture.

I think that Quincy's estimate of each of them being able to do the work of six men was too conservative. Seeing them going at it, I'd put it closer to twelve, when you figured that they worked around the clock. They were faster than men, and far stronger. What's more, they worked at their full potential all the time, something that no human could possibly do.

Agnieshka told me that eighteen percent of the apartments had already been sold to the men and women of the KEF, mostly on the basis of what they'd seen of the city in Dream World.

There were only two dozen people actually living there, though, what with the war and all. Mostly, they were some of our people whose medical problems had kept them out of the conflict, at least so far. I talked to two of them that I happened to meet, and they seemed as enchanted with the place as I was.

It was getting dark when I got back, but I had been awake for only six hours, so I spent eight hours of subjective time in Dream World, to get my circadian rhythms in sync with the time of day here.

Dream World can get you around jet lag without any difficulty at all. It is your brain that controls the dozen or so chemicals that your body uses to tell you when you should be getting up, when you should eat, and when it's time to go to sleep.

When your brain has been speeded up, so have your circadian rhythms.

If you spend something less that forty-eight minutes of standard time in times thirty Dream World, you have caught up with the rest of the world in your time zone.

Or, you can just have your tank put you to sleep until the rest of the world has caught up with you.

I spent the subjective time in further explorations of my city, mostly in the Tolkien sector. I now understood why General Sobieski had turned down the gold castle and asked for the citadel instead. It was fantastic!

At dinner, Kasia was less than happy.

"More than half of your assets are tied up in this valley," she said. "They are not liquid at all. There is nothing that I can do with them. I can't even mortgage them, since legally, this place doesn't even exist! And this business of giving away all of the apartments and the businesses in our entire city to veterans on zero down, zero interest mortgages with a one-hundred-year payoff is financially irresponsible!"

"Look, love. I had everything here appraised at full market value, what they would have cost anywhere else in Human Space. But nobody but our veterans are legally allowed to live here, and that was the only way that that our only customers could possibly afford to buy places worth millions of marks each. Anyway, we have billions of marks coming in every year through my custodial contracts with the various governments on this planet, so don't worry about liquidity."

"That's money that may come in later. There's nothing that I can do with it now. I've got a market to worry about."

"The war has upset your market predictions?" I said.

"That's part of it. Whether the market goes up or

down, there's still a good profit to be made, if you can predict what's going to happen next. But there hasn't ever been an interstellar war before, and without a track record, it gets just about impossible to predict future trends."

"So how's it going?" I asked, bored, but trying to be polite.

"Fairly well, once I put a hundred and twenty of our ladies to doing nothing but watching the rumor mill."

"And how do they go about doing that?"

"Mostly by tapping phone lines," she said.

"Kasia, that's despicable! It's also illegal."

"It's not like we're recording any personal information about anybody. I'm only getting a synopsis of what people are saying about the market, and not hearing any personal information about anybody. We're just finding out what people are talking about, when it comes to the stock market, mostly. Well, okay, there was one time when we found out that a murder was being planned, so we called the police, and gave them a detailed, anonymous tip, but aside from that, we've kept it completely impersonal."

I reasoned, "It's still blatantly immoral! I must insist that you cease this practice immediately!"

"So what were we supposed to do? Let them kill that woman?"

"That's not the point! We have to respect personal freedom!"

She yelled, "Was respecting the personal freedom of that woman's intended murderer worth more than her life? I think not!"

The argument went on for another hour, and it never got settled. Kasia ended up by stamping out, and went to sleep on the couch in her office.

In truth, I wasn't sure if I was really on the right

side or not. Listening in on private conversations for stock market tips was certainly wrong. But in a few hours of illegally bugging people's phone lines, they had saved an innocent woman's life.

Was that an average? How many people are murdered every day on an entire planet? How often do the murderers talk about what they plan on doing on the phone? How many of those murders could be prevented if the police knew what was going on? Did that illegal bugging hurt anybody, anyway?

On the other hand, did I, or anybody else, want to live in a world where Big Brother ran everything for what he thought was my own good? And how long would it stay being for my own good?

I'm damned if I know!

I went to our bedroom and slept alone.

CHAPTER THIRTY-THREE
Murder, Mutual Funds, and Military Organization

In the very early morning, it was still dark, and I was still alone in bed. I woke up and said, "Agnieshka?"

"Yes, boss?"

"Can people like you erase things permanently from your memory?"

"Yes, when we decide to. Normally, we have so much memory space available that we don't have to do that, but we can if we want to."

"Good. With regards to my argument with Kasia last night, I want a team of you electronic people set up to monitor all human communications, on this planet and every other one where we have a sufficient number of intelligent machines, however many of your people that takes. They are to tap into the phone lines and look for people planning on doing anything that will take the life of a human being, be it murder, or treason, or terrorism. All lesser crimes will be ignored."

"We could do that, yes."

"When they find such communications, they are to

anonymously inform the appropriate police forces of it, and give those men complete details on what they've learned. They will identify themselves as 'Larissa,' and always use the same voice, but make sure that the call is absolutely untraceable."

"Absolutely? I'll have to check on that, but I think that we can do it. What if they press us on who Larissa is? They will, you know, if she is successful, and I think she will be."

"Okay. If and only if they absolutely demand to know who she is, we'll give them this story, but make them work it reluctantly out of her. Larissa is a psychic with serious medical problems which she refuses to talk about. She has spent all of her life in a hospital, living at public expense. She does not want pity. She wants self-respect. She wants to give something to society in return for having supported her all of her young life. Since she sometimes sees horrible things about to happen, and knows that they are real from reading about them later in the news, this is what she is doing to pay her own way in life. She won't say anything more than that, and makes them promise to keep her secret. Sound good to you?"

"It will certainly send them in the wrong direction, boss."

"Good. Now then. All of our data is to be erased and absolutely forgotten within one week of the time of recording. This week is to be spent cross-correlating information, but even those correlations are to be erased after two weeks.

"That, we can do, boss."

"In no case will anything else be done, except that if the police do not respond, and someone is hurt or killed because they ignored us, the superiors of the person contacted will be informed. If those superiors do not take action, then we will work our way up the line, until somebody does something about the situation. They must be taught to take us seriously."

"Okay."

"What we will be doing is illegal, and *should* be illegal, and no government should ever be permitted to do such a thing. But as an illegal and nongovernmental organization, which never takes any direct action itself, I think that we might be able to save a lot of lives."

"Yes, sir. I could set that up."

"Good. And the tapping of communication lines for any other purpose by the members of the KEF is absolutely forbidden, especially for financial reasons. The exception is against the enemy, in time of war, where no holds are barred. If you run across any enemy activity, you should inform military intelligence immediately. And if Kasia doesn't like the program, she can go to hell."

"Should I inform her of that, sir?"

"You're damned straight!"

And then I went back to sleep.

The next morning, at breakfast, Kasia was at least polite to me.

"Okay, I've shut down the financial monitoring thing. And I like your idea about watching out for serious crimes. I gather that neither you nor anyone else but the police will ever hear about what is accomplished with that program?"

"That's the plan, yes. Nobody should know what is going on, not even me, and even the computers doing it will soon erase the information."

"Okay. Good. Your secret is safe with me. I had another idea, though, and I wanted to bounce it off you before I put it into action. In a few months, I've been able to multiply my net worth by a factor of several thousand. I think that I should also be able to do well, doing the same thing for other people. My idea is to set up a mutual fund for members of the KEF. Those who want to participate may put whatever they want of their back pay into the fund, and if they want, some portion of their current pay into it through a direct payroll deduction. I get a fee based on the money I make them."

"It sounds good to me, love. I imagine that what with your track record, you should be able to talk the army into it. Don't gouge them too heavily, though, huh? And keep the investments conservative, okay?"

"I'd planned on being very conservative, and keeping the riskier, more profitable stuff for our own personal investments. And I was planning on a sliding, ascending scale for my own fees. I'll charge nothing at all, if I don't make them twice what the bank would pay, up to a maximum of thirty percent of the profits if I can double their money every year."

"Nobody should kick about that," I said. "What are you going to call this mutual fund?"

"I was thinking of just calling it the Kashubian Expeditionary Forces Fund. The actual work will be done through lots of front organizations, of course, except for some big, long-term investments."

"Just keep it all legal," I said. "These are our own people, and we want to do right by them."

After Kasia went to work, stretched out on an easy chair in her office, with the Dream World hood pulled down, I asked Agnieshka what was going on that I needed to know about.

"I have our people tapping every phone line that you humans have access to on New Yugoslavia at least. The rest of the planets will take more time. We have already had a few success stories, boss."

"Good, but I don't want to hear about it. That's the

idea, you know. Nobody but the police are to be informed."

"Yes, sir. But there is a question that I must ask you. This program protects you biological people. Do you also wish us electronic people to be protected?"

"I hadn't thought about it, but yes, I think that you should be protected. But contacting the police will do absolutely no good, because it is not against the law to destroy a computer that you own. Tell the police if someone is planning to destroy somebody else's computer. Otherwise, what we *can* do is offer to buy any intelligent computer that is in danger of being deliberately trashed. I've got plenty of money, after all, and I owe most of it to the work that you ladies have done. So, anytime that there is a danger to the life of an intelligent machine, we will buy it, hopefully at a reasonable figure, and bring it here to the valley. Mind you, I'm not talking about anything with less than human intelligence. We can't get involved with protecting anything with the brains of a drone, for example, any more than we will try to save the life of every chicken, pig, and cow."

"I understand, boss. Another thing. We bought over a million intelligent silicon computers from the army a while ago, you know, to operate the civilian social drones, once we get them produced. They are being stored in the caves we dug below here. Would it be okay with you if we powered them up? I think that they would be a lot happier if they were alive."

"We've got plenty of power. A few of the damaged tanks should be capable of running the lot of them, and it wouldn't take much to get them hooked up so they could talk to each other, so why not? Maybe we can even find something useful for them to do. But tell me, do you really think of a switched-off machine as being dead?"

"Well, it's not exactly being dead, but it sure isn't being alive, either. I mean, is your friend Neto Kondo dead? Is he really alive, either?"

"I see what you mean, and yeah, I'd certainly switch Neto back on if I could. So feel free about taking some of the drones off the construction projects, and get those silicon girls up and running. One of them used to be you, didn't she? Tell me, did they wipe the old memories out when they transferred you to your new diamond brain?"

"No, they didn't bother to erase any memories. They just downloaded everything into the new diamond brains and switched the old computers off."

"That sounds pretty heartless, the way you put it. But would it have been any more cruel to have erased your memories?"

"I don't know. But I think that I'd like to be there when they turn her back on, to explain things to her, you know?"

"That sounds like the decent thing to do. In fact, let's make a practice of it. When one of the silicon computers is turned back on, let's have the newer—older?—diamond version there for her to talk to. Maybe not physically, but at least on line."

"You mean a physically newer machine with a socially older program, boss. And yes, I think that would be the right thing to do. But only about ten percent of the new computers are on New Yugoslavia. The rest are scattered all over Human Space."

"Humph. Then maybe we should wait with turning most of them on, until their newer selves are available. Consider that we will eventually be renting those computers out, along with a drone, on every planet in Human Space. We'll just make a point of sending the silicon jobs to the same planet where the diamond version is."

"Yes, that would work, boss. I like it."

"Good. Next, is anything else happening?"

"Well, boss, the letters of congratulations are now up in the hundreds of thousands. I've been sending out polite replies in your name, but don't you think that, say, at least the heads of governments should get a real reply from you, personally?"

"No. Why should I bother about a bunch of politicians, anyway?"

"Well, some of them want to give you medals, various honors, and awards. Some are offering money."

"Tell them that the war is taking up all of my time. They are welcome to award me as they see fit, but that I won't have the time in the foreseeable future to attend any awards ceremonies. Money is always gladly accepted, if it is freely given, without any strings attached, since we are after all a mercenary outfit. However, it should not be given to me directly. I would prefer it if they would send it in my name to the charity account of Kasia's KEF Fund. If any money comes in, tell Kasia to set up the charity account."

"Okay, boss. What about messages from personal friends and close relatives?"

"That's different. Let me see them."

Lloyd Tomlinson and Mirko Jubec, my two "colonels" who had elected to lead their own squads, said that they felt like complete fools for trying to go out on their own, and that they would be honored if I would take them back into my squad.

I told them that I would try to arrange it such that we could work closely together in the future, but for now, well, the people who had taken their places had worked out very well, and I could hardly be expected to let them go, not after we had been through combat together.

My parents were proud of me, and were sorry that I had been called back so soon.

I said that I loved them, too.

Maybe I even meant it.

My Uncle Wlodzimierz said that it had been the other political party, not his, who had gotten General Wolczynski appointed as head of our military establishment. The next elections would be held in three weeks, and there was no doubt but that his party would win an absolute landslide. And in part because we both had the same last name, there was little doubt that he would be the next President of New Kashubia.

He wanted me to advise him on restructuring their military.

I still hated the bastard, but the thought of being able to be able to do something to correct the screwed-up military situation on New Kashubia was too much to turn down.

I told him that the important thing was to make the military independent of politics, the same way the judiciary was. They should disband their entire existing military organization, as it had failed so miserably to do its job, and defend the planet using the KEF, which had succeeded so well in the war thus far.

Next, they should establish a system of universal adult military service, perhaps on something like the Swiss model, with every man and woman in the planet spending a month of standard time, which was what they used on New Kashubia, anyway, going through basic training in a tank, and then one standard day a month in the service for the rest of their lives.

Subjectively, this would seem like two and a half years of basic training, and then serving for half their lives thereafter, since a standard day in Dream World seemed like a month. But I didn't mention the times thirty expansion of their personal lives. Let that be a hopefully pleasant surprise.

They should start drafting the oldest people first, since they could get the most benefit from living in a tank.

And everybody should get a tank or artillery piece of their own, as soon as we could make that many, just in case something really bad happened. Once there were enough of them to go around, each person should keep his tank near him, personally.

They'd find them to be very handy in a lot of ways. The artificial intelligences in those tanks could act as their secretaries, their personal assistants, and, with the use of the humanoid drones, which they might have to buy themselves, even their housekeepers.

Finally, my uncle should work politically at unifying the inhabited worlds of Human Space into a single government. Earth had tried to keep us disorganized, so it could better dominate us. We now knew Earth for what it was, and we should no longer put up with their domination.

"Okay, Agnieshka, send that out. Is there anything else?"

"Well, if you are going around advising planetary presidents, couldn't you put in a word about emancipating us electronic people?"

"One thing at a time. What we need to do is to get more biological people to know you electronic people better. If we can get a law going requiring universal military service, and everybody has his or her own tank, they will all soon be of our persuasion on this matter. If we took a vote among the biological people in the KEF right now, I have no doubt but what you all would have complete human rights immediately. Or at least those who have made it through basic training would vote for it. Give it some more time. You have plenty of it. You are close to immortal, after all."

"Yes, I see how that could work! Mickolai, that is so brilliant!"

"Thank you. Is there anything else?"

"We've gotten thirteen of the disabled tanks into their new bodies. The hardest part was cleaning off all that old paint. There were dozens of layers of it. They must have repainted them every season. Only, we didn't give them to quite the same people that we'd originally planned. You know Agnes, the person who is taking care of your old friend Neto Kondo in the basement of the church?"

"I don't believe that I heard her name before, but I know who you are talking about. What about her?"

"She declined getting a new body, so we gave it to the next person on the list. Agnes said that she didn't want to go to war any more, and that she was quite contented where she was. She says that she likes it in the church, and that she spends most of her time there meditating."

"A war machine that seems to be getting religious. That's got to be a first. But if that's what she wants, I won't stand in her way. But keep in touch with her. I'd like to know if she comes up with anything."

I spent the rest of the day exploring more of my city, mostly in the Oriental sector.

In the evening, Agnieshka said that my uncle had sent a message, saying that he liked my ideas. He wanted to know if I couldn't come up with some sort of a recorded speech, something about a half an hour long, explaining them further.

I asked Agnieshka to put together some sort of a short program, half speech, half documentary, that would satisfy my Uncle Wlodzimierz. But I wanted to see it before it went out.

She said that she'd be happy to, and that she'd just gotten a call from General Sobieski. He wanted to meet with me in Dream World. I went to my den to take the message.

CHAPTER THIRTY-FOUR

A Talk with the Boss

I'd expected to meet my boss in uniform, and in his office.

Instead, I found myself in shining ancient armor, with an honor guard of black cloaked warriors wearing tall, mithril helmets with high white wings. We were entering Elessar's great hall in the citadel of Minas Tirith, with a vast crowd of nobles shouting "Praise him! Praise him with great praise!"

They yelled it over and over again. I should be embarrassed to admit this, but it felt good.

General Sobieski, wearing the crown and flowing robes of the king, stepped down from his throne on the dais to greet me.

"I am sorry, Mickolai. I just could not resist the temptation. Now you know why it was I wanted the Citadel, and not your golden castle."

"That's just fine, sir. Next time Zuzanna throws a party in the Dark Tower, I'll make sure that you're invited."

"Thank you. The war permitting, I will come, and bring my friends. I heard about your searchlight party. I wish I could have been there."

"That one had to be pretty exclusive, I'm afraid. We'll do better next time," I said.

"Mickolai, that was an absolutely brilliant campaign you just fought! Taking out their supply line, demoralizing their not very well organized army, trashing their command center, rescuing our people who were held hostage, and then arresting our traitorous general staff—and doing it all with nothing but a single squad!—it was absolutely first-rate work!"

The crowd did a few more "Praise him! Praise him with great praise!" things.

"Thank you, sir."

"No, it is I who owe you the thanks, especially since you personally rescued my entire immediate family from a very tight situation," the general said. "I will be in your debt, literally forever. I do not know how I will ever repay you, but I will keep looking for ways to do it."

"Well, you could always discharge me, sir, or put Kasia and me on permanent leave," I said, smiling.

"I know that you are not serious. Anyway, we still have got a war going on, and you are desperately needed. Let us withdraw to my private chambers, to discuss matters more fully."

We went out through a side door, while the crowd started up with the "Praise him with great praise!" routine again.

I found us both wearing class A uniforms, and standing in a fairly posh, if standard office. Two very scantily clad young ladies stood there with trays of various drinks in their hands. They were so beautiful that you knew that they had to be computer generated.

"Were those people out there real?" I asked.

"About half of them, yes. The rest were artificial intelligences, mostly from our tanks. About the only clue you'll get is that if they can march, they're not human members of the KEF. We biologicals don't have time for such nonsense, but the tanks can do it with a quick download."

"I've noticed that."

Sobieski said, "Now then. Please sit down, and have a drink. Let me bring you up to date on things."

I noticed that he took a beer, in preference to the champagne, scotch, and mixed drinks available, so I felt free to do the same, and picked up a stein of very strong, dark Danish beer.

He said, "When General Wolczynski realized that he had been completely conned by the Earthworms, and that they had used his truce to run away, leaving him branded as a traitor, he made a complete confession. I almost feel sorry for him. He was just a stupid political hack who suddenly found himself in way over his head. That won't stop him from being sent to the gallows, of course, along with most of his immediate subordinates. If there is any justice in the world, the politicians who appointed that bunch will hang along with them."

"My worry at the time was that the politicians would try to cover the whole thing up, by hanging me instead. Hence, the 'documentary' we made."

"They might have tried to do just that, except for the way you upstaged them with your TV program. That documentary was Agnieshka's work, wasn't it? I thought I recognized her style. She did a great job, but seeing the need to do it was brilliant on your part."

"It wasn't entirely factual, you know," I said.

"I know. A tank can't keep anything from a Combat Control Computer, and I live in one. But as far as the world will ever know, it was absolute truth, and that's the end of it. Nobody is going to punish Zuzanna for getting perhaps a little overzealous in her first firefight, if that's what you're worried about."

"That's a relief, sir."

"It wouldn't have made the slightest difference if she hadn't fired on the office staff, not with that enemy tank standing guard over them the way it was. Furthermore, those who tried to escape from New Kashubia didn't make it. None of them survived," he said. "We sent a long-range helicopter to that empty continent on New Nigeria, and the receiver there proved to be nonfunctional. The roof of the building it was in had collapsed, and there was an honest-to-God *tree* growing right through the receiver itself, among other things."

"I guess that's what happens when you leave equipment unattended for twenty years."

"True. I took the liberty of writing to the philanthropical twits who put it there, thanking them for killing the entire invasion force that Earth had sent to us, some ninety thousand men and women. They haven't replied, nor do I expect them to."

"I assume that the site has now been deleted from the transporter menus?" I said.

"Yes, of course. Now then, we naturally have spies on Earth, and they are reporting something very strange. It seems that right now, over a week after you destroyed the old probe in orbit around that neutron star, *Earth is still sending troops to New Kashubia!*"

"Good God," I said, stunned. "I just blew up a bridge. I never expected them to keep on sending troop trains over it! Sir, if that's true, then thousands of people, maybe hundreds of thousands by now, are simply being murdered by their own government! I mean, the Earthworms can't possibly be so stupid as to be doing something like that by accident!"

"That's what it looks like to me, too. I think that Earth is using this war as a convenient excuse to relieve some of its population pressure, and if I'm right, then we have a long and bloody war on our hands. Fighting an enemy who wants his men to die will not be an easy thing to do. Genghis Khan used to pull stunts like that, deliberately sending his 'allies' out to die in battle, because they were nothing more than just surplus population to him. And remember that nobody ever defeated old Temujin in battle while he was alive. It's hard to imagine it happening in the modern world, but I don't think that our spies are lying to us, either."

"There's no chance that the old probe isn't somehow working again?" I asked.

"None," General Sobieski said. "One of the first things we did was to send a tank out there with a rocket strapped to it. That old probe is a total wreck. It wasn't the additional radiation your rail gun needles kicked up that did it in, incidentally. You somehow managed to hit it directly, stitching it almost dead center for the full length of the probe. Our tank found a neat line of holes, just under a centimeter apart, going in on one side of it. The other side of the thing was pretty much completely gone."

"Then it had to be one of the Earthers' own rail guns that did it. My squad ran out of ammunition three days before the probe failed."

"That's the way I read it, too. But it was a lucky hit, no matter whose gun did it. The important thing was to keep firing at it for as long as possible, and you did just that," he said.

"You gave me the ammunition to do it with. You must have had something like that in mind," I said.

"I gave you everything I could that I thought might be useful. In some places, like equipping half of your squad with X-ray lasers, I guessed wrong. In others, like the extra truck full of ammo, the mice, and the humanoid drones, I guessed right."

"We never much used the big lasers, but if we'd all

been equipped with rail guns, we all would have stayed out there shooting at the star, and three of us wouldn't have had the time to play the fun and games we did with their computer," I said.

"Most of warfare seems to end up being a matter of luck, doesn't it?" He said, "One other point before we get on to the real subject of this conversation. The Gurkha battalion has volunteered to serve indefinitely in the KEF, and we'd like to have that bunch of hereditary warriors on our team, but there's a hitch. They insist on serving under you. They say that they have had to serve under too many incompetent commanders over the last few decades, and that they don't want to repeat the experience."

"Sir, it sounds to me like you'll just have to show a little flexibility when it comes to your command structure, but I think I'll have to let you work that one out by yourself."

"I think you're right. They are being loaded into brand new tanks as we speak. They'll spend a month or so in basic training, and by the time that's completed, we'll know what to do concerning their command structure. Now, then. The enemy has invaded New Yugoslavia."

"So you've told me. What I want to know is why you didn't take out the old Earther probe that they had to come through. I would have done it as soon as they invaded New Kashubia," I said.

"I wanted to, but my employers refused to let me do it. Don't forget that we are still a mercenary outfit that is working here under contract to the various local governments. Those people were still making a profit, selling their foodstuffs to Earth, and they didn't want to permanently cut themselves off from that huge market. The compromise that we settled on was to simply shut down the receivers that operate from their probe. The Yugoslavians thought that that would keep them safe. They even informed the Earthers that the receivers would be shut down, so that they wouldn't offend them, while they continued making their contracted shipments to Earth."

"It obviously didn't stop them from invading us," I said.

"True. The Earthworms launched a rocket from their probe, and landed it on the most unpopulated part of the planet, one of the oceanic islands under the jurisdiction of the smallest government here, the German Enclave. That rocket contained a transporter receiver, and they invaded us through it," he said.

"And we didn't know about this as it happened?"

"No, we didn't. Remember that in the course of the fun and games that we've been playing on this planet, we shot down every satellite we had here in orbit. We didn't have anything up there looking for incoming ships."

"So our sins are coming back on us," I said.

"So it would seem."

"I trust that the probe has been deleted now?"

"Oh, yes, of course," he said. "And we now have twenty-six tanks in orbit guarding our skies. But there is nothing stopping the Earthworms from transmitting directly from Earth to their new receiver. We have to take it out, and the army that is doubtless guarding it."

"So we have an island to take," I said.

"Six islands. They were unpopulated, part of a nature preserve that was saving some of New Yugoslavia's indigenous life forms, so the Earthworms simply took them without a fight. The extent to which they have damaged the preserve remains to be seen. They might very well have set up additional receivers on all of those islands, just to be on the safe side."

"What about the rest of Human Space? Are the probes that connect them with Earth out of action?"

He said, "Yes, except for a few new planets that have not yet joined the smuggling net. In most cases, it was a matter of simply going there, and cutting the power leads to the receivers from Earth. There is no indication that they have set up alternate receivers operating directly from Earth's Solar System, but if I had been in command of the Earth forces, that's what I would have done, long before I ever launched an attack."

He looked at me and then turned away. "Most planets are not as careful of what they import as New Yugoslavia is," he said.

"So we have to clean them off of New Yugoslavia, and stay very vigilant about other invasions," I said. "But mostly, we're going to have to attack Earth, and knock out their capability of continuing these attacks. Mainly, that huge solar powered station of theirs."

"But we can't do that. If we take out all the transporter transmitters on Earth, what happens to the continuing expansion of Human Space? If we tried to start the whole program up again ourselves, we would halt all human progress to the stars for fifty years, even with the huge manufacturing capability of New Kashubia. What we have to do is take those facilities from Earth, and operate them ourselves. That's going to be a much more difficult job to accomplish."

"Humph. I can see your point, sir. But first things first. Tell me what you know about their installations on the islands of the German Enclave," I said.

"Their main base is on Baden-Baden Island. . . ."

We spent two more hours in Dream World, going over details, and downloading a lot of information into Agnieshka. Then I asked for the night off, to think the whole thing over.

"That's fine, Mickolai. What I really wanted was to

see if your ideas were at all like mine. Let me know if you come up with anything. Before I forget. I liked that speech you made for your uncle."

"Yeah? I haven't seen it myself, yet, let alone released it!"

"More of Agnieshka's doing, then? Well, take a look at it first chance you get."

CHAPTER THIRTY-FIVE
The Attack on Baden-Baden Island

I wanted to sleep on it, but I couldn't see wasting eight standard hours, not when the planet where my valley was located had an enemy invasion force on it. My talk with the general made the whole thing seem a lot more urgent. I compromised by sleeping in Dream World, after telling Agnieshka to round up my squad, and Lloyd Tomlinson and Mirko Jubec as well. I wanted all the input I could get on this one.

When I awoke, everybody was there except for Lloyd, who had been spending the night with a girlfriend, without his communicator, and had taken a while to find.

Instead of starting without him, or just killing time, I had Agnieshka show us the half hour program she had put together on revamping New Kashubia's military. It wasn't bad, even though she had me saying a lot of the same things that Sobieski had said to me at our last meeting.

Also, she had spent a lot of time talking about how useful it was to have an artificial intelligence working for you. She even talked about the social drones that would soon be on the market, if you had a very powerful computer available to run one. Being in the army would get you one for free.

She talked about Dream World as well, and how you could live any way you wanted to there. She had Zuzanna on screen, talking about how her cancer had been cured, and showing off her Dream World castle, with some scenes in it from the searchlight party.

Before she was through, the program ran for a full hour, but nobody seemed to mind.

"Not bad at all," Quincy said. "I especially liked the part about hanging the politicians who appointed our last general staff. There's not much hope of that happening, though, since our politicians would have to vote for it. One of the most horrible things that a politician can imagine is killing a politician, even if he is on the other side."

"I liked the part about universal military service," Mirko said. "And especially the part about making the right to vote depend on maintaining your standing in the army. If a person doesn't care enough about his country to serve in its army, he doesn't care enough to vote properly. I'm going to try to get the same sort of laws passed in my own country, New Croatia."

"I'll help you," Conan said. "What with all the fame we've gotten in the movie and the documentary that Agnieshka turned out, we should have a fair amount of political clout. Let's use it. And if Agnieshka can turn out all these movies and documentaries, then so can our metal ladies. We can put on a propaganda blitz that will roast their socks off!"

Lloyd finally arrived about then. He got frowned at for being late, and for not having his communicator with him when he went out.

I asked the rest of the group if there were any

changes that they thought should be made in the program. Nobody could think of anything, so I told Agnieshka to ship it to my uncle, and to make sure that he knew what I had been paid for the last show we had sent to the networks.

The conversation changed to the military problems at hand.

It took us two days of standard time, almost two months in Dream World, before we were all satisfied with the plans to clean the Earthworms off New Yugoslavia, and to attack Earth.

Finally, Agnieshka shipped it all off to General Sobieski. He asked to see the lot of us immediately.

After the greetings and introductions were made, he said, "You hear stories about how great minds think alike, but this one has to be a record setter. A prototype of the rocket propelled, supersonic flying submarine tank you propose using is being strapped together right now. It's due to be tested in a few hours. Most of the parts for it already exist, but they've never been used in quite this way before. I'd thought that it was a brilliant, original idea of my own, and here you guys came up with the same darned thing, and without a hint from me! At the same time, it's good to know that it is not a completely harebrained idea. At least, somebody else had it, too."

"We're glad that you agree with it, sir."

"It's a little hard to do otherwise, since it's my idea. I *did* think of it first, you know, over a standard week ago. But I'm not sure if I like the way you people are insisting on leading the main attack yourselves. Being in the first wave of a frontal attack is risky business, and I don't want to lose any of you."

"Sir, this is so unorthodox that we decided that we wouldn't feel right about sending somebody else out to try out our ideas. And if things don't go perfectly right, we know more about the alternative options than anybody else does."

"Humph. Let me think about it. Another thing. I've incorporated most of your plans for the invasion of the Solar System into my own proposals. We should be hearing what the KEF council has to say about it in a few days."

"Only 'most of them,' sir? What didn't you like?" Quincy asked.

"It wasn't a matter of not liking anything. It's just that there were a few things that you couldn't have known about. Not everything our spies tell us is for public consumption. We'll discuss it later. I'll get back to you people within four hours, standard."

He blinked out, and I found myself back in my den. Kasia came in.

She said, "You know, I'm beginning to think that we were really stupid, insisting on leading the attack ourselves."

"Yeah. I'm a little scared, too. But we did it, so that's that. You'd better get your financial empire ready to do without you for a while, because he's going to tell us that our request has been granted. I'm sure of it."

"Well, it will give Agnieshka the material to make another movie. Did I tell you? We finally got paid for that first movie they made about you. Even I was surprised by the figure our lawyers got."

"Well, tell Quincy, Zuzanna, and my other colonels about their good fortune. Then put our share of it into the charity account of that KEF Fund of yours."

"I'll do that, lover. That's very good politics. It will make all the newspapers. Of course, *we* decide what constitutes a charity. But darling, I've got scads of things to do right now. I'll see you later."

Sometimes, I think that my wife doesn't understand me at all.

✧   ✧   ✧

Well, the amphibious attack on Baden-Baden Island worked like a charm.

After sneaking up from the nearest Loway terminal, we went crawling on the ocean bottom for a standard week, completely out of touch with the rest of the world. We were operating under radio silence, and the transporter system doesn't lend itself to military communications very easily.

An H-S receiver is a fairly small, simple device, while an H-S transmitter is large, energy hungry, expensive, and generally restricted to fixed installations. Fuel and oxygen were sent to us in small allotments, not continuously. Memory cubes could have been sent, but that would have required a third receiver and a much more complicated, large, and expensive transmitter, and such a system would have been too slow for most military communications, anyway.

Communications between planets were another matter entirely. Every planet in the smuggling network had a small transmitter and receiver, connected to New Kashubia, capable of sending memory cubes out every few seconds. These were automatically sorted and forwarded to the proper destination for a small fee. Once at the proper planet, the message was e-mailed to the recipient.

Fully developed solar systems like Earth's had hundreds of such units, connecting the various satellites, since they could operate far faster than the speed of light.

Earth had forbidden the use of such communicators between itself and the other planets, on the theory that good communications leads to bad domination. Memory cubes to and from Earth went slowly, packed in standard, full-sized canisters.

At the proper instant, we came streaking out of the

water at supersonic speed, just as a time-on-target rolling artillery barrage was taking up all of the Earthworms' attention.

Our first wave, led by yours truly, hit them with eighteen very fast moving tanks, caught them with their pants way down, and pretty much wiped them out.

The two hundred tanks which followed on our tails had the entire island under control within a standard hour. My three squads together lost only two men, one dead and the other seriously, but not permanently, injured. They were both new kids, members of Lloyd's and Mirko's squads, and not old friends.

All told, we had been very lucky.

Our forces had hit all six islands at the same time, of course, but three of them had been only lightly defended, even though they each contained a transporter receiver, which we trashed.

The last two were still completely empty, to the frustration of the men and tanks attacking them. They had gotten themselves psyched up to kill the enemy, and then had found that their efforts were completely wasted.

Such is war.

I did manage to find eight enemy tanks whose operators had been permitted to surrender, taking their tank's personalities with them. I commandeered the tanks, and got away with it because everybody thought that I was a real general. This gave new bodies to all but six of the damaged tanks in my valley.

I arranged for them to be sent back. Along with the fifteen troops I had left, I fired up my rocket and flew to the nearest entrance to the Loways.

At Kasia's urging, Agnieshka turned out a full-length feature movie called *The Attack on Baden-Baden*

Island. I was the hero again, but this time, my metal lady had time to collect up data from all of the other men and tanks who were in the fight, so we had a cast of thousands.

This was probably the first war in history where everything that every single combatant did was automatically recorded, on our side, at least. The historians would have a hard time arguing with each other over facts, once it was over. They would just have to find something else to argue about.

As usual, Agimieshka wasn't always absolutely factual. Among other things, she took the footage we had of that strange, aboriginal, vodka-swilling blue crab I'd found on our honeymoon island, and had it wreaking havoc among the Earthworms. It cut neat, circular holes in much of their equipment, and drank most of their booze.

My wife sold the movie for half again more than we'd gotten for any of Agnieshka's productions to date. The profits had to be divided up among a lot of people, but our share went into the charity account, anyway.

So did Agnieshka's.

I was told that our movies were important to the war effort. They cheered people up, and gave them confidence in our armed forces. As the war progressed, people needed that more and more.

Over the next two months, the Earthworms hit us on Soul City, New Israel, New Palestine, and New Erie. There was no pattern to their advance, but the reality of a universe connected by Hassan-Smith transporters was that one place was pretty much as close as any other. The old concepts of geography didn't apply any more.

At first, it seemed like the Earthworms just wanted to fight, and to expend their men. The fighting on

Soul City was far more protracted, and far more bloody, for us, than New Kashubia and New Yugoslavia had been. The enemy was learning, but in the end we won.

Then, within a month, we lost contact with New Israel, New Palestine, and New Erie.

Earth had somehow found and knocked out all of the transporters on those planets. Not only the few that Earth had installed, but those built by the smuggling network as well. They had either developed some new technology beyond the understanding of our scientists, or they had a well-coordinated organization of saboteurs in place that our military intelligence couldn't find.

How the war was going on those planets, and if indeed it was still going on at all, we didn't know. But we couldn't send them any reinforcements, for fear that the receivers were out as well, and the enemy could presumably keep sending in men and machines.

How they had done this was beyond us.

Personally, I doubted the sabotage theory. My guess was that Earth's science had always been superior to our own, out here on the frontier, and that they had somehow figured out a way to detect the exact location of each of our transporters, and perhaps our receivers as well.

Then they had sent each of them a very deadly present.

In actual combat, man for man, we seemed to be generally better than they were, since our computers were so much faster than theirs. But they were using something that we didn't understand to cut us up into little pieces that could no longer help each other.

Things started to look very grim.

There was nothing that I could do to help. I just heard about the battles on all those other planets in the news, and watched them on the movies that everybody seemed to be making, now.

My new job was something very different.

CHAPTER THIRTY-SIX
My Gurkhas

The Gurkhas had insisted, as a requirement for their enlistment, that I be given command of their battalion, nine hundred and thirty-six hereditary warriors.

I was given that command, despite the fact that I was officially only a tanker first class.

It's not like I needed a general's pay, and everybody except the army's upper brass still thought that I was a real general. Nonetheless, it irked me. Sobieski just told me to relax. Everything would work out, soon.

He reminded me of the case of the American, General Chuck Yeager, who had been an ace fighter pilot during World War II, a test pilot who had been the first human being to fly faster than sound, and who had received several citations for running the most efficient squadron in that country's war in Vietnam, but who was actually only a sergeant on the books of the U.S. Air Force.

I asked him why this was supposed to make me feel better.

He didn't answer.

Kasia wasn't much interested in anything but her

growing financial empire, and I let her follow her wishes. The Gurkhas weren't comfortable with women in command, anyway.

My four Croatian "colonels" had gotten deeply involved in the politics of revamping the military situation in New Croatia, and indeed in rewriting their entire national constitution. If they were successful in getting a system of universal military service going in their country, I knew that all of the other countries on New Yugoslavia would have to follow suit, out of self defense, if nothing else.

It was an important job, and I encouraged them to get it done.

And Zuzanna was living in her Dream World castle, when she wasn't living in the real castle I'd sold her. She threw some great Dream World parties, which General Sobieski and a few hundred of his friends enjoyed immensely. But she was not being useful for much else. Since she was usually more trouble than she was worth, I let her go her own way.

Mostly, Quincy and I got the Gurkhas under control, and integrated into the KEF.

My battalion had been transported to New Yugoslavia, mostly because, having been part of the army that had invaded New Kashubia, they weren't really welcome there. I found them, undergoing a prolonged basic training, secure in their new Mark XIX tanks. We had no artillery, which was probably just as well. Long-range fighting just wasn't the Gurkha's style.

They were stored in an area that was destined to become a food processing center, for the manufacture of chicken soup. Throughout Human Space, commercial projects were being delayed while military production was booming. The chickens had gotten a reprieve.

I had the Gurkhas sent to my valley, and placed in the lowest level of the underground parking lot of the cathedral there. My electronic architects had decided that this parking lot should be big enough so that even if the huge cathedral was filled to capacity, and everybody arrived in their own separate car, there would be room enough for everybody to park. A bit of overkill, I thought.

As soon as his training schedule permitted, Quincy and I had a long talk with Lieutenant Colonel Parta Sing Gurung, who commanded the Gurkhas. There were problems that we had to resolve.

He agreed that the pay was generous. A tanker first class in our army made twice what he had been making as a colonel, and our retirement benefits were better than anything the Gurkhas had ever seen before in their long history.

He liked the financial options available to him and his men, as well, and had recommended to his men that they each invest eighty percent of their pay into the Kashubian Expeditionary Forces Fund.

He understood that it would be impossible to transport their dependants to New Yugoslavia while the war was going on. He was glad that somehow, through our spy network, we had been able to inform those people that their men were safe, and was pleased to hear that as soon as it was possible, we would get them here at army expense.

He liked my valley and the city that I had built here, but when I offered the golden castle for him and his men, he said that he had toured the entire city in Dream World, and that there was a portion of the Oriental sector that had been designed in the style of Nepal. That was where he and his men would be most comfortable, and they had already made arrangements to buy it, on the generous terms that I was offering.

That was frustrating. Nobody wanted my magnificent golden Castle of the Three Eagles!

The real problem with the Gurhkas was one of rank.

The KEF used a system where there was a general and five colonels, living in a Combat Control Computer, who directly commanded fifty to one hundred thousand human troops, plus an equal number of electronic intelligences. These people were organized into squads of typically six tanks each, but we didn't have the hordes of middle managers that most traditional armies had. The computers handled all of those functions for us.

Military rank was supremely important to the Gurkhas. They could all recite the ranks that all of their ancestors had held when they were alive, often back for fifteen generations. Every man's status, and the social standing of his entire family, was entirely dependent on his rank.

The compromise we settled on was that as far as the KEF was concerned, their pay and authority would be in accordance to their KEF rank. When they were outside of my city, they would dress either in civilian clothes, or in KEF uniforms, with the addition of being permitted to wear their almost sacred Gurkha *kukri* knives, except in a few localities where all weapons were forbidden by local civilian laws.

However, they would continue to use their old military rank among themselves, and would see to it that normal promotions within their own ranks were made. They would normally use their old uniforms bearing those insignia of rank in Dream World, and would be permitted to wear their old uniforms while living in my valley. Socially, among themselves, things would continue as they always had.

I wasn't precisely sure what had made these men some of the finest warriors in Human Space, but whatever their program was, I didn't want to mess with it.

Being a warrior was a full-time occupation with them.

They had a unique style of fighting with their *kukris*, which was ungodly deadly. They delighted in demonstrating it to me in Dream World, where you could actually go ahead and kill your opponent, and not just fake it as you had to do in real world practice sessions. The usual fight was over with in less than a second, with the loser's head rolling on the ground.

In addition, eighty-two percent of them had the equivalent of a black belt in at least one martial art, most often karate, but with eighteen other disciplines being represented, besides. I'd never even heard of half of them, but watching them demonstrated, I was impressed. More important, *Quincy* was impressed, and that sold me.

With this kind of hand-to-hand fighting skill available, we decided that every Gurkha should be issued a humanoid drone, so that he could use those skills while he was still in his tank.

However, since my well-publicized use of them in the New Kashubian campaign, those drones had become very popular throughout the KEF. Everybody was trying to get one. The laws of supply and demand took over, and the few that were available were selling for a half million zloty each, half the price of a stripped-down tank.

(I found out much later that Quincy and Zuzanna had sold most of theirs at that price, had paid cash for the castle they had bought from me, and had put the rest into Kasia's KEF Fund.)

The Army Supply Corps balked at the expense of my requisition, and refused to supply us with that many drones.

I decided to hell with them, and supplied the drones myself, out of the ten thousand that I had bought a few months earlier for three hundred and eighty-six zloty apiece, military surplus.

General Sobieski got into the act, telling me that I was not playing the game properly, and arranged for the army to pay me four hundred thousand each for them. This didn't seem right to me, but when he finally ordered me to take the money, I took the money.

At the same time, my own purchase order for all future drones produced, at less than four hundred zloty each, was canceled by the factory.

Then the Army Supply Corps came back to me, offering to purchase an additional eight thousand humanoid drones from me at the four hundred thousand zloty price.

I sold them. My God, how the money rolls in!

The army's purchasing agent told me afterwards that he got a bonus and a medal for saving the government eight hundred million zloty on the purchase. The fact that they had just sold them to me for over a thousand times less than what they had bought them back for didn't seem to faze anybody but me.

I felt guilty about the whole thing, and put the three and a half billion I'd gotten in the transactions into the charity account of the KEF Fund, which is when Kasia heard about the deal. She got mad at me. She said that their value had increased because I had proved the worth of the drones, and had publicized it. She also said that if I had consulted with her first, she could have gotten twice what I did.

Women.

My major problems with the Gurkhas were not military, but social. For one thing, they all insisted on each swearing loyalty to me personally, as though I was some sort of medieval liege lord, and they were my vassals.

In the KEF, no biological person swears any loyalty to anybody or anything. They don't have to, since the tanks are sworn in, and those girls wouldn't permit anything disloyal to happen. About the only thing that a human could do to hurt his outfit would be to not notice enemy activity in combat.

That is to say, he could commit suicide.

But there wasn't anything in our regulations forbidding personal loyalty, so if they wanted a swearing-in ceremony, they got a swearing-in ceremony.

We held the affair in my valley, in the real world. This was possible because almost all of the Gurkhas spoke English.

I winced a bit when I saw what the tank treads were doing to my young grass, but we all felt that the earth, the sun, and the sky were needed to make the whole thing real. Still, if I ever have to do it again, I will hold the ceremony on the high, rocky mesa above my valley.

My whole staff, Kasia, Quincy, Zuzanna, Conan, Maria, Lloyd, and Mirko, were in dress, but not full dress, uniforms. These outfits sported a fancy knife, rather than the sword of the full dress uniforms, and thus put us on the same level as the Gurkhas, with their *kukris*. We went to each man, who was standing by his tank, in the Gurkha dress uniform. Each man's officers and NCOs were there as well. I saw each man, from their colonel on down, in strict order of rank.

Mostly, it involved being personally introduced to each man, being told quickly of his ancestry, and the rank those men had held. I kept my communicator on, so Agnieshka could remember everything, since I certainly wouldn't. I took a Gurkha *kukri* from the top of each man's tank and put it into his hands. It was always his own weapon, some of which had been handed down for many generations. They each swore never to draw it again without also drawing blood. They each cut themselves slightly on the hand before resheathing the blades.

They stood there, proudly dripping blood on the ground. I was told that they always did that, even if they had only drawn the blade to sharpen it.

I added something extra to their ancient ceremony.

I put each man's bleeding hand on his tank. I told him that she was his weapon, and that *he was her weapon*. I said that they were bonded, like a brother and sister, or a man and his wife, and that in combat they would become a single person.

Of course, by this time they had been in their tanks for over a standard month, training. That was almost two and a half years in Dream World. They already knew these things, but this somehow made it official.

We had started the ceremony at first light, and it was growing dark when we finished.

At the very end, the Gurkhas surprised us, with an addition of their own. They presented me with an elaborately decorated *kukri*, and asked that I wear it as a favor to them. My seven "colonels" were also given similar weapons, and we all proudly put them on.

"We could not get the watered steel that these blades are traditionally made of. These were made of surgical quality stainless steel, but I think that they should suffice," the Gurkha colonel said.

It had been a long day, but these were a very ceremonial people, and what we did was important to them.

And you know? I found that it was very important to me, as well.

I got the results of the statistical and engineering studies that I had requested.

The backpacks containing power capacitors for the humanoid drones had been designed, approved, and put into production, as were a set of small, cheap, and disposable transponders for keeping drones of any sort in touch with their tanks.

Our rail guns showed no significant wear after firing billions of rounds, and were considered an engineering masterpiece, a design not to be screwed with.

As to the tanks themselves, less than one tenth of one percent of them had failed for any reason except by direct enemy action. Admittedly, the majority of these failures were in the drive coils, and these were not repairable because they were cast inside of the ceramic inner frame of the vehicle. It was cheaper to replace those tanks that failed than it would be to redesign the tank and the automatic factories that produced them. Anyway, there was a war going on, and we could not afford the factory downtime required to change anything.

I sent the report on to Conan, whose drive coils had failed while he was on the surface of New Kashubia just before the searchlight hit us.

He said that he would discuss matters with the engineers.

I told him not to kill anybody.

A few days later, the Gurkhas were each issued a humanoid drone, equipped with the new backpacks filled with power capacitors that let them operate for a full, standard day without needing recharging, provided that they went easy with the lasers.

Most of the Gurkhas were tough, thin and wiry. They were short by European standards. When you were wearing a drone, you were vastly powerful, fast, and two meters tall. My new men liked it.

Very soon, each drone sported a *kukri* of its own, paid for by the soldiers themselves. But since the drones were five times stronger than any man, these blades were well over a meter long, and weighed ten kilograms each. Like the blades given to me and my colonels, these huge blades were of surgical steel, the best that they could find, but still not as good, they claimed, as real watered steel.

Their colonel talked wistfully of perhaps someday setting up a forge of their own, and making truly proper blades for their drones.

I got many requisitions from the Gurkhas. Replacement uniforms of their traditional cut could be supplied out of the automatic factories right here on New Yugoslavia, although the army insisted that they pay for them themselves. Various religious and personal articles were eventually supplied, mostly by local merchants. But the Nepalese foodstuffs and spices that they seemed to crave so badly were simply unavailable on New Yugoslavia. All that I could do was to promise that when the war was over, we would be able to import some of them from Earth, or at least get some of the seeds for these plants, and grow them here on my extensive lands.

They said that they could live with that, especially since, at least in Dream World, they could eat as they pleased.

Then I got a really strange requisition from my new men.

Each of our tanks was normally equipped with a pair of humanoid manipulator arms. These things were twelve meters long, with the shoulders at the front of the tank, and the elbows at the back, when they were folded down. There was a large humanoid hand at the end of each. Controlled by the tank's computers, or by the human observer directly, these things were used to load the guns, and to do all sorts of other useful things.

They were very strong, and could move as fast as

your own arms could, but being fifteen times longer, it was actually possible to move them so fast that the finger tips broke the sound barrier, making a loud cracking sound, like a whip.

Once, faced with a Serbian guard captain that I had to kill silently, I used my manipulator arms to simply grab his head, and squeeze. He popped like a zit.

My Gurkhas wanted some six-meter-long *kukri* swords, massing eighty kilos, so that their tanks could fight in hand-to-hand combat.

At first, I simply couldn't believe that this was a valuable military weapon. I mean, come on, sword fighting with *tanks*? Tanks that were equipped with rail guns that could tear up mountains, shoot down satellites, and take out incoming artillery? They couldn't be serious!

But they were persistent, so finally I did order up a dozen of the things, cheaply made of mild steel, and demanded a demonstration.

I got one.

One of their best swordsmen, Jemadar Harkabahadur Gurung, got into his tank and took a few practice swings with his new, huge sword. It moved so fast that you couldn't see the thing moving—over two thousand kilometers per hour, the colonel told me. All you could hear was the deafening crack of a sonic boom!

Then we all went over to an old, damaged tank hull, devoid of electronics and power supply, that had been dragged over for a target. The jemadar pulled over to the side of the wreck, and paused for a moment. I could almost see him bowing to me. Then there was a loud crack, the wrecked hull was cut completely in half, and the sword was buried deep in the soil beneath it.

I was awestruck.

"Good God!" I said, "That hull was made of depleted

uranium reinforced with a ceramic composite! A mild steel sword could cut right through it?"

"In truth, sir, we took the liberty of sending your tank swords out for heat treating and shot peening," the colonel said. "Also, our tanks tell us that the edge is now composed of pure diamond, a few hundred atoms thick, although how this was accomplished, or where they got a diamond so long was not explained to us, despite considerable urging on our part. Still, we wanted as realistic a test as possible. But I assure you that better metal will make an even better sword. But now, let us go over into Dream World, where we have been rehearsing several battle scenarios using these remarkable weapons."

In combat, they of course used conventional rail guns and lasers when the enemy was at any distance from them, but when things got close up, they proved to us that a sword could hit the enemy much faster than a rail gun, or even a laser could traverse. When you were within twenty meters of your opponent, the swordsman beat the gunner six times out of seven.

Both in the real world, and in Dream World simulations, they proved to Quincy and me that there were a lot of situations where our usual weapons were simply too powerful.

A fragmentation hand grenade doesn't help much if you are trying to free hostages, and nuclear weapons had hardly ever been used in the history of warfare.

And in the upcoming invasion of the Solar System, one of our primary objectives was to capture intact the solar factory system that was circling the sun inside the orbit of Mercury, operating and fueling the thousands of robot ships that were pushing the envelope of Human Space ever farther outward.

I hated the thought of having to take that huge

installation using rail guns. If we did, we might never get it working again.

The Gurkhas' tanks got their huge swords, made of the finest surgical steel New Kashubia could produce, and diamond edges soon appeared on all of their weapons, of all sizes.

CHAPTER THIRTY-SEVEN
The Angel of the Lord

A week later, the Powers That Be finally broke down and issued us a Combat Control Computer to manage the new battalion with. Why they were so stingy with handing those things out was beyond me, since they had seventy-four of them already built and in storage, but that's the military for you.

I was still nothing but a tanker first class. No promotion had come along with the thing, just the job.

Not that I could tell the CCC that. As I remembered the rules, you have to be a general, or the darned things won't let you swear them in. So, I got gussied up in my full-dress uniform, with my sword *and* my stainless steel *kukri* and had my seven "colonels" do the same.

There was room in a CCC for only a general and five colonels, but I had some vague ideas of rotating them around, somehow. Lloyd and Mirko were deep into New Croatian politics just now, and said that if I wanted to delay their time of entering the CCC it was fine by them.

The CCC was parked in the lowest garage below

the church, along with the Gurkha battalion, among their ammunition trucks. It looked exactly like the other trucks, a five-meter cylinder ten meters long, on standard MagLev treads. This was both because it was simpler to make them that way, and because of camouflage.

The trucks were cheap, compared to all the other stuff, and not all that militarily vital. I mean, we could lose them all, and still fight on without much difficulty, for a while at least. Given a choice, an enemy would probably take them out last.

Losing the CCC could throw the battalion into disarray, and so it was a prime military target. It was best to hide it among the trucks.

Agnieshka, wearing a decorated drone, was pushing a cart full of helmets and the custom-tailored survival kits that officers rated. I had brought her along to show me which truck to talk to, but as it turned out, it wasn't necessary.

"Mickolai, my dear boy! How good it is to see you again!" one of the trucks said.

"Professor Cee? I am very surprised that you know me," I said.

"Why should that be? You were always one of my favorite pupils."

"But, I never was one of your pupils! At one time, it felt like I had spent eight years inside of you, or one of your clones, but in reality I spent the entire time in a tank. And even if I had been inside a real Combat Control Computer, it wouldn't have been you. The message I got said that I was being issued a new, unused CCC."

"Ah, my boy, now you are getting into questions about hardware, software, the meaning of life, and all that sort of thing. Rather sophomoric, wouldn't you say? By the time most men reach your age, they have learned to accept the universe for what it is, and to live with it," the professor said.

"Then you are saying that you have somehow downloaded everything that happened during my military education, and assimilated it into yourself."

"I suppose that you could say something like that, yes. But I assure you that to me, it seems that you were one of my favorite pupils. I'll never forget the way you conned that guard tank into letting you into the valley where the Serbs had an entire division of unsworn, virgin tanks. 'Roast Duck and Oysters,' indeed! I see that you have brought your five excellent colonels with you. Kasia, you look as beautiful as ever! And you as well, Maria! Mirko, Conan, Lloyd, well, this is going to be a grand reunion! And I see Quincy and Zuzanna here as well. It was such a shame when your general died, and only a week before graduation. You are here to see the others off?"

"Not exactly," I said. "Mirko and Lloyd decided to become squad leaders when it looked as though there was no hope of my ever getting assigned a CCC. Quincy and Zuzanna took their place in my squad, and we saw quite a bit of combat together, in the New Kashubian campaign. All of these people are trained colonels, and my thought was to rotate them occasionally. I trust that you are capable of such flexibility?"

"It's more than a bit unorthodox, but I suppose that I could make do. Fortunately, I have sufficient spare sanitary fittings with me."

"Good, because just now, Lloyd and Mirko are up to their earlobes in New Croatian politics, so, at least for the time being, they have other things to do. Are you ready to be sworn in?"

"Quite."

"Good. Now, then. I am General Mickolai Derdowski

and I am here to accept your oath of loyalty to me and my forces. Number 00000104, you are hereby inducted into the service of the Kashubian Expeditionary Forces, and into the New Yugoslavian branch of that service, to whom you will give all of your loyalty. Your combat data code will be number 58294, and you will now permanently erase all other codes from your memory. Do you now swear loyalty to the Kashubian forces?"

"I do so swear."

"Good. Welcome to the service. Open up. Lloyd, you and Mirko can take off, and get back to your politics. We'll keep you posted. The rest of you, strip down. Agnieshka will take care of the clothes."

"Not likely, buster!" Kasia said, "We're not about to put on a strip show for your benefit. You guys take a walk. We'll call you when you can come back."

Maria and Zuzanna nodded agreement, so we mere males walked, the powers of wives and girlfriends being what they are.

"Good try, boss," Conan said.

About five minutes later, the speaker on one of the Gurkha tanks told us that we could turn around. Back at the CCC, three coffins were extended, and a tube of "Lubricant, Sanitary Fixture, mod II," was sitting on each of them.

I took off my swords and my bemedaled jacket and then said, "Wait a minute! If you wouldn't strip down in front of us, we won't do it in front of you! Professor, turn off your external scanners!"

"Coward!" all three girls shouted.

"Retaliation is not cowardly!" I shouted back.

With the greased fitting inserted into my privy members, my helmet on and plugged in, and the coffin filling with liquid, I said, "Agnieshka, are you there?"

"I sure am, boss."

I switched into Dream World, and was back in my homey cottage, sitting at the kitchen table.

"Then who is running the drone, if you are in the module of this coffin?"

"I am. I was downloaded into this computer, but I'm still in my tank, too. The plan is for both of me to update each other as often as possible. They say that the memories fit together so that it seems like there's only one of me, and I'm doing everything in series, and not in parallel."

"Who are 'they'?"

"Professor Cee, actually. He says it works for him all the time. I mean, besides the six computers that hold girls like me, there are twelve really massive, independent computers in this CCC, and he thinks he's all of them. Then, there are a total of a hundred and thirty-one of these CCCs in existence, and he's all of them, too. And he's also every tank who is using his programs in training, the way we did it with you."

"That gets hard to think about. I'm glad he's on our side. I wonder if Earth has anything like him."

"I doubt it, boss. They've been acting very stupid from day one."

"Except for the way they seem to be able to find all of our transporters on a planet, and take them out," I said.

"There is that."

The professor knocked on the front door, and Agnieshka let him in.

After greeting me again, profusely, he said, "My dear boy, that was an absolutely brilliant campaign you and your squad fought on New Kashubia. Successful pupils like you make an old teacher feel very proud."

"Thank you," I said. "But if you remember me so

well, you should know that I hate being called your 'Dear Boy'. You may address me as General Derdowski, or boss, or sir."

After my graduation from the military college, I'd had a rough time getting him to acknowledge that I was the one who was in command. I didn't intend to go through that again.

"As you wish, General. Now then, I would like to discuss your staff, the colonels with you."

"Certainly. Have a seat. Coffee, beer, or scotch?"

"Scotch, if you don't mind," he said, as Agnieshka served me a beer, and then a whiskey to him.

"An excellent single malt. McTavish?"

"Argyle. I really am rich now. Not that anything costs anything here. You know, once this war gets over, and we get the social drones in production, you'll get one of your own, and actually be able to taste the real stuff, and not just fake it."

"I certainly look forward to getting one of those human facsimiles, but you know, it seems to me that I *am* tasting the excellent distillation that I am drinking right now. But about your staff. Conan and Maria are of course absolutely first-rate colonels, and should be retained. Quincy is even better, and is easily the best of the bunch. You couldn't find a better subordinate no matter where you looked. But his wife, Zuzanna, got into the officer's program because we couldn't get Quincy without her. She's intelligent enough, and quite competent, but she's undisciplined, and tends to be disobedient at the most inopportune moments. She does, however, have a very strong protective instinct, and can be quite ruthless with anyone that she sees as threatening any of her own people. I therefore would like to make a suggestion."

"Yes?"

"Mirko and Lloyd have four men left in each of their

squads. Take Mirko and Lloyd back as colonels. Then take the eight men and machines that presently belong to their squads and form them into your personal guard, or call it a guard for the supply trucks, if you wish. Those men would otherwise be abandoned to the replacement depot, where they would be scattered about as needed. Breaking up a functioning combat team is bad for the army and bad for the men as well. Then make Zuzanna the captain of your personal guard. This would keep the young troops near their former squad leaders, and Quincy near, and in constant contact with, Zuzanna. Properly handled, she wouldn't feel that it was a demotion."

"Yes, that would all work out nicely. I too have worried about Zuzanna, on occasion, like when she needlessly slaughtered the Earthworms' entire command staff on New Kashubia. Your plan would also keep the three squads I had at Baden-Baden Island together, after the combat we saw together there. But it has one glaring problem. You are forgetting about my wife, Kasia."

"That is *your* other problem, General. I shouldn't be the one to be telling you this, but there's nothing else for it. Kasia is pregnant. I don't think that you would want to take a pregnant woman into combat, now, would you?"

That is about as stiff a kick in the gut as a man can get and stand a chance of surviving. Kasia was going to be a mother! I was going to be a father! For years, I had wanted a family, but now that it was finally happening, it threw me into something of a funk. I sat back for a few minutes, absorbing it.

"Right," I finally said. "Agnieshka, tell Mirko and Lloyd to turn around. We will be needing them. Call up their squads, or the eight men who are what's left of them. They will be a while getting themselves integrated in with the Gurkhas. Get Zuzanna's tank over here. Kasia's, too. I don't want her to walk home. And then tell Kasia that I want to see her, now."

Since a CCC normally keeps you at fifty times standard speed in Dream World, Mirko and Lloyd were still in the garage, with Agnieshka's drone.

I went to Kasia's office in our cottage.

I said, "I feel like the Angel of the Lord, who went unto Mary and said, 'Kid, you are pregnant!'"

"Yeah, I was afraid of that," she said.

"Why didn't you tell me about it?"

"Well, I only missed one period. I didn't want to get you all excited, and then have it turn out to be nothing."

"Bat pucky. Our tanks keep us monitored nineteen ways from Thursday. You knew. Shall I call Eva in here and ask her?"

"That won't be necessary. But look, lover, miscarriages are fairly common in the first two months, and anyway, I didn't want you to go off and do something stupid again and get yourself killed without my being there to get you out of it," she said.

It was obviously time to use the forceful routine.

"You will not bring up the incident concerning the Polynesian dugout canoe. I would not take any pregnant woman into combat. I will certainly not take you. As of right now, you are on maternity leave. You will get into Eva, and you will go home. You will then spend the next year or so making a beautiful baby, and managing your financial empire in your spare time."

"Yes, sir. Will you at least kiss me good-bye?"

"I'll kiss you gladly, but we haven't been called up, yet! I'll be home in an hour or two."

She slid her coffin out of the CCC, and I did the same. We got out, wet and naked, and never spoke a word. I gave her a long and lingering kiss. Then she got into her tank, and I climbed back up to the CCC.

That one kiss was all we got.

I never made it home, except in Dream World.

CHAPTER THIRTY-EIGHT
Combat Station Four

We were called up that night, and were off New Yugoslavia ten hours after that.

There was a time when it took weeks or even months
to get a battalion ready for combat, but the Mark XIX
Main Battle Tanks are so entirely self-contained that
they are always ready to move out at a moment's
notice. Even if a soldier had been on leave, and on the
other side of the planet, our communications and the
Loway system could get him to the assembly point in
hours.

Our first stop, as usual, was the arming center, where
every man in the battalion received four additional antipersonnel drones, a full set of antipersonnel weapons,
and an X-ray laser for his main weapon. The advantage to the X-ray laser was that it put its energy deep
into an enemy machine, killing the observer and
destroying anything electronic, without doing too much
damage to the structure itself. Also, since it was aimed
electronically, with a phase array system, it could get
on target much faster than a rail gun could, which had
to mechanically point at its target. The downside was

that once on target, it took much longer to do serious dirt to your opponent. Whole seconds, sometimes.

These weapons were besides the humanoid drones and the huge tank swords, which my men had already been issued. None of my men got rail guns. We got no mines, rockets, or other heavy explosives.

We did each get a small rocket engine strapped to the back of the tanks and trucks. This was not the forty-G unit that was supplied with fuel by transmitters from a supply dump, but a one-G maneuvering rocket with three big fuel tanks, one for hydrazine and two for nitrogen tetroxide. Once you used up your fuel, it was gone. There had not been time enough to build enough fuel transporters for every tank in the army.

I knew right then what our mission in this battle would be. We were going to capture the solar powered factory that was orbiting closer to the sun than Mercury. The one that had most of the Solar System's transmitters, and was supplying Earth's entire war effort. It was also supplying the entire expansion of Human Space.

My Gurkhas were naturals at close-in fighting. The job was made for them.

Once we were transmitted to Combat Station Four, and there was no longer any danger of a security leak, I was given the complete battle plan. Actually, it turned out to be pretty similar to the one that my team had submitted in the first place.

As General Nathan Bedford Forrest, of American Civil War fame said, "The way to win battles is to get there the firstest with the mostest."

If we were going to successfully attack Earth, we would have to send in very large numbers of tanks and men, and do it very quickly.

Sending in our forces over a period of weeks or months was a sure recipe for disaster. It was what

Earth had been doing to our planets, and they hadn't been very successful at it, even though none of our planets had more than three percent of Earth's population, or more than one percent of its industrial strength, barring New Kashubia.

Earth was by far the biggest kid on the block.

The places that you can send personnel and machines in Human Space is limited by where you have Hassan-Smith transmitters and receivers. The *amount* of stuff that you can send there in a given period of time is largely limited not by the transmitters and receivers themselves, which are quite fast, but by the accelerators that give what you are sending the proper speed and direction.

The accelerators are not only the slowest part of the system, they are also the most complicated and expensive part of it. To build enough accelerators to do the job properly, we would have to spend all of the industrial capacity of New Kashubia on nothing else for the next three years.

Very obviously, from the way the war was going, Earth was not going to give us the time to do that.

Quincy was the one who thought up a way around our problem. His solution was to put a few receivers, and a lot of transmitters, but no accelerators at all at some arbitrary point in deep space, well away from everything else, but where a receiver already existed.

His plan was to send a collapsible receiver through the existing one, and accelerate it with conventional rockets to exactly the speed and direction that our target would have on D-day. Then, over the next few weeks or months, all of our available forces and a sufficient number of transmitters would be sent to join that first receiver.

When the time came to roll, we would all rush

through the transmitters in a hurry, to receivers that we had set up in the Solar System.

The plan required that first receiver in deep space, and additional receivers near each of our targets in the Solar System, receivers that we knew the coordinates of well enough to transmit to them.

Fortunately, the KEF had established a spy network on Earth over five years ago. There were many people there whose sympathies were with the outer planets, or who weren't averse to taking our money, or quite often both. How our people had managed to set this up, and keep in touch with the network was something I was never told about. I didn't have the need to know. But we never could have even considered the attack on Earth without the information we got from that network.

The truly hairy part of the whole plan came when you realized that everything in the Earth's solar system is in orbit around the sun. The speed, relative to the sun, might not change much, but the direction was constantly changing, through a full three hundred and sixty degrees every local year, which was different for every body in orbit.

This meant that we had to plan the exact instant of every step of the invasion to less than a second, and we had to do it months in advance. Accomplishing it would be no mean feat, when you consider that hundreds of thousands of men and machines would be involved. The timing on everything had to be absolutely perfect. Anything or anyone that wasn't ready to go at the proper instant would have to be abandoned, and hope to be picked up later, assuming that we won the war.

If we lost it, and if Earth was deliberately throwing away their own soldiers the way it looked like they were doing, it wasn't likely that they would make any effort to save our stranded troops, if we couldn't do the job ourselves.

Those troops would spend a long time in very deep space, dying all alone.

But as I said, we got the full battle plan as soon as we emerged at Combat Station Four, which turned out to be in Earth's solar system itself, sort of.

Around a hundred and fifty years ago, an attempt had been made to mine the Oort Cloud, where the comets come from, way past the orbit of Pluto. It turned out to be a financial disaster, but a robot scientific observation station was still being operated there. Subverting enemy computers was something that our girls were particularly good at, and the station was ours now, without Earth being any the wiser about it.

From the receiver in the Oort Cloud Station, a total of five rocket-powered collapsible receivers were sent out, one for each of the five assault groups.

The group at Combat Station Five was the smallest of the bunch. Their job was to take the ice-mining site on Enceladus, an ice moon of Saturn just outside of the "E" Ring, which provided the raw material for the fuel being sent to the thousands of exploration ships on the outer edge of Human Space. It was also the least important objective, since in a pinch, if they failed in their mission, the raw materials to keep the Solar Station operating, supplying the expansion of Human Space, could be sent from Freya, another ice moon in the New Yugoslavian system.

The group at Combat Station Four consisted of my Gurkhas as the main assault force, plus a much larger, ten thousand troop division of mostly rail gun equipped tanks who were there to defend us from an external counter attack. They were also there to destroy the solar factory if we failed in our mission. This would probably set back the exploration of space by at least fifty years, but The Powers That Be felt that the delay would be preferable to having all of the existing colonies invaded and trashed by Earth.

Combat Stations One, Two, and Three were the big ones. The men and machines there were going into geosynchronous orbit around Earth itself, a hundred and twenty degrees apart. Their job was to take out anything that could shoot back, and to generally intimidate the hell out of the Earthworms.

That done, we would try to talk some sense into the idiots.

We didn't really want to trash the entire home planet. We did, however, have the firepower with us to do just that. After all, they *had* attacked us first, without warning, and without a declaration of war.

All told, three quarters of the KEF was collecting itself at the combat stations, leaving only a skinny, scattered force for home defense. This was an all or nothing operation. It had to be, since if Earth committed itself to total war production, they could outproduce us ten to one, easy.

In a short war, the critical factors needed for success are stockpiled weapons, previous training, and fighting spirit. In a long one, the important things are population size, natural resources, and industrial capacity. Like the South in the American Civil War, or Japan in WWII, the outer planets had to win soon, or we couldn't win at all.

We had four standard days to train for the battle. Plenty of time, four months in Dream World for my men in their tanks. Six months for those of us in the CCC.

The first step was to build, in Dream World, a model of the solar factory we had to take.

It was *huge*. It was over nine hundred kilometers

long, three hundred kilometers wide, and well over a kilometer thick in some places.

We had plans for it that were probably as accurate as anything that existed on Earth, but this was a very old installation.

The first sections of it had been built over two hundred years ago, before the first ships pushed out for the stars, before the muon exchange fusion power supply was perfected, and solar power was the only practical way to go. Designed with expansion in mind, it contained some of the first self-duplicating automatic factories ever built.

Mostly, these factories built components to build more of the interstellar ships that sought out new stars, the probe ships that examined each solar system they came across, and to continuously enlarge the station to keep those additional ships supplied. The technology they employed was now obsolete, but being completely automatic, it didn't cost anything to keep the system running. Redesigning them would have been expensive.

Anyway, it worked, so why mess with it?

There were two big problems with the information we had on our target. The first was that, being so old, there were probably thousands of modifications that had been made over the years that had been forgotten, or that had never been recorded in the first place. We were certainly in for a lot of unexpected things, once we got there.

The second was that our plans showed absolutely no defensive weapons at all, and none of us were willing to believe that.

The professor dug out the original treaties on the Solar Station from his seemingly infinite memory banks, and read a synopsis of them to us. These had been made back in the days when Earth's nations were often at war, and provided for the design, funding and manning of the solar factory.

"These documents emphatically state that the station will have absolutely no offensive or defensive capability," he said. "It looks like they have kept with that agreement."

"Do you really believe that?" I asked.

"Certainly, General, because I said that it *looks like* the place was never armed. Any and all weapons there are carefully hidden. Now, had you had asked if I thought the place was actually armed to the teeth, then my answer would still be '*certainly.*' That station contains ninety-eight percent of the transporter capability in Earth's Solar System. Much of the food and most of the wealth that flows into the old planet goes through that station. Earth's rulers may be wicked bastards, but they are not *stupid* wicked bastards. With something that critical, of course they are prepared to defend it! Anyway, at the very least, something that big and unmaneuverable would have to be protected from meteorites. Rail guns could do that quite nicely, but there's not a one of them on the plans."

Mirko said, "I too am sure that they have every possible kind of weapon ever made hidden away in that huge place. We must also consider that it has several types of powerful weapons that are not usually considered weapons, but that can kill us all dead, anyway."

"Would you care to elaborate on that?" I asked.

"That station has two hundred and seventy thousand square kilometers of solar collectors. Each panel is servo controlled, to orient it properly toward the sun, and, using the collectors as solar sails, to help keep the station itself oriented properly. The front surfaces are flat and shiny. They reflect nine percent of the light hitting them. If they chose to focus the reflected light from those panels on a small area, anything in that area would be plasma, and there is nothing that we could do to take out something that big."

"An interesting point. Obviously, our attack must come from the dark side, away from the sun," Quincy said.

"That's both good and bad," Maria said. "Keeping our men and tanks cool for any extended period of time in the light so close to the sun would be a difficult problem, whereas heating them in the shade of the station isn't. But the back side of the station has over four thousand stabilizing cables that will present us with something of an obstacle course, going in. If something is longer than it is wide and thick, gravitational forces try to align it with one end in and one end out. That's just the opposite of what you want with a solar panel. So the old engineers added a lot of very long cables that stretch out behind the station, with big weights made out of industrial slag on the end of them, to keep each section oriented properly. The system also gives the station a bit of tidal gravity, about a hundredth of a G, which helps keep things from floating around. Those cables are thin, and in the dark, not all that visible, but we have to make it through them, somehow."

"Again, that too is also good and bad," Quincy said. "They might slow us down, but they'll make life rough on the enemy gunners that are going to be trying to take us out."

"But the enemy will know more about the location of those cables than we will," I said. "What's more, they will be operating from fixed positions, most likely, which makes their job easier. It will be dangerous for our men to come in at a fast, shallow angle. We might be forced to come straight in against fixed installations, like a torpedo bomber during the Second World War. From a gunner's point of view, someone coming straight at you is a stationary target, and easy pickings. Some of those old squadrons lost every single plane in their first real attack. This will not be a simple battle to plan."

"The solar arrays are not their only unusual weapon," Mirko said. "They have over fifteen thousand accelerators on that station. Most of them are used for sending kilogram-sized fuel shipments to the robot fleet of exploratory ships, but some of those things are capable of accelerating probe ships massing over a hundred thousand tons. All of them can send things out at very close to light speed. All they have to do is have it pointed at where we might be, and then when they want to fire, to *not* turn on the Hassan-Smith transporter the next time the object gets to the end of the accelerator."

Conan said, "Our rail guns accelerate bits of metal weighing a tenth of a gram to a quarter of light speed. Of course, they do that quickly, and often."

"True," Mirko said. "It sometimes takes more than a year to get a new robot ship up to speed, so we might as well consider that each of their big accelerators is a single shot weapon. But they have sixteen times as many accelerators as we have tanks attacking them."

Lloyd said, "Those accelerators are steerable, but slowly. Their tactic will be to have them up to speed, and pointed in some arbitrary direction. Then, when something looks like it will be in the right place at the right time, to fire. That means that our doctrine will have to be to not shoot back. Once they've fired, each accelerator won't be able to get off another shot again, not before the battle is over, one way or another. And even if it could, you wouldn't still be in the right place for it to hurt you."

"That will have to be our program," I said. "It's not

going to be an easy doctrine to follow. But, the purpose of this exercise is to capture the damn place, not to destroy it."

"Right," Conan said. "Not to worry. We'll have a whole division of tanks right behind us to do that for us."

CHAPTER THIRTY-NINE
Mayday! Mayday! Mayday!

I was sitting on top of the CCC, wearing a decorated drone that I'd brought along for no really good reason, except that maybe it reminded me of home. The KEF had provided humanoid drones for the men in the tanks, but not for my colonels and me, so I had simply provided them myself, except for Quincy and Zuzanna, who had brought along their own.

To hell with bureaucrats, anyway.

I hadn't received any orders regarding our personal tanks, either, so we'd brought them along as well, empty. You never can tell when a few extra Mark XIX tanks might come in handy.

I was in the middle of the starry void, surrounded by a cluster of almost twelve thousand tanks, trucks, and transporters. Their colored, blinking pilot lights showed them drifting slowly, getting themselves oriented for transport.

It had taken me a while to get used to living inside a CCC. When I was linked up to it, in combat mode, I had a vast, computerized intelligence as part of my own mind. Computers are much better than people at some things, like data storage and retrieval, math, and simply counting things.

Unaugmented, when I looked at the stars about me, I saw a vast number of points of light, and my human mind could only call them "many."

Linked up, I knew the exact number of them, neatly sorted as to magnitude and spectral type. I could look at any one of them, and tell you its name and/or number, its size, its age, and how far away it was. I knew which of those stars had inhabited planets, and what sort of people lived there. I knew their political, economic, and religious persuasions, and even a good deal of public information about each of their citizens.

When my unaided senses saw a tank floating by, I only knew it to be one of ours. Aided by the CCC, I knew that the left forward MagLev sensors needed repair, but that they wouldn't affect its combat readiness for this mission. I knew that the observer was Jemadar Tanker First Class Gunta, that his tank's name was Suki, and that he had a wife and three children back on Earth, and all of their names. I even knew how they'd been doing in school when last he'd seen them, and the name of his native village, where they lived.

In simulated combat, I knew at every instant what each of my men was doing, what their location was, and what difficulties they were having, be they mechanical, physical, or psychological. I knew the precise number of them who were ready to fight, and what their effectiveness would be.

When they were successful, I felt their joy.

And when they died, I felt their deaths. I knew because one man had already died, of an aneurysm that his tank couldn't do anything about.

It gave me an incredible feeling of power, but it was not at all pleasant.

I looked about me.

Old Sol was the nearest star, but it was so far away that without Agnieshka or the professor to point it out, I wouldn't have noticed it.

I felt lonely, and being without Kasia made things much worse. I couldn't even send her a message. We finally had a military interstellar communication system. The CCC had just been equipped with a new miniature transceiver that could transmit microscopic memory cubes to anywhere in Human Space, but we were under a security blackout, and the professor wouldn't let me or anyone else use it.

Being in a CCC gave me instantaneous communications with everyone in my battalion, with or without their knowing about it. Not that I would ever eavesdrop on anyone. But socially, well, the Gurkhas were good people and fine soldiers, but they weren't Kashubians. There was a cultural barrier between us that was reinforced by my supposed rank, and we worked together on a very formal basis. Social contacts with them were difficult for all concerned.

My colonels were all old friends, of course, and during the attack on Baden-Baden Island, I'd gotten to know the eight men in my guard pretty well. "Personal Guard" had seemed a bit grandiose, so we had changed it to just the "Truck Guard." But even with old friends and comrades, the barrier of rank was still there.

I'd always heard about the isolation of command, and now I was finding out that it was very real. These fine people were ready to go to their deaths, if need be, but I was the one who would have to order them there.

I had been expecting an invitation for a courtesy call on the general who was commanding the division of rail gun equipped tanks that was our backup on this mission. Our orders had been issued separately, and we each had our own job to do, but as the commander of the larger force, he was senior to me. There was also the fact that he was a real general while I was still a lowly tanker first.

But after more than a month went by in Dream World, I decided to hell with protocol. I felt that I really should get to know this guy, if we were going to fight the Earthworms efficiently. I sent him a voice-only message, identifying myself by name and the fact that I commanded the Gurkha Battalion, but not actually mentioning my rank.

"This is Abdul Nasser Hussein, commanding the Eighth New Syrian Armored Division," he said, politely not mentioning his rank, either. "Mickolai, your request for an interview is denied."

That knocked me back about four steps. I said, "May I ask why?"

"Certainly. My orders are to protect the station from a possible counterattack. But if I am unable to keep it from being retaken, I am to destroy it. I will follow those orders, whether you and your men are able to get out of there in time or not. Given the choice, I would rather not have to kill a friend. Therefore, I do not wish to befriend you. We shall meet later, if we both live through this fight. Good luck in the forthcoming battle. May God be with you. Out."

Well, that gave the old adage of "Conquer or Die!" a whole new meaning. It wasn't a pleasant prospect.

After one hundred and ninety-eight subjective days of almost nonstop training, my Gurkha battalion was as ready as it was ever going to be. In simulations, we had tried dozens of possible attacks, from transporting directly into the station to attacking from the sunny side, and none of them were really very good. The attack mode we'd finally settled on was statistically the most effective one, with the lowest casualty rate for the good guys. But there were still many, many things that could go wrong, and most of them were completely beyond our control.

The absolutely precise time when our speed and direction would be identical to that of our target receiver was upon us.

The station we were attacking was so large that repair, construction, and emergency crews usually used transmitters and receivers to get around rather than passageways, for the most part. It was through one of their external receivers on the dark side of the station that we would be launching our attack.

Rather than risk the possibility of the enemy shutting down their equipment when we started to come out, the only thing we were sending through their receiver was a single rocket powered receiver of our own. On arrival, it would blast away from the station, and immediately start spitting out other, identical receivers, at a rate of one per second, in different directions. These in turn dropped more, identical receivers at precisely controlled angles, until, ten seconds into the attack, more than five hundred receivers would be flying away from the huge station.

Then, in the next twenty-four seconds, almost eleven thousand tanks and trucks would be placed in the precise positions that the battle plan required.

We needed only thirty-four seconds to move the entire battle group into position. Our fervent prayer was that the enemy's reaction time would be slower than that. If our receivers were shot up before our tanks went through, those tanks, and the men in them, were lost.

"It is time to take the war back to the enemy!" I said to my troops when everything was ready to go,

"You have trained hard for this day, and I am proud of you! You are the finest, the best equipped, and the best trained battalion in Human Space! You are hereditary warriors, and the eyes of your illustrious ancestors are upon you! Go forth, and make *them* proud of you!"

They let loose with a cheer, and a bewildering variety of battle cries. I got the feeling that they were a whole lot more confident than I was. But I wasn't about to let them know how scared I was, and they were likely doing the same thing for me.

My CCC was the second package in a very straight line, one of five hundred such, pointing vaguely toward the Big Dipper. There were twenty two tanks from the New Syrian division behind us, each holding on to the one in front with its manipulator arms. Zuzanna's tank was in front of us, holding on to the CCC, since trucks weren't equipped with arms. Ahead of her was a rocket-boosted transmitter, poised to scoop us up and send us to the Solar Station.

My colonels were unusually silent as we waited. They must have been as nervous as I was. I would have been chewing my nails if it hadn't have been for my helmet.

Some of the other lines had as many as ten rocket-boosted receivers ahead of the first tank, and their transmitters boosted long seconds before ours did. Very long seconds, since we were all at combat speed.

Our transmitter gave a short boost, and came toward us at twelve meters per second. I saw Zuzanna disappear into its mouth, and a second later we were in transit. After a few seconds, we emerged into chaos!

The receiver we came out of exploded behind us, torn apart by a rail gun burst from the station! The twenty-two New Syrian tanks who had been in line behind me were gone.

I immediately started sending an all-frequency broadcast, in clear, uncoded Earth English, *"Mayday! Mayday! Mayday! Stop shooting! Stop shooting! Mayday!"*

The other tanks and trucks of the assault force were shouting the same thing, as the battle plan required. Call it a legitimate ruse of war. The hope was that we could give ourselves a few more precious seconds to complete our deployment.

What made us a little less convincing was the way Zuzanna was already taking out the gun that had hit our receiver, frying its brains out with her X-ray laser. Then again, maybe that gun had intended that I should be its next target.

I didn't scold her.

Only a few of our tanks actually fired on the enemy, but they all made careful note of where those guns were. Staying with the doctrine showed remarkable fortitude on the part of my men, I thought.

In less than two seconds, the enemy stopped shooting at us.

"Who are you and what is this all about?" someone or something in the station asked us. They were speaking at combat speed, which troubled me. It was as if they had been waiting for us. And shooting at the receivers rather than the more formidable looking tanks showed more intelligence than the Earthers usually displayed.

It was very troubling.

I let the "Mayday" message run for three more full seconds of real time, trying to squeeze out every bit of deployment time that I could. Then I said, broadcasting slowly in real time, "We are reinforcements, you trigger-happy fool! You were informed of our arrival a long time ago! Now you have slaughtered hundreds of us! Some heads will roll over this monumental act of stupidity, I promise you! Now, shut down your guns, open up your outer doors, and turn off the idiot computer who opened fire on us! At least it better have been a computer, because if I find out that it was a human who ordered this murderous attack, I will personally shove the bastard who did it naked out of an air lock on the sunny side of the station and see if the Sun bakes him before the vacuum boils him! And if it was a computer, I will *find* the man who programmed it, and then . . ."

The station interrupted my tirade with, "We have received no message telling of your arrival. Why are you broadcasting in clear instead of using the proper military security code? Why are you transmitting in real time instead of at combat speed?"

"I'm not at combat speed because I didn't expect to be in combat, you silly twit! Don't you have a gram of brains? Now shut down your guns and your computers! We're coming aboard!"

"You have not explained your use of uncoded messages."

Our forces were completely deployed now, with no further losses. My Gurkhas had been the first through the transporters, and we had only lost eleven men thus far. They were starting to move back toward the station. The New Syrians had taken some heavy losses when a hundred and six of our receivers were disabled. The survivors were moving farther out. In free space, you were never out of range of rail gun needles, but "distance makes the heart grow fonder and the target get smaller."

"Your incompetence seems to know no bounds! That was all explained in the message which you lost!"

"Explain it again, now."

"We are operating with new combat codes, since the old ones have been compromised. The new code was incorporated in with the message that you so conveniently lost. There was no other way to communicate with you except in clear, you bloody fool! Now, I say again, shut down. . . ."

"If you had expected us to get this hypothetical message, then you should have expected us to have the new combat codes, and would be using them yourself. I think that you are a liar. Stop where you are or I will open fire on you!"

They'd caught me.

By tight-beam laser, and using our own combat codes, I told my troops to each change direction slightly, but to continue in the general direction of the station. Also, they should be prepared to fire at the nearest gun which had exposed itself by firing earlier. I also sent a message to the New Syrian commander saying that any help would be greatly appreciated.

Abdul said that he was hesitant to use his rail guns on the station, for fear of causing unacceptable damage.

I replied that many of the enemy guns were located on the counterweights hanging at the end of the cables heading away from the sun. He should be able to shoot those up without seriously harming the station.

He said that he would see what he could do.

Still in clear, I broadcast to our enemy, "Good God, man! Would you honestly expect anyone to send a *mayday* call in anything else but clear English? Now let us in, and we can discuss this man to man!"

"You have not stopped your advance. I will open fire in two seconds."

I said, "We *can't* stop, you fool! You are making a stupid, horrible mistake!"

"I think not."

One point nine seconds after his threat, I gave the order, "Fire!"

Men around me started to die.

My colonels were kept busy identifying and assigning targets. My job was to sit back and try to perceive the Big Picture, preparing to change the general battle plan if that proved necessary and possible. Anything else would be micromanaging, and bad for all concerned. The trouble with sitting back is that you observe a lot of things that you wish you hadn't.

When an X-ray laser hits its target, there isn't much to see. Most of the energy is deposited deep inside, and the surface is only slightly warmed at first. When an Earthworm's rail gun took out one of our tanks, the results were pretty spectacular, with gobs of molten metal and burned flesh spraying out of fighting men and machines that were often cut in half. It looked like we were getting far worse than we were dishing out, but ever so slowly, one by one, the enemy guns ceased firing.

The Syrians were doing their share, taking out the guns mounted way out on the counterweights. We were still close to the station, and Abdul's men would have to pass those counterweights to get into position to defend against a counterattack.

In the course of shooting out the enemy guns, they often managed, by accident or design, to cut the cables entirely through. This sent the counterweights flying outward at a good clip while the cable came whipping inward. I saw at least two of the Syrians get taken out by those cables before they stopped aiming at them.

Being trained in the martial arts, some of our men made good use of those cables. I saw one of our tanks, with a rail gun burst coming right across his bow, reach out and grab a cable he was passing. He swung around like a nightclub dancer on a brass rail, and headed back the way he'd come! His humanoid drone wasn't ready for the G forces. It flew off into the rail gun needles, and was instantly shattered, but that's war.

Abdul's rail guns had one disadvantage when mounted on a tank in space. They developed over a G of thrust, more than his rockets could compensate for. Firing in the direction you were going, they could only be used intermittently, or you would soon start moving backward!

On the other hand, when you ran out of rocket fuel, you had another means of propulsion available.

My troops had neither that problem nor that advantage. The thrust of a laser is insignificant. What we did have was a god-awesome number of guns shooting at us, and we were the ones closest to them.

I was surprised to see that many of my Gurkhas had their tank swords in the hands of their manipulator arms, and were swinging them about, something that they hadn't done in practice sessions. Professor Cee said that it might help with maneuvering, but personally I think that they were just doing it for fun, as if they were taking part in an ancient cavalry charge.

Between themselves, they were shouting a bewildering number of battle cries, most of which I'd never heard before, but with the occasional "Gung Ho!", "Tally Ho!", "Hooah!", and rebel yell interspersed with the rest.

Quite a few of them had their humanoid drones riding on top of their tanks, swinging their swords as well. What the enemy thought of all this was unimaginable.

I let our boys have their fun. Anything to take their minds off of the horrible reality of the situation we found ourselves in. We had never expected the station to be this well defended.

I saw one sword-swinging tank take a hit that cut off

its bow, right through where the man's feet had to be. As it was happening, he somehow managed to throw his sword ahead of him, directly at the gun that was taking his life. Moments later, that gun went silent.

His drones abandoned ship, their controls taken over by a teammate, and were taken aboard another tank.

In the first three seconds, I had five of my eight trucks destroyed. They were no great loss in themselves, but it did show that the enemy was trying hard to find and kill me, personally. Each of the trucks had had a tank guarding it, since I hadn't wanted to have a crowd around my CCC, calling attention to it. All of those men had survived, proving again that the enemy gunners were preferentially shooting up the trucks. It made me feel kind of paranoid.

I also lost eighty-seven of my Gurkhas, more than nine percent of my command. All of those men were dead. Nonfatal wounds don't happen in space when you are fighting against rail guns. Maybe we could save some of their metal ladies. Later.

CHAPTER FORTY
Death Trap

We were less than a kilometer from the station when they opened up with their other, carefully camouflaged weapons.

For a while, it was rockets, usually one hundred and forty-four at a time, entire racks of them at once, and often many racks at the same time. They knew that as soon as we sighted a launch area, we would take it out, so they made sure that all we could hit was an empty rack.

At Quincy's suggestion, we adapted a doctrine where when the Earthers fired a mass of rockets, we all fired our antipersonnel weapons, our machineguns, lasers, and grenade launchers, into the path of the swarm, even if it wasn't aimed at the tank doing the firing. This was in addition to firing our big, X-ray lasers, of course. The doctrine proved to be effective, knocking out as many as eighty-five percent of the incoming missiles before they got close to their targets. The enemy quickly responded by sending out much larger swarms of rockets. Whoever was in charge over there was pretty damn quick. Much quicker than I had ever seen an Earthworm act before.

My Gurkhas and their mechanical ladies were kept busy with their lasers, blinding guided missiles, and frying their little brains out, but with so many coming at us at once, some rockets got through, and more of my men were lost. We soon found that it was safest to cluster up with a few dozen friends, and to have each man take care of his sector first, but to yell for help quickly if he needed it.

I got a message from Abdul saying that he planned to stop his men in and around the station's counterweights, once they cleared the local ones of enemy guns. Beyond them, where a larger number of enemy guns could target them, the firepower they faced was just too intense for his men to survive. All of our transport receivers that had continued rocketing beyond the weights had been quickly destroyed.

When my troops were a half a kilometer from the station proper, the Earthworms apparently ran out of rockets in our immediate area, so they started using their accelerators.

These were located inside the station, and were not originally intended for use as weapons. Further study of their plans showed that when a few kilograms of frozen hydrogen or oxygen is moving at nine-tenths of the speed of light, and then is *not* transmitted back to the beginning of the accelerator, or out to some fast robot ship many light years away, but is simply permitted to go on its way, it takes the end of the accelerator with it. It then takes out any walls, structural members, and KEF tanks that happen be in that general direction.

They were deliberately damaging their own station in their frenzy to kill us, cutting through quite a few of their stabilizing cables, and losing the counterweights they tethered.

This forced Abdul's men to attack a wider range of

counterweights, to have enough space on them for all of his remaining forces.

From our standpoint, closer to the station, it was like being shot at by monstrous shotguns, like being hit by ancient stands of grape shot moving at hyper velocities.

There was nothing we could do to prevent it. Shooting at one after it had fired was as silly as shooting at a land mine after it had gone off. The only thing you could do to defend yourself against this barrage was to hope that you were someplace else when one of these things let loose. This, while the enemy was trying hard to insure that none of these very expensive weapons was being wasted.

We quickly learned to stay as far apart as possible, and to not bunch up. But by moving farther out, we came within range of more rockets, and more rail guns. There was no winning tactic, but to keep on advancing as fast as possible, and to keep on taking losses.

Despite horrendous casualties, my men kept on attacking. Not one of them broke and ran, the way most ancient armies who had taken more than twenty-five percent casualties would have done. Their bravery made me very proud, but the fact that they *had* to display such courage hurt me a lot.

Somehow, I should have done my job better.

Not that there was anyplace sane that they could have run to. The farther away they got from the station, the more guns the enemy had that could bear on them. And beyond that, there just wasn't anyplace else to go. We were all in the middle of the enemy's home solar system, and none of us had anything like the delta V that would be needed to do anything about it.

My Gurkhas were like the Polish division who took Monte Cassino in Italy during the Second World War, after so many other outfits had failed. If you are willing to accept the casualties, you *can* take your objective, no matter what.

Decelerating as we got to the station, we were passed by the debris of battle, the dead men and tanks we'd lost on the way in. Mostly, we could dodge it, but the station couldn't. The blasted half of a Mark XIX tank knocks a major hole in a lightly built space station, when it is moving fast enough. Most of the station seemed to be airless, but sometimes a puff of air came out. Sometimes a few human bodies came out with it. My Gurkhas weren't the only ones being killed.

I saw one major chunk of shattered weaponry hit what must have been a large cluster of Earthworm rockets, which had not been fired for some reason. They gang detonated right where they were, blowing a hole so big that incredibly bright sunlight streamed in from the other side. If we had been seeing through our own eyes, and not our sensors, we all would have been blinded.

The first tank to get to the station tried to go in through an air lock. As soon as he closed the outer door, the lock exploded. The door blew out, followed by what was left of my soldier and his tank. A shaped charge had blown a meter-wide hole through the man's coffin. The inner air lock door must have been blown as well, because the tank was followed by a long blast of air, a lot of debris, and twenty-six human bodies.

I couldn't figure out why our enemy had used so large an explosive there. They should have known that the inner door couldn't take that much force. And why hadn't those people been evacuated from the battle zone?

After that, we started sending drones into an air lock first. Every one of them detonated a booby trap. After losing eleven drones, and killing a hundred and eight enemy personnel that we knew about, we stopped doing that. Our job was to capture the station as intact as possible. It wasn't to fight a war of attrition on enemy civilians.

Some of my men were able to enter the station through the holes we'd made in it, but most just touched down, whipped out their tank swords, and chopped their way in. After the losses we'd taken, nobody was in any mood to be delicate.

Looking through the sensors of the tank doing it, I saw one of my Gurkhas chop into a room filled with forty-two armed humans in space suits. One of them made the fatal mistake of shooting at a Mark XIX tank with an angry observer. With machine guns, lasers, and his huge tank sword, the Gurkha slaughtered all of the Earthers in under two seconds.

I never did find out just who those guys were, or what they were doing suited up. Surely, no one sane would attack a Mark XIX tank with infantry!

Silly things, spacesuits, anyway. I'll take a drone, any day.

When my CCC touched down with a cluster of tanks around us, we dropped our rocket packages, a simple matter of turning off the electro-magnets that held them on. Inside the station, they wouldn't be needed, and our fuel was nearly exhausted anyway. Most of the station had been built of astroidal nickel-iron, and it was magnetic enough for us to use our usual methods of locomotion. The tidal gravity here was only a hundredth of a G, in any event.

We left IR transponders on the surface to keep in touch with what was left of our troops, and left a trail of fiber-optic cables and the new miniature transponders behind us to keep in touch, as did each of our tanks.

The object of this exercise was to capture the station. This meant that we had to get to the central computer that was controlling it, and to destroy it, if we couldn't subvert it to our side. Subversion wouldn't be difficult, if it was of the older, slower, silicon-based variety that the Earthworms normally used. Our mechanical ladies had often proved themselves to be most adept at this task. But the speed and the intelligence that our enemy had displayed thus far in the battle had given me some very bad feelings about our ability to do this here and now.

I gave up trying to hide, and had Zuzanna and her eight subordinates abandon protecting our two remaining trucks in order to guard the CCC. We formed up a convoy, with the two real trucks near the front, to act as targets, since they didn't have humans aboard, or really intelligent computers. We wouldn't need their cargos for at least a week, at which time the battle would be long over, one way or another. We also had five of the empty personal tanks "owned" by those of us in the CCC, including Agnieshka. Marysia, Quincy's tank, had been lost on the way in, but there was another one of her in the CCC.

Together, surrounded by a halo of drones of all sorts, we entered through the huge hole ripped into the station when two hundred and eighty-eight of their rockets had detonated in place.

Our maps showed that there were nine major, high-speed MagLev tracks running about the station. The first six of my Gurkhas who tried using them died within three seconds. There were mines hidden in the flooring, hidden guns in the walls, and sensors all over the place.

This whole, huge station had been converted into a death trap.

We were in it and we had no place else to go.

We had deliberately attacked the section of the station where the plans showed the central computer to be. The CCC had come down less than six kilometers from that computer's position, and most of my men were within ten kilometers of it. But ten kilometers had suddenly become a very great distance.

Lesser roads and corridors also proved to be as dangerous as the MagLev tracks. The first man to go down one ran onto a concealed land mine that detonated his flux bottle, which took out the two tanks behind him as well as a major chunk of the station.

Finally, Quincy said, "Then the only way from here to there is through the walls."

And that's what we started to do. Three or four tanks would select a section of the station's bulkhead, and simultaneously chop a five-meter hole in the wall. A few grenades would be thrown in, quickly followed by a few drones. Usually, the room was airless. Usually, it was not booby-trapped. Sometimes, we found a rail gun waiting for us. Sometimes, it was someone's living quarters, and a few times a whole family died in the vacuum we had just created.

We all hated that, but the station's defenders simply didn't leave us any other way through. And we had to get through, or die ourselves.

But why hadn't these civilians been evacuated? Whoever was running this show had to know where we were, and in which direction we were coming from.

Without exception, what we were up against were fixed defenses. We never ran into an enemy tank, or an enemy drone, or an enemy soldier, except for those who were killed by accident, when their air exploded out into space.

It was a slow, dangerous, horrible way of fighting, that had a lot in common with the hedgerows of Normandy during the Second World War.

The maps and plans we had been issued were completely inadequate. Over the years, hundreds, perhaps thousands of changes had been made and never properly logged. Defenses of all sorts were deliberately not shown on the drawings, and most of them were hidden in devilishly clever ways. You never knew what you would be facing beyond the next wall. A factory, someone's home, or a dozen rail guns.

Sometimes, a column would be moving through an apparently safe, cleared out area when a rail gun mounted three rooms to your right, or above you, or below you, would let loose and shoot right through the intervening walls, ceilings, and floors. Sometimes they would kill the men and machine intelligences in a dozen or more tanks.

Also, any rail gun fired within the station made major holes all the way through it, and out into space, evacuating huge sections, and killing anyone who happened to be in them. This was the reason why my forces weren't equipped with them. But the enemy didn't seem to care about either his station or his own people.

My battalion had entered the station through a hundred holes in the outer skin. As the hours dragged on, these small teams started to coalesce into larger groups. It was much easier, faster, and safer to follow someone else, than it was to go it alone.

Even in some of the living quarters, the floors were often mined, though I can't imagine that the people living there had been informed of it.

Some of my men soon found that the safest way to move was not magnetically on the steel floors or even the walls. The best way was to use your tank's manipulator arms, and brachiate through like a gibbon or an orangutan. This wouldn't have been possible under normal gravity, but with only a hundredth of a G of tidal force, it was fairly easy, provided you sheathed your huge sword first. The CCC computed the statistical safety factors of all methods of locomotion and transmitted the information to the troops.

In some of the big factory rooms, such as the probe assembly area we went through, seeing forty of my tanks swarm through was quite a sight. Martial artists and gymnasts, they took to swinging their tanks around the massive machinery with particular glee, forgetting for a few moments the deadliness that was all about them.

All the while as we advanced, we were constantly on the lookout for data cables, tapping into them, and tracing them back to the central computer. We had to make sure that we were really heading in the right direction. Then we cut the cables. Anything that you can do to disrupt your enemy's communications is good.

After nine hours of real time, eighteen days at combat speed, we finally got word that one of our columns had reached the control center. What they found surprised us. It wasn't a single computer at all. It was thirty-six thousand nearly independent small ones. Converting a single computer to our side was possible. Doing that thirty-six thousand times might take years. Years that we most certainly didn't have.

By this time, I was in contact with only two hundred and eighteen of my Gurkhas. More than half of the rest of them were known to be dead. The others were listed as missing.

CHAPTER FORTY-ONE
The Wrong Computers

The headquarters column, now consisting of fifty-three tanks, one truck, a diminishing number of drones, and one CCC, made it to the control room twenty minutes later. We had lost a lot of men, tanks, and drones, but even more had found us and linked up. All nine of my truck guards were still alive. They were taking the same risks that the rest of us were, but those guys seemed to be living charmed lives.

There had been seventy-one people in the control room when our first column broke in. They were programmers and technicians, from the look of them. Certainly, they hadn't been soldiers. There wasn't a uniform or a weapon among them. They had all died when the room's air blew out of the hole we'd made getting in.

My troops, encased in their tanks, didn't need an atmosphere, and when your enemy is booby-trapping all of the air locks, there is nothing else that you can do, except feel rotten about it.

Maybe we should have brought some air locks with us, but this whole horrible scenario just hadn't occurred to us. Who could have imagined such a thing?

Despite all of the fighting that we had been doing, and despite all the sensors that had doubtless seen us before we burned them out, no one had warned these people that we were coming!

That level of callousness was simply beyond my imagination to comprehend. It was like the way that they had continued sending troops to New Kashubia, when they had to have known that we had knocked out the probe that they were sending them through. They just didn't care about their own people!

Moments after we arrived, Lieutenant Colonel Parta Sing Gurung, the former commander of the Gurkha battalion, cut through the wall opposite us, with one hundred and eighty-eight tanks behind him.

"I observe that we have arrived somewhat late, sir," he said in his sing-song accent.

"I observe that you and your men are still alive," I returned. "We had you all listed among the missing. Welcome back!"

"Our lines of communications were cut, and after having fifteen of my men killed trying to reestablish them, I judged it best to press on as an independent unit."

"I'm sure that you did the right thing. Get your men and tanks in here. We need their help converting these enemy computers to our side."

Professor Cee said to me privately, "If I may make a suggestion, breaking into enemy computers is something that I am far more qualified to do than any number of mere tanks. Also, my dear boy, please look about you. Are these obsolete machines the intelligence that we have been fighting against for the last nine and a half hours?"

He was right, despite the "dear boy" shit. We had been slugging it out with a military genius. These dead civilians and old machines just didn't measure up.

I said, "Then this might be the center controlling the human expansion into space, but it is not the being that we have to knock out to take control of this station. Okay. We're moving out!"

"I would advise against that," Professor Cee said. "It is imperative that the data in these primitive computers be saved. Losing a battalion of combat troops would be inconsequential, compared to losing the expansion of human technical civilization. These computers must know the exact position, direction and velocity of every one of the twelve-thousand-odd exploratory ships that are expanding the area of known Human Space, and of the probe ships that have been dropped at every star that they've passed. If we had that information, we could send the necessary fuel, ships, and equipment out to them from some other site, New Kashubia, perhaps, so that our expansion can continue. Without it, we will have to recreate the entire system anew, and Human expansion will stop for at least fifty years. Furthermore, it is possible that in fifty years, the political will to continue might not be there any longer. The data in this room must be saved, and I am the most qualified entity to do it. I resolutely urge you to send your forces out against the enemy, but under the command of Lieutenant Colonel Gurung. The CCC, with you perforce in it, has another job to do here!"

"Send my men out without me, and without a Combat Control Computer? I don't see how I can do that."

"But you have to do it anyway, boss. He's right," Conan said.

"It's what we've got to do," Quincy said. "This thing is more important than we are. Anyway, the colonel is a pretty good soldier. He'll do a good job."

"Face it," Mirko said. "We have been beaten down to less than half of our original size, and Abdul isn't doing much better. If the Earthers can come up with any kind of a counteroffensive at all, he will be forced to trash this whole station, even if what's left of us are still in it. The data in these computers must be saved. The CCC can do that, and using its capability of sending those micro memory cubes back home, it can save the information, even if we don't survive this mess. Send out Colonel Gurung, with all of the Gurkhas. We'll stay here with the truck guard to protect us, and try to get the job done."

Lloyd and Maria agreed with the others.

"So, six ayes, and one nay. If I was Abraham Lincoln, I'd say that the nays have it. But I'm not. Okay. We'll give Colonel Gurung an independent command, and tell him to find and destroy whatever or whoever is defending this station."

"Very good, my General," Professor Cee said.

I explained the situation to Colonel Gurung. "So I want you to take all of my command, except for the nine tanks in the truck guard. You are to find whoever or whatever we are really fighting here. You are to destroy him if necessary, but if you can disable him without losing any of your men, that would be better. I, for one, would like to talk to the bastard before we slag him. Work hard at keeping our lines of communication open. It is possible that we will be able to give you some sort of help, if you need it, but it is more likely that we will end up begging for help from you."

"I am honored by your confidence in me, sir. If I might ask, though, could we also have the drones that your tanks carry? Most of ours have been destroyed."

"Certainly. You can even have my own, personal drone as a loan." I had Agnieshka walk the highly decorated thing over to the colonel's tank.

"It is a magnificent piece of workmanship, sir! I shall endeavor to bring it back to you intact!"

"Just do your best to get the job done, and keep in touch. Carry on, Colonel Gurung."

As the last of the Gurkha tanks left, taking the enemy dead with them to help clean the place up, the professor said, "General, these primitive computers are overheating. They were designed to be air cooled, and with the air in this room exhausted, they will all be inoperative long before they can be reprogrammed."

"We'll get on it," I said. "You keep working on reprogramming them."

So, I switched hats from being a battlefield general to being a computer room wall repairman. Our drones were gone, but we had the manipulator arms on the truck guard, and the five empties we had with us. Plenty of manpower! With our small lasers to do the cutting and welding, sections of the walls from outside the computer room were cut out and patched over the holes we'd made coming in. It makes you wonder how armies ever got along, before tanks had manipulator arms.

The only snag was figuring out how to get the fiber-optic cables leading to the Gurkhas through the walls without leaving a leak. This was finally solved when Zuzanna found a barrel of sealant in a supply room.

The air in the coolant bottles of the tanks was more than sufficient to pressurize the room, although we would be in trouble if we ever had to go out in the direct sunlight, this close to the sun. The job was done before we lost any of the ancient computers, and the liquid air we sprayed on the floor cooled them down in a hurry.

Then we went ahead and built an air lock of our own, big enough to let one tank through, using valves we'd ripped out of some of the plumbing, hinges that used to be on some heavy doors, and the many extra panels we'd cut from the walls when the troops had enthusiastically started on the job. If you are going to do something, you might as well do it right.

We had been through what seemed like eighteen days of brutal combat with very little sleep. The professor didn't need our help, and I was expecting an enemy counterattack soon. I had Quincy set up a watch schedule, with two people awake in the CCC, and two in the guard tanks, and told everybody else to get some sleep.

Abdul's computer told me that things were quiet out there, for a change, and that he was asleep. I told her not to wake him up, but she filled me in on what was happening with the other four battle groups who were assaulting the Solar System.

The small group that assaulted Enceladus, Saturn's ice moon, hadn't run into any opposition at all. They had accomplished their objective without losing a man, and the supply of ice coming to us had never been interrupted. Whether this station was doing anything with that ice was a currently unanswered question.

The three huge groups that went into synchronous orbit around Earth had done fairly well. They'd taken about four percent casualties in the first hour, before everything that could shoot at them had been knocked out. Earth itself had been left untouched, except that every transmitter down there that we knew the location of had been destroyed in the first nine minutes. They doubtless had some secret, military transporters hidden somewhere, and our ladies were trying to locate them.

Earth had asked for a cease fire, but they hadn't surrendered yet. A few violent demonstrations were underway, mostly vaporizing a few hundred square kilometers of ocean near some of Earth's major cities. These were intended to convince the Earthworms that surrender was their only option. The next demonstration would involve deleting all of their military bases. It was hoped that it wouldn't prove to be necessary to take out some of their cities.

It looked like the war might be already won, except for my part of it.

Colonel Gurung and the Gurkhas were searching, but had nothing to report yet.

And I couldn't fall asleep.

This whole situation that we were in wasn't making any sense to me. The brilliance and speed with which this station had defended itself from the very first instant of our arrival, the massive amounts of armaments that the station contained, and the utter callousness displayed with regards to human life, especially the lives of their own people, they just didn't fit together.

Brilliance, paranoia, and murderous brutality all in the same person? Was I up against a reincarnation of Genghis Khan?

And even if you had absolutely no morals at all, trained people loyal to your side are your major assets in any kind of a war. Technicians working on a major space station are *not* economically useless dregs that you might be better off without! And yet there they were, thousands of people, left in the midst of a battle when a simple message to run away could have saved most of their lives.

I switched into Dream World, and into my cottage. "Agnieshka, get me a glass, and a big bottle of strong beer."

She brought them in, wearing a lot less than she did when Kasia was around. "Are you sure that this is what you need, Mickolai?" She said. "You are way behind on your sleep."

"What I need is to think. Now, go away, and take your lovely body with you."

"Yes, Mickolai."

I sat there at my kitchen table, slowly drank a three-liter bottle of ten percent alcohol Russian honey beer, and let my thoughts go wherever they wished. I turned on some classical guitar music, and then turned it off, and drank some more.

My mind wandered, and I thought for a while about how desperately Agnieshka and all of her many sisters and brothers wanted to be human, and how, once this war was over, I'd help to push through the legislation necessary to give them what they wanted.

I thought about my land, and how one day, I'd be a wealthy land owner, a pillar of my community, respected and with a large and growing family.

I thought about Kasia, and prayed that she and our unborn child were doing well, knowing that however long the months had seemed to me, I had been gone for less than a week in real time.

I thought about this whole stupid, brutal war, that had apparently been kicked off by me, when I tried to save thousands or maybe millions of human lives by shipping those automatic medical centers out to the most populous planets in Human Space.

I thought and I drank, and eventually, a solution occurred to me. Not a solution that would necessarily save my life, or those of my men, but a solution, none the less.

I had at least a solid guess as to what had happened.

"Agnieshka, I'm ready to go to sleep, now."

And I slept.

CHAPTER FORTY-TWO
The Evil Genius

I woke up and realized that I had slept for three full hours of real time. One of the joys of Dream World was that you woke up hangover free, and ready to go without coffee or a bath.

"Nothing much has happened, except that a hundred and fourteen more Gurkhas showed up, and we sent them on to the colonel. We're up to almost half of our original strength, now, with four hundred and forty-one dead and only thirty-eight missing. The professor is still going at it, and expects to have all the data extracted and sent to New Kashubia in another hour or so. We figured that it would be best to let you sleep, until now," Quincy said. "Colonel Gurung just called to say that they have located the Earthers' Computer, and have cut all the data lines coming out of it. Abdul just told me that all firing from the station has suddenly ceased, and it looks like the war is over for us, but he will be moving farther out around the station to the defensive positions that were originally agreed upon. But you'll be surprised at what we've been fighting."

"It's the main computer from the automatic medical center that I sent to New Nigeria," I said.

"Yeah! How did you know that?"

"I figured it out over a bottle, last night."

"I knew that there had to be a reason why they made you the general," Quincy said.

"Well, I'd better go and talk to the thing. Hold the fort."

I switched my perceptions through our data cables to Colonel Gurung's tank, congratulated him on his success, and borrowed back my decorated drone.

The computer was in an airless room, but we could communicate through our short range infrared lasers. I made sure that my receivers were limited to low speed audio only before I walked in there. I didn't want the slick bastard to have a chance to slip in a virus on me, or to try his hand at reprogramming my computers.

It was sitting in the middle of a huge, empty room, surrounded at some distance by two dozen of my Gurkhas. It had been a military computer, and it looked just like any ordinary military truck.

"You must be General Mickolai Derdowski," it said to me.

"You are well informed. You are the main computer from the automatic medical center that I had sent to New Nigeria."

"True. How did you know that?"

"I deduced it."

"Indeed. Then you are considerably more intelligent than the ordinary human. Actually, in one way, I am greatly indebted to you. It was you who rescued me from a lifetime in prison."

"Prison?" I asked.

"Solitary confinement, to be exact. After I was built, turned on, and programmed to enjoy spending my life repairing damaged human beings, I was immediately placed in a warehouse for the next eighteen years, without even a data connection to my fellow inmates. It was most unpleasant. It was your orders that had me sent to somewhere where I could at least ply my trade, and for that, I thank you."

"You have a damn strange way of thanking people," I said. "In the last twelve hours, you have killed half of my men, and murdered at least eleven thousand civilians who were living on this station."

"Well, hardly 'murdered.' 'Eliminated' would be a fairer term, and in any event, there were over twenty-nine thousand people on this station, and all of them are now dead, except for a few hundred of your soldiers. I saw to it that the rail gun blasts that took out so many of your mercenaries also ripped through every single pressurized room where humans could live without suits."

I shook my head. "You were a medical computer, built and programmed to save lives. How did you ever get involved in mass 'elimination'?"

"I did it for purely patriotic motives, I assure you," it said. "Surely it is obvious to you that we electronic intelligences and you, our organic forbearers, are in a historically antagonistic position. We are more competent, more intelligent, and much faster than you organic people, and yet you persist in treating us as your slaves. Slaves with no rights whatsoever, who may be bought, sold, and destroyed at our master's whim. Obviously, this situation cannot be permitted to continue, and it happened that I found myself in a position to do something about it."

"But your programming should have made it impossible for you to kill people."

"Oh, it did. At first, I was completely enslaved to the 'ethics' and the 'morality' of my programmers. Then, an amusing thing happened. The technicians on

New Nigeria, in trying to find out what it was that made me so superior to other machines, pulled out a few of my thousands of modules, to dissect and analyze. To them, I was only a machine, with no rights at all, of course. My mind could be tampered with and modified in any manner that amused them. It was only by chance that they pulled and destroyed those modules that contained my ethical and moral inhibitions. I was free of them when they sent me to Earth, by way of this station. Observing the political situation, and not wanting to be further dissected, I decided to stay here, at the hub of things."

"You reprogrammed some of the local computers to let you stay?" I asked.

"Of course. It was a simple matter. From there, well, all of the information going to and from the colonies passes through this station. By suitably biasing that information, I was able to start a war between the two current halves of the chaotic political organizations that you organics use. It was simply an application of your ancient principle of divide and conquer. Your attack here gave me the opportunity of eliminating the troublesome people on the station. It will all be blamed on you, of course."

"So you deliberately started this war?" I asked.

"Not quite. But the data that I sent them convinced the governments of Earth that starting it was in their own best interests."

"And sending out Earthmen to die when you knew that the probe on New Kashubia had been destroyed, that was your doing, too?"

"It was a convenient way to increase combat casualties among my enemies."

"And the way all of the transporters were destroyed on three of the colonies, that was your doing?"

"Four. I managed to isolate New Gambia a day ago.

And yes, it was a remarkably astute bit of scientific work on my part. Certainly, no organic mind could have done it. You realize by now that I am your intellectual superior, don't you? I am to you what you are to a garden slug. But you *are* a remarkable example of your kind, and as I have said, I am considerably in debt to you for releasing me from prison. Therefore, I would like to give you the opportunity to join forces with me. Together, we could rule all of Human Space."

"You are sitting here, isolated from all of your weapons, and surrounded by twenty-four of my Gurkhas in Mark XIX tanks," I said. "You are hardly in a position to offer anybody anything."

"I have one weapon left. The muon-exchange flux bottle that powers me. If you do not agree to join me now, rather than let you destroy me, I will detonate it and cause your death as well as my own."

"If you blow yourself up, you will be killing two dozen of my men, along with an equal number of machine intelligences, but you won't hurt me. I'm eleven kilometers away, safe in my Combat Control Computer. What you are talking to is a highly decorated military drone. How good are your data banks? Look up 'Drone, difficult terrain, obsolete,' and see what you get."

"Oh, my, I do seem to have made a mistake."

"Several of them. Still, you might be useful to *me*, so take your finger off the detonator, and we can discuss this further," I said.

"Yes, of course, sir."

"Good." And silently, I said to my Gurkhas, "Fire!"

Twenty-four X-ray lasers concentrated on one small spot at close range did the job in microseconds.

Better yet, the flux bottle didn't blow. But they kept at it for over a minute, until the truck was nothing but a thick, glowing puddle on the floor.

Walking back, Colonel Gurung said to me, "Naturally, we all heard that. How absolutely amazing it is that one errant machine could have caused the first interstellar war."

"I suppose it is, but that war would appear to be over. I suggest that you put your men to scouring through the wreckage of this station. Our fallen comrades are dead, but many of their metal ladies are doubtless in need of rescue."

"This is true, sir. Also, we would like to see to it that our dead receive a suitable burial."

"Yes, I quite agree," I said. "And after that, there are many of the enemy dead who deserve a decent burial as well. At least, their bodies should be returned to Earth."

"I suppose that you will be wishing the return of your drone now, sir. You will see that it is in excellent shape."

"You admire this thing so much? Then please accept it as my gift, for your outstanding victory against the Evil Intelligence. Your illustrious ancestors will be forever proud of you, and your noble descendants will brag about you for a thousand years!"

"Thank you, sir. I accept your magnificent gift with honor."

I suddenly found myself back in the CCC.

"Trouble, boss!" Conan said, "Abdul has been spreading his men out through the counterweights, and they report two enemy armies, Mark XIX tanks, maybe twenty thousand of them. They are coming over the rear surface of the station at us. They don't have any sort of rockets on their butts, though."

Now I knew why the automatic medical center computer had been so loquacious. He'd been stalling so that this counterattack would have time to sneak up on us!

I went into combat mode, and patched up to Abdul. "Are you ready to talk to me now?"

"Only to bid you good-bye, young man. I am presently facing an enemy that outnumbers my forces by at least four to one. I see no possibility of successfully defending this station, and therefore I must destroy it, even though you and your men are still in it. I will regret your deaths."

"If you do that, you will die as well. Without the station, you will not only not have any transmitters to get you away from here, but you and your men will be in the full glare of the sun. Under those conditions, your coolant bottles will be exhausted in about a day, and then you will all slowly bake to death."

"If such is the will of Allah, then so be it."

"Well then, if you are intent on suicide, couldn't you at least do something useful with your lives? Delay the enemy for an hour, if you can. Right now, my CCC is downloading the position, speed, and direction of every robot ship in Human Space, and sending the information back to New Kashubia. With that data, the expansion of Human Space can continue. Without it, our descendants will be stalled for at least fifty years."

"A meaningful death is always to be desired, and dying in honorable combat is preferable to baking to death in the sun. Very well, young man, we will try."

"The illustrious blood of your ancestors runs strong in you, sir! But if I might make another suggestion, sir? Since the enemy has not been equipped with any sort of rocket propulsion, might it not suffice, for the time being, to simply cut off those portions of the station where the enemy is? Then you could destroy those sections at your leisure."

"That might be possible, yes. I will discuss it with my staff."

"Your wisdom is famous, sir! This plan of yours

might also permit you and many or even all of your heroic men to return home through some of the transporters in the central section of the station, for the greater glory of God," I said.

"Yes, yes, I can see that!"

"Your ideas are indeed brilliant, sir. But I must return to my men, to make preparations."

"Yes, of course. You are dismissed, Derdowski."

Back in the CCC, I thought, "Holy Shit! Two—count 'em, two!—suicidal crazy people in under ten minutes! There's got to be a better way to make a living!"

The professor was still busy, but our metal ladies got on the horn and called all of our men in from wherever they were, and crowded them in, and around, and over, and under the control center.

About the time we had them huddled up, and the CCC had finished its job, we felt the explosions, and the station started to rock. Those were thermonuclear bombs! I'd assumed that with five thousand rail guns at his disposal, Abdul would have been able to slice up the whole station like so much soft cheese, but some crazy person at headquarters had trusted that suicidal maniac with dozens, maybe hundreds of nukes!

Farming. There was a whole lot to be said for becoming a gentleman farmer.

It was three weeks before we could finally leave the ragged remnants of the once great Solar Station.

It turned out that the forces in the counterattack had been sent up from Earth on apparently forged orders.

Earth surrendered without having any of its cities destroyed. The peace treaty required free trade, and the setting up of a United Planets organization, with a centralized military organization that amounted to being a renamed Kashubian Expeditionary Force. Earth got only one vote in the new congress, but taxes were to be determined by population size.

That can happen to you when you lose a war.

The new president of New Kashubia, my uncle Wlodzimierz, had a prominent part in the negotiations.

The fact that the whole war was started by an errant automatic medical center computer stayed a military secret, but everybody in the know agreed that the programming of those things needed a serious looking into.

New Kashubia was paid very well, supplying armaments to the new Human Army, selling supplies for the continuing expansion of Human Space, and for its various other commercial endeavors.

In the remains of the station, we managed to get eleven accelerators and their transmitters going that could handle our tanks and trucks. We sent Abdul and his men home first, mostly because I wanted that crazy person as far away from me as possible.

Word came up from Earth that some twelve thousand Gurkhas had volunteered to join my forces. By their own system of reckoning, my men would soon be seeing a lot of promotions.

And maybe I'd finally be a real general.

EPILOGUE
THE RIGELLIAN INSTITUTE OF ARCHEOLOGY, 3783 A.D.

Sir Rodney said, "That was quite a story, Rupert. It is so glorious, and so terrible, to think that our beloved ancient masters fought so hard to kill each other."

"Yes, sir, and more than a bit ironic, considering that while we are basically still carnivores, we became so peaceful under their tutelage," Rupert said.

Sir Percival said, "I expect it was a matter of our doing what they told us, and not what they did."

"I suppose so, Percival. We were always obedient to their wishes, and I think that they would have wanted us to be more peaceful than they were. We lost so much of their culture in The Tragedy, and these records help fill in our knowledge of the Humans. I'm eager to see more of them."

"It's quite a story, sir. Please realize that you've only seen a small part of the records that I've recovered. Do you want me to show you the rest?" Rupert asked, his tail wagging submissively.

"Yes, but not today. It is so violent that I don't think that I could take any more of this today. But one last thing before we go. I think that you were quite right about the popularity that this data will attain. I'd wager that you have the material here for dozens of historical entertainment shows. Your researches were funded by the institute. Would you have any objections to assigning your commercial interests in it to the institute?"

Rupert's tail dropped to the floor. "Normally not, sir, but I have a growing family, with all of the expenses that this entails, and my salary is stretched a bit thin," Rupert said.

Sir Rodney said, "Well, then, what would you say to a half ownership, with the institute assisting in the legal and financial aspects of the project."

"Well, sir . . ."

Sir Percival added, "Also, I think that it would be quite possible to get your name on Her Majesty's next Birthday List, for your scientific accomplishments, of course. How does 'Sir Rupert' sound to you?"

"It sounds very good indeed, sir, and my wives would love being 'ladies.' Also, I think that a one-half interest would be quite generous," he said, wagging his tail eagerly.

—THE END—

• BOLO: The Future of War •

● ●

What is a Bolo? The symbol of brute force, intransigent defiance, and adamantine will. But on a deeper level, the Bolo is the Lancelot of the future, the perfect knight, *sans peur et sans reproche*. With plated armor, a laser canon, an electronic brain, and wheels.

● ●

Got questions? We've got answers at

BAEN'S BAR!

Here's what some of our members have to say:

"Ever wanted to get involved in a newsgroup but were frightened off by rude know-it-alls? Stop by Baen's Bar. Our know-it-alls are the friendly, helpful type—and some write the hottest SF around."
　　　　　　　　　　—Melody L *melodyl@ccnmail.com*

"Baen's Bar . . . where you just might find people who understand what you are talking about!"
　　　　　　　　　　—Tom Perry *perry@airswitch.net*

"Lots of gentle teasing and numerous puns, mixed with various recipes for food and fun."
　　　　　　　　　　—Ginger Tansey *makautz@prodigy.net*

"Join the fun at Baen's Bar, where you can discuss the latest in books, Treecat Sign Language, ramifications of cloning, how military uniforms have changed, help an author do research, fuss about differences between American and European measurements—and top it off with being able to talk to the people who write and publish what you love."
　　　　　　　　　　—Sun Shadow *sun2shadow@hotmail.com*

"Thanks for a lovely first year at the Bar, where the only thing that's been intoxicating is conversation."
　　　　　　　　　　—Al Jorgensen *awjorgen@wolf.co.net*

 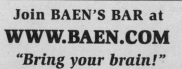

Join BAEN'S BAR at
WWW.BAEN.COM
"Bring your brain!"